In Greene Pastures

Also by Kendra Norman-Bellamy

For Love and Grace
More Than Grace
Crossing Jhordan's River

In Greene Pastures

Kendra Norman-Bellamy

www.urbanchristianonline.net

URBAN CHRISTIAN is published by

Urban Books, LLC
1199 Straightpath
West Babylon, NY 11704

ISBN-13: 978-1-60162-930-2
ISBN-10: 1-60162-930-3

First Trade Printing January 2007
First Mass Market Printing August 2009
Printed in the United States of America

10 9 8 7 6 5 4 3 2 1

Submit Wholesale Orders to:
Kensington Publishing Corp.
C/O Penguin Group (USA) Inc.
Attention: Order Processing
405 Murray Hill Parkway
East Rutherford, NJ 07073-2316
Phone: 1-800-526-0275
Fax: 1-800-227-9604

Dedication

I thank my God upon every remembrance of you.
(Philippians 1:3)

Jimmy Lee Holmes
Clinton & Willie Mae Bellamy
Valeria Bellamy Bryant
Tonja Holmes

I didn't really lose any of you because I have no question about where you are.
I find comfort in knowing that you are rejoicing and at peace in His arms.
Even so, I miss you all.

Acknowledgments

In everything give thanks for this is the will of God concerning you.
(I Thessalonians 5:18)

As always, I first thank **God**, because without Him I can do nothing. This gift that He has given me has brought me such joy and satisfaction, and for that I will be eternally grateful. I will always write for Him.

I'm thankful for my husband, **Jonathan (aka Spiderman)** for all that he does to make this journey easier for me. It's not every man who will work a nine to five and still come home, take care of the kids, clean the house, wash and fold laundry and even cook, if necessary.

I am so proud of and thankful for my daughters, **Brittney and Crystal** for their constant honor and superlative status in school and at home. I am indeed a blessed mother and they are my greatest gifts.

Indebted doesn't quite describe how I feel when it comes to my parents, **Bishop H.H.** and **Mrs. Francine Norman**, but it's the most appropriate word I can think of at the moment. They believed in me even when I doubted myself. It is their prayers that have gotten me through the most difficult times of my life and brought me into the most rewarding. I owe them so much and my desire is to always make them proud.

If the phrase "siblings extraordinaire" was in the dictionary, the definition would be four simple words: **Crystal, Harold, Cynthia** and **Kimberly**. I feel blessed to be the middle child, sandwiched between such goodness.

I am thankful beyond measure for my cousin, **Terrance**, who constantly helps me make my dreams come true. He is worth his weight in gold.

I am appreciative of my in-laws from both the **Holmes** and the **Bellamy families.** For those who embrace me, wish me well and support me unconditionally, I am grateful.

I am thankful for the love and guidance since infancy that I've received from my godparents, **Aunt Joyce** and **Uncle Irvin** and embrace the opportunity to be a role model and offer support to my own godchildren, **Mildred, Courtney, Jon-Jon, LaMonte** and **Cayla**.

Much appreciation goes to my attorney/agent, **Carlton**, the best legal mind in the business, and my publicist, **Rhonda**, for helping me gain mass exposure.

I am thankful for my longtime best girlfriends, **Gloria, Deborah** and **Heather**, for a lifetime of love, laughter, and memories and for my spiritual reinforcements, **Lisa** and **Dama**, for being a sacred sisterhood in those times when I needed it most.

In the few short years that I have walked in the

fullness of my calling, I have gained priceless literary friends and I am grateful for each of them. **Victoria, Jacquelin, Tia, Patricia, Vanessa, Hank, Eric, Timmothy, EJD, Keith** and **Maurice** are just a few authors who serve as a source of constant support and encouragement.

For *In Greene Pastures*, I must give special recognition to authors, **Travis, Jihad** and **Toschia**, who gave me inspiration, insight and ideas that helped to bring it all together.

I'm grateful for the opportunity to work with **Joylynn** and the **Urban Christian family** in this newest stage of my career and I am appreciative to **Carl** for seeing my gift, acknowledging it, and giving me the opportunity to expand it on a new level.

I don't take for granted **KNB Publications**, the independent self-publishing company that God inspired me to establish. And I appreciate all of the wonderfully **gifted writers** who have entrusted their works to my hands.

A literary family was gained when I founded **The Writer's Hut** in 2005. I am thankful for the encouragement that I draw from all of those who make up this unique online writer's group.

Special thanks goes to all of the churches within the **Revival Church Ministry** where my dad is overseer and where my spiritual roots will always remain, and to **Bishop Johnathan** and **Pastor Toni Alvarado** and the **Total Grace Christian Center family** for making me feel welcome each time I enter the doors of your worship facility in Atlanta.

For my home book club family, **Circle of Friends XI,** and to all of the wonderful **book clubs**

and individual readers across the globe that have purchased my novels and supported my destiny, I am eternally grateful.

As I never forget those who shared my beginning, I know that I will always be grateful for **Shunda, Jamill** and **Booking Matters, Inc.** We've come a long way, baby! (smile)

Finally, every book that I write begins and ends with music that inspires me. With that said, I am grateful for those whose music I listened to most while writing this book: **Brian, Fred, Musiq, Fantasia, John, Mary Mary** and **Take 6.**

If I have missed anyone, it is not intentional. If I can be just a portion of the blessing to them that they have been to me, my living will not be in vain.

In Greene Pastures

Prologue

"Mrs. Tides, are you okay?"

Mildred Tides saw the small-framed uniformed police officer that stood at her door and she heard the words that the woman had spoken, but Mildred's response was trapped somewhere between her stomach and her throat. Her body trembled and she could feel beads of perspiration breaking through the skin at the edges of her graying hairline. Mildred repeatedly tried to speak, but all that could be heard were heavy pants as she struggled to catch her lost breath and form words through lips that felt numb and useless. The female officer spoke again.

"Mrs. Tides, I know this is shocking for you and I am so sorry to disrupt your evening with this news. If you wish, I can radio an ambulance as a precautionary measure. I know this is the last thing you expected or wanted to hear this evening. Mrs. Tides? Do you want me to summon medical help?"

What Mildred wanted more than anything was to awaken and find that the happenings of the last five minutes were no more than the details of a horrible nightmare. She shook her head with vigor while at the same time squeezing her eyelids shut and opening them again. Pains shot through her stomach as it became clear that this was not a dream and the woman standing in her still open doorway was not a hologram.

"Oh, dear God," Mildred managed to whisper through a gasp of air.

"Mrs. Tides, I'm going to have someone come to your home. Okay?"

"N . . . No," Mildred responded, still trying to gain some sense of control over every muscle in her body that seemed to tremble within.

"Mrs. Tides, I can transport you to the scene," the woman offered. "I can get you there quickly."

"I need to call my children." Mildred managed the words through burning tears. "I . . . I need them with me."

"I understand, ma'am. Come on; let's call them now."

Placing a tender hand on Mildred's arm, the officer led the flustered woman toward her living room where a telephone rested on a stand near the arm of her couch. For a few silent moments, Mildred stared at the piece of equipment as though it was a foreign object that she'd never used before.

"Mrs. Tides, do you want me to dial the number?" the policewoman offered.

By now, there were so many tears in Mildred's eyes that she could barely see. A mother of three, she spoke to her children often, but as she continued to stare at the telephone in front of her, Mildred was unable to recall any one of their numbers, thrusting her into a feeling of helpless panic. The armed police officer awaited her answer, but Mildred had none to give.

For a moment, she sat in the chair, weeping heavily into the palms of her hands and moaning the prayers that her mouth couldn't utter. The day had started out like any other and had been pleasant throughout until the knock at her door disrupted everything. Now the dinner that was heating in the oven would go untouched and common things such as the contact numbers of her own children had become foreign.

"I'm sorry, Mrs. Tides." The woman's voice was soaked with genuine pity, and with light strokes of her hand, she rubbed Mildred's back, hoping to give some comfort.

The sound of the telephone ringing caused both their bodies to stiffen. In her years as the first lady of New Hope Church, Mildred had seen God perform incredible miracles; maybe this would be one He'd execute just for her. Perhaps this was the police station calling to tell her that the woman who sat beside her was mistaken. It was a long shot and highly improbable, but that's what miracles were made of.

After the third ring and with mounting hope, Mildred grabbed the phone and brought it to her ear and said, "Yes? Hello?"

"Hi, Mother. Jackson and I are on our way over. I made the cheesecake that Daddy said he wanted. I decided to bring it on over tonight. If he eats it all, I don't mind making him another one for Sunday. I just wanted to be sure you guys were home before driving . . ."

A burst of tears from Mildred silenced her youngest child who, just today, had arrived in Atlanta to spend Father's Day weekend with her dad.

"Mother? What's the matter? Why are you crying? What is it, Mother?"

"I need y'all, baby," Mildred responded through sobs that had reached a point of being beyond her control. "The police are at my house. Please hurry!"

Chapter 1

One Month Later

Hunter Greene reread the letter in his hand and recalled the four-week-old event as if it had happened yesterday. He knew that lingering heartache and desperation was the motive behind the unexpected correspondence. What he didn't yet know was how he would go about refusing the delusional woman's plea without causing her even more pain.

The famed preacher's funeral services had been held three weeks ago. Hunter had been one among the hundreds who attended and viewed the large framed photo displayed on the stand by the closed casket. It had been a sad, dismal day, but surely the letter-writer couldn't be serious in her request. Hunter's eyes were focused on the words on the paper but his mind traveled back to the happenings of Thursday, June 14th.

The flashing lights on the half-dozen or so police cruisers parked alongside the once-peaceful stretch of Interstate 285 looked like splashes of lightning that rhythmically cut through the darkness of the midnight skies. Traffic was generally sparse that time of night, but the swarm of emergency vehicles coupled with the closing of all but one of the highway's lanes was causing quite a traffic jam among the late night travelers. Water from the hose of a fire engine blasted through the stubborn flames that engulfed the wrecked van that had been the cause of the mass confusion. Although uniformed officers stood at the edge of the road and used flashlights in an attempt to urge the inquisitive drivers to keep the traffic flowing, it was a lost cause.

In a lavish brick home that was surrounded by six acres of land, three of which housed the prized horses he bred, thirty-five-year-old Hunter Greene sat forward in his chair. His residence, nestled in quiet suburban Stone Mountain, Georgia, was miles away from the televised chaos of downtown Atlanta, but the breaking news on the screen in front of him had absorbed Hunter, taking his attention away from his ten-year-old son's summer vacation studies.

When the story first broke, Hunter immediately picked up the telephone to call Diane Vickers, Managing Editor of the *Atlanta Weekly Chronicles*, the newspaper Hunter founded nearly fifteen years ago and now the most subscribed to weekly news periodical in Atlanta and neighboring areas. This wasn't just the average run-of-the-mill vehicular fire. The picture before Hunter's eyes and the story surrounding it were hot in more ways than one and he wanted his paper to be among the first to capture the details for the next day's edition.

"Have the police been able to decipher whether or not there was anyone in the van at the time of the fire?" The question had been posed by Monica Kaufman, a thirty-year veteran of Channel 2 Action News and arguably the most noted African-American news anchor in Atlanta.

The blonde woman who responded was a regular too, and Hunter found himself turning up the volume to drown out whatever it was that Malik was asking concerning his assigned work.

"No, Monica." The reporter on the scene's voice boomed through the surround sound speakers. "So far the investigators haven't been able to verify that due to the continuous battle to put the fire out. Early speculation is that the reverend somehow lost control of his vehicle and it veered off of the main highway and into the embankment that you see here. The van apparently slammed into one of the trees and burst into flames. This inferno has been too intense for the attending firemen and other officials to see whether or not the driver was able to escape. I must say that it's not looking too promising, Monica. There are no signs of the reverend anywhere near the area and the anonymous caller who reported the accident and blaze stated that no one got out of the van after impact.

"It would indeed be a devastating blow to the Stone Mountain community as well as Atlanta's church community as a whole if evidence of a body is found when the smoke finally clears. As we stated a few moments ago, from the tag number provided by the 911 caller, this vehicle belongs to Reverend B.T. Tides, the highly esteemed pastor of New Hope Church in Stone Mountain. Officials told us that Mrs. Tides was notified of this incident about half an hour ago but she has not arrived on the scene as of yet. We can only imagine how devastated she and her family must be and the police hope to be able to provide them with more answers soon.

"We don't have much more information than that to give, Monica, but as you can imagine, the news of a probable fatal crash involving this well-loved pillar of his community is spreading fast and we presume that this unusual high-volume of traffic is in part due to church members or affiliates trying to get to the accident scene. Additional police have been called upon to help keep order and ensure the safety of those who are determined to try and get a closer view."

"Daddy!" Malik wasn't pleased with being ignored and raised his voice to compete with the level of the television's volume.

It was times like these that Hunter was most grateful for TiVo, a luxury that he'd once branded "an unnecessary waste of money." He had used the remote that night to pause the news report while he forced his eyes away from the screen in front of him and on to the paper that his son was holding up for him to view.

"Is this right?" Malik asked.

It only took a moment for Hunter to scan the mathematical equation. Unlike his son, he'd always been good with numbers. "Good job, sport,"

Hunter said with a pat to Malik's head. "I knew you could do it."

The boy beamed at his father's praise and Hunter knew that his approval meant a lot to Malik. For more than five years now, Hunter had been his sole parent. Malik was barely a toddler when his mother and Hunter severed their romantic ties. The courts granted them joint custody, but in the two years that followed their breakup, Hunter noticed that Yvonne chose to spend less and less time with their son. Even now, every time Hunter looked into his only child's eyes, he saw reflections of Yvonne. It was a mixed blessing. There were certainly enough good memories of his three-year involvement with her to make him not turn his eyes away from Malik, but the memories that were the freshest and had lingered the longest were the ones Hunter didn't know about until just two weeks before she died.

Yvonne's death changed Hunter's life completely. Being thrust into full-time fatherhood at a time when his livestock business was in high demand and during the construction of the office that would house the production of his dream newspaper was challenging. But it faded in comparison to his having to come to grips with the fact that he had unknowingly dated an addict whose dependency gradually worsened until it eventually devoured her. Throughout their entire relationship, Yvonne had been addicted to pain killers she had begun taking as a teenager and Hunter hadn't a clue. Feeling herself losing the last bit of grip she had on reality and frightened for her own well-being, Yvonne had confided in Hunter and told him only days before she took a lethal combination of pills. For the sake of their son, Hunter set aside his personal grudges against her, and with the offer to pay, convinced Yvonne to enroll in a highly recommended rehabilitation program. She died forty-eight hours before she was to begin her road to recovery.

Malik's toddler years were particularly tough, and there were days when Hunter rethought his decision to fight Yvonne's parents for custody. Being a single dad hadn't been easy, but in hindsight, Hunter wouldn't have had it any other way. Just like the years had dissolved his animosity towards Yvonne for the lifestyle she'd led behind his back, they had also softened the anger that Malik's maternal grandparents had at one time harbored for the man who was awarded full physical custody.

"Time for bed, kiddo," Hunter told Malik on that memorable night after looking over his son's other practice papers for accuracy. "It's way past your bedtime."

The news report had started at ten forty-five and Malik's bedtime during the weekdays was nine o'clock sharp. It was a rule to which Hunter seldom made exception.

"That's 'cause you gave me a lot of work this time, Daddy," his son griped. "You don't usually give me that much."

Hunter often wondered if he was pushing his son too hard, but he found that when he gave Malik scheduled work to do during the summer break from the regular school year, he performed much better when classes resumed. Each summer since Malik had completed second grade, Hunter purchased learning materials so that his son would be up to par for the next grade level. Grooming his son to become a well-educated man was important to him even if Malik couldn't appreciate it at this young stage of his life.

"Don't try and blame this on me," Hunter responded. "You didn't get started on your lesson right after dinner like you were supposed to. You only have to do this twice a week, but if two days a week is a problem, we can up it to four. It's your call."

"It's not a problem," Malik quickly decided.

"I didn't think so."

When Malik rose from a kneeling position after gathering his work papers, Hunter stood with him. At six-feet-two-inches, he towered over his son by more than a foot. Placing his hand on the back of the boy's neck, Hunter pulled him in for a hug and then kissed him on the top of the head.

"Love ya, sport," Hunter told him.

"Love ya."

It was then that Hunter was able to get back to the story that was being aired on all the local stations. For the next few days, the tragedy also took up the front pages of all of the area newspapers, and every Friday, buyers of the AWC were purchasing multiple copies to send to non-subscribing family members and friends who lived elsewhere but knew of the famed preacher.

The city went into mourning when the report came that charred remains were mixed in the ashes of the van's interior. Just the thought of this reputable minister, with one of the most watched television broadcasts in the city, dying in such a cruel manner seemed both unbelievable and unjust.

Reverend B.T. Tides was an unselfish man of God who spent his time away from church ministering to the homeless, feeding the hungry and visiting the hospitals to pray for the sick.

The droves of people who traveled from near and far to attend his funeral were evidence of the widespread admiration in which he was held. Hunter's paper was given exclusive rights to cover the services. Hunter credited the favor shown by the family to the fact that his paper had been a source of many supportive contributions made to the church. The AWC was the only one to have photographs of Reverend Tides' grieving family and church members plastered throughout the local section in a special edition that was printed the day following the internment. For the first time in its existence, the *Atlanta Weekly Chronicles* sold every single copy of its print run.

After the funeral, the major hype fizzled. The Sunday after his homegoing services, Reverend Tides would have turned sixty-five. In its twenty-two-year existence, New Hope had only had one pastor and now he was dead. Hunter recorded the media's actions on that day. Channel 2 spent some time showing excerpts of the church service and pondering who it was that this body of worshipers would choose to replace the man they loved so dearly. It was a question that would go unanswered. None of the members of the board even wanted to discuss it. However, there were lay members who seemed more than pleased to have one last opportunity to shower their former leader with high praise.

"I know heaven's always been a place of unending joy," one hat-wearing woman said as she stood in the main entranceway of the church that seated fifteen thousand members. "But with B.T. Tides up there, I know Jesus and the angels are just straight up showing out!"

There was no music to keep her feet in perfect timing, but with those words, the news reporter had to step back. The woman let out a loud squeal and then broke into a holy dance, never letting go of her purse or her Bible. Other nearby members rushed to her side just to be certain she didn't lose her footing and take a spill, but in Hunter's eyes, she seemed to have everything under control.

A straggly-looking fellow, who was probably younger than his hairy face let on, dabbed at the corners of his eyes with a handkerchief while the reporter waited patiently for him to voice his thoughts. A child stood beside him with his head lowered, almost seeming afraid to look into the camera.

"God don't make no mistakes," the man said after gathering himself. "So we got to believe that there is a reason why the good Master saw fit to take him this-a-way. Reverend Tides was a good man. Many, many times he gave me money from the benevolence offering to pay my bills when things got tight with my family. I know we all got to go some time, but it's a shame he had to suffer like this. It's a doggone shame."

Even after the television networks and rival newspapers stopped their frenzy over the death of the preacher, Hunter continued to spotlight letters in a special editorial section of his paper. Letters had been pouring in and the more he featured them, the more they continued to fill the mailroom of the

Atlanta Weekly Chronicles. Finally, beginning with last week's edition, he made the decision to end the special feature and move forward to other topics. Reverend Tides was dead, and to continue the letters made Hunter feel as though he was playing a part in slowing down the healing process for the family. That is, until now. Hunter looked back at the two-page letter that had come, not to the newspaper, but in his own private mailbox today. The postmark indicated that it had originated in Virginia Beach, Virginia and the name in the top left corner of the envelope read: Jade A. Tides, Ph.D.

Dear Mr. Greene,

I am the daughter of Pastor and Mrs. B.T. Tides of Atlanta, Georgia and a second-year subscriber to your weekly newspaper. Let me first express my appreciation to you for printing a paper of such high quality that keeps me in touch with my hometown. I look forward to its weekly delivery to my office.

For the last few weeks I have, with mixed emotions, enjoyed reading the thoughts of the community about my father and his legacy. As his daughter, of course I thought he was a great man; but hearing it from others really adds to my knowledge of the soundness of his character. I noticed in the last edition that you are now printing reader letters that are geared toward other matters. I would like to thank you for the extended highlights that you did in honor of Daddy and although I understand that it was never your intent to continue them forever, seeing them removed from your paper has left me with a feeling of perplexity and I had to at least try and reach out to you for help that only you can give.

Just as he had done the two previous times that he'd read the letter, Hunter took a moment to pull his eyes away from the words on the paper in front of him and take a breath. It wasn't that the letter was hard to read, per se; but from this point on, the words took on a pleading tone. In a sense, Hunter felt as though Jade Tides was desperately petitioning for his help. He could feel her pain and knowing that he would have to turn her down was almost heartbreaking, but he had no other choice. Slowly, Hunter brought his attention back to the stationery in his hand.

Mr. Greene, what I am about to disclose to you I've not told anyone—not even my family members. As I read the letters that you featured in your paper, I would have constant visits from my father in my dreams. At first, I thought it was just a byproduct of my sorrow, but his last visit forced me to think otherwise. Daddy's last appearance in my dreams came the night before you discontinued the features. In that dream he told me that the answer to who did this to him and why could be found in the letters.

Mr. Greene, I can only imagine how insane this must sound, but I must be open with you if you are to understand where I'm coming from. I am not crazy. I know that Daddy's death was ruled an accident, but from the underlying message in his visits to me, I am certain that my father was murdered. I don't know by whom or why, but I do know that this was not an accident. At this point my greatest fear is that whoever purposefully ignited the fire that took my father's life will never be found if you don't continue printing the letters that your newspaper has received.

The case is closed as far as Atlanta authorities are concerned. But there is someone out there who is getting away with cold-blooded murder because they succeeded in making it look like my father had an automobile accident.

As unbelievable as it may sound, my father had never had an accident in his fifty years of driving and he didn't have one last month either. I need to find out who killed my father and the only way I can do that is if you will continue printing the letters. Somewhere in them lies the puzzle piece that will give me the answer that I need. If you need to speak with me in further detail for clarification, please feel free to call me day or night at 757-555-9014.

Sincerely,
Jade Tides

Throughout the letter she addressed Hunter as though they were complete strangers. It was clear that Jade didn't remember him but Hunter recalled meeting Jade and her brothers when they were all elementary and middle school-aged children. It seemed like a lifetime ago—before Hunter and his family moved to the thriving city of Roswell, Georgia, and before the Tides finally made their ascension to the upscale Stone Mountain subdivision known as Shelton Heights. For about four years, the Tides and the Greene families lived next door to each other in the same low-income housing complex where the Tides were known as "those crazy church folks in apartment 280." They were the only black children Hunter had ever known to refer to their mama as "Mother."

For poor kids, the Tides children used extremely proper speech and always used respectful terms like "Yes ma'am" and "No sir" when talking to adults. Still, "crazy" was how almost everyone began referring to them after Reverend Tides started sticking flyers in all of his neighbors' doors inviting them to attend weekly prayer service in the small living room of his two-bedroom apartment. None of the neighbors ever accepted the invitation, but it didn't stop Reverend Tides from getting his family together for prayer anyway. Sometimes Hunter, his brothers and a few of their friends would assemble outside the door of apartment 280 at 8:00 on Friday nights just to listen for one of what they called "Reverend Tides' fire and brimstone prayers" so that they could quietly mimic him and draw laughs from one another.

Hunter could still remember the day he stopped poking fun at the reverend and his family. That particular night was cold and rainy and Hunter had stood alone outside of Reverend Tides' apartment door and heard him praying. His snickering came to an abrupt end when he heard the preacher specifically call out apartment 278. Reverend Tides asked God to bring the family living there a special blessing. That was where Hunter lived with his mother who was a single parent, working two jobs to provide for herself and her four young sons. Hunter had never heard anyone pray for his family before. Never again did he meet his friends outside of apartment 280 for a laugh at the preacher's expense.

Six weeks later, Hunter's mother performed the Heimlich Maneuver on an eight-year-old boy who had begun choking on something that he was eating at the restaurant where she waited tables. The boy turned out to be the grandson of one of the high-ranking officials at a prominent financial institution. The grateful grandfather rewarded Patricia Greene by purchasing her a five-bedroom home on the "good side" of town. When the Greenes moved into their new home, it marked the last time, in childhood, that Hunter saw the Tides family.

Hunter had known for years that Reverend Tides' humble beginnings had flourished into the mass congregation that he had led for more than two decades before the accident that silenced his voice from the pulpit. Never forgetting the prayer that the aging preacher spoke on behalf of his family, Hunter sent regular donations to New Hope even though his church membership was elsewhere. He had even visited the church on a few occasions and took pride in the fact that he'd known the preacher when Reverend Tides' congregation consisted of only his own wife and kids. However, prior to the funeral, Hunter hadn't seen two of the pastor's three children in more than twenty years.

The eldest, Jackson Tides, was the one that Hunter had seen during his sporadic visits to New Hope. In childhood, Jackson had been the athletic one in the family, but had traded in his football jersey for a minister's collar. Not only was he following in his father's footsteps, but he even managed to be strong enough to eulogize his dad. Had the preacher's second son, Jerome, completed high school, he would have graduated one year ahead of Hunter. Instead, he chose his own path in life and because of it Jerome had been forced to come to his father's funeral accompanied by an armed guard. They'd let him out of prison long enough to help bury the man whose teachings he'd rebelled against almost all of his life. At the funeral, Jerome cried more than any of the others—probably more out of guilt than anything else.

Physically, Jade had changed the most. At the funeral, she was poised and looked chic in her ivory suit, in spite of her tears. Ironically, she was the only one of the Tides children whom Hunter had ever even spent any time around as a youngster. She was three years his junior, but they attended the same school and caught the same bus each day. On Saturdays, while Jackson played football with the bigger boys and Jerome was on lockdown as punishment for whatever he'd done at school during the week, Jade would wander out on the apartment complex' playground where Hunter and his friends would be shooting baskets. Her mother always watched from a distance.

Perhaps he felt sorry for her, seeing that she had no sisters or friends her age to play with. Hunter was never sure of his motives, but every now and then when he got the basketball, he would hand it to her despite the protests of his friends and allow Jade to take a shot at the basket. She never scored, but she enjoyed trying.

At the funeral, it was hard to envision the woman who sat next to her mother, holding her head high despite her quiet flow of tears, as the same chunky girl next door who always wore hand-me-downs and thick pigtails.

Clearing his head of memories that seemed more distant than they actually were, Hunter folded the letter and replaced it in the envelope before setting it down on the coffee table in front of him and taking a long sip from his glass of cold milk. As genuine as it all sounded, Hunter was unsure of how to handle what he had just read. His heart went out to the Tides family as a whole, but they could not expect him to continue the written tributes forever—and certainly not based on something as ambiguous as words spoken by a dead man in a dream to a daughter who was obviously still distraught. Insane didn't come close to describing how her revelation sounded. The other local periodicals, as well as radio and television stations, would have a field day if they caught wind of Jade's belief that her dead father's spirit had come to her in her dreams to tell her that he had been murdered—especially in light of the fact that there was absolutely no evidence to corroborate her theory.

Hunter continued to look at the ink on the outside of the envelope as he deliberated what he could do for or say to Jade that would pacify her. It was apparent that she was in a fragile state of mind. No clear-headed person with Jade's advanced education would ask him to keep running letters in his paper in hopes of making a murder case out of a death that even the authorities had ruled accidental. To try and find some kind of verification of a perpetrator in letters that did nothing but extol the pastor was ridiculous. It seemed that only someone whose ability to think rationally who in question could suspect foul play.

Pushing the envelope aside and out of his view, Hunter finished the last of his drink and headed for his room to prepare for bed. His intent was not to make light of the suffering of the family that Reverend Tides had left behind. Hunter imagined that little, if anything, could be worse than losing a loved one at the hands of a killer and being left without true closure or answers; but trained professionals had combed the accident scene and found nothing suspicious. So, what was he to do? As fatigue from the long day finally took its toll, Hunter knew that it wasn't a matter that would get settled tonight.

Chapter 2

"Girlfriend, you need to lie down on your own couch and charge *yourself* a hundred and fifty bucks an hour."

Jade had just opened her door to allow her best friend Ingrid to enter, but if the remark had been made while Ingrid was still on the other side of the entranceway, Jade would have closed the door in her face and engaged both locks. Instead, she accepted the envelopes that Ingrid handed her and closed the door behind her before heading toward the kitchen for a glass of water. Her outspoken, no-nonsense, but loyal best friend made herself at home on the sofa.

"I checked your mailbox on the way up," Ingrid said. "I still have the key you mailed me when your Father's Day trip turned into a ten-day stay in Atlanta. I was thinking that I should give it back to you, but since it appears you'll be leaving on another trip in a strait jacket soon, I'll just hold on to it."

"Thank you very much for your unyielding support, Ingrid. I can't tell you how much I appreciate it," Jade said in mock sincerity.

"I'm sorry, girl. I don't mean to sound like I don't care 'cause you my girl and you know I got your front and your back. But I'm 'bout to be scared to come in your house. First, it was just that big ole poster size picture that you hung on the wall—now *this.* It's starting to feel like you got ghosts living here or something."

Biting her bottom lip, Jade held her peace and decided not to reply immediately to the heartless-sounding remark. She knew what Ingrid was making reference to, but in spite of how it sounded, Jade also knew that her friend meant no harm. Looking over the kitchen counter at her, Jade drank from her glass and watched as Ingrid grimaced at the display in the corner that had been set up two days ago.

"Girl, this don't scare you?" Ingrid said, not taking her eyes off of the table that had been decorated with photos, letters, flowers and candles.

"It's a memorial to Daddy. Why would it scare me? I wasn't afraid of him."

Jade's response was met with quick patting noises caused by Ingrid's hand making repetitive contact with the leather that covered the empty space on the couch beside her.

"Come over here and sit down, boo," she said.

Not in the mood for another one of Ingrid's talks wherein she was referred to as "boo," Jade turned her eyes toward the ceiling and released a lung full of air through her lips.

"No need for the attitude, girlfriend," Ingrid told her. "Just come sit down like I said. We need to talk for real. All I need is one uninterrupted minute of your time."

With her glass of water in hand, Jade took lazy steps toward the couch. She could protest, but that would just extend the agony. In a word war, she could never outtalk the native New Yorker.

"Now, you know I would never intentionally do anything to hurt you," Ingrid started.

"Ingrid . . ."

A swift swat was delivered to Jade's arm. "Ouch!" she said, grimacing as she grabbed the target spot and tried to rub away the stinging sensation.

"Didn't I just say I needed one *uninterrupted* minute?" Ingrid pointed out.

"You also just said that you'd never do anything to hurt me," Jade shot back. "You think that didn't hurt?"

"I said I'd never do anything to *intentionally* hurt you," Ingrid corrected her, tossing her lengthy cornrows over her shoulder. "I didn't mean for it to hurt, I just wanted to shut you up. Sorry."

Jade rested her back against the cushions of her sofa and brought her glass to her lips for a moment, only taking in a small amount of the cold liquid. Then she pulled the glass away and tried to be inconspicuous as she folded her arms and used the glass as a cold compress to calm the continued burning of the spot where Ingrid's hand had landed moments earlier.

"Listen, Jade. You know I'm only thinking of

what's best for you. I'm not trying to say that I can relate because I know I can't. My father is still alive. At least I think he is," she added after giving her words some thought. "But the point of the matter is that it's not healthy for you to be so absorbed with what happened to Reverend Tides. We have to accept whatever God allows to happen as a lesson of strength and trust. That means you have to be strong enough to know that God would not put more on you than you can bear and trust Him enough to know that your father is in His arms and resting well."

"I know all of that, Ingrid." Jade shook her head. Ingrid always became "saved" when she wanted to, but would lay her religion down in a heartbeat if someone crossed her the wrong way.

"Then why the shrine? That freaks me out. It's like I can see you, when you're all alone at night, sitting Indian-style on the carpet with those candles lit conjuring up your daddy's spirit."

Jade chuckled and shook her head at her friend. "Your imagination is *your* problem, Ingrid, not mine. I set up that memorial in honor of Daddy, not to try and bring him back to life or to summon up his ghost."

"Well, can you at least move it to the back of the apartment somewhere so that it won't be the first thing that captures the attention of whoever is visiting you?"

Getting up from the sofa and heading back in the direction of her kitchen, Jade replied, "If *whoever* is *visiting* doesn't like it, they can always not visit."

"Are you referring to me?" Ingrid's tone was defensive.

"Only if the cap fits."

There was a brief silence before it was broken by the sound of the television that Ingrid had used the remote to power up. Although she lived alone, Jade always felt like she had a roommate. She and Ingrid Battles had been friends ever since the two of them met on the first day that Ingrid was hired as the receptionist at the quick copy business next door to the doctor's office where Jade worked. They had met in the parking lot that morning, and by that afternoon they were having lunch together and laughing like old buddies.

They'd seen each other through some rough times during their relatively short friendship, but the tragedy that Jade went through last month left wounds deeper than she had even made known to Ingrid. It was something that Jade just couldn't bring herself to talk about, so she chose to pretend that she understood God's purpose and plan for snatching her father away and succeeded in wearing an invisible mask of strength in front of her family and her friends. Disappointed in what she didn't find as she sorted through the envelopes that Ingrid had given her earlier, Jade tossed them aside on the counter and drank the last of her water.

Hunter Greene was the only person that she'd even come close to baring her soul to. Unlike the people closest and dearest to her, he knew about her lingering anguish and her recurring dreams that had now ceased. Jade had sent the letter to Hunter's home address with tracking services so she knew that the newspaper Editor in Chief had received it. By now, she'd hoped to have gotten a call or at least a written response from him.

He thinks I'm crazy. I know he does. Hunter Greene thinks I'm crazy just like Ingrid does. But I'm not. I know I'm not. The thoughts ran through Jade's head like cheap, thin syrup. She glanced toward the table that housed most of the personal memories of B.T. Tides and blinked back tears before looking away and nibbling at the fingernail that covered her thumb. *Maybe I am. Oh, God, please don't let me be losing my mind. All I know is what Daddy told me in the dream. Or maybe it was just what I wanted to hear.*

"Earth to Jade!"

Ingrid's raised voice broke Jade's train of thought and she turned from the stove and looked in her friend's direction.

"Did you hear a word I said?" Ingrid asked.

"I was . . . I was just finishing going through my mail. I guess I wasn't listening," Jade admitted. "What'd you say?"

"I was asking whether or not you wanted to go and grab a bite for dinner instead of ordering in like we usually do on Wednesday evenings. Aside from work, you haven't been out of this place since you returned from Atlanta."

Jade quickly opened her mouth in preparation to dispute her friend's allegation but immediately came to realize that Ingrid's statement was true. During her extended stay in Atlanta, Jade had spent most of her time being strong for her mother's sake. Jackson was there for Mildred as much as he could be, but as a long distance truck driver, uninterrupted time to spend with his family had been limited to two days. Jerome had been ushered back to prison following their father's burial to continue serving out his sentence for the part he'd played in a drug-related armed robbery and shooting ten years ago, so he was of no good use to his mother.

Jade hated to leave her mother alone with no immediate family there to keep her constant company, but Jade had other pressing obligations, including her job. Renee, Jackson's wife of four years, agreed to be available to Mildred if any need arose; that was the added comfort that Jade needed so that she wouldn't feel any guiltier about leaving than she already did.

"Well?" Ingrid pressed. "Are you game for going out or not? You really need to get out of this apartment and relax a little."

Before Ingrid could finish her sentence, Jade was already shaking her head in preparation for a negative response. "My stay in Atlanta put me behind on everything, Ingrid. I really need to prioritize so that I can get caught up."

"On what?" Ingrid was not convinced. "I can understand that you might need to play catch-up at the office, but what you got to catch up on around here? You want to put out more pictures? More flowers? More candles?"

"That's enough, Ingrid!" Jade's tone was harsh, but she had no apologies. "I didn't ask you to stop by, so if you don't want to be here in my home then you're welcome to leave. I just don't feel like going out and relaxing or celebrating right now, okay?" Tears welled in Jade's eyes as her speech began sounding more like a tangent. "Party, party,

party, that's all you want to do! Everyday is just a big party to you and I'm sick of it. All you can think of is what you can do or where you can go to celebrate next. Well, you can go right on, Ingrid. Do whatever it is that makes you happy. If I'm bringing you down, then there's the door! Go hook up with one of your friends whose father didn't just get murdered four weeks ago. I'm sure he or she will be more than happy to share your need to paint the town red."

"'*Murdered?*'" A look of shock could be seen on Ingrid's face as she repeated the one word that stood out more than any other in what her friend had said. "Jade, what are you talking about? Your dad wasn't murdered, he—"

"Get out, Ingrid. I just want to be by myself, okay? Is that too much to ask?"

Ingrid stood and began to walk slowly. Her steps, however, weren't toward the door, but instead, in the direction of the kitchen where Jade stood with her elbows propped on the counter and her face buried in her hands.

"Okay, Jade, I'm sorry. I shouldn't have invited you to go out and relax. If staying here is what you want to do, then that's fine. I'll stay here with you. We'll watch a movie or something. That's fine."

"Stop talking to me like I have loose screws, Ingrid!" Jade yelled as she snatched her hands away from her face.

"I'm not . . ."

"I'm a s*hrink,* Ingrid! I know what professional patronizing sounds like. I'm not crazy."

Ingrid inched closer. "I know you're not crazy.

There's a difference in crazy and just not thinking straight, Jade. I know you're still feeling the loss of your dad, but you can't go around creating something to justify what happened. It was an accident."

Jade walked quickly from the kitchen to the front door and opened it. Then tossing a brief look at Ingrid, she made a sweeping motion with her arm indicating the open door.

"What is *wrong* with you, Jade?"

Ingrid's question was met with complete silence. Jade continued to point at the door, all the while praying that Ingrid would exit before the flood of tears that pressed against the back of her eyeballs broke through. After a few seconds of motionless silence, Ingrid walked back to the sofa, grabbed her purse and walked through the open doorway. Just as she began her descent of the staircase that had brought her there less than an hour earlier, Ingrid turned to face her friend.

Jade saw her mouth open and knew that there was more that Ingrid wanted to say, but before a word could be spoken, Jade closed the door and locked herself inside, forcing Ingrid to speak to the door.

"God don't like ugly, Jade; and you might not want me here but I'm coming back!" she called. "Don't you go and do nothing stupid either. I still got your spare key at my house and I'm gonna give you about an hour to cool off and then I'm coming back. And you betta be here, too. I ain't playing with you, Jade Tides!"

Her back pressed against the door and fresh tears streaming down her cheeks, Jade could hear Ingrid mumbling words of displeasure as the heels of her mules made loud clunking noises with each step she took down the wooden stairs.

When Ingrid made it to the bottom of the staircase, Jade heard her raised voice call out, "Fifty-nine minutes, Jade!"

Chapter 3

Hurricane Dennis whipped through the Florida Panhandle and seemed to herald what would again be a string of storms to hit the southern-most state. Last year, a history-making four hurricanes ran amuck in the same area, causing the President of the United States to declare much of Florida a disaster area. Although the worst of Dennis didn't reach Georgia, a lot of the rain and winds that came along with it did resulting in a series of rainy days, making daily rush-hour traffic a dreadful chore. Tonight, though, rainfall didn't seem to be all that was on the horizon.

Hunter stood at the windows that overlooked his deck and watched the lightning as it flashed in the distance. Thunder rolled overhead and its magnitude caused the double-plated windows in his kitchen to vibrate. Hunter hadn't seen a storm like this one brewing in quite some time. The Weather

Channel had announced a severe thunder-storm warning for all of Atlanta: a storm that had the potential to bring not only torrential rains but golf ball-size hail. It was going to be a long night.

"Daddy, can I sleep in your room tonight?"

Hunter turned to face Malik, whose face had taken on the look of a frightened toddler as he stood by the bar near the kitchen's entranceway. In the boy's hand was his favorite blanket, which, along with his pajamas, depicted a picture of superstar WWE wrestler, "Edge." The sight of Malik wearing the image of a strong man while looking helpless had his father on the verge of laughter when the lights blinked simultaneously with another roll of thunder. Through the temporary darkness, he saw his son wince before running to him for protection.

"Come on, sport," Hunter said, hoisting the ten-year-old up in his arms as though he was at least five years younger. "You can crash with me tonight if you're scared. That's cool."

"I'm not scared," Malik quickly said as he wriggled from Hunter's arms onto the bed and put his legs beneath the covers. "I just didn't want you to be scared so I wanted to be here just in case you were."

The laughter that the thunder had stolen from Hunter just a few moments earlier found its way back. Malik laughed with him and struggled to free himself from his father's tickling hands.

Ending the brief game, Hunter stood over his son and helped him straighten out the covers. "Did you say your prayers already?"

"Uh-huh."

"Good. I'm going to be out in the den for a while before turning in, but I'll come back and check on you in a few minutes."

Leaving Malik, Hunter made his way back to the kitchen and returned his attention to the darkness outside the window. With each passing moment, the winds outside seemed to gain strength. Four hours earlier, when the news first broke of the impending storm, Hunter had gone to his pasture and gathered his horses. There were twelve of them in all, but they were well trained and it didn't take long to get them into the shelter that had been built for nights like this one.

Sipping a glass of cold milk, Hunter gazed through the window into the nighttime sky. A vanilla milkshake was his drink of choice, but at night, chilled milk made for a viable substitute. Through the light that the moon provided, he could see angry clouds forming. A noise from behind him caused him to turn quickly. He thought that Malik had become panicky again and had come to sit up with him, but as Hunter walked from the window into the open den, he saw no one. When he took the short walk down the hall, Hunter found his son lying comfortably in the king-size bed where he'd left him just minutes earlier.

As he did most nights, Hunter rechecked his security system, making certain that his house alarm had been activated. It was a habit that was hard to break. His mother had diagnosed him early in life with obsessive-compulsive disorder, or what she called the "gotta-keep-checking-for-the-same-stuff-over-and-over disease." As early as his son's age, Hunter recalled the need to check his book bag several times before leaving for school to make sure that all of his books and homework were tucked inside. As a teenager he would repeatedly check his pockets for his wallet or his keys. It was a habit that annoyed Yvonne during their relationship, but Hunter's efforts to break the strange addiction were unsuccessful.

Assured once again that the monitoring system was doing its job, Hunter made his way back into the den and looked up at the high ceiling as the lights threatened once again to plunge his home in total darkness. There was something different about tonight's storm. The wind had been blowing and it had been thundering and lightning for well over two hours, but no rain had fallen. Every once in a while he would turn on his television for an update on weather conditions, but there was never anything said that hadn't been reported before.

Due to Hurricane Dennis, there had been scattered thunder-storms all week long, but no other night had come close to what seemed to be looming tonight. Walking back into his kitchen, Hunter placed his empty glass in the dishwasher. Just as he closed the door, he heard a swishing noise and then a knock . . . or maybe a thud. The series sounded much like the eerie combination he'd heard coming from the living room area a short while ago.

For a moment, Hunter stood still—not moving an inch, but listening closely. All he could hear was the wind as it blew through the trees that surrounded his property and the sounds of his own heart pounding. When Malik had teased him before about being afraid, Hunter was able to laugh. Now, however, he experienced a sense of elevating panic. While he knew it was impossible for anyone to be inside his home, Hunter couldn't dismiss the reoccurring, unexplained noises.

This time as he walked toward his den, his steps were cautious, as if he expected to sneak up on an unsuspecting prowler. But just as before, the den was empty and the source of the strange sounds was undetectable. It was just after ten o'clock and unusual for Hunter to go to bed this early. However, the uneasy feeling that had crept in made him want to sleep the rest of the night away and awaken to a fresh day with sunlight and only the noise of Malik getting ready for school while he himself prepared for a morning meeting with the staff of the *Atlanta Weekly Chronicles.*

Walking into his bedroom to prepare for his shower, Hunter paused and looked at the lump that Malik's body had formed under the comforter. Unlike his father, the boy was a restless sleeper. It was one of the reasons that Hunter had insisted that Malik, even as a small child, sleep in his own bed. Hunter didn't look forward to the tossing and turning tonight, but he would manage.

The shower water was hot and Hunter adjusted the setting on the showerhead massage so that the water pulsated over his tired body. He hadn't gotten much sleep last night as he sat up late to write a column that had to be turned in to the production department today to make tomorrow's printing deadline. As owner of the AWC, Hunter stressed the importance of prioritizing and getting articles complete and submitted in a timely manner. Generally, to be an example to the others, he was first to turn in his editor's column, but this week his mind had been scattered and he'd found it difficult to write. Last night, he finally regained his focus, but inspiration's late arrival caused him to miss several hours of sleep.

As a college student, Hunter's two loves were writing and music. He majored in English and thought his destiny was to teach at his Alma Mata or perhaps find a career in songwriting. But against his mother's wishes and for reasons that he mostly kept to himself, Hunter chose to walk away from Morehouse College despite his 3.8 GPA and the fact that he was less than two years from obtaining his degree. Just a few weeks after withdrawing from Morehouse, Hunter ran into two of his old friends who used to play basketball with him in the backyard of the low income housing where they all lived as children. The men had made nothing of themselves. Even in their early twenties, they still clung to childhood fantasies of playing beside the NBA's and NFL's greatest, but were doing nothing to accomplish their goals. Even worse, they had children . . . sons, who were still early in grade school, but already showing signs of becoming the low achievers their fathers were.

Hunter immediately felt a need to reach out and help the youngest victims. His first thought was to open a youth center where he could work to thwart the vicious cycle that no one other than he seemed to detect. But taking on such a challenge was much easier said than done. One afternoon of factoring the bottom line of what an undertaking of that magnitude would cost him, and Hunter began looking for other ways to reach the lost boys of his community.

The *Atlanta Weekly Chronicles*, at that time, was still in its infancy. He had started the paper in the middle of his sophomore year and ran the entire non-profit, amateur operation from the spare room of his two-bedroom apartment. In the paper, Hunter started a column called "From the Heart of a Man." In it, he wrote articles that reached out to black men in particular, in hopes of getting them to be examples, especially for the next generation. Soon, businesses were calling him for ad space in the paper and making sizable donations for him to expand what started out as an eight-page periodical.

His written messages urged men to spend time with their children. That prompted support from area theme parks and sporting arenas. Hunter's calls for brothers to be spiritual leaders for their families gained the citywide attention of pastors and churches. The determination to succeed made Hunter a workaholic who never took a day off from the job for leisure. Before long, he had to hire employees to help with day-to-day operations, buy a larger press and eventually move into an independent office space to handle the growing demand.

Now, fifteen years later, the paper, although no longer non-profit, remained a hot commodity and local churches and businesses still applauded the man who saw a need and did something about it. Although his own youth center dreams never materialized, Hunter donated frequently to other organizations that carried out the vision that he once had.

The AWC had long ago expanded beyond preaching dignity and responsibility to the black male. Now, there was something inside the six-section, sixty-page weekly periodical for readers of all ethnic groups. With the profits that the paper brought in, Hunter was able to pay a staff of three full-time and six part-time employees and offer compensation to free-lance staff writers who joined him in making the newspaper a page-turner for weekly readers.

A loud crack of lightning, followed by the deep sound of thunder and the storm finally made good on its threat to put Hunter's entire house in absolute darkness, bringing his mind sharply back to the present. His mother would be livid if she knew he'd showered with such unfavorable weather conditions prevailing. Hunter finished drying himself and slipped on his pajamas just in time.

"Daddy!" Malik called just as Hunter entered the bedroom.

The booming sounds of thunder had awakened Malik and Hunter quickly climbed onto the mattress and pulled his son close to him.

"It's okay, Malik. I'm here. It's okay."

Feeling his father beside him calmed the boy a bit, but he still clung to Hunter in fear. All of a sudden, the skies seemed to open up. As the combined sounds of rain and hail began beating on the roof, Hunter lay back on the pillows and tightened his hold on Malik. They were so close that Hunter couldn't tell if the pounding he was feeling in his chest was due to his son's heart or his own. In all the years that he had lived in Atlanta, he couldn't remember a storm that paralleled this one. Silently, he prayed for the safety of his family as well as the well-being of his livestock. No doubt, the cataclysmic conditions had frightened the horses as well.

With the house without power, the lightshow on

the outside could be seen through the corner of the security blinds that covered Hunter's bedroom windows. In spite of the fact that the meteorologist warned of heavy rains and wind gusts, Hunter doubted that he was the only Atlantan who wasn't prepared for the surprising strength of the storm. Even within the sturdy walls of his home he could hear the might of the winds, and the falling hail sounded like discharged bullets trying with all their might to penetrate his ceiling and walls. The storm was getting worse.

Since Hunter's child-rearing beliefs meant that he seldom physically disciplined his son, Malik rarely cried. But his fears had escalated once again and now Hunter could hear his son whimpering through anxious tears. He wanted to once again assure Malik that all was well, but the continuing sounds of what appeared to be nearby lightning strikes and constant thunder rolls were causing Hunter's own uncertainties to multiply. Atlanta was taking a fierce beating and there was nothing he could do about it.

"Daddy!" Malik screamed.

His cry was an appropriate reaction. Even Hunter's body tensed when the entire bedroom lit up momentarily. The lightning seemed to touch the grounds right outside of the window beside them. But as quickly as the room brightened, it returned to its dark state. Thinking that the lightning may have struck his home, Hunter jumped to his feet.

"Daddy, no! Don't leave me!" Malik begged.

"Come on, son," Hunter said, reaching for the boy's outstretched hand.

Hunter held Malik close beside him as he walked

to his bathroom. Hunter knew exactly where his candles and matches were kept and it only took a moment to feel for them in the cabinet. As he lit the candles, Hunter looked in the mirror in front of him and saw a look of terror on his son's face.

"Everything is going to be okay, sport," he reassured him, while trying to do the same for himself. "See? We can see a little bit now. Daddy just needs to check around the house. I'm going to put two candles on the dresser so that the room won't be so dark. You can stay in here and I'll take the flashlight with me while I check the other rooms, okay?"

"Can I go with you?" Malik's eyes were pleading even more than the words he spoke.

"Sure you can," Hunter said as he pulled the flashlight from the floor of the bathroom closet.

Hunter's home consisted of five bedrooms and three bathrooms. The den was the most spacious part of the house with its glass-top coffee table surrounded by two sofas, a loveseat and a lazy boy. A marble fireplace decorated one wall and a full entertainment center was the focus of the other. The kitchen and dining room were adjacent to one another and shared the same blue and beige decor. Off from the den was an office where Hunter did much of his reading, writing, and other at-home business. It was where he did most of his praying too. His office was his favorite space in the house. Hunter carefully looked over each room before starting up the stairs that led to the bedrooms.

Wrestling was Malik's most-loved sport and his room told the story. His curtains and his bedding accessories bore the same federation logos as the pajamas that he wore. After leaving Malik's bedroom, Hunter thoroughly checked the other three. After closing the last door, he breathed a sigh of relief.

"See," he told Malik. "I told you everything was cool. Come on. Let's go back to bed."

Malik didn't verbally reply, but when Hunter climbed into bed, the ten-year-old followed and positioned himself close to his father. As Hunter wrapped his arms around his son, he felt Malik's body relax. It wasn't long before the sound of soft snoring indicated that Malik was asleep. Knowing his child felt safe with him meant a lot to Hunter. With his son resting comfortably in his arms, Hunter found a new level of serenity, despite the raging storm outside.

Suddenly realizing that he'd not said his own prayers for the night, Hunter closed his eyes, spoke silently with God, and drifted off to sleep.

Chapter 4

Lightning had disabled the power in Shelton Heights early in the night and as the hours ticked away, darkness seemed to take up residency in the quiet suburban neighborhood.

"Mother, it's almost one o'clock in the morning. You really should get some sleep," Jackson said as he walked into the dimly lit living room where Mildred had insisted upon sitting up late into the night.

"I'm fine, son," she responded. "I won't be able to sleep in this weather anyhow. Might as well just sit here and think. Don't let me keep you up, though. You go on back to bed."

Nothing had been the same since Reverend B.T. Tides' van had been spotted engulfed in flames after it veered from the main highway that fateful Thursday evening. Jackson and Renee had tried to get Mildred to move in with them, at least for a few months, but she wouldn't hear of leaving the home that she and her husband had shared for forty-five years.

Jackson found his way to the sofa and sat down beside Mildred. He looked at his mother for several moments, watching her as she stared at the set of glowing candles on the table in front of her. It had only been about five weeks since his father's death, but to Jackson, his mother seemed to have aged five years. Jackson sometimes wondered if he was the only child who cared anything about his mother. Why couldn't Jade have taken a leave after their father's death and spent more time in Atlanta? As for his brother . . . well, Jackson had stopped feeling like he had one years ago.

"Mother, why don't you stay here with us for a while?" Jackson figured that it couldn't hurt to ask one last time, but he wasn't at all surprised when he saw his mother shake her head in protest.

"I'm fine over there in my house. I have everything I need right there—except your daddy. And my moving in here with y'all ain't gonna give him back to me so . . ."

As her voice drifted, leaving her sentence incomplete, quiet tears began rolling down Mildred's cheeks. Jackson reached over and placed his hand on top of hers and gave it a quick squeeze.

"If you ever change your mind, there is always room here."

"I know," Mildred replied with a forced smile. "I appreciate it, son. You know I do. It's just gonna take a while, that's all. God just didn't give me no time to prepare for your daddy dying like he did. This one has been a real test of faith for me."

Jackson nodded. "I think it has been a test for all of us, Mother. Even Jerome."

Mildred lowered her head at the sound of her middle child's name. "It's a shame before God that that boy had to come to his daddy's funeral in such a manner. I don't know where we went wrong with that one. I'm glad we didn't let any cameras in the church other than the people at the AWC. Those other folks would have had a ball taking pictures of Jerome sitting next to that policeman who we had to share the family pew with. Your daddy and I tried so hard to keep him out of trouble. We warned him over and over again when he was a boy. But he couldn't hear us for listening to those hardheaded friends of his. And where did that get him? Some of those same so-called friends are running the streets as free men while he's locked up in a cage like a rabid animal, all because he wouldn't listen."

Jackson watched the shadows that the candlelight cast on the walls and revisited his teen years. Jerome was just a year younger than he, and Jackson could remember days when both of them left the house for the bus stop and as soon as Jerome knew that they were no longer in their parents' view, he'd take off, looking for whatever trouble he could find. Many days Jackson covered for his younger brother and didn't tell on him when he'd show up at the bus stop in the afternoon just in time to walk home with Jackson as though he'd been at school all the while. It wasn't until the teachers reported Jerome's absenteeism that their parents became aware of the extent of his mischief. Jackson, drawn into the web of deceit, had to take his lashes right along with his brother. To their father, it mattered not that they were fifteen and sixteen years old at the time. It taught Jackson a valuable lesson about honesty, but being punished for covering for his brother had also made Jackson harbor anger for Jerome.

Jerome got more whippings than Jackson, Jade and half of the other neighborhood children combined, but it did little good. As a preacher, their father carried an unspoken shame for not being able to tame his wayward son, but unlike Mildred, he never gave up on Jerome. Reverend Tides always said that there would be a day when his prodigal son would come to the knowledge of Christ, but even locked in jail, Jerome never admitted his wrongdoings. He never even owned up to the crime he'd been charged with nearly a decade ago. Jerome constantly denied being a part of the armed robbery that he'd been convicted of, but the judge could see right through him. The evidence was overwhelming. Jerome wasn't the triggerman but he'd been sentenced to ten to twenty-five years for his role in the offense.

"He told your daddy and me that he has his first parole hearing coming up soon," Mildred stated. "But if he don't allow the Lord to work in him, your brother is going to be put right back in jail again." Mildred shook her head. "If Jerome don't do no better *if* he gets out of jail, y'all gonna be burying me next to your daddy 'cause my heart is too weak for all that nonsense."

Jackson looked at his mother's shadowy image and knew that she meant what she said. He wanted to tell her to take back her words, but Jackson remembered too well the havoc that Jerome had wreaked on their family. Many days, Jackson had seen his father comfort his mother because Jerome insisted upon going against every good thing that they had taught him. B.T. Tides had been the only reason that Mildred survived those years. With his father gone, Jackson knew that the words his mother spoke were true. Just the thought of it made him angry. For years, only the strength of God prevented him from hating Jerome. Even now, he struggled with the disturbing emotion toward his brother.

The rain that had slowed was now falling heavily again. The constant thunder had disturbed Jackson's daughter's sleep earlier in the night, and Alexis called for comfort, her cries awakening her parents, but for her grandmother sleep had become a rare thing since that night when the policewoman came knocking at her door; she was already awake.

"Go on and help Renee with the baby." Mildred gave her son a nudge as she spoke the order. "I'll be alright. I just want to sit out here for a few more minutes."

"Mother . . ."

"Do as I said, Jackson," Mildred told him. "Sitting out here with me won't accomplish much, but holding my grandbaby will help both her and Renee. Go on now."

After a moment of hesitation, Jackson rose to his feet. He tried to walk away having seen the tears in his mother's eyes, but his heart wouldn't allow it. After taking a few steps, he turned to face her.

"I know you miss him, Mother. We all do. Maybe

we need to consider making a change that would better help all of us cope. I especially think it would be good for you."

Mildred dabbed the corner of her eyes with her finger and said, "Change? What kind of change? I know y'all want me to move from the house, Jackson, but I don't want to. I can't leave Shelton Heights. That house is my home. That house is where . . ."

She fell silent suddenly when Jackson raised his finger to his own lips and blew through clinched teeth. Returning to the space on the sofa that he had just vacated, Jackson gently took his mother's hands in his. What he was about to suggest was difficult even for him. He knew the likelihood that his mother would see eye-to-eye with him was slim to none, but he had been secretly pondering the issue for weeks and telling her now felt like the right thing to do.

"I'm talking about the church, Mother," he said. "I think that maybe we, as a family, should consider moving our membership elsewhere."

"What?" Mildred snatched her hands from Jackson's grasp and pulled backward, putting several more inches between the two of them. "What?" she repeated.

"Mother, church is supposed to be a place to go for refuge, joy and peace. It's supposed to be a place where people unite to worship God together in the beauty of holiness. New Hope doesn't do that for you anymore, Mother. It doesn't do that for any of us."

"What?" Mildred said for the third time, seemingly unable to think of any other words.

"Going to New Hope is just a constant reminder of what happened to Dad," Jackson further explained. "Every Sunday when I'm off from work, I sit in church and watch you cry your way through the entire service, Mother. And they're not tears of joy, either. It *pains* you to see another man sitting in Dad's chair and standing in his space. It hurts me too, Mother. I just think a fresh start would be just the thing we all need. There are a thousand other churches in the city of Atlanta. Let's just take the next few Sundays to visit and then, as a family, we can make a . . ."

"Stop it!" Mildred's voice rose in indignation.

Jackson had been rambling, trying to make his words come quickly so that he could say everything on his mind before his mother could stop him. He thought that if he was able to make his full point before being interrupted, there might be at least a possibility that she would see his line of reasoning. But his words didn't come fast enough. Mildred's countenance was completely transformed and the look of sadness had been replaced by one of exasperation.

"Jackson Andrew Tides!"

The only time his mother called any of the children by their full names was when she was completely fed up with whatever it was that was transpiring. More times than Jackson cared to count, he and his sister had heard the name Jerome Abraham Tides repeated during their younger years. But tonight, hearing his own full name caused Jackson to settle back into the cushions of his couch and prepare for a tongue lashing.

"I can't believe the words I hear coming from

your mouth," Mildred scolded. "How could you ever shape your lips to speak such foolishness? Your father worked hard to build New Hope and now that he's dead you want us to walk out on the vision that God gave him? Do you know how many days of fasting and praying went into that ministry? If you count all the raindrops that have fallen on Atlanta this night, it still don't add up to the number of tears and the amount of sweat that B.T. and me shed while working together to get that church to where it is right now. Your daddy would turn over in his grave if he could hear you now!"

Mildred's rejection of his idea was no surprise, but her level of fury was. Jackson knew that getting his mother to admit that walking through the doors of New Hope was no longer a joy wasn't going to be easy, but he'd not expected her to take such a solid stand on behalf of the ministry that her husband was no longer alive to lead.

"Is everything okay?" a soft voice spoke.

Jackson looked up and saw Renee standing in the shadows that the candlelight cast. In her arms she held Alexis, the little girl who hadn't had the chance to get to know her grandfather before he was taken from them.

"Yeah. Everything is fine," Jackson said. "I was just telling Mother . . ."

"He was just telling me goodnight," Mildred interrupted.

"Mother, all I was saying was . . ."

"Goodnight, Jackson," Mildred said while returning her eyes to their earlier stare at the candle that was burning in front of her. "I heard loud and clear, everything that you said. Now, please do what your mama said and go help your wife with the baby. I need to be left alone."

There was so much more that Jackson wanted to say but he looked at Renee and saw her silently beckoning for him to comply with his mother's request. Picking up Mildred's right hand, Jackson brought it to his mouth and lightly pressed his lips against it before returning it to her lap.

"I love you, Mother," he whispered.

"I know, son."

The quivering in her voice tugged at Jackson's heartstrings, but he said nothing more. Getting up from the sofa, he quietly followed Renee as she led the way into the bedroom. Stopping at the door, Jackson turned. In the flickering dim light Jackson watched as his mother slowly buried her face in her hands and wept. Seeing her hurt, Jackson was unable to hold back his own emotions and silent tears streamed down his face as he pressed his back against the wall.

"Come on, sweetie," Renee whispered in his ear. "It's gonna be okay. I promise."

Chapter 5

"Hunter, I hope you don't mind, but I couldn't reach you on your cell yesterday before giving the word for the pressroom to go ahead and print last night so that we could have the issues on the stands and in the mail by this morning. I don't know what happened; somehow I didn't get the fax from you signing off everything as okay, but I figured that you must have gotten sidetracked. Can you shoot that to me real quick for my files? Or, I can just get it from you right now if you have the original handy."

Kwame Akil Williams was the first employee that Hunter hired when demand for his newspaper became too much for one man to handle. It was a risk at the time, but it turned out to be the best business decision Hunter could have made. At that time, Kwame's name was Thaddeus Lee Williams, but two years ago, he decided to change his name to express the pride he had in his heritage and to get away from what he often referred to as "the man I once was." Kwame explained to Hunter that his chosen first name was rooted in Ghana and meant "born on a Saturday" and his middle name was Swahili for "intelligent." After knowing him as Thaddeus for so many years, it had taken some time for Hunter to get used to it, but calling his best friend Kwame finally began to feel natural.

Although Malik's name was also of African decent, Hunter and Yvonne decided upon the name simply because it was the one that Hunter chose and one that they both liked. It wasn't until after Yvonne was dead that Hunter realized that his son's name was Somalian and meant "king." Although it wasn't intentional, he loved that he'd chosen such a strong name for his only child.

As editorial director, Kwame held the highest position among the relatively small staff, second in command only to Hunter. What had come to be known as the Tides Tragedy had hit close to home for Kwame. Reverend B.T. Tides had been his pastor for as long as he'd been a devoted Christian.

"Close the door for a minute, will you?" Hunter said just before removing his suit coat and sitting in the chair behind his desk.

From the expression on Kwame's face, Hunter knew that his simple request had raised immediate concerns with his friend. It wasn't often that Hunter closed his office door. It was always his intent to paint a picture of his availability to his staff whenever they needed him. Only special circumstances made him forgo his unspoken policy.

Kwame did as he was told and then sat in the seat across from Hunter. "What's up, man?"

Hunter's thought-flow seemed to travel at a speed faster than he could form words. For more than a day he had held his uncanny experience inside. He was tempted to bring it up in yesterday's staff meeting, but chose not to disclose his thoughts to everyone at once. Hunter pondered whether it was wise to reveal it at all, but he knew he had to tell someone and Kwame was his first and only choice.

"You didn't get the sign-off sheet because I never sent it to you." Hunter's voice was just above a whisper, as though he thought someone might hear him despite the door that separated them from the eyes and ears of the other workers.

"What's up?" Kwame repeated. "Was something not cool with the layout or one of the articles? Should I not have given the go-ahead?"

Getting up from the chair he'd just occupied, Hunter briefly paced the floor behind his desk before coming to a stop in front of the window that gave him a broad view of the busy street beyond the parking lot. "No, it wasn't that. I'm glad you took the initiative to make sure we made print in time."

"What, then?"

Hunter was beginning to second-guess his decision to confide in his friend, but in order for anything he did from this point to make sense, Kwame had to know. "Several days ago, I got a letter from your late pastor's daughter."

"Jade?"

"Yeah," Hunter nodded. "It was weird and at first I just thought she was reacting like any heartbroken woman would if her father was all of a sudden taken from her and her family, but now . . ."

"What are you talking about, Hunter. What did the letter say?"

Opening his briefcase and reaching into the pocket, Hunter pulled out the unsealed envelope and laid it on the desk in front of him. "First, I need you to give me your word that this conversation will not be shared with anyone else in or outside of the AWC family. For now, I need it to be confidential until I fully figure out what I'm going to do."

Kwame's tone was guarded. "Okay. It doesn't go beyond us. You have my word."

It was all Hunter needed to hear. He knew that if Kwame gave his word, he could be trusted to keep it without question. "In a nutshell, Jade said that Reverend Tides' spirit had been visiting her in her dreams and that he told her that he was murdered and that his death wasn't an accident."

"What?" Kwame sat up straight in his seat, eyes widened in disbelief.

"Like I said, I didn't give it too much credibility at the time, but now, I don't know."

At the sound of Hunter's words, Kwame joined him in his stance in front of the office window and looked him directly in the face. For a moment, neither one of them spoke and Hunter had the feeling that Kwame was waiting for the crack of a smile or any hint that he was somehow being sarcastic. Kwame was the first to speak.

"What do you mean, you don't know?" Now his voice's level was low too, reflecting that of Hunter's. "There was nothing to indicate otherwise, was there? Do you know something that I don't know that would make you think that my pastor was murdered?"

"No; not really," Hunter said. "But something strange happened the other night when that storm blew through here. All of my power went out in my house."

"Mine too," Kwame interjected. "But what does that have to do with . . ."

"Let me finish," Hunter said, holding up his hand. "I kept hearing these strange noises in my house but I never could find the source. It was the creepiest thing I've ever felt. I almost had the notion that someone else was in my house aside from me and Malik. I could almost *feel* the presence of someone else there, but I never saw anything. But the noise was real, Kwame. I *heard* noises."

"Did Malik hear it, too?"

"No. But that don't mean nothing," Hunter quickly added when he saw the expression on Kwame's face. "Malik was so frightened by the thunder and lightning, that he wouldn't have noticed the noise even if he had heard it, I know what I heard, man."

Kwame walked the length of the office floor and then stopped suddenly and shook his head in confusion. "Okay, so let's just say you heard a strange noise in your house during the storm. So what? What does that have to do with Jade thinking her dad was murdered?"

Hunter stepped closer to his desk and tapped his index finger on the envelope, drawing Kwame's attention back to the letter that had been placed on the desk moments earlier.

"I read this letter some days ago and placed it back in the envelope and left it on my coffee table.

It's been lying in the same place ever since I read it. I even looked at it before the storm peaked on Wednesday night. I was reading a book at the time and I placed the book on top of the envelope when I finished the chapter that I was reading.

"Yesterday morning when I woke up, the storm was over, the power was back on, and this letter was outside of the envelope, lying open on top of the book that I had covered it with the night before. It was *open*, Kwame," Hunter stressed. "I promise you, I hadn't opened it since I placed it down on the table last week."

The brief silence that followed was broken by the sound of Kwame's hysterical laughter that seemed to radiate off of the walls of the office space. "Man, you sound like that guy who was talking that day at the mystery theatre dinner that we went to last year. What are you getting at?" he asked between gasps of breath. "Are you saying that you think something or *someone* was actually in your house and whatever or whoever it was pulled that envelope from underneath the book, opened the letter and laid it out on the table so that you could see it the next morning?"

When Hunter didn't join in Kwame's laughter or offer an immediate response, the room returned to its silent state. Taking slow cautious steps, Kwame rounded his friend's desk and came to a stop just a few inches from where Hunter stood staring out the window with his hands shoved in his pants' pockets.

"You're kidding, right?" Kwame's voice had reverted to a whisper. When Hunter's silence persisted, Kwame continued. "Hunter, you can't be saying that Reverend Tides' ghost came in your house and opened the letter. You have to know that there is some other explanation. Maybe Malik got up during the night and was pilfering around and opened it."

Hunter responded with a shake of his head. "I'm not saying it was done by a ghost. I don't even believe in ghosts, but I know for sure that Malik didn't do it. I told you he was scared stiff. Malik wouldn't leave my side that night. He never would have gotten up and opened the letter."

Kwame made his way back to the chair he had been sitting in at the start of their conversation. Hunter turned from the window and looked at him. He could only imagine the thoughts that were going through Kwame's mind and he couldn't blame him. If the tables were turned, he'd probably think the same if Kwame were telling the tale. Hunter had already told him the most farfetched part of the story, so he figured that this was as good a time as any to explain it all.

"In the letter, Jade said that she'd been having consistent dreams of her father visiting her and telling her that the answer to who had done this to him was somewhere to be found in the letters that we were printing in the paper. She was pleading with me to continue to post the letters so that she could find the answers that would lead to her father's killer. That was the reason for my hesitation in signing off on this week's print. I was trying to decide if I should honor her wishes."

Kwame was back on his feet and pacing the floor once again. "Hunter, the competition will kill us if we do this; you know that, right? They'll tear into us like a hungry gator. We'll be accused of using the

Tides Tragedy for profit. Everybody knows that our sales skyrocketed during that time, and if we go back to those features after ending them, it's gonna look like some kind of marketing strategy to keep our sales at that record high."

"I know." He had considered all of the possible repercussions.

"Hunter, New Hope is my church," Kwame continued. "I can't have them thinking that I'm capitalizing on Reverend Tides' death. I'm not the best of friends with Reverend Jackson Tides, but being on the deacon board, I know him and his mother well enough. Every Sunday, Mother Tides cries during services and I know her heart is still torn about all of this. Doing what you're contemplating would be like . . ."

"*I know*, Kwame. I *know*," Hunter reiterated. "Don't you think I've thought about all of that? Man, I don't know what to do. I think this open letter on my coffee table was a clear message sent to me. And call me crazy, but I think God is trying to tell me something here."

Kwame's pacing continued and he murmured to himself as he walked. Next to Hunter, Kwame was the most passionate about the *Atlanta Weekly Chronicle*. Hunter knew that he was thinking of more than his personal ties to the Tides family. Kwame was looking into the future and seeing the paper take a beating for reopening deep wounds within the community that were just beginning to see signs of healing. It had been hurtful enough to find out that Reverend Tides died tragically. If New Hope and the citizens of Atlanta were suddenly told, despite investigation results, that there was a chance that the preacher had been murdered, the survival of the AWC would be put in jeopardy once the stone-throwing subsided. And, as with all of the full-time staff members who ran the weekly periodical, the AWC was Kwame's livelihood.

"What if you just gave Jade the letters?" Kwame suggested. "Instead of printing them in the paper, why not just dump all those letters in a big ole Hefty bag and give them to her? That way, she can sort through them herself and find whatever it is that she thinks she's going to find. There are ways to get around this, Hunter. We can't start a campaign that is going to be the death of us. We *can't*."

"When readers send us letters, Kwame, they are letters to us not to someone else. We can't just send Jade those letters. We haven't read them all and we don't know what's in them. Sending them to her and exposing the identity and whereabouts of all of the writers could pose a bigger problem for us than printing the letters would.

"I know what you're thinking, man, and believe me, I've thought about every way this could backfire. If I'm just letting my imagination get the best of me and Jade is letting her grief get the best of her, then we could lose our shirts over this. But what if she's right? What if God is trying to tell her something in her night visions and your pastor was actually murdered? What if the letter being opened on my table is a sign that God wants me to fulfill Jade's request? And if her daughter is right, wouldn't it be better for Mrs. Tides to know the truth and wouldn't she be relieved to know that the killer was no longer roaming the streets? I've got all the questions," Hunter admitted, "but I don't have any of the answers."

Running his hands through the short dreadlocks on his head, Kwame released a lung full of air and for the first time in several minutes, he stood still. "Here's what I suggest. How about we don't do anything right now? How about you just sign off on the papers for us taking this week's edition to press, and over the next few days, we'll talk about this some more and pray about it to see if we can get some real guidance. To be honest with you, Hunter, I find it hard to believe that Reverend Tides was murdered and Atlanta's finest didn't see any evidence of that. But for the sake of argument let's just say that there is more to the story than any of us know. Before we start printing letters and starting a scandal that we won't be able to control, let's take a step back and use the next week or so to get some direction. Okay?"

Hunter nodded. Kwame was right. They had to be careful and they had to make sure that whatever steps they made next were in order. Once the decision was made, there would be no taking it back and too many lives would be affected for them not to move forward with caution.

"And for now, let's not talk to Diane or any of the other staff members," Hunter added. "If I decide to reopen the section of the paper that served as a tribute to Reverend Tides, then I'll also decide on how to break it to everyone else."

Kwame's reply was a silent nod of agreement, but Hunter could still see the concern on his face. Without saying another word, Hunter picked up the white envelope from his desk and took a long thoughtful look at the return address before slipping it back into the pocket of his briefcase. Although he would never admit it to Kwame, Hunter's gut-feeling told him that the decision of what he would do had already been made by a power higher than himself.

Chapter 6

While most of her colleagues were very vocal about their disdain for Monday mornings, for Jade, Mondays were just like any other weekday. Five days a week, her schedule was almost set in stone. She woke up, took a shower, ate a slice of dry wheat toast and drank a cup of green tea before getting dressed and making the twenty-mile drive from her home in Virginia Beach to her office in Norfolk. Most weeks, she had her patient load memorized and knew that an hour after she walked in her office door, her first client would arrive and be ready to sit on the couch and allow Jade to pick her brain. Ninety-eight percent of Jade's clients were women and oddly enough, Jade's specialty was grief counseling.

Being a psychologist wasn't a boring job. In fact, it was quite the opposite. Every day posed a new challenge and no one client's story was the carbon copy of another's. When she began her career after graduating from Clark Atlanta University with a Bachelor of Arts Degree in Psychology, Jade immediately gravitated toward working with women wrestling with grief. After all of the anguish she'd been struggling with, it all seemed ironic now. Having been faced with the biggest grief of her lifetime, Jade understood first hand what it meant to feel as though she couldn't talk to anyone.

For over a month she had been forced to harbor most of her feelings on the inside. Ingrid was the one person that she thought would understand, or at least pretend she did in the name of friendship. But her last exchange with Ingrid, coupled with the silence she construed as rejection from the founder of the *Atlanta Weekly Chronicles*, induced mounting feelings of dejection and loneliness.

Funny how I can advise people all day long on their issues and yet when I needed some of my own expertise, there was no one to be found.

The thought ran through Jade's head as she parked her car in the lot of West End Edifying Practitioners, the counseling center where she had practiced her profession for the past few years. The acronym for the business was W.E.E.P. and in Jade's experience as a counselor, it couldn't have been more appropriate. Just before entering the building, she scanned the parking lot to see if she saw Ingrid's Jeep. Its absence meant that her best friend was running late for work once again.

"Good morning, Dr. Tides," the receptionist greeted as Jade headed for her private office.

"Good morning," Jade replied.

Working in a place such as this and having talked to so many women who had gone through pain, Jade felt surprised that she had been living in her own world for all of the weeks that had passed since her family tragedy. Jackson said that it was time to heal. Her mother had been trying to convince her that her father would have wanted them to heal. But as much as Jade knew that they were all still hurting, she was certain that her pain was of a greater magnitude. The fact that she had convinced herself that there was more to her dad's death than what the world knew was proof of that. It took yesterday's sermon to shake her out of her grieving coma and make her see her own foolish ways.

"That's why God can't use some of us the way He wants to," Pastor Clifton Rhodes had said into the microphone as he stood behind the pulpit of Gospel Tabernacle of Praise. "We're so busy trying to hold on to our dark pasts that He can't lead us into the bright future He has prepared for us."

Agreeing responses of "Amen," "Yes suh," "That's right" and Deacon Burgess's favorite, "You preaching now, Doctor!" made Jade feel as though every member of her church was ganging up on her. Thinking realistically, she knew that her pastor didn't know the inward battle that she'd been fighting since her father's death and Jade also knew that he didn't hand pick today's sermon just to bash a hole in her skull and tattoo the words "move on already, will ya?" on her brain, but that was exactly what it felt like.

From her seat on the third-row pew, Jade had a

good view of the preacher and he had a good view of her as well. As the sermon entered its second half-hour, it seemed as though Pastor Rhodes was directing all of his words at her. It was Sundays like that one when she missed the luxury of being able to hide in a congregation of fifteen thousand like the one her father'd had at New Hope.

Pastor Rhodes continued. "God didn't promise any of us that life would be easy. All of us have ups and downs. All of us have heartbreaks and tragedies, but we still have to be able to put our faith in God and move forward. Can I get an amen?"

"Amen!" The voices around Jade echoed in her ears.

"When we stop stressing and rest in the Lord, God will work things out in our favor," Pastor Rhodes continued. "He is our shepherd and He won't lead us astray. The Bible says that God will give us rest. Psalm chapter twenty-three and verse two tells us that He'll make a way for us to lie down in green pastures and He'll lead us to still waters!"

"That's what the Word says," someone replied.

"Teach us, Pastor," another called out.

Perhaps it was all in her mind, but Jade was sure that Pastor Rhodes never took his eyes off of her as he preached. The walls of the one thousand seat edifice felt as though they were closing in on her and Jade forced her eyes to remain glued on the pages of the Bible on her lap to avoid the glare of her pastor and those around her.

"If you need healing, if you want deliverance, if you're looking for peace of mind, if you want the answers you've been searching for. . . . run to the green pastures He has prepared for you and find rest!" the preacher said pounding his fist on the pulpit in front of him. "God has given you peaceful waters and He's given you fertile grounds. You might walk through the valley where death is all around you, but you don't have to fret because God is right there. Rest!"

"You preaching now, Doctor!" Deacon Burgess said.

Those who had been sitting around Jade had long ago risen to standing positions as they cheered Pastor Rhodes on. Jade remained in her seat and hoped that their shadows were helping to hide her face and the tears that she couldn't withhold. Whether the preacher had really been looking at her or not and regardless of whether he had tailored his sermon specifically for her, Jade couldn't help but think that the message was a direct command from God.

Ever since her father's death, she'd been struggling just to get three or four hours of sleep per night. And the level of anxiety had only heightened over the last two weeks. From the time she placed the letter in the mail to Hunter Greene, she had done little else than worry over whether or not he would even take the time to read it, let alone give her request any consideration.

After hearing Pastor Rhodes' sermon, Jade was finally convinced that she had allowed anxieties and worries over her father's death to take full charge of her life. The dreams of him taking her by the hand and hinting that he'd been murdered had all been self-inflicted. The nightmare she'd had a few nights ago wherein she was running barefoot through the forest with a faceless man chasing her and calling her name—it too had emerged from her own troubled mind. All along, Ingrid, the police, the investigators and everyone else who had said that her father's death was an accident had been right. Jade couldn't see it or accept it because she didn't want to. Had she been resting in God instead of stressing over the situation, she wouldn't have lashed out at her best friend or been frustrated over not receiving a reply from Hunter.

When the congregation was finally given the official dismissal, Jade exchanged greetings with the people nearest her and then worked her way through the crowd and out the exit doors. On the outside with no walls boxing her in, she was able to breathe freely. Once inside her vehicle, Jade turned the key to start the engine and then relaxed against the headrest while the uplifting sounds offered by Star 94.1 streamed from her speakers. It was the station she always listened to in her car. Many of the choirs that they played reminded her of her teenage years, growing up in Atlanta and attending New Hope. But the choir at the church her father founded hadn't always sounded so glorious.

As Jade sat in her car in the church parking lot, she reminisced about the time her father first began having services outside of their living room. Their first real church was a little storefront building that was attached to a liquor store on Memorial Drive in Stone Mountain. She was only about six years old then, but she was still able to recall images of her and her family having to pick up empty beer cans and liquor bottles that had been discarded at their church's front door before they began morning worship. In those days, the choir was her brothers, her mother and herself. In fact, the members of Jade's immediate family were everything back then, from the ushers and the armor bearers to the announcer and musicians. They didn't have an organ or piano, but a set of drums was erected in one corner of the small building, and each Sunday, Jackson sat on the raggedy stool behind them and did his best to keep time.

In her youth, Jade remembered being picked on by schoolmates about the location and cosmetic shortcomings of the humble building that her father had chosen. Ironically, their first member was the wife of the liquor store owner. Less than a year later, after the proprietor of the package store gave his life to Christ, he closed down his thriving business and donated it to the church, making it possible for New Hope to expand its narrow room. At first there seemed to be no need for the extra space, but God must have realized their sincerity and chose to honor their efforts.

Before long, people began stopping by on Sundays just out of curiosity. They wanted to know more about the preacher whose presence in the neighborhood had made such a marked change in such a short time. In two years, the number had increased to fifty faithful worshipers and by the end of their fifth year they were forced to move from the location that could no longer accommodate the growing membership. By the time Jade was thirteen, they were laying the foundation for what was now the New Hope Church.

Late. Jade hated that term used to describe the deceased. Before the death of her father, she'd not even given the word much thought, but over the weeks since his accident, she had seen the term attached to his name in more news articles than she cared to keep count of. In life, her father was the most time-conscious man Jade knew. Now, in death, when getting anywhere was no longer an issue, he was referred to as "the late Reverend B.T. Tides" and Jade despised it.

For more than one reason, Jade chose to move away from north Georgia years ago. And while going home was something she seldom did, when Jade was there she always looked forward to hearing her father expound on the Word of God. Without him around, everything was different. A knock at her office door snapped Jade back to the business at hand.

"It's open," she called.

"Good morning." It was Demetrius Miller, a fellow psychologist whose office was across the hall from Jade's. "I picked up the papers this morning and yours was among them. I just thought I'd hand deliver it to you."

"Thank you."

Jade tried not to notice that Demetrius purposely touched her hand as the exchange took place. Though he was a handsome bachelor, apparently unattached, Jade felt no real attraction to Demetrius. Recently celebrating his second year at W.E.E.P., Demetrius was the newest member of their practice, and the tall, fair-skinned, smart-dresser had made his interest in Jade clear from his first day of employment. After declining many offers, Jade had gone out to dinner with him once, but had no desire to repeat what was in retrospect an error in judgment. She concluded long ago that there could be no real room for her in Demetrius' life because he was already full . . . of himself. His favorite subject was him and he never seemed to tire of trying to convince others of how worthy a man he was.

"Nice suit," he said, eyeing the lavender satin pantsuit that Jade wore.

"Thank you. Can you close the door on your way out?" Jade gave the response without looking at him. She was way past the days that she felt obligated to be nice and/or professional in her rejection of Demetrius. He used to just get on her nerves, now his simple presence irked her to no end. There were dozens, perhaps hundreds, of women out there who would probably jump at a chance to be attached to his arm. Why he continued to pursue her escaped Jade's reasoning.

"I'm surprised you're not wearing a wool coat with the chill that's in this office," he responded sarcastically.

Still looking at the front page of her copy of the *Atlanta Weekly Chronicles,* Jade responded. "I'm sure it's a lot warmer in your office. Why don't you go test it out and see?"

The timing of her telephone's ring couldn't have been better. Jade immediately picked it up, halting whatever response Demetrius was about to offer. Noting her business-like tone, he reluctantly gave her the respect of stepping out and closing her door. After counting to ten to be sure her unwanted guest was actually gone, Jade sighed and placed the phone back in its place. Upon her greeting, the caller had apologized for dialing the wrong number and had immediately hung up. The entire dialog to the imaginary "Mrs. Kirkpatrick" that followed was just Jade's way of getting rid of Demetrius. It worked beautifully.

A relationship was the last thing on Jade's mind and one with Demetrius Miller was even further down on the list than that. Jade had just turned thirty-two in May. As a child growing up, she thought that by this age she would be married and have fulfilled her desire to have a family. But with two relationships ending up to be two missed marks, she was in no hurry to take on what could possibly be strike three.

Love interest number one had been a college sweetheart that she met at Clark Atlanta University. B.T. Tides wasn't one to hear of his children dating in high school. As far as he was concerned, absolutely nothing should be on their minds at that age other than finishing their education and pleasing God (and not necessarily in that order). Her father's rules were fine by Jade because as a late bloomer, she had no real interest in dating as a teenager. But once she entered her sophomore year in college, one man appeared who made her want to give love a chance. His name was Oscar and he was a third-year Chemistry major. They were only three months into their courtship when he was arrested for being eight months behind in financial support for a child Jade didn't even know he had. She had been a bit injured by Oscar's dishonesty, but because the relationship was still young, getting over him wasn't too difficult a task. In the long run, she felt more embarrassed than heartbroken.

Jade's second failure in the love department wasn't nearly as uncomplicated. George Bannister had not only been her steady for over a year, but he had also had the rare pleasure of meeting her family, talking to her father, and gaining permission to pop the question. He had done so and presented her with a breathtaking solitaire diamond ring as a gift on her twenty-ninth birthday. A year later, thousands of guests were gathered at Jade's father's church while she sat nervously with her maid of honor in one of the back rooms, waiting for her cue to approach the entrance door for her long-awaited bridal march.

If there was any man that seemed "safe," George was his embodiment. Jade had known him for two years as a faithful Christian. George was a member of the men's ministry and each month the group, supposed to consist of spirit-filled brothers, visited the men's homeless shelter and fed the residents both physically and spiritually. George had all the qualities that Jade thought she wanted in a husband, but she never became his wife.

They didn't have an argument or even an official breakup. George simply never showed up for the wedding. The night before, during rehearsal, he was nervous, but not to any level that wouldn't be expected of a future groom. No one would have guessed that his cold feet would have sent him running in the opposite direction, but they did. He didn't even give Jade or her family the courtesy of calling or giving any explanation. It was a month later when she finally got a letter of apology from him in the mail. In it, he stated that he realized at the last minute that he just wasn't ready for "that level of commitment." He still loved her though, he'd insisted. His prescription for treating the problem was that they continue to date for a little longer and plan the wedding for a year later.

Jade didn't agree; she chose instead to send back the ashes of his letter as her only response. She'd contemplated returning the two carat ring to him or pawning it for half of its worth, but she did neither. Perhaps knowing that he still had multiple payments to make, Jade's choice to keep the gift was partly made out of spite. For a while following the breakup, looking at the jewelry renewed bitter, painful memories. George had broken her heart in the worst way. He'd betrayed her trust and made her feel unimaginable anguish. The ring, at first, was a constant reminder of that but over the months as she found comfort in God's grace, Jade chose to cherish it as a reflection of her own inner beauty and substantial self-worth that George had almost caused her to lose sight of.

After several weeks of trying to get in touch with Jade, George finally accepted the fact that the relationship he'd shattered could not be salvaged. Considering the circumstances, Jade was shocked that he'd ever thought she'd give him another chance. She later learned that George's job had relocated him to Gary, Indiana. If she had had her way, he would have been relocated to Cambodia or better yet, Pakistan or some other country where they tortured and killed people who professed to be Christians. For George, it would be a fitting punishment as far as Jade was concerned.

At the buzzing of her telephone, she picked up the receiver and placed it to her ear. "Yes?"

"Dr. Tides, Mrs. Anderson is here to see you." the receptionist said.

"Thank you, Cassandra," Jade responded. "Give me five minutes and send her in."

Jade had been so engrossed in her own thoughts that she hadn't even pulled Mrs. Anderson's file in preparation of her arrival. Thumbing through the drawer of her file cabinet, she retrieved the manila folder and placed it on her desk where the newspaper her colleague had brought in earlier still lay. Instinctively, Jade opened the paper to Section C, which had at one time been filled with tributes to her father. Although she had heard Pastor Rhodes' message on Sunday and had already made the decision to concede and move on, a bizarre sense of sadness engulfed her at not seeing any mention of the man she respected more than any other.

Taking a deep breath and blinking back the threat of tears, Jade tucked the newspaper in her drawer and made final preparations for her first therapy session of the day. Just as the expected knock came at her door, the sounds of her cell phone ringing came from the same drawer she'd just closed.

"Come on in, Mrs. Anderson," Jade called while simultaneously reaching for her purse which was now buried beneath the newspaper.

"Hello?" she said while silently motioning her client to take a seat.

"Dr. Tides?" querried an unfamiliar voice on the other end of the line.

"Speaking."

"Do you have a moment? I need to speak with you."

Chapter 7

Going through B.T. Tides' things and boxing them up for storage had been the hardest thing Mildred had ever done, aside from enduring the funeral itself. She and her husband had created so many memories over the past forty-five years that everything she pulled from the closet and the dresser drawers seemed to have a story behind it.

Mildred remembered the day she bought him the blue shirt that she was now folding. It was three years ago during a sale at JC Penney when they traveled to Florida for a week-long vacation. The grey pants that she picked up next were one of B.T.'s favorite articles of clothing. The right pocket had a hole it in and there were permanent paint stains near the hem. Her husband had had them for more than twenty years. They had gone out of style, come back in style and gone out again, but he didn't care. They were the pants that he wore when they were painting New Hope in preparation for the grand opening of the newly-constructed edifice.

"B.T., you just got paint on your new pants!" Mildred remembered exclaiming when she saw him accidentally brush against a can of paint that sat on the floor.

"Did I?" He looked down and saw the ivory stain that clearly marked the spot.

"If we go in the bathroom right now, I might be able to get most of it out with a wet cloth," Mildred offered. "We need to hurry before it starts to dry."

B.T. had laughed in that carefree way that Mildred had come to love over the years. Then he said, "Don't worry yourself, honey. They're just pants. Besides, ain't nothing wrong with a little paint. Every time I wear these, I'll remember the day I was anointed with a bit of the paint used to cover the walls of God's house."

And he wore them often. They became his work pants—the ones he wore whenever there was work to be done around the house, and he wore them to youth outings and church barbecues. Mildred used to immediately begin fussing when she saw him pulling the outdated garment out of the closet to wear. Now, as she folded them to put them away for the final time, she'd give anything for a chance to see him slip them on again.

"Give me strength, Lord," she prayed while using the fabric of the pants to clear the moisture from her eyes.

It was a prayer that she had uttered many times in the six weeks that had passed since she last saw her husband alive. Reverend Alfonzo Knight, the preacher who had recently been permanently assigned to the leadership role that B.T. Tides had left open, told her just two days ago that God was going to give her a renewed level of strength. While Mildred didn't doubt God's abilities, her strength, both mental and physical, seemed to be waning more with each passing day.

This past Sunday, she sat in church and tried to imagine herself occupying a pew amongst another congregation of worshippers. Mildred didn't want to admit it, but Jackson had been right when he said that attending New Hope no longer felt the same.

There was a time that whenever her name was called, Mildred felt a sense of reverence from the person who had felt the need to recognize her presence. Now, when the new pastor and the members acknowledged her, she felt as if she were being put on the spot. Reverend Knight was a gifted teacher and Mildred had no qualms with the board of directors' choice to place him in leadership position. She, too, had signed the dotted line, giving her approval for the assignment. But as well-versed in the scripture as he was, Reverend Knight couldn't adequately fill the shoes that B.T. had left void; at least, not in Mildred's eyes.

There were times during yesterday's service that she felt like a stranger in the ministry that she had helped her husband build, mold and nurture. Although she knew that there was probably no true way to prepare for B.T.'s demise, Mildred always thought that when it was time for her husband to go, she would be at peace, knowing that he was resting in the Lord. But she hadn't had a day of peace since the tragedy. Sometimes she felt like her dreams were being interrupted by unseen forces. All of her nights, since the accident, had been restless and not once in the past month and a half had she slept in the bed that she and B.T. had shared. Without him, even the normal felt strange.

"Lord, you promised never to leave me or forsake me," Mildred said while folding another article of clothing and using it to wipe away another tear before adding the shirt to the stack.

At first, she had made a decision that she wouldn't change anything about her life or her home. The way B.T. left it was the way that she'd let it remain. But after weeks of not being able to sleep, Mildred decided that she had to make some changes if she was ever to find the serenity that she needed. She reasoned that being forced to look at his shoes by the bedside and his clothes in the closet was contributing to her tension. Earlier in the day, she'd put all of his shaving items and hair care products in a box and sealed it for storing. It had been harder to motivate herself to remove his garments, but Mildred finally forced herself to begin emptying the dresser drawers.

Ridding the closet of his Sunday suits and the tie and handkerchief sets that she loved so much would be even more difficult to do. Mildred had already decided that the closet would have to wait for another day. In the beginning, doing it all at once seemed like the route to take, but as she used the sleeve of her bathrobe to wipe new tears, Mildred knew that for her, it was too big of a task to take on.

The ringing of her telephone startled her and caused her to drop the socks that she'd been knotting together. After taking a moment to calm herself, she took a deep breath and put on her best telephone voice. "Hello?"

"You have a collect call from Phillips State Prison," the automated voice responded. "To accept, press one, to decline the call, press two."

Mildred closed her eyes and released a heavy sigh. She loved her children dearly, but Jerome had been such a colossal disappointment, and on days like today, she was in no mood to deal with him. Reluctantly, she pressed one and waited to hear her son's voice.

"Mother?" Jerome's voice rang through the receiver.

"Hi, Jerome." She tried not to sound as let down as she felt.

"Hi, Mother. I just wanted to call and see how you were doing. How is everything?"

"As well as to be expected, I suppose. How are you?"

Jerome was quiet for a moment and then brought his voice to the level of a whisper and said, "I miss him, Mother."

On the inside, Mildred felt a twinge of anger brewing and she was glad that Jerome couldn't see the grimace on her face. She wanted to scream at her son who never seemed to show any appreciation for anything that his father had done for him in the past. At the funeral, she noted his steady flow of heavy tears and had an urge to leave her seat to slap Jerome across the face, despite the presence of the officer who sat beside him. It offended her that he would be so emotional about the death of a man he rarely honored in life.

"Jerome, all of us miss B.T.," she responded, swallowing back the words she really wanted to say. "We're going to make it through with the help of the Lord."

There was another brief silence, but the stillness was broken by a defined sniffle coming from Jerome's end of the line. Mildred shook her head in disgust but chose not to speak in fear of what she might say.

"You know I saw him the evening before he died," Jerome said.

Mildred stiffened. She didn't know that her husband had gone to the jail that Wednesday. They usually went together every Friday for a visit with their son.

"I think he knew he was gonna die, Mother," Jerome said, taking his mother's emotions to a whole new level.

"What?"

"Listen," he said. "Dad said that he stopped by to see me because it might be a while before he got back this way again. He said God had a special assignment for him so I thought y'all were planning a trip or something. But now that I think about it, I think God was speaking through him and having him tell me goodbye."

"Jerome Abraham Tides, since when are you the expert on God speaking?" Mildred had heard all she could take and the words jumped from her lips before she could stop them. "In all the years you've been on the face of the earth, you've never heard one word that God spoke to you through your daddy and now you want to try and tell me that B.T. knew his days were numbered and God had him to tell *you*? If B.T. was getting ready to go and be with God and he knew it, *I* would have been the one he would have told, Jerome, not you!"

Her outburst had rendered Jerome speechless. For several moments, all Mildred could hear on his end was breathing and the occasional voice of someone talking in the distance.

"What are you saying, Mother? Are you saying that because of who I was God can't speak to me? Are you saying you're better than I am?"

"Boy, don't you get smart with me," Mildred warned. "I'm not talking about who you *were* Jerome. You act like you've changed. You haven't changed. You've been locked up in jail for ten years and you haven't changed a bit. You still haven't even owned up to your mistakes and now all of a sudden God is speaking to you?"

"God can speak to me just like He can speak to anyone else, Mother."

"You know what? If you have never told the truth before, you just did," Mildred said after a dry laugh. "God spoke to Satan himself, so yes, He could speak to you, Jerome. But my point is this. If God were going to speak through your father about premonitions of his death, out of *all* of us in the Tides family, I don't think He would have given you first dibs."

"I thought I could talk to you about this, Mother, but I see that I can't."

"Jerome, as long as you are being honest, which by the way is something you've always had trouble being, you can talk to me about anything. But you'll have to excuse me for not taking kindly to this particular conversation. Let's just say that your daddy felt the need to divulge information like that to someone other than me. We had two sons, Jerome. One of them not only followed B.T.'s teachings, but he's walking in his footsteps. The other one is . . . well, the other one is you, Jerome. Do you really believe that your daddy would have come to you instead of Jackson?"

"He would if he didn't see me as unworthy as you apparently do."

Mildred sighed as deeply as she could. She was in no mood to argue any further. "Let's just change the subject, Jerome. It's apparent that we're getting nowhere."

"That was what I called for, Mother. So I have nothing to change the subject to. I gotta go now. My telephone time is up. Talk to you later."

Before she could respond, Jerome hung up the phone. Mildred did the same with hers. When she thought about all the times she was contacted by school teachers, neighbors and even family members about Jerome's behavior, she couldn't help but feel angry.

"I think he knew he was gonna die, Mother."

"I think he knew he was gonna die, Mother."

"I think he knew he was gonna die, Mother."

Jerome's words seemed to bounce around in Mildred's head, reverberating from one ear to the other and making her more disturbed with each echo. How could her son even say such a thing? Was this just another way to annoy her? Jerome had been harboring anger against her and B.T. for years. When he was arrested years ago, he told the police that his parents were the alibi he needed to prove his innocence. Mildred still remembered the day that she and her husband had been visited by two detectives; one male, one female.

"Your son says that he was with you at Bible Study on the night in question," the man had revealed to them. "We need you to verify that for us."

Mildred and B.T. could only exchange silent glances. Neither of them wanted what their son was being accused of to be true, but they knew they couldn't lie for him. Jerome was twenty-six years old at the time and he hadn't set foot in New Hope Church in at least three years.

"It's true that we had Bible Study that night," B.T. had said while shaking his head slowly, "but Jerome wasn't there. I wish to God that he was, but he wasn't."

For the first six years that he was in jail, Jerome openly blamed his parents for his incarceration, but Mildred and B.T. were sure that his fate would have been sealed regardless of whether they'd been honest or not. His face had been picked from a photo album of mug shots by the man who had been pistol whipped and held up at gunpoint by Jerome and his friends and ultimately shot by one of the men who was now serving twenty-five years to life.

In a strange way, Mildred had been relieved when her troubled son was put behind bars. When Jerome was free, she was in constant fear of his safety and had fully prepared herself to receive a phone call that he had been killed. She knew that life behind bars wasn't easy, but Mildred felt that he was safer there than on the streets.

"I think he knew he was gonna die, Mother."

"I think he knew he was gonna die, Mother."

"I think he knew he was gonna die, Mother."

Mildred couldn't get the words out of her head, but she refused to believe them. For nearly fifty years, since they were teenage sweethearts, Mildred and B.T. had gone through everything together. She tried always to be honest with him and she trusted him to be the same with her—especially when it came to matters that would affect both of them. Dying easily fit that bill. There was no way that B.T. would somehow know, or even *think* that he would lose his life that night and not tell her. He wouldn't knowingly rip her heart out without any warning.

"You should be ashamed of yourself, Jerome!" she said in a harsh whisper. "You mocked your daddy's teachings when he was alive and now you're trying to ridicule his reputation as an honest man. B.T. wouldn't have ever kept something like that from me."

Mildred grabbed a handful of her husband's clothes from the drawer and resumed her task of folding them, all the while wiping away more tears that clouded her vision.

"He would have told me!" she exclaimed. "He would have told me!"

Chapter 8

Hunter sat at a corner booth at Vivo Cucina, an Italian eatery located in Virginia Beach. Even when he wasn't at work, he wanted to be there, so now his mind drifted between his reason for being in Virginia and the things that needed to be done at work. Only important issues kept him from the office, and like most of them, today's issue was work related. With his elbows propped on the tabletop and his hands clasped together, he stared at the door of the restaurant, searching the faces of all of the patrons as they entered the establishment and waited to be seated. Either Wednesday was an exceptionally busy day for Vivo Cucina, or it was a thriving spot.

Although Italian food was his favorite, Hunter had never eaten at this restaurant. In fact, when he stepped off of the Delta flight after landing at Norfolk International Airport, it marked the first time he'd set foot in the state of Virginia. Once he'd endured the crowd at baggage claims, Hunter picked up his reserved rental car and driving along, began enjoying the sight of the beautiful bodies of water and the distant mountains. He followed the directions that he'd been given that would guide him to the popular dining spot.

When he telephoned Jade two days ago to set up the lunch meeting, Hunter immediately judged from her tone that she wasn't expecting his call. The sound of his voice seemed to almost startle her, and Jade's level of uneasiness had left Hunter confused. At one point, her hesitation prompted him to think that she was going to turn down his lunch invitation. When the conversation ended, Hunter spent some time questioning whether he'd made the right decision. Jade was the one who'd set the stage. She had written him and made the request that he alter his decision to cease printing the newspaper tributes to her father. But suddenly, Hunter was led to consider the possibility that she had, for some reason, changed her mind. In the end, Jade accepted his suggestion that they meet over lunch, but . . .

"Mr. Greene?"

Hunter's thoughts had him so many miles away that he had not noticed his lunch companion enter the restaurant. She had walked across the floor, led by the hostess, and was now standing right beside him. Masking his embarrassment, Hunter stood and extended his hand toward her.

"Thank you for making time for me, Dr. Tides," he said. "Please call me Hunter."

"Nice to meet you, Hunter; and you're welcome to call me Jade." As she spoke, she made herself comfortable on the bench across from him in the booth that they now shared.

Hunter almost laughed out loud, but instead he flashed a broad smile. It amazed him that he could remember so vividly their childhood days as neighbors, whereas Jade couldn't. After giving the waitress their drink orders, they were left alone.

They engaged in conversation and by the time the glasses of tea arrived and they had given the waitress their lunch orders, Hunter felt as though he had been given the opportunity to catch up on the more than twenty years that had passed since he'd spoken to Jade. He found himself fascinated by her life. Not that he'd ever given any consideration to what she had grown to become, but Hunter never would have guessed that she would have gone into psychology. When he saw the abbreviated Doctor of Philosophy title on the envelope of the letter she sent to him, Hunter had envisioned her as a university lecturer. To find that she was a clinical psychologist was something of a surprise.

"I was the only one of my parents' children to complete college," she explained as their plates of food arrived. "My oldest brother, Jackson, had dreams of becoming a professional football player almost his entire life. He completed two years at Notre Dame but then said he felt a calling to do God's work. To everyone's surprise, he opted to refuse the rest of his athletic scholarship and instead, go into the ministry. I always wondered why he didn't do both."

Jade's next few words brought a burst of laughter from Hunter that he was unable to suppress.

"You'll think I'm saying this just because I'm his

sister, but Jackson had the potential to be a star NFL quarterback. He was something fierce on the football field."

The outburst from Hunter caught Jade by surprise. Hunter could tell she was unsure of how to interpret his reaction.

"I'm sorry," he said.

"You don't believe me?"

"No, no, no," Hunter said while shaking his head. "It's not that at all. I'm just very amused by the fact that we've been sitting here chatting for over thirty minutes and you have absolutely no recollection of me."

Jade removed her glass from her lips and gently placed it on the table beside her plate. Hunter watched as she searched his face for signs of familiarity. True, it had been two and a half decades since the last time he handed her a basketball on the playground of the housing project, but Hunter didn't think he'd changed that much over the years. Certainly, Jade hadn't. She still had the same thick, curly hair and coffee-colored skin. Her eyes still carried that charming hint of innocence that all those years ago, had pulled at his heartstrings and made him give her the basketball for a shot that had no chance of making its mark.

"I'm sorry," she said, surrendering. "Do I . . . Do I know you?"

"Think grade school," Hunter hinted.

"We were in the same class in grade school?"

"Strike one," Hunter said, enjoying her struggle to remember. "Think of the old Perry Homes."

"That's where I lived when I was a little girl," Jade said.

"I know," Hunter nodded. "Back in the days before it was demolished and replaced by the nicer West Highlands development."

"You too?"

"For a while, yes." Hunter was happy to put the pieces of the puzzle together for her. "My family lived right next door to yours, but we moved away before you all did."

"Hunter Greene," Jade said thoughtfully.

"I was a couple of grades ahead of you," Hunter pointed out. "I guess it's not odd that you don't remember me. It's not like our families interacted much with each other. All the guys I hung out with idolized Jackson. He had a mean right arm back then."

Jade smiled at the accolades for her brother. "So you did understand when I said that he could have made it in the NFL."

Hunter nodded. "There are two things that made me remember you so well."

"What?"

"You used to like to follow the guys outside to play basketball."

Jade's face lit up. "Now, I *do* remember that. I used to have to beg Mother to let me go out and watch the boys shoot hoops. Most days she'd allow it, but only for a little while and only when she had the time to stand there and watch me. She said the boys played too rough and when they scampered for the ball, I could get hurt if I stood too close," Jade paused to laugh and then she continued. "Now, I understand her concern, but back then I thought I was a big girl. In reality, I was very small compared to the boys who were really there to play. Most times I'd just watch but every once in a while, one of the guys would take pity on me and give me the ball and . . ."

She stopped when Hunter broke into a grin and held his arms out as if to say "ta-da!"

"You?" Jade asked, sitting forward in her seat. "That was you who used to hand me the ball?"

"Guilty as charged."

The two burst into simultaneous laughter, two old friends reunited by an amusing memory. For Hunter, it was the first time that he noticed just how much Jade had grown to look like her father. They grew quiet as their food was delivered to their table and when Hunter bowed his head to say the grace, Jade followed his lead. After he had prayed over their meal, Jade broke the brief silence that followed.

"What was the second thing that made you remember me?" she asked, picking the conversation up where they'd left off.

"Your name," Hunter said. "It's green like mine."

Jade looked perplexed, so he explained.

"Hunter is a shade of green and so is Jade. I always thought it was crazy that my mom would give me a first name like Hunter when my last name was Greene. So my name is actually Green Greene."

A thoughtful expression covered Jade's face, followed by a smile; then she said, "I think Hunter is a strong name. I like the name Hunter Greene."

Hunter felt a warm feeling flush through his body. "Thank you."

"In one of my psychology courses in college, we read that names had so much more bearing on children than parents even gave consideration to. Children with stronger or more meaningful names sometimes find greater success in life. They survive better than others. You might be one for the win column on that one."

Hunter's smile broadened. "And you as well."

"I try not to think like this," Jade said, "but sometimes I think my family would have survived better had we relocated elsewhere when we moved from Perry Homes."

"How so?"

"Shelton Heights," Jade pointed out. "You haven't heard the legend behind it?"

Hunter knew the myth very well, but he sat silently and looked at Jade, hoping that she would continue so that he could hear her thoughts. She did as he'd hoped.

"People say that strange things have happened to the residents of Shelton Heights from the time the subdivision was built. The homes are very nice, but they sell and rent for much less than they're worth because of the tales surrounding it. We knew of a couple of incidents that happened to people who lived there, but we never gave them much thought. Daddy would always tell us that God was greater than any foolish superstition and we believed him."

"And now?"

She looked at Hunter following his probing question and at first Jade's only response was a shake of her head that was barely detectable. After a brief silence, she spoke again. "We were so poor growing up in Perry Homes. As far as I was concerned, nothing could happen in Shelton Heights that would even come close to being as bad as that was. Honestly, I don't know what to think now."

"People die everyday, Jade," Hunter said. "They die of diseases, accidents, old age and some are even murdered. In any case, all of those people don't live in Shelton Heights. That whole myth started because Shelton Heights, the man, was said to be some kind of warlock. It's all just talk, Jade. You know that, I hope."

"Yeah." Jade's response was soft-spoken and Hunter wasn't at all convinced that she was being completely honest with him. When Jade spoke again, she changed the subject completely. "Were you in the grade with Jerome? Do you remember him? He's my brother too."

Sensing that her abrupt change was deliberate, Hunter didn't press the former issue. The last topic had obviously made Jade uncomfortable, but the new one now did the same for Hunter. He discerned immediately that he needed to approach his answer with caution. His first thought was to pretend he knew nothing of Jerome's incarceration, but most likely Jade would see right through his fraud. When her brother was arrested, it was major news given the prominence of her father. All of the local newspapers, the AWC included, had featured the story of the robbery and shooting. For Hunter to put on an act would do more harm than good.

"No, I was not in the same grade with Jerome, but I do remember him. How is he?"

Jade's hesitation was a bit longer this time, but

after drinking from her glass, she answered. "I haven't seen him since Daddy's funeral, but I've spoken to him a couple of times. Jerome and I were never really all that close, even though we're closer in age than I am to Jackson."

She paused a moment and appeared a bit nervous as she used her hand to tuck strands of hair behind her ear. Hunter was almost sure that he saw moisture gathering in her eyes, but she quickly hid it behind her glass as she drank more of her tea. Changing the subject seemed like the right thing to do, but Hunter sensed that she wasn't finished talking.

"Jerome has always been a bit standoffish in my opinion. Maybe it was just that he didn't feel he could bond with a little sister, I don't know," Jade said while staring at the food that remained on her plate. "He never bonded all that well with Jackson either, though. Jerome just didn't seem to fit in with the rest of the family. He stayed in trouble. I don't suppose I have to tell you that he's in prison."

"I'm aware," Hunter admitted.

"I get by to see him every time I make a trip to Atlanta, but he never really says much to me. I mean, he talks, but he doesn't really *talk*. You know what I mean?"

Hunter nodded in silence.

"The last time I saw him I told him that he needed to call me more often. I really don't mind the collect calls. But for some reason he won't really talk much to me. I think he and Daddy were just starting to get closer when the accident happened.

Mother . . . well, Daddy's death has really hit all of us hard. Daddy was everything to our family. For him to die . . . it just doesn't seem real, you know?"

All of the earlier laughter was gone and the tears that Hunter had seen building were now spilling down Jade's cheeks. His first impulse was to reach across the table and place his hand on top of hers. After a moment of reconsideration, he decided that the move would be too intimate, and the diamond on her finger that sparkled from the beam of the overhead light suggested that doing so might not be the best idea. Instead, Hunter reached into his suit jacket, retrieved a white handkerchief and offered it to her.

"Thank you," she whispered, taking the cotton cloth the size of a bandana. "I'm sorry."

"Don't be. I know how dear Reverend Tides was to the community so I can only imagine how difficult this whole situation has been to the family that loved him even more. I could feel the pain at the funeral and even in your letter."

"Oh, that?" Jade said, dabbing away the last of her tears. "I guess I should apologize for the letter. Although you wouldn't go into details over the phone on Monday, I know that's the reason you called for this meeting. I really did have good intentions when I wrote it. I don't know . . . I guess maybe I was hoping for an understandable reason for what happened to my father. His being killed in an accident just didn't seem logical. Maybe I thought that a murder made more sense."

Hunter interrupted. "Are you saying that you no longer believe that there was some foul play involved?"

Jade looked away and crossed her arms in front of her body like she felt chilled all of a sudden. Quietly Hunter watched her, waiting for her to answer. Jade closed her eyes and exhaled. It was a quiet sigh, but one that was deep enough for Hunter to see the rise and fall of her chest. The word difficult didn't seem to adequately describe how she felt about talking about this subject.

"I'm trying not to," Jade finally said. "A few days ago I gave in to what everybody else seemed to believe so I could try and find closure and move on with my life. Realistically speaking, it was the only thing to do. Police reports proved everybody right, but yet I was stupidly holding on to something that I had no proof of. The few people to whom I made my feelings known thought I was crazy. I only disclosed a bit of it to my best friend and she basically told me that I needed to hire myself for some counseling," Jade said with a short laugh. "And then, there was you . . ."

"I never said you were crazy," Hunter quickly defended.

"Some things don't have to be verbalized," Jade responded after a brief silence. "But it's okay. I understand, really."

"Do you?"

"Yes."

Hunter sat back in his chair and looked at the woman sitting across from him. Jade had opened a door for him and if he played his cards right, he could bail without so much as a graze. Tomorrow, he could catch his morning flight back to Atlanta, tell Kwame that he could stop worrying about the paper going under, and return to business as usual. No one would be the wiser.

"Do you know why I called you and set up this meeting with you today?" He might regret it later, but Hunter had to follow his instinct.

"Uh-huh," Jade nodded.

"Why?" Hunter challenged.

"You don't need me to tell you why you came here."

"Indulge me."

"You came here to tell me that you weren't going to be able to fulfill my ludicrous request."

"I could have done that over the phone, couldn't I?"

Jade pushed her plate aside and used the increased space as a prop for her elbows as she leaned in closer. "You see this?" she asked, repositioning the band on the ring finger of her left hand so that the diamond was directed toward her lunch companion.

"Even if my name was Stevie Wonder, I couldn't have missed it," Hunter said, drawing a brief laugh from Jade.

"Well, I had it appraised before deciding to keep it and what I found out was that it's a very clear, flawless diamond. The man who gave it to me, however, was a jerk."

She had Hunter's full attention.

"He left me at the altar."

"I'm . . . sorry."

"Why?" Jade asked. "I'm not. At least, not any more. After he left me, quite some time passed before he ever gave me an explanation. When he did decide to own up to his inexcusable stupidity, he did so by writing me a letter. Daddy said that if he was of any worth, he would never have done that by letter or by telephone. He would have met with me, perhaps invited me to lunch, and explained his actions to me in person. Not that that would have made a difference to me, mind you," she added quickly. "But at least there would have been a smidgen of a chance that I could have viewed him as a man again."

Hunter smiled, looked up into the ceiling and shook his head all at the same time. The door was still open. In fact, she had just made the escape route wider. He could end the conversation now and do so without her having ill feelings toward him. Jade had all but said that she respected him for having the decency to meet her with his declination. With that knowledge, Hunter wouldn't have to feel that he'd left her with eternal scars. Still, he couldn't do it.

Bringing his eyes back to hers, Hunter said, "In your letter, you mentioned dreams . . . visits from your father that indicated . . ."

"I know what I said, Hunter."

"Shhh," he responded before pushing his plate aside and leaning in closer too, putting their faces within inches of one another. "Jade, when you told me that you felt that your father's spirit was trying to send you a message, I'll be the first to admit that my immediate thought was that you were behaving like any unstable, grieving daughter would. Reverend Tides was your father. He was the man who loved, raised and nurtured you. It was understandable that you'd have dreams, hallucinations or any other type of vision that would keep him alive in your heart. Back then, although there was some logic in it, yes, I have to admit I thought it was crazy."

"What are you saying?" Jade whispered back. "You don't think it's crazy now?"

"If, as his daughter, what you were experiencing was craziness, then there would have to be a different word for my encounter."

Jade's eyes widened and Hunter remained silent while she stared him straight in the eyes with a look reminiscent of a woman watching an intense scene unfolding in a horror flick. She looked as if she was afraid to ask, but curiosity got the best of her.

"Hunter, what are you trying to tell me? Did you have a dream too?"

"A dream? No. A dream probably wouldn't have freaked me out nearly as much as what happened to me the other night. Before you make the decision not to pursue your intuition and the interpretation of your dream, I think you need to hear this. Or maybe I just need to tell you; I don't know, but in any case, just be glad you're sitting down."

Chapter 9

"You did *what*? I thought we were going to talk about this first, man."

All morning Hunter had kept to himself the meeting he'd had with Jade. It wasn't until the lunch hour and he and Kwame were sitting across from one another at Maggiano's, a popular restaurant on busy Peachtree Street, that Hunter decided to fill his editorial director in on his out-of-town business.

"We did, Kwame. You and I talked about this last weekend. I made the appointment with her on Monday morning."

"Did we come to a decision over the weekend that nobody bothered to tell me about?" Kwame asked. "Yeah, we talked about it, but I didn't know a decision had been made."

It was true. Hunter realized that there was no real agreement made during their two-hour leisure time at the ESPN Zone and he felt that there would be no true meeting of the minds where this particular subject was concerned. The ultimate decision was his anyway and Hunter had taken it upon himself to speak to Jade, realizing that it was the right thing to do despite the fact that it wasn't the safest decision for the survival of the *Atlanta Weekly Chronicles.*

"Hunter, I can't believe you did this without my knowledge. When you called me on Tuesday night, you said you weren't going to be in the office on Wednesday because you didn't feel well. I should have known better. You never take a day off. You can be blind in one eye and can't see out the other and you'd be here. I can't believe you lied to me, man. You intentionally did this without telling me. That's just not right."

Feeling the need to defend himself, Hunter finally spoke up. "Hold up. First of all, I didn't tell you that I didn't feel well, so I didn't lie to you. I said I didn't feel like coming into the office, which was the truth. Did I intentionally keep this trip from you? Yes I did. I knew you were never gonna think I should go to Jade with what happened. You know why? Because all you can do is think of what the church folks will think and your job at the AWC. If you think for one second that I'm not concerned about that, you're wrong. I'm *very* concerned, Kwame. Especially about the impact it will have on the paper.

"I've devoted much of my adult life building the reputation of the AWC, so believe me when I say I'm *more* concerned than you are. But you know what concerns me even more? The belief that God was sending me a message about Reverend Tides' death and what my disobedience of His direction might cause. I could lose more than my paper if I defy God, Kwame, and pardon me for being just a tad more mindful of Him than I am of you or your church. What happened in my house last week was way too powerful to ignore, so I will apologize for misleading you, but I think I did the right thing and I'm confident that the AWC, and your paycheck that is provided through the success of it, will remain intact."

Hunter finished his speech only seconds before their entrees arrived. Both men remained quiet while the waiter removed the appetizer bowls that had held their minestrone soup and carefully set their lunches in front of them. The combined smells of Kwame's shrimp oreganata and his own chicken parmesan filled Hunter's nostrils and reminded him that this was his first meal of the day. After ensuring that his customers had everything they needed, the waiter hoisted the tray over his shoulder and walked away, leaving the friends to themselves.

Hunter graced his food and began eating. Maggiano's was one of his favorite eating spots, and he'd often visit when he was in the mood for Italian. It was a place that satisfied both Hunter's craving for the specialized seasonings that they offered, and Kwame's desire for seafood.

"So is that why you were late for work this morning? Because you caught an early flight back from wherever you went?" Kwame chose not to look at Hunter when he posed the questions.

"My flight from Norfolk landed this morning at

six o'clock. I got a few hours of shut-eye before driving in to work."

Hunter could sense that there were more questions where those had come from, but he resumed eating once he saw Kwame doing the same. The silence looming over them was awkward. Conversation was rarely scarce on the days that they chose to eat lunch together away from the office. Something had generally happened at work that morning or elsewhere the evening before that they would chat about while they dined.

"So are you going to start running the letters again or not?" Kwame suddenly asked while scooping up pieces of tomato with his fork.

Hunter used his napkin to wipe his mouth before answering. "Yes. I'm going to spend some time this afternoon going through the letters and I will have Lorna type them up for inclusion in tomorrow's edition."

"Tomorrow?" This time, Kwame looked directly at Hunter. "You're implementing this with this week's run? Why so soon?"

"Putting it off isn't going to make it any more or any less shocking to our readers, Kwame. I've decided to move ahead with this right away. If it's your church associates that you're worried about, don't. Everyone who reads the paper will know that bringing back our tributes to Reverend Tides is my doing. I'll make it very clear in my weekly letter and there will also be a notation in the section itself. Plus there will be no mention of the possibility that the pastor was murdered. All we'll do is the same thing we did a few weeks back. We'll run the letters as a special homage."

Kwame shook his head slowly, but said nothing as he nibbled on the remainder of his lunch. Hunter was quiet too. The explanation he'd given Kwame for the rush was only partial. A lot was at stake and the thought of losing the respect, not to mention the income, from his paper's readers was unnerving. The biggest reason for Hunter's haste was so that it could be done before he changed his mind. He was certain that he was doing the right thing, but knowing that didn't make doing it any less stressful.

It was after one o'clock by the time they returned to the office and Hunter knew that he was working against time. The box that he'd asked to be retrieved from storage was sitting beside his desk, waiting for him to begin his task. Hunter arbitrarily pulled ten envelopes out of the box and began reading the letters. Most of them were brief, and that was ideal. The shorter the letters were, the more of them he could fit in the allotted space. As Hunter read through the notes, he still wondered within himself how any of the tributes could finger a supposed killer. All of the notes were filled with honors and praises for the deceased preacher.

Reverend B.T. Tides was the best pastor a church could have. We at New Hope are more than a membership, we are a family. And Reverend Tides was more than a shepherd and leader, he was a father to all of us and we respected and loved him as such.

Regards,
Betty Floyd

It was notes like that one that threatened to make Hunter rethink a decision that he was as unsure of as he was sure. The possibility that this would have a negative impact on the AWC was great. By now, even the people who had written the letters might not want to see them in print. Kwame had told him that a new pastor had been named and that the church was slowly becoming accepting of Reverend Knight, who had served well under the guidance of Reverend Tides.

The Lord recruited a mighty soldier when He took Reverend Tides. We miss him and we always will. But knowing that he is in the arms of the Lord gives us the comfort and courage that we will need for the weeks and months ahead. Go on, Reverend Tides, and take your rest. We loved you but God loved you best.

Love,
Ernest Wilford

With the notes being as short as they were, Hunter decided that they could fit more than the planned ten in tomorrow's edition. The more that could be included in each edition, the shorter the time span that he would have to continue the section. There had to be two hundred letters in the box, and at one time Hunter thought that his paper would have to continue the feature for the better part of five months. If he could double the number of letters that he'd planned to print each week, the job could get done in ten weeks or less. The sooner he could fulfill his promise to Jade, the better it would be for the *Atlanta Weekly Chronicles.*

"I got your voice message. You were trying to locate me?"

Looking up from the mountain of envelopes that covered the middle of his desk, Hunter took note of Diane Vickers standing in his doorway with her hands perched on her hips. Diane was a reasonably attractive forty-five-year-old divorced mother of two college students. In the six years that she had served as managing editor, Diane's skills had helped to make the paper the success that it was. For nearly all of that time, she'd also vied for Hunter's heart. Her hints of interest were subtle, but Hunter was well aware.

"Hi, Diane," Hunter said.

"Hi yourself," she replied with a wide grin, approaching his desk with swaying hips. "Missed you yesterday and haven't seen much of you today. How are you?" She asked the question with concern, but all the while, Diane's eyes skimmed the envelopes curiously.

The news that illness was what kept him away from work yesterday was the shared belief around the office and Hunter wasn't about to give his actual whereabouts to anyone who didn't already know. Instead of addressing her query, Hunter grabbed a few of the envelopes and motioned for Diane to sit in the chair across from his desk. She obeyed without hesitation and immediately reached forward to relieve him of the still-sealed letters.

"Starting with tomorrow's release, we're going to bring back the section on Reverend Tides."

"What?"

"You heard me," Hunter said, while scanning the words of another letter. "We're not going to accept any letters that we don't already have, but at some point over the next few weeks, all of these correspondences will be printed. I need you to look through the ones I just handed you to be sure that there is nothing in them that goes against our printing guidelines. These have to be typed and sent to production . . ."

"Did I miss a meeting or a memo?" Diane said, obviously not pleased at the way she was being informed. "When was this decision made and why?"

In moments like this one, Hunter wondered if his open door policy and his efforts to treat his employees as his equals were the best ideas for business. With calculated movements, he placed the envelopes in a neat pile and then resituated himself in his chair before looking at the woman who sat across from him.

"*I* made the decision, Diane. I don't owe you, nor will I give you an explanation. I did it based on my own reasons. These people took out the time to write these letters and send them in to us. I think they merit printing just as the others did. Now, can you look through the letters as I asked or do I need to call Lorna in here to do it for me? I'm sure she wouldn't mind the added responsibility."

That last comment was a cheap shot and Hunter knew it. Although Diane and Lorna were cordial to one another most days, it was no secret that neither of them cared much for the other. Kwame had long ago determined that it was because both women were attracted to their employer, but because Lorna hadn't given any clear signals to justify Kwame's conclusion, Hunter couldn't readily agree. Hunter's determination regarding their rivalry was that Diane's business skills and educational credits far exceeded that of his assistant's, leaving Lorna feeling a bit subordinate. On the other hand, he concluded that Lorna Adkins' defined curves, and the fact that she was half Diane's age, threatened Diane and somewhat evened the playing field. Whatever the case, Hunter knew that bringing up Lorna's name would be intimidating.

Without verbally responding, Diane tore away a corner seam of one of the envelopes and pulled out the folded paper inside. Hunter resumed his task as well, reading each letter quickly, but with care. In the earlier years, he would print a letter just because it was sent in to him. Now, Hunter was far more selective of what he would allow in the paper he'd established. The media business was a very cutthroat one. Atlanta's other news periodicals hadn't expected the *Atlanta Weekly Chronicles* to last, let alone be competitive. Hunter's success story had made him the subject of several national magazine features. He had long ago proved himself worthy of the decade-ago inclusion in *Ebony's* "100 Leaders of the Future" article.

"Well, this one's sweet in an innocent kind of way," Diane said, breaking Hunter's attention from the paper in front of him.

"What?"

"It's a letter from a little boy."

"What does it say?" Hunter asked.

Like most of the others, the boy's letter was brief. Hunter leaned back in his chair and listened while Diane read the words that had been written in pencil on a sheet of paper that had been torn from a spiral notebook. Hunter agreed that the letter, though juvenile, was touching. When Diane placed it in the pile with the other letters to be printed, Hunter retrieved and reread it silently.

My name is Kobe and I am eleven years old and I go to New Hope Church. Reverend Tides christened me when I was a baby. I have the pictures in my drawer. He's a very, very, very nice man and I cry every day for him. I just want Sister Tides to know how sorry I am. Sister Tides, if you are reading this, I am sorry and I pray for him and for you every night.

Love,
Kobe

With a quiet sigh, Hunter replaced the letter in the pile and continued sorting. He had never given much thought to how Reverend Tides' untimely death might have affected the youngest members of his congregation, but the fact that the man was well loved by almost everyone was obvious. Knowing that made the hunt for a killer seem even more senseless.

"This one is rather lengthy," Diane announced as she held up a two-page letter for Hunter to see. "I mean, the lady says some nice things, but the word count might be too much to include in this week's run if you're actually going to go for printing twenty."

Hunter's response was delayed by an unexpected interruption.

"Hunter?"

Diane stiffened at the sound of Hunter's name articulated in an almost lyrical manner. She didn't speak nor did she turn to acknowledge the secretary who had just interrupted her and Hunter's meeting, but a clear expression of displeasure could be noted on Diane's face.

"Yes, Lorna?" Hunter said, ignoring the silent protest of his managing editor.

"I'm done with the dictation of your letter for tomorrow's paper," Lorna reported. "Do you want to look it over before I forward it to Kwame? He's already called once to ask if I had all of your things together to send over."

"Let's have a look," Hunter replied while stretching out his hand to receive the printout that Lorna extended toward him.

His eyes skimmed the words on the paper, but Hunter was fully aware of the tension that seemed to hover in layers over their heads. It was a familiar presence that always set up shop whenever both women were in close proximity to one another.

"That looks good, Lorna. Thanks."

"You're welcome," Lorna said with a sweet smile. She accepted the paper from Hunter and added, "Is there anything else I can do for you?"

Diane released an exasperated sigh and this time Hunter found himself having to forcefully extinguish a brewing laugh. From the coy tone of Lorna's question, it was clear that her offer was made more to agitate her rival than it was a genuine offer of assistance.

"As a matter of fact, yes," Hunter said, "I need you to type these letters for me. I'll have a few more for you so check back with me when you're done with these."

"It would be my pleasure," she responded just before excusing herself to begin her new task.

Alone once more, Hunter looked across the desk and noted that Diane was still holding the same two-page letter that she had been referencing when Lorna entered. Her eyes were fixed on the papers in her hand, but it was obvious to Hunter that she wasn't reading.

"About your earlier question," he said, breaking her mindless stare. "You can put that one to the side. We'll consider it for next week. Meantime, let's move on, shall we?"

Nodding in agreement, Diane placed the letter on the corner of the desk and reached into the pile for another.

Chapter 10

"I will enter His gates with thanksgiving in my heart. I will enter His courts with praise. I will say this is the day that the Lord has made. I will rejoice for He has made me glad . . ."

The praise and worship team sounded heavenly as Kwame made his way to his seat for Sunday morning worship. Every voice was in perfect harmony, every note that the musicians played was on key. But to Kwame, it also felt as though every eye in the building was staring at him, burning holes into his flesh.

As a child, his grandmother had told him that rain was a sign that God was crying because of the sins that had overtaken a world that He had created to be a perfect dwelling place for mankind. If she was right, God had been crying almost every day for the past two months and today's downpour was so intense that New Hope was still half-empty at a time when it was generally full almost to capacity.

When the choir finished singing and Reverend Knight took the stand, the tension magnified by ten. The newest edition of the *Atlanta Weekly Chronicles* hit the stands on Friday and when the feature on Reverend Tides was discovered, the edition became a hot commodity. Kwame hoped that the resurrected section would be viewed as something honorable. After all, the letters that were posted were favorable ones and Hunter made good on his promise not to mention Jade's murder theory. But Kwame's hopes of a peaceful reception were dashed when Reverend Knight stood behind the podium holding a copy of the AWC instead of his Bible.

Kwame didn't own the paper and returning the feature on his deceased former pastor was not his idea, nor one that he approved of. But nearby members of the congregation stole periodic glances in his direction as Reverend Knight openly expressed his denunciation of what he referred to as "a dastardly attempt to use the tragic death of a man of God for the sake of money." *Filthy lucre* was what he called it and his declaration drew loud responses of agreement from the congregation.

Why didn't I stay home like I started to? Kwame questioned himself. His mouth was so dry that his tongue seemed to swell; and although the temperature in the church was always at a comfortable level, Kwame could feel sweat building at the roots of his locks.

Last night, he'd had horrible nightmares that would not allow him to sleep peacefully. More than once, Kwame had awakened to chills from the sweat which had formed on his skin. In Kwame's dreams, he was running from the church building trying, without success, to dodge the painful hits of the stones that were being thrown at him by the members of New Hope. They were angry at him for something and once he was awake, Kwame reasoned that they were angry with him for the decision Hunter had made. And as he now listened to Reverend Knight sputter from behind the speaker's stand, Kwame realized that the only thing that real life was missing were the actual stones. The anger could be heard and seen and the feeling of being under attack was certainly genuine.

"Be not deceived. God is not mocked," Reverend Knight said. "Whatever a man sows, that's what he's gonna reap."

"Amen!" the crowd shouted.

"The Lord giveth and the Lord taketh away!" the preacher said as he leaned in close to the cordless microphone in his hand. "New Hope is a big part of why this paper is successful. Our very own Reverend Tides, along with many of the businesses in the area, planted seeds in this paper. We supported it because it was honorable. But now look at what they've allowed greed and hatefulness to do. They've allowed the devil to creep in and use this paper as a weapon to kill our beloved Reverend Tides all over again!"

"Tell it! Tell it!" someone sitting near Kwame called.

"Y'all see that empty seat over there?" Reverend Knight said while pointing to the second row of pews on his left-hand side. "That seat ain't empty 'cause of the wetness that the rain is causing. That seat is empty 'cause of the wetness that tears are causing. Our church mother is so broken that she couldn't even come out of her house this morning. God is not pleased, sisters and brothers, and He ain't gonna let His children go on hurting. I decree the fury of God upon this paper! I curse it in the name of the Lord!"

Kwame sat still and closed his eyes as he listened to the pastor speak with such harshness. A part of him was angry. As much as Kwame had been against the decision to bring back the feature, he knew that Hunter's intentions were honorable and nothing had been done because of greed, as the preacher had accused. The AWC was already successful. They had no need to play games for the purpose of gaining fortune. But in spite of his anger, Kwame could also feel the hurt and the pain that surrounded him. All of Kwame's worst fears were becoming reality.

All of a sudden, the church that had been Kwame's place to worship for all of his Christian life, felt foreign. He felt ostracized and unwelcome in the very place where he'd stood at the altar and given God his heart. The edifice that had been a safe haven for him in the time when his life had been the most chaotic now felt like a den of lions—and he was the raw meat thrown in for them to devour.

Reverend Knight finally tossed the paper aside and began his sermon, but even then, the dark cloud of contempt hovered more heavily on the inside than those that delivered the rain on the outside. For the duration of the preacher's sermon, Kwame considered leaving. He wished a million times that he'd sat closer to the rear so that an abrupt departure wouldn't be so conspicuous. He hardly heard any of the message and his eyes stayed fixed on the newspaper that Reverend Knight had partially ripped before throwing on the floor of the platform like a worthless piece of garbage.

As soon as the benediction was given, Kwame avoided all eye-contact as he made his way to the exit doors. Once he was safe inside of his car, Kwame pulled his cell phone from the inside pocket of his suit and pressed a speed dial code before backing out and heading toward the street.

"Hey," he said, even before Hunter could begin speaking. "Meet me somewhere for an early dinner. Your treat."

"*My* treat?"

"Yeah, man, *your* treat. You owe me big time for what I just had to go through."

Chapter 11

Jade watched as Ingrid dug her hand into the jar of colorful assorted Mike and Ike candies that sat on the corner of Jade's desk. Ingrid didn't ask if it was okay to munch on the treats, but then again, she never did.

"So let me get this right," Ingrid said through a mouthful of the chewy fruit-flavored candy as she held up the most recent copy of the *Atlanta Weekly Chronicles*. "You asked the owner of your hometown paper to do something like this and he just did it because you asked him to?"

Closing her eyes to block out the brightness of the overhead light, Jade took a slow, cleansing breath. She could understand the logic behind having clients lie down on the couch while they shared their darkest, deepest secrets. Something about lying there caused the mind and body to relax and it was just easier to talk when there was no feeling of threat.

The burgundy leather sofa matched the warm, relaxing colors of Jade's office décor perfectly.

The walls were covered in tan wallpaper with thin burgundy stripes. The hardwood floors matched her mahogany desk and brass floor lamps were set strategically around the space so that there was just the right amount of light for her patients' comfort for their therapy sessions. Never were her overhead lights used during sessions, and as she opened her eyes and closed them again, Jade understood the logic behind that as well.

"I told you, Ingrid. He did it because he, too, felt there was a need. I had given up on the idea of him running the letters, but when I met with him he renewed my faith in my hunch about Dad's death."

It hadn't been done without apprehension, but on Monday night, Jade finally opened up and told her best friend about her dreams and the interpretation of which she was convinced. To Jade's surprise, the revelation didn't send Ingrid into histrionics or a fit of uncontrolled laughter.

"Listen, boo," Ingrid had said two nights ago. "I can't say that I agree with you. I mean, truth be told, I don't think for a minute that your daddy was murdered. But if this is what it takes for you to find closure, then do what you gotta do. I just want you to be happy."

The normal workday for both women had ended hours ago, but the conversation that they'd started as Jade was gathering her items to leave had held them over. For both of them, the commute home was easier if they allowed the rush-hour traffic to clear up first. Therefore, choosing to stay a little later had its benefits.

"So this guy thinks your daddy's death was something other than accidental?" Ingrid asked.

Swinging her legs around, Jade brought herself to a seated position and then used her fingers as a brush to tame hairs that had gotten out of place during her moments of relaxation. Before she answered, Jade gave Ingrid's question more thought. Hunter never said that he believed her father was murdered, but he did indicate that he thought there was more to the story than anyone knew. Jade had been caught totally off-guard when he revealed the strange happenings of that stormy night when the letter she'd written him mysteriously lay open-faced on the coffee table in his living room.

"Hunter thinks there are some things that both the police and media don't know or maybe just chose not to reveal."

Ingrid dipped into the candy jar once more. "Hunter? Is this the same guy who used to be Mr. Greene just a few days ago?"

"Oh, I didn't tell you," Jade said, intentionally glossing over the suspicious tone in Ingrid's voice. "I found out that I actually know him. We grew up in the same housing project as kids. He was a couple of grades ahead of me, but we went to the same school and everything. We lived right next door to each other and I used to follow him and his friends to the basketball court. Those are some really nice letters he printed in that issue, aren't they?"

"I hadn't really taken the time to read them yet," Ingrid answered. "This is a really nice picture of *him*, though. He's handsome."

"Whatever," Jade shrugged. "Read the letters. I thought a couple of them were particularly sweet."

As she spoke the words, Jade slipped her feet into the high-heeled mules that she'd abandoned earlier and walked across the floor to the only window in her office. She had closed the shades earlier, but opened them to look out onto the street that ran in front of the office park. Traffic had decreased, but observing the volume of cars on the road wasn't Jade's real reason for standing there. It was more of a ploy to hide her face from Ingrid, who was very good at reading facial expressions that people weren't even aware they were showing.

Although Jade had spoken little to anyone about her meeting with Hunter, she'd done little else than think of it. Ingrid was right. Hunter Greene was an attractive man—a *very* attractive man. The picture in the paper only told half the story. In the straight-faced pose, Ingrid and other readers who'd not had the opportunity to meet the man behind the AWC couldn't see the million-dollar smile that Hunter possessed. He had grown into a man only distantly resembling the skinny boy that she vaguely remembered from the playground. Now, though the height still remained, bulk had been added to Hunter's once excessively lean body. He wasn't what Jade would call a particularly muscular man, just pleasantly solid and aside from a neatly trimmed mustache and goatee, he was clean cut right up to his bald head.

"These *are* nice letters," Ingrid said, pulling Jade's attention from the window.

"I told you they were," Jade responded while closing the window shade.

"Is he married?"

"Who?"

"Hunter Greene," Ingrid said. "Is he married or single?"

"I didn't ask, Ingrid, but I think he's married. Hunter talked quite a bit about his children, or at least a son who he described as looking more like the boy's mother than him."

"That doesn't mean he's married. Did he have on a wedding ring?"

Jade wanted to tell Ingrid that she hadn't paid attention, but that would be a lie. She noted very early in their meeting that aside from a gold watch, Hunter wore no jewelry.

"No; but neither did my dad and he and Mother were married forever. So the absence of a ring is not necessarily a clear sign of whether or not a person is married. Why are you asking anyway?" Jade probed. "Are you interested?"

Ingrid shrugged her shoulders before responding. "Not particularly. I was just wondering. But now that you mention it, and since you're still treating all men as if their names were *George*, maybe a sistah might make the next trip with you to Atlanta." Ingrid sighed. "When are you gonna let it go and try for happiness again, Jade? I still can't believe that you won't give that fine Demetrius Miller the time of day."

Since the termination of Jade's relationship with George, she and Ingrid had had this conversation more times than Jade cared to recall. "Demetrius is not my type, Ingrid." It was her standard answer.

"Why? Because he's not in the church like you are?" Ingrid challenged. "You know my Uncle Rufus wasn't saved when he married Aunt Josephine, but after a few years he made the step that she'd been praying for. Sometimes that happens, you know."

"Not for this lady," Jade said in a matter-of-fact tone as she began packing papers into her attaché in preparation for leaving. "When I'm ready to do so, *if* I'm ever ready to do so, I will move on. But one thing for sure; I won't be moving on with someone who's not already moving in the same direction as I am. If your aunt chose to go that way, more power to her. But marriage is tough enough when two people are in sync. Why add the unnecessary headache of hooking up with somebody that you know doesn't share your level of commitment?"

"Touché," Ingrid said. "Aunt Josephine did go through quite a bit before Uncle Rufus finally came to his senses. So you have a point. You ready to go now?"

"Not really, but do I have a choice?" Jade said with a chuckle. "It's been a long day and I'm dreading this ride. If I had a set of spare clothes here, I think I'd sleep in the office tonight."

"I hear ya," Ingrid agreed as she gathered her purse and car keys and stood behind the desk waiting for Jade to join her.

One at a time, Jade blew out the candles that she lit every day to give her office the vanilla scent that she loved. Her clients often complimented her on the fragrance when they walked through her door.

"Okay, I'm ready," she told Ingrid.

With their belongings in hand, both women headed to the door. The ringing telephone stopped them in their tracks. Turning, Jade noticed Ingrid reaching for the desk that she still stood near.

"Don't answer that," Jade said.

But her command wasn't faster than Ingrid's hand. As a receptionist, it was an automatic response for Ingrid to answer. She froze for a moment as if contemplating whether or not she should hang up without speaking. Then, after tossing an apologetic look at Jade, Ingrid brought the telephone to her ear.

"Good evening; Dr. Jade Tides' office. May I help you?"

Planting her hands on her hips, Jade locked her knees into position and smacked her lips in disapproval. Office hours were long over and had Ingrid not been so fast, the answering machine would have kindly delivered that message to the caller.

"I'm sorry," Ingrid said into the telephone. "The office is closed right now. If you'd like to leave a message or make an appointment, you can give me your information and I'll be sure that she gets it."

A broad smile quickly swept away Jade's earlier look of disappointment. Ingrid was handling the situation perfectly.

"Hunter Greene?"

At the sound of the name, Jade's eyes locked into Ingrid's.

"Hold please."

As soon as Ingrid pressed the button to place the call on hold, she turned to Jade with widened eyes. "What do you want me to do? You want to take this or you want me to just take a message and you call him back later?"

"Well, you've told him that the office was closed,"

Jade said. Both women whispered their words as though Hunter might be able to hear them despite modern technology. "If I get on the phone now, it's going to look like you were lying."

"I said the office was closed. I didn't say you weren't here."

Jade stared at the telephone that Ingrid still held in her hand. In the conversation that she had on Monday with her mother, Jade had been informed that the resurgence of letters in the AWC hadn't gone over well with the community. Jade hadn't taken it too seriously at the time. Her mother sounded a bit distant, but she didn't seem angry about the feature. In fact, she stated that she wasn't sure what to think. Jade could decipher that Mildred wasn't overjoyed, but as long as she wasn't angry, Jade could handle it. The letters would only run in a few more copies and it would soon be over.

Still, the handful of disgruntled customers may have spoken to Hunter. There were several reasons that could have motivated his call to her and one of them could be anger. What if he was calling because he was mad at her for planting the seed of suspicion in his mind concerning her father's death? Sure, Hunter had told her of the frightening incident that took place in his house during the blackout, but maybe he now thought that he'd let his imagination get the better of him. If buyers of the newspaper threatened to withdraw their support, Hunter would be put in a major hot seat.

"What do you want me to do, Jade?" Ingrid asked again. "I can't keep him on hold forever."

Jade took a deep breath and then walked slowly

towards her desk. Extending her hand toward Ingrid, she took the telephone and released the call from hold.

"This is Dr. Tides." Jade kept her voice calm and steady, but on the inside, her nerves were anything but.

"Jade," Hunter said. "I'm glad I caught you. I tried to call your cell, but I got no answer so I found your office number and took a chance that you were there. Is this a bad time?"

"Uh, no. I was just preparing to leave, but I have a moment."

"Listen," Hunter said. His sober tone told her the news wasn't good. "I need to meet with you, but with the new school year just beginning, I can't leave Atlanta right now. Is there any way possible that you can take a couple of days and come this way so we can talk?"

A couple of days? Jade's uneasiness heightened and her parched throat begged for water. Hunter hadn't asked for a moment or even a few hours; he'd asked for a couple of days. In Jade's mind, things descended from bad to worse. She walked to her cooler, filled one of the cone-shaped cups and took a sip before answering.

"I don't have a full schedule tomorrow," she said, hopeful that the length of time he'd requested was just a figure of speech. "You want to do a conference call in the afternoon?"

Jade held her breath. If Hunter agreed to the conference call, she would feel a bit of relief. Knowing that whatever it was could be discussed and put to rest by telephone would mean that it wasn't as serious as she'd thought. Any problem that could be solved without a face-to-face meeting would have to be one that was less critical than one that required eye-to-eye contact.

"No," Hunter said, causing her heart to sink deeper. "We need to sit down and talk. If you can't come here then I'll have to make the sacrifice and meet you in Virginia. How's tomorrow night? I need to see you before we go to print on Friday evening."

Before we go to print on Friday? Now there was no doubt about what Hunter wanted to discuss. The water wasn't offering much relief, but Jade took another sip. "Is something wrong, Hunter?" Jade already knew the answer, but like a glutton for punishment, she needed to hear the words from him.

"I can be there by six o'clock tomorrow evening," Hunter said, not giving a direct response to her inquiry. "Does that work for your schedule?"

Jade felt as though she were primarily to blame for whatever small friction was resulting from the letters printed in the *Chronicles.* Her letter to Hunter was the start of it all and running away from responsibility had never been her way.

"No," Jade said after a brief pause. "You just sit tight and I'll make arrangements to meet you there in Atlanta."

"Are you sure?"

"Yes. It's time for me to check on Mother anyway, so I'll just make a weekend of it. I'll arrange to take a flight out tomorrow evening. Is a breakfast meeting on Friday convenient for you?"

"That's fine. I'll make it work."

"Okay," Jade said as she tossed a look at Ingrid. "Where should I meet you and what time would be best?"

"Ten o'clock," Hunter replied. "Let me give you the address."

Chapter 12

Friday morning couldn't come soon enough for Hunter. The after-effects of Hurricane Dennis had passed more than a week ago, but the rainfall continued. It was going to be another one of those seasons where one storm after the other would pass through Florida and other areas, wreaking havoc not only on the citizens of one region, but all of the neighboring areas as well. Right now, some tropical storm that would not reach hurricane status was completing its trek and the soil in Atlanta remained wet because of it. This was the first week of school for the children in Dekalb County, and Malik had grimaced every day this week, disappointed that he wouldn't be able to ride the horses in the afternoons once his homework was complete.

The weather wasn't the only complication for the ten-year-old and Hunter couldn't help but feel responsible for his son's dilemma. Last school term, Malik was a popular boy; son of the owner of Atlanta's hottest newspaper; son of the man who owned Greene Pastures, a horse farm that opened its doors each fall for an annual visit from the students at the elementary school that Malik attended. This year, he was shunned for the same reasons that had made him popular in the preceding years. Malik still had friends, but he was feeling the heat of a decision that his father had made and Hunter wasn't oblivious to what was going on. The community's in-your-face disdain for the *Atlanta Weekly Chronicles* couldn't be mistaken.

Yesterday, for the first time, Hunter came face-to-face with his growing mass of enemies. When he pulled into his parking space at the AWC, he first had to pass a mob of men and women who stood at the mouth of his business, screaming words at him that he couldn't even understand while they held signs that urged consumers to no longer patronize his business. Hunter didn't look at their faces as he emerged from his BMW and headed into his office. He didn't really want to know who had turned on him.

His staff got very little work done yesterday. Diane had called the authorities and the police responded by coming out and forcing the protesters to move farther away from the building, but throughout the day, the people remained. Even the cloudy skies and the threat of rain didn't discourage them. It was evident that their sole purpose was to make sure that nobody purchased Saturday's edition. Hunter didn't want to admit it to his employees, but he was just as unnerved as they were.

"Hunter, what are we gonna do?" Kwame had

asked behind the closed door of his boss's office. "They're going to kill us. I know how sold you are on us continuing this feature, but you have to at least consider the community's wishes."

Not directly answering his question, Hunter instead requested to have time alone. He didn't want Kwame to see the struggle that was going on inside of him. It was only after he was alone in his office yesterday afternoon that he peeked through the blinds and took a long look at the crowd outside. There were at least a hundred of them . . . maybe two. And equipped with a bullhorn and a Bible, Kwame's new pastor was leading the campaign. Some of the participants carried signs of protest, but others carried enlarged photos of Reverend B.T. Tides. To them, Hunter's decision was an attack that they were taking personally.

Now, looking out of the blinds that covered his living room window, Hunter could only imagine the even larger crowd that Kwame had informed him was convened outside the AWC headquarters today. Hunter broke away from his thoughts for a moment while he flipped the last of the buttermilk pancakes that were cooking on his stovetop griddle. All that was left to cook were the eggs, and since he was unsure of how Jade liked hers, Hunter decided to wait until she arrived to prepare them. The aroma of the pancakes and sausages filled his home, creating a delicious mask for the anguish that he felt on the inside.

The beeping of the intercom meant that his guest had arrived. Hunter looked at the clock on the wall and saw that she was right on time.

"Yes?" he called as he pressed the button to

communicate to the occupant of the car who waited at his security gate.

"Taxi cab driver for Ms. Jade Tides," the male voice responded.

"Come on in," Hunter said while remotely commanding the gate to open. He took a quick moment to wash his hands in the kitchen sink and again check to be sure that the stove was off before stepping outside and watching the cab make its slow journey up his winding driveway. The clouds above that hovered in the distance were beginning to darken. Whether or not it would rain today was no longer in question. Hunter only hoped that the rain would fall hard enough to run away the crowd that was, no doubt, still growing in front of his place of business.

"I have it," Hunter said as he walked to the car, interrupting just as Jade was about to hand the cab driver his fare.

"Thank you, sir. Have a good day," the driver replied, grinning at the generous tip Hunter had given him.

After helping Jade remove her shoulder bag from the backseat of the car, the two of them watched the driver maneuver the car back down the paved surface.

"Thank you," Jade said, looking up at him through shaded glasses.

Very little sun was out with the overcast skies, so Hunter concluded that the eyewear was more of a fashion statement than protective gear. Jade had made a good choice, though. The brown-tinted sunglasses were very becoming on her face.

"No problem. I hope you're hungry," he said

while leading the way to the door that immediately placed them in his living room.

Hunter noted the look of awe in Jade's expression when she removed her glasses and captured a clear picture of her surroundings. Hunter kept his decor simple, but elegant. His living room furniture was tan leather. The glass top table that was the centerpiece of the surrounding sofas sat on a brown bear-skinned area rug. The rest of the flooring around it was polished wood. His cream-colored walls were bare except for two large photos: one, a painting of a faceless jazz musician playing a saxophone, and the other, a painting of a white Baby Grand piano.

"You didn't eat already, did you?" Hunter asked, trying not to show pleasure in seeing that Jade liked his home.

"No," she responded. "I came here straight from the airport. Check-in time at the hotel isn't until three o'clock, but when I made the reservation, they told me that I would be able to get in by noon."

"I see."

"Your home is beautiful," she added. "So is your landscape."

"Thank you," Hunter replied.

"I'd heard that the owner of the AWC was a horse breeder, but I'm still getting used to the idea that you, the boy from Perry Homes, are that man I've heard and read about over the years. So, I was a bit taken aback when the cab driver first pulled onto your property."

He smiled and then gestured toward the sofas. "The horses are put away right now due to the pending rain, but maybe you'll have the chance to see them another time. Please make yourself at home. I imagine that you're tired."

He watched as Jade made her way to the loveseat. She was dressed comfortably in a hot pink blouse and black Capri pants. Neatly manicured toenails, painted with clear polish stuck through the opening of her high heeled pink sandals. Everything Jade wore, she wore well and Hunter noticed every detail.

"I didn't get much sleep last night," Jade confessed as she sat and tucked thick strands of auburn hair behind her ears. "I admit that I'm a little concerned about this meeting. You sounded very serious on the phone."

There was a reason for his grave tone during Wednesday's phone call, but Hunter didn't want to get into it with her just yet. Instead, he excused himself and retreated to the kitchen to finish preparing breakfast. Upon his inquiry, Jade told him that she liked her eggs scrambled, "soft scrambled" to be precise. With everything else already done, the eggs didn't add much time to the wait.

While Jade followed Hunter's instructions on how to get to the restroom to wash her hands, he prepared their plates and set them with two glasses of orange juice on the dining room table. The large mahogany table was designed to seat up to eight people. Hunter and Malik rarely used it, opting to eat in the living room using trays instead. The table got good use when Hunter's mother, his siblings and their families gathered at his home for Thanksgiving. It was an annual event that Hunter looked forward to.

Deciding to set their places opposite each other so that they would be facing one another, Hunter was just putting the silverware in place when he heard Jade's voice coming from behind him.

"Smells wonderful."

His grin was almost boyish as he turned to face her and shrugged. "Just a little something that I threw together."

Before walking to the other side of the table to take his seat, Hunter pulled out the chair nearest him and allowed Jade to sit. She almost seemed made a bit uneasy by his gesture, but Jade thanked him before he took the short walk that delivered him to his own chair. Immediately after sitting, Hunter bowed his head to grace the food. Jade thanked him for that as well. She took her first bite from one of the pancakes and Hunter couldn't help but smile when she closed her eyes for a moment and quietly savored the taste.

"Good?" he asked, hoping it wasn't obvious that he was fishing for more compliments.

"A man who rose from poverty, started his own business, doesn't mind helping with the cooking and plays an active role as a father. Whenever I meet your wife, I'll have to ask her which end of the ocean she cast her line when she caught you."

Jade laughed when she finished her statement and for a moment, Hunter thought that she was joking. When it finally became clear to him that Jade actually was unaware of his marital status, he broke into a laugh as well.

"When *you* meet her?" he said. "When *I* meet her, I'll be sure to tell her what you said."

A look of bewilderment covered Jade's face for

a second, but that look was quickly overtaken by one of shame. Hunter was almost sure that he could see her brown skin flush.

"I'm . . . I'm sorry," she stammered.

"Don't be," he said, waving his hand in a carefree manner. "I've been told that I act like an old married man, so I guess it must be true."

"I'm sorry," Jade repeated. "You mentioned having a family . . . a child, before when we spoke. You said he looked like his mother . . . I just assumed . . ."

"So I did," Hunter interrupted. "Malik is my ten-year-old son. I don't have to tell you that marriage and children don't always happen in that order."

"I know," Jade said, looking as if she wished she could erase the entire conversation. "I'm sorry. I didn't mean to pry or be judgmental. I just . . . I'm sorry."

It was her fourth apology inside of one minute. In the brief silence that followed, Hunter reviewed his words and the accompanying tone that was distinctly harsh. All of his life he'd been defending Malik and his decision to become a custodial parent. When Hunter's mother first learned of Yvonne's pregnancy, she was livid. Ironically, her anger wasn't toward Hunter, but Yvonne. Patricia Greene accused the girl of getting pregnant just to entrap her son. When Hunter came to Yvonne's defense, his mother was even more displeased.

Learning of Yvonne's addiction was all that Patricia needed to hear. Hunter heard all of the "I told you so" speeches that he could stand. By then, he and Yvonne had already severed their romantic ties, but Patricia didn't hold back on her lingering displeasure for the girl who she believed used Malik to remain a part of Hunter's life. Patricia begged Hunter not to become the custodial parent. She voiced concerns that the child, who bore a strong resemblance to his mother but very little to Hunter, was probably not even his son. For a while, Patricia's indignation put a wedge between her and her son, but after building a strong spiritual foundation, Hunter had found the peace and strength to forgive her, in spite of the fact that his mother never asked him to.

Still, whenever he felt that someone was saying anything that even resembled something negative about his relationship with Malik, Hunter's defenses shot up. Recalling the conversation that he'd just had with Jade, Hunter knew that she meant no harm. In the short span of time that had passed since her final apology, he realized that in this case, he was the one who was out of line. Looking across the table at his guest and clearly reading her level of discomfort, Hunter made the decision to break the tension.

"I don't think you ever knew Yvonne Glossier."

His words brought Jade's downcast eyes from the table. She looked at him and shook her head.

"I met her after my family moved away from Perry Homes. She was a nice girl from a low income family. I think once we became what most people categorize as middle class, my mother forgot where we came from. She thought I was too good for Yvonne and she never accepted my relationship with her."

"But doesn't every mother think her son is too good for the women he chooses to date?"

Hunter released a brief laugh and then shook his head. "I know what you're getting at, but believe me; Mama just wanted us to leave everything about poverty behind us. She met a stroke of good fortune and really became a different woman. Yvonne qualified for free lunches and her folks had meager jobs. By this time, my mom didn't really have to work if she didn't want to. Pretty much all of our needs were being met. We weren't rich by any stretch of the imagination, but our house and car were paid for and our utility bills weren't even in my mom's name. They went directly to the man who had given us our new standard of living."

"Your mom married rich?"

Hunter paused before answering Jade's newest question. This was a conversation that he'd never before engaged in with anyone. Not Kwame. Not even any of his siblings. Sometimes he wondered if not talking about it and getting clarification directly from his mother, he'd allowed his imagination to get the best of him over the years. But deep inside, Hunter knew the truth. Certain happenings in his childhood and teen years were too obvious to ignore.

"No," he answered after taking a drink from his glass. "My mother has never been married. She had five children from three different relationships, but we never had a stable father figure in the home. The man that provided our standard of living and paid my college tuition was married, but not to my mom. They never made their relationship public, but I think all of my siblings and I knew that Dwight Rollins was doing more than just rewarding my mother for saving his grandson. It started out as that, but I'd bet my life on the fact that Mama was, and still is, a kept woman."

Neither of them was doing much eating now. Hunter had put his fork down minutes earlier, and now Jade was doing the same. He watched her watch him as he spoke. Hunter surprised himself when he opened up even further, exposing his whole life to this woman he barely knew. Talking to Jade felt comfortable and safe. Hunter didn't even preface any of his disclosures by asking her to keep his family secrets to herself. Something inside of him felt assured that she would and he believed it. The rain had begun to fall outside and sounds of the downpour could be heard beating on the windows and the rooftop.

Before long, Hunter and Jade had abandoned the dining area and their half-eaten meals and retreated to the living room where they kept talking over drinks: tea for Jade and milk for him. Hunter told her how much of his decision to leave college was based on the fact that he despised the man who was paying his tuition. Hunter was the only one of his mother's children to go to college instead of jail and she wasn't at all happy about his decision to "throw his life away." Still, Hunter decided to walk away. He couldn't control the fact that his mother would always have to attribute her so-called success to a man who used her for his own sexual gratification, but Hunter would not allow Mr. Rollins to wear that same crown in his life.

"I needed to be able to make it on my own," Hunter told Jade. "I didn't want to feel liked I owed him anything. Mama looked down on Yvonne, but in reality, she had no right to. Yvonne had her issues and they ultimately took her life, but in the scheme of things, whatever life she lived, it was no more of a disgrace than the one Mom led and still leads."

Jade seemed surprised at his last remark. "She's still with him after all these years?"

"With him? No, she's not with him, Jade. Mr. Rollins controls my mother without her even recognizing it—or at least she won't admit to recognizing it. Mama only sees him when he wants her to. Mr. Rollins is *with* his wife. Mrs. Rollins is the one who gets to accompany him to his business parties and on his posh annual vacations. Does my mother still *serve* him? Yes."

Hunter hoped that the hurt that he felt on the inside couldn't be seen by Jade, but if it could he wouldn't be too concerned. He'd stopped trying to get his mother to shake herself loose from the man who Hunter saw as little more than a slave master. It had been the subject of many past arguments that Hunter still hadn't won. In the last three years, he'd chosen to leave it alone, but he still prayed daily that his mother would see the light and face the truth.

"Don't get me wrong," Hunter added. "I love my mother and I'd do just about anything for her, but . . ."

"But you can't condone her wrong?" Jade guessed.

Hunter nodded.

Jade spoke again. "Fortunately for me, my parents not only taught us the right path to follow, but they also lived model Christian lives in the presence of their children. We didn't always walk the straight and narrow or always make the right choices, but whatever wrong we did . . ."

"It wasn't because they didn't do their jobs." That time it was Hunter who finished Jade's thought.

Jade continued. "I can't remember much about your mother, but I do remember a little about your brothers. Mostly from the basketball court," she added with a laugh. "It just seems like the units at Perry Homes were full of boys. There just weren't many girls for me to play with. At least not girls my age. I lost track of all of the kids who grew up in that area when I left for college."

"Most of the ones I knew became dependents of the State," Hunter informed her.

"Well, God smiled on you in spite of the choices your mother made," Jade said. "I'm sure she did what she thought was best for her children. Sometimes parents make mistakes too."

Hunter nodded in silence again.

"The best part of all is that your courage paid off," Jade continued. "You moved from under the control of Mr. Rollins and you proved that you could make it on your own. You stepped up to the plate when your son needed you the most and now you are a successful father for him to model himself after. She may not have agreed with all the choices you made, but I'm sure your mother is proud of you."

"Maybe," Hunter shrugged, "but she's never said so."

"Well, I'm *very* proud of you."

Hunter wasn't certain, but he was almost sure that his heart went into a brief double-time at the sound of Jade's words. He looked at her and for a moment, their eyes locked. His body's desire to slide closer to her almost materialized, but Hunter pulled his eyes away and instead took another sip of his milk.

Jade was different from any woman he'd ever known. She was the first woman to ever express admiration for his accomplishments. His mother never had. Yvonne never did. Even the women Hunter worked with had never complimented him on his achievements. He wanted to thank Jade for her kind words, but other issues began to return and weigh heavily on his mind. Now, with her being so supportive of him, it was even harder for Hunter to express his reason for asking her to make the trip from Virginia.

"My job . . . what I do means a lot to me, Jade," Hunter started. "I've worked hard to get to where I am and the churches and the communities surrounding Atlanta are a big reason for my success."

"I know. The *Atlanta Weekly Chronicles* offers something that its competitors don't. There's something different—something special about it," Jade said.

"Let me finish," Hunter pleaded. He knew that if she continued the path she'd started, he would never make his point. "Those same people who helped me get where I am have turned on me, Jade. Right now, if the rain hasn't run them away, there are a hundred or more people picketing outside my office and holding up signs displaying words of hostility."

Jade placed her glass on the coaster provided and repositioned herself on the sofa so that she looked directly at Hunter. Her expression told Hunter that she had been totally unaware of the magnitude of what was taking place because of the decision they'd made.

"Why? What's going on?" she asked.

"They are protesting the letters."

"For my father?"

"Yes. I had prepared my staff to expect some backlash, but nothing on this scale. The community thinks that I'm resurrecting the letters to raise the bottom line of my business. The other papers are having a party at my expense," Hunter explained further while pulling a copy of his largest competitor from underneath a book that lay on his coffee table. He handed the paper to Jade and continued. "They are enjoying every minute of it—making the anger of the community towards my paper the front cover news of their local section. The AWC is taking a pounding and we haven't even begun to feel the agony yet. The low numbers we sell of tomorrow's issue will tell the real story. That's why I needed to talk to you before we went to print, Jade. You needed to hear it from me; not find out when your subscription issue arrived in Virginia. I have to do something and quickly. I need you to understand that I can't continue the feature. I have to remove it beginning this week."

"But you can't, Hunter."

"I *have to,* Jade. If I don't, I'm going to lose everything and my staff will as well."

"But I thought you believed in the cause. This wasn't just my idea, Hunter. You told me that *you* believed that there was more to my father's death than any of us knew."

Hunter took a deep breath and settled back against the leather covering of his couch. "I do, Jade. I do believe that there's something more. But am I supposed to let my business and my employees suffer for my personal beliefs? There's got to be another approach."

"No. There is no other way," Jade stressed, raising her voice in the process.

"Yes there is," Hunter insisted. "There has to be."

"But Daddy said that the answer would be in the letters you printed in your paper."

Hunter's frustration was heightening as well. He leaned forward and said, "It was a dream, Jade. Your daddy didn't *say* anything. He's dead, remember?"

He jolted back into an upright position with his cheek bearing the sting of its sudden contact with Jade's hand. Hunter couldn't remember the last time he'd been slapped. He recalled it happening once or twice as a child when his mother would reprimand him for misbehaving, but in his adult years, he couldn't recall ever experiencing it. Hunter narrowed his eyes in disbelief and in the next moment, they both sat speechless and without motion.

Just as he was about to verbalize his displeasure of her reaction, Jade jumped from her position on the sofa, grabbed her overnight bag and dashed toward the front door. Hunter watched in temporary confusion as she disappeared through the opening, not at all deterred by the falling rain. There was no waiting cab for her to jump into and other than the stall that the horses used for shelter, which was inside a locked fence almost an acre from the house, there was no available covering to protect her from the elements.

Realizing that Jade wasn't coming back, Hunter got up from the sofa and stood in his open doorway. The white sheets of rain were so dense that it took a moment before he spotted the black in Jade's outfit in the distance. She seemed to be running with no plan or purpose.

"Jade!" Hunter yelled, darting blindly into the rainfall.

Chapter 13

Jackson Tides shook the excess water from his umbrella as he allowed his mother to pass before closing the door behind them. The protest that they had taken part in had been abbreviated due to the rain, but he felt a sense of accomplishment. His father would be proud of the way they stood up in his honor.

"Renee!" he called out.

"Hush, Jackson," Mildred warned. "The baby might be sleep. The only rest Renee gets is when Alexis is sleeping. You're going to disturb everybody with all that yelling."

By the time Mildred finished her sentence, Renee was rounding the corner that led to the bedrooms. "It's okay, Ms. Mildred," she said. "The baby is still asleep. I'm glad y'all came on home. I put some hot water on the stove for tea just in case, but I was wondering if you were going to try and outlast the rain."

"If I had gone by myself, I would have," Jackson said. "I didn't want Mother out in the weather like that, though. Reverend Knight was still there when we left, just kind of sitting in his car like he was going to see how long the rain lasted. So he may be ready for round two as soon as the rain slows down."

In Jackson's home, the kitchen and the dining room shared one large space with no dividing wall to separate them. He and his mother immediately moved toward the dining area where Renee was putting steaming cups on the table for them. For bodies that had been dampened by the rain, the hot liquid came in handy.

"We got the right one to take over as pastor," Jackson remarked. "I wasn't sure at first, but Reverend Knight has proved himself. He ain't no joke. He served under Dad for years and you can see it in the fire he has for the ministry and his leadership skills. He stepped right in to head the fight against what those people at the AWC are trying to do."

"Yes he did," Mildred agreed. "He didn't waste no time letting both the media and the community know how we felt. I admit that in the beginning I was just a bit disturbed about the letters because I wanted B.T. to be able to rest in peace," she added. "I didn't even consider that the paper was doing what they were doing for profit until Reverend Knight said it. That's just how your daddy was. He had a gift for discerning the things that were hidden to others too."

Jackson got up from the table and made the short trip to the stove to refill his cup with hot water and to get a fresh tea bag. Mildred's words were true and forced his mind to travel back to yesteryear. Even when he and his siblings were youngsters, they were able to get over on their mother much easier than they could their father. Fooling their mother was a scheme that Jackson's younger brother seemed to master.

Many days Jerome would come home from school, or wherever he'd chosen to spend the course of the school day, with suspicious cuts or bruises on his arms, legs and sometimes on his face. Being the active child that he was, Jerome's stories sounded believable when he would tell Mildred that he'd fallen or that the marks on his body had been acquired during horseplay in gym class. Most times his mother would buy the lies, but B.T. Tides knew the difference between a bruise caused by the hit of a football and one that had come from the hit of a fist. Their father also knew cuts that derived from scraping the edge of the door of a locker and a cut that came from scaling a fence or breaking a window.

Jerome's cases were always the extreme ones. Jackson and Jade had less dramatic instances, but no matter the level of deception, B.T. could rarely be fooled. His limited formal education may have left his book-smarts lacking, but no matter how many degrees the members of his family or congregation obtained, they were no match for the gift of discernment that God had given Reverend Tides.

"I knew if we just hung in there, the Lord was going to make New Hope feel like home again," Mildred said with a slight, but noticeable upward curl at the corners of her lips.

From the stove where he remained standing, Jackson nodded before bringing his cup to his lips. It was good to see his mother smile again. She still got sentimental when she thought of her husband, but Jackson had taken note of Mildred's slow return to her normal self. It angered him when he thought of the healing process that had now been disturbed by the *Atlanta Weekly Chronicles* and its mounting mischief. The last thing his family needed was a setback in a still painful tragedy.

"Do you think the AWC will remove the letters now?" Renee's question reeled Jackson back in to the kitchen from which his thoughts had drifted.

"Lord knows I hope so," Mildred said.

The sadness in her voice heightened Jackson's irritation. Although Mildred had assured him repeatedly that she was alright, he knew the feature had blindsided his mother and had forced her back to a place of mourning from which she'd barely had time to recover.

"They'd better," Jackson said in no uncertain terms. "One thing about it; money speaks. Before anyone purchases the paper they will turn to Section C, and if there are letters printed, they're not going to buy them. If the AWC loses the money that they hoped to gain by using Daddy's death as a sales pitch, then they'll stop. This community made that paper and just like we made it, if we band together, we can shut it down."

Kwame had been standing in the same spot for the last hour—maybe even longer. When the rainfall began to decrease, he vacated his own office and took his present stance by the window in Hunter's. His prayer that the rain would continue to pour through nightfall had apparently fallen on deaf ears. Kwame was sure that the crowd that had been assembled outside during the early morning hours would return at the first hint of sunshine, but so far, they had not. There was still a light shower sprinkling outside, but Kwame knew that it was not enough to keep the determined protesters away.

"Have you heard from Hunter?"

Turning away from the window where he had been watching and waiting for the worst, Kwame faced Diane. She looked about as worried as he felt. The entire staff, including the men in the pressroom, was on edge as they waited for Hunter's call to give them the go-ahead to begin printing.

"Not yet," Kwame answered.

Diane released a frustrated sigh and then sat in the chair that was nearest the open door. Kwame wanted to ask her to leave. What he wanted right now was to be left alone with his own thoughts, but he chose not to make his feelings known. There was enough tension in the room without him adding to it. Instead, he turned his back to her and resumed his outside watch.

"I don't understand why we can't just move forward," Diane said, breaking the silence. "Hunter already made it clear that he didn't want to continue the letters. You're in charge when he isn't here, Kwame. Why can't you just use your authority and tell the press room to go for it?"

Kwame tightened his jaws and took a deep breath. He knew if he didn't take at least one before speaking, he'd probably regret the words that came from his mouth. Diane knew the protocol. The presses at the AWC didn't run without Hunter's nod. And although it was true that Hunter had made his intentions known, Kwame wasn't at all convinced that his best friend wouldn't change his mind. There was little or no certainty in Hunter's voice this morning, when they last talked.

"We don't go to press without Hunter's say-so, Diane. You know that," Kwame finally said.

"He stood right here in this office Wednesday and told all of us that the letters had to discontinue. I think . . ."

"Maybe so," Lorna said as she walked in and interrupted Diane's speech. "But he also gave me twenty-two letters to type."

Kwame turned from the window for the first time since Diane entered. Usually when things took place that he hadn't been made aware of, Kwame remained calm, giving the illusion that he'd known all the while. The expression on his face now was a dead giveaway that Lorna's announcement was news to him. From Diane's reaction, he could tell that it was her first hearing of it as well. Kwame figured that Diane was more devastated than he was about Lorna's knowledge of something concerning which they'd been left in the dark.

"What did you do with the letters once you typed them?" Kwame asked.

"Gave them back to Hunter like I always do," Lorna answered. "But, so what? I don't know what y'all getting all worked up about. Hunter is gonna make the right decision. He's got more to lose than any of us if anything happens to the *Atlanta*

Weekly Chronicles. This paper is his baby. Do y'all really think he'd take a chance at seeing it die? Hunter is a very smart businessman. I can't believe y'all sweating over this mess."

"Mess?" Diane stood from her seat and her tone was saturated with venom. "*First of all,* I have known Hunter Greene a lot longer than you have and the level of *my* business relationship with him is certainly on a higher plane than yours. So I don't need you to tell me how intelligent he is. What he does in this case that Kwame and I were discussing before you so rudely interrupted, is no slight against Hunter's business sense. So, nothing about this is mess, as you so *eloquently* put it. Apparently, in your position behind your little computer that is used mostly for email and playing solitaire, you can't comprehend the severity of the impact of whatever decision Hunter makes. We could *all* lose our jobs over this, Lorna. Now, maybe with the minimum wage that you make, you can't see how that might be devastating. But those of us who actually make *real* money do."

Diane had spoken without fear during her rant, but as Lorna gave her a sharp threatening look and began taking slow steps toward her, Diane couldn't hide her panic. She took a few steps back to preserve the safer space that Lorna had narrowed and looked as if she wanted to make a mad dash for the door. But in order to do so, Diane would first have to get around the woman whose facial expression held menace. As much as Kwame knew that he needed to step in before the threatening movements became an actual confrontation, he watched in silent amusement.

Lorna finally spoke, losing whatever trace of professionalism she generally portrayed in her workplace dialogue. "I tell you what, *trick*; open your mouth to say one more word and I promise you, you gonna need every dime of yo' *real* money just to get my *real* five-inch stilettos removed outta yo' *real* . . ."

"Hey!" Kwame barked. A part of him wanted to see how it all would end, but he knew he couldn't allow the women to come to blows. Lorna ignored his warning and continued.

"Come on, ya lil' Condoleezza Rice wannabe," she said, slipping out of her pumps and stepping closer to Diane, beckoning with hands that sported long nails with diamond studs at the tips of each one. "Say something. Anything. I dare you. All I need is a reason."

"That's enough, Lorna," Kwame said as he moved from behind Hunter's desk and stood between the women. He'd never seen them physically fight before, but Kwame had a hunch that doing so wasn't even close to being beneath Lorna. And if her bite was anywhere near the strength of her bark, Diane wouldn't have a fighting chance.

"Lorna's right," Kwame said, after successfully bringing the brewing confrontation to an end. "Hunter will do the right thing. All arrows are pointing to us going to press without the feature, but that doesn't change the drill. I can't give the print department the green light until Hunter gives it to me."

"That's a cop out, Kwame, and you know it," Diane charged. "It's not like you haven't done it before."

Kwame gave her a cold stare. He had a half mind to just walk out, close the office door and let Lorna have an early birthday gift. Proceeding instead with more logic, he replied, "The only time I've taken that step is when Hunter didn't get back to me by the deadline. The guys who run the machines need an allotted amount of time to get the job done. There have been only two occasions when I've given the word without Hunter's approval, and both times we were past deadline and I couldn't get in touch with him. We're not past deadline, Diane, and even if we were, I know where Hunter is and would be obligated to call him first. So, give it up. We're not taking it to print until he says so."

"I agree," Lorna said, slipping her feet back into her shoes, but all the while, casting Diane a glare that told her that she had no problem taking them back off again if Diane dared to give a reply of any sort.

"Let's get back to work," Kwame said. "The day isn't over yet."

The nearly three-hour rainfall was over and with the women gone, Kwame was once again left alone to stare out the window and pray silently that the picketers would not return. It was upsetting enough that his livelihood was in jeopardy. Having it threatened by so many familiar faces, many of whom he respected and admired, was heart-rending. There were still more than two hours left before the absolute deadline for print and Kwame knew that they would be the longest hours of the day.

* * *

It had been another bad day for Malik. He didn't say so, but glancing at him through the rearview mirror while his son sat in the backseat, Hunter knew it had. On the ride from school, Malik was generally talkative—anxious to tell his father about his day's experiences, but for this first week of the new school year, those days were rare.

"What's going on, sport?" Hunter asked, taking a brief look over his right shoulder.

"Nothing."

Although the volume of his stereo system was lowered, Hunter could barely hear Malik's mumbled reply. It was clear that his son didn't want to talk, but Hunter pressed for more.

"All your classes straight now?"

"Yes sir."

"You still like all of your teachers?"

"They're okay."

Hunter knew that he needed to get back home as quickly as possible to take care of unfinished business, but the wellbeing of his son took precedence. Taking a different route than normal, he steered his Range Rover to the drive-in window of Chick-Fil-A. It was Malik's favorite fast food joint. He loved their chicken strips.

"Let me have a six-piece order of strips with buffalo sauce and a number one combo with a lemonade," Hunter called into the microphone. It was the same order he always got when they went there.

"Will that be all for you, sir?" a voice asked.

Hunter paused to think and then replied, "Let me have a dinner salad. The southwest chargrilled salad will be fine."

"Who's that for?" It was the first piece of conversation that Malik had volunteered since getting inside the truck.

"We have company."

Malik looked at Hunter with curious eyes as his father handed him the large bag for safe keeping, but no other words were spoken between the two of them for the duration of the drive. When they entered the house via the garage, Hunter pointed toward the sofa and placed his finger to his lips, motioning for Malik to remain as quiet as possible.

"Who's that?" the boy whispered.

"She's a friend I knew from a long time ago," Hunter whispered back. "Go on upstairs and put your things away. Then you can wash up and come back down and eat your lunch."

Hunter watched Malik disappear up the stairs and then he turned his attention to Jade. It seemed that she hadn't moved since he left her nearly an hour ago. When she darted out into the rain following their brief heated exchange, Hunter followed, calling her name with every few steps that he took in pursuit. Jade had made it to the wooded area just beyond the pasture by the time he caught up with her.

She was hysterical, screaming and swinging at him in her failed attempt to get away from his grasp. Both of them had collapsed on the ground during the tussle and after a moment of holding her so tightly that she couldn't move, Jade gave up the struggle and instead surrendered to a flood of tears that couldn't be distinguished from the rain water that soaked her face.

When Hunter was confident that she was calm

enough for him to relinquish his hold without her running deeper into the thickness of the trees, he stood and pulled her up with him. Draping her carry on bag over his shoulder, and with a tight grip of his arm around her waist, he led the way back through the drenching rain. From the woods to his house was a long walk but they were already sopping wet, so there was no need to hurry.

Once back inside, Jade collapsed on the sofa, making Hunter grateful for the leather that covered the furniture. He left her there and went into the downstairs guest bathroom to draw a tub of hot water. Hunter was additionally grateful for the leather that Jade's luggage was made of. It was wet on the outside, but all of her clothing had been protected. After placing a fresh towel set on the bathroom counter, Hunter coaxed Jade off of the couch and took her in the bathroom where her luggage awaited her. He left her there, standing silently in the middle of the bathroom floor with a puddle forming beneath her where the water dripped from her clothes.

"Get a bath and put on some fresh clothes," Hunter had instructed. "If you wait for me in the living room, we'll talk. Okay?"

Since Jade didn't reply, it wasn't really an exchange, but it was the last thing he'd said to her before leaving to pick up Malik. Hunter took a thick, cotton towel and dried the living room couch and the floor and then went into his own room to change his wet clothes and to shower away the mud he'd picked up from the ground where he was forced to sit while he restrained Jade. By the time Hunter had emerged from his room refreshed, Jade had made a bed of the sofa and was sound asleep. At the time, Hunter had chosen not to wake her. As upset as she had been, he thought that the rest might be what Jade needed. That had been some time ago, and now it was time to talk.

Moving closer to the sofa, Hunter reached forward to wake her, but stopped before his hand reached her shoulder. From his squatting position, he looked at Jade and for the first time, Hunter found himself paying attention to the details he hadn't noticed before. Upon seeing Jade from a distance at her father's funeral, his eyes captured grace and elegance, and during their first meeting he'd been drawn in by her warm personality. But now was the first time Hunter really appreciated her natural beauty.

The rain had washed away all of the curls that Jade had used a hot curling iron to create and had forced it back to its naturally wavy state. Jade had brushed it into a neat ponytail that was beginning to dry into a thick, curly mass that fell just below her shoulders. There was no visible makeup on her face, but to Hunter, Jade's skin appeared flawless. Thoughtlessly, he reached out to stroke the side of her face with his hand.

"Can I eat now, Daddy?"

Gasping, Hunter pulled back his hand, and in an instant, he was standing upright. He hadn't even heard Malik's footsteps as the boy began his descent from upstairs. Jade's sleep had been disturbed by the call from the stairwell and she stirred before slowly opening her eyes.

Hunter took a step back from the sofa before

answering his son. "Yeah, Malik. Come on down. The food is on the table."

Hunter tried to shake off the embarrassment and guilt that he felt inside. He was embarrassed because he was sure that his son had seen him admiring the woman who slept on their couch; and Hunter's guilt derived from knowing that he had almost touched a woman in an affectionate manner without her consent or her knowledge.

"Hi," Malik said to the stranger as he stopped beside his father en route to the dining room.

Jade wiped her eyes with her hands and replied with a groggy, "Hi."

Like Hunter had taught him to do when he greeted visitors, Malik extended his hand in Jade's direction. "My name is Malik Greene."

Jade smoothed her hands over her hair to be sure no strands were out of place and then offered her hand and a weak smile in return. "Hi, Malik. I'm Jade. It's nice to meet you."

"Go on and eat your food before it gets cold, sport," Hunter said as he nudged his son toward the dining room.

After Malik had rounded the corner, Hunter sat on the loveseat adjacent to the sofa where Jade was still gathering herself. As self-conscious as he felt, Hunter knew that it could have been worse. At least *she* didn't know what he'd almost done. As they both sat in silence, neither of them seemed to know what to say or where to begin in the first conversation they would have since their earlier dispute.

"I'm sorry," Hunter said, only to hear Jade saying the same words at the same time. Their eyes met for an instant, but Jade turned away before Hunter could voice his next thoughts.

"All of this that's going on with the paper has me a bit on edge," he admitted. "But that was no reason for me to say what I said."

Nodding in slow motion, as if she understood, Jade stared at her clenched hands. "My father's death is still a very sore spot with me, but that was no reason for me to do what I did either. I'm. . . . so sorry for hitting you. It was more than wrong. It was disrespectful and . . . "

"It's okay." Hunter sat up straight, casually rubbed the side of his face where the sting had long disappeared, and then allowed his back to rest against the cushions of the sofa. Staring into the lighting from the chandelier above them, he said, "The paper is suffering and I just don't know what else to do, Jade."

Although his eyes remained fixed on the high ceiling, Hunter could feel Jade's eyes on him. Too sure that he would see the same hurt in her eyes that he saw when he made his decision known earlier, Hunter couldn't bear to bring himself to return her gaze. Jade broke the silence.

"How is it that the world saw these letters as an honorable gesture just a few weeks ago and now they see it as a ploy? I know this has been rough for you and the AWC, Hunter, but please let me talk to Mother and the new pastor of the church. I know I can get them to speak up and calm the community."

Hunter laughed out loud, but there was no sign of amusement on his face when he brought his eyes to meet hers. "*They* are the leaders of the uprising, Jade."

"What?"

"Reverend Knight is the one who organized the protest," Hunter clarified. "It's all right there, written in the story in my competitor's paper. Most of the people who have been spending their day hours outside my business are members of New Hope and they are gaining support from other community leaders and businesses. I'm sorry, Jade, I truly am; but I have to make a move before it gets any worse. I know you don't agree with it, but I *need* to hear you say that you at least understand it."

Chapter 14

Jerome Tides lay on his bed and stared into the ceiling. The six by eight-foot space had been his living quarters for more years than he even wanted to calculate. Sometimes he struggled to know what day of the week it was; the year would sometimes escape him too. Everything was kept in order in his mind by each day's happenings. For instance, Jerome was only sure that today was Friday because Wednesdays and Fridays were the visiting days for the men in his unit. He knew it wasn't Wednesday because one visiting day had passed already this week. His cellmate, as well as others around him, had gotten visitors today, but Jerome hadn't. He wasn't overly disappointed though, because he really hadn't expected to; and with today's final chance for visitation just minutes away, Jerome didn't anticipate any surprises.

When he thought about all the years he had lost

entrapped behind doors that gave him no privacy, Jerome cringed. He'd heard someone say once that after doing something for twenty-one days it became a habit—a natural occurrence. In Jerome's opinion, that person had never spent those twenty-one days waking up in prison. For him, nothing inside the walls that surrounded him felt natural. Even the things that were routine often felt foreign. He just lived from day to day as best he could, and in the process, tried not to lose his mind and his manhood.

The issues that kept him preoccupied had changed many times over the years. At first, Jerome was haunted by anger and relentless hatred for his parents whose statement to the police had helped to seal his doom. Then when he realized that the friends he had on the outside were no longer anywhere to be found, Jerome came to understand that family was all he had. From that point, he began feeling sorry for himself and picked up a habit of blaming whomever he could for his incarceration. The system, society, "the white man"—anybody he could find to point the finger at, Jerome did. Facing the truth was just too hard.

All those years of trying to prove himself to be something that he wasn't; acting as though he was a perfect fit for the group of hoodlums that he ditched school, divided drug money and committed thievery with, now meant zilch. Behind iron walls, he'd been reduced to nothing. In prison, there was no such thing as safety. Whether compound officers were present or not, Jerome knew that he was in constant danger. The criminals who shared his address had long ago proved to Jerome that he wasn't nearly as big or as bad as he thought he was when he existed on the outside.

He'd taken everything for granted when he lived in his parents' home, and if Jerome could relive his life, there was hardly a day of it that he'd repeat in the same manner. Since his incarceration, Jerome couldn't even count the many times he'd had to fight just to hold on to the little dignity that he had left. Growing up, his parents tried to tell him about the woes of serving time, but Jerome never listened because he viewed it as only a scare tactic. Now he wished a million times over that he had. But now it was too late. Because of his constant rebellion, he was now forced to live in a place that he could only compare to hell. A place where it mattered not whether he slept on his back or his stomach; either way, he had to do so with one eye open and one eye closed. A place where friendships came with a price that was sometimes too high to pay.

Carefully, so as not to disturb his sleeping cellmate, Jerome brought himself to a seated position and looked around. The consistent rainfall had cut down on the allotted outside time given to him and the other inmates. The outside time was all that kept Jerome from losing his sanity. Every day was a test of wills and strength. In the nearly ten years that he'd been in the Phillips State Prison in Buford, Georgia, there had been very little to look forward to. With his first parole hearing approaching, for the first time, Jerome felt a level of hope. It had been a year since his last brawl. He knew that if he could stay out of fights and clear of trouble for just a few more days, he had a good chance of sleeping in a real bed for the first time since he was twenty-six.

Every week since the beginning of his sentence, Jerome had been visited by his parents. Even in those early weeks when he hated the very sight of them, they'd been there. Jackson would come by about half as often and he saw Jade even less. Since his father's death, Jerome's mother had adopted Jackson's schedule, only coming to visit when she was accompanied by her *good* son. The thought of it irritated Jerome. It was almost as if his mother was afraid to visit him without the protection of another family member. He wondered if her fear was of the other men in the compound or if it was directed toward him.

Walking to the slit in the wall that the outside world called windows, Jerome peered through. The daylight had faded and darkness was beginning to overtake the city. He could see lights shining from the buildings in the distance. Life on the other side of the concrete walls went on as if neither he nor his colleagues mattered. It was the heart of rush hour and Jerome could see the cars whiz by on an isolated road as people went about their daily lives, giving little or no thought to the citizens that could only admire free life from afar.

Tears formed in Jerome's eyes, but he immediately wiped them away before they could fall to his cheeks. The worst thing that could happen would be for a guard or a fellow inmate to see a sign of weakness. In jail, that was like having the emblem of a target painted on his back. He was already known as "church boy." Jerome didn't want any other epithets linked to him that would cause him any more trouble. Just a few more days and he could be free of this hellhole. He had to keep reminding himself of that. If he could get past the parole board, Jerome's only disappointment would be that his father didn't live to see him make the emergence.

Nothing about being in prison was good, but Jerome couldn't deny that being in there had taught him some valuable lessons. On the outside, while he was terrorizing innocent people, he had placed very little value on life. But having met people whose lives had been cut short by more than two thousand volts of electricity caused Jerome to think differently. Sometimes he didn't even like the guy whose lawyer's last ditch effort for a stay of execution was rejected. Still, whenever the lights at the prison would dim because of the powerful surge that the punishment would call for, Jerome's heart would sink. A few years ago, Georgia had outlawed the electric chair and replaced it with lethal injection. The end result still meant that somebody had been put to death, but Jerome found this means easier to stomach. Perhaps it was just because he didn't have to see the lights blink.

Another lesson he'd learned behind bars was the appreciation for decent employment. Before his arrest, Jerome never kept a job—not an honest one anyway. He stole and sold drugs to sustain himself. It was easier than getting up every morning and fighting traffic to get to a job that he hated. He made more money stealing and dealing than he ever did when he worked honestly, but Jerome had come to the hard conclusion that money wasn't everything. It was another lesson that he would not have had to learn the hard way had he listened to his parents.

At Phillips State Prison, every inmate had a job and it wasn't one that he wanted or got paid fairly for working. Jerome's assignment was scrubbing toilets, but as disgusting as it sounded, his job was simple in comparison to the jobs of some of the others.

His learned lessons seldom came easily, but Jerome was learning them one at a time. Since his father's death, he had been making a greater effort to be a better person. Freedom was so close that Jerome could almost taste the flavor of it on his tongue, but he didn't intend to get out just to be brought back. Somehow he had to make his experiences work in his favor. The last visits from his father had turned into haunting recordings that played themselves over and over in his dreams at night. Jerome knew that the only way he could honor his father's memory was to consider B.T.'s words. But how he'd get himself together enough to follow the path that his father had only partially directed him toward, Jerome didn't know. All he'd ever been any good at was hustling.

Just when it seemed that he and his dad were making a breakthrough connection with one another, tragedy snatched B.T. Tides away. Using the back of his hands, Jerome wiped away the threat of more tears. He couldn't tell whether they were angry tears or the result of sadness. It was like God had played a cruel joke on him . . . like another addition to the sentence that been handed down to him ten years earlier. As soon as Jerome took note of the thought that had formed in his mind, he pushed it away; all the while, reminding himself not to try to find others to blame. This wasn't God's fault and Jerome knew it. But he missed his father in such enormity that it often brought on physical pain. The last few times B.T. was there, he spoke to his son about the desire to start a prison ministry within the church. He'd told Jerome that God had been speaking with him regarding the many lost souls that were tucked behind prison bars, starving for something that wasn't readily available to them.

At first, Jerome had selfishly opposed the idea, thinking that it could only result in more trouble for him. Almost all of the inmates already knew that he was the son of a preacher. That alone made him the object of mockery and ridicule. To them, a preacher's kid in jail was an oxymoron. Jerome figured that if his father and members of the church started visiting and witnessing to the men in his cell block, he would never be able to live it down. But during his father's final visit, one of the few visits where he'd come alone, Jerome agreed.

"I think these guys could really use something like what you talked about the other day, Dad," Jerome had said. After a moment of thought he added, "I think *I* could really use something like that."

B.T.'s pleasure in his son's acceptance could be seen all over his face. He had smiled and then pulled Jerome in for a lengthy embrace. It was a good visit. By far, one of the best that they'd had. But it was what B.T. said next that prompted Jerome to reveal his inner thoughts to his mother.

"I'm glad to hear you say that, son, but the prison ministry may have to come a little later than planned. Perhaps with someone else heading it instead of me."

"What are you talking about?" Jerome asked, disappointed by his father's sudden revelation. "You mean you're not gonna be the one to do it?"

"I'd planned to; but as I was in prayer at the church earlier tonight, I got the feeling that God has a special assignment for me that I won't be able to avoid. It may be awhile before you see me again. I think He wants to use me . . . take my life and use it in a different way."

"What do you mean by, 'in a different way'?"

"I wish I could tell you more, Jerome. But I can't. I don't think my telling you would lessen your disappointment in the details of the prison ministry. Besides, I can't even say that I'm totally clear on the purpose that God has for me. But whatever it is, just remember that where He leads me, I must follow. And if He leads me there, He will take care of me. The prison ministry will still go on and I want you to be an intricate part of it."

"Me?" Jerome was confused by his father's words. "How am I gonna be a part of a prison ministry? I'm a part of *prison*. I'm in here just like the rest of these cats. What can I tell them?"

"Experience is the best teacher, son. And who can teach better than he who has learned? Your life can be a mighty testimony. *That's* how you are to be a part of the ministry."

Jerome had been left baffled by the exchange with his father. It wasn't until after the accident that B.T.'s words began making sense. Jerome hadn't meant to upset his mother when he called her to share his thoughts, but it was apparent that she was not pleased with what he had said. The week was almost gone. This was the week for her and Jackson to visit and Jerome hadn't seen or heard from either one of them. With B.T. gone, Jerome had already begun preparing himself for the lonely days leading up to his hearing.

The names of inmates who had new visitors were now being called over the loud speaker and Jerome was caught off-guard when he heard his own. As much as he had prepared himself for the probability of not seeing his mother and brother tonight, knowing they were there made him happy. It seemed like ages since he'd seen them.

The room where tables and chairs were set up for prisoners to talk to guests had very little privacy, but when they got as few visitors as Jerome did, they didn't care. Each table was separated by a few feet of spacing and armed security never left the room, so privacy was a treat that the inmates were never truly given. They'd given up that luxury when they decided to live lives of crime that ultimately got them caught.

Jerome quickly scanned the busy room and then spotted his guest in the distance. As soon as the woman rose from her seat to capture his full attention, Jerome broke into a wide grin and rushed to meet her with open arms. He hadn't seen his sister since they'd buried their father.

"Hey, Jerome. How are you?"

"Girl, you are a sight for sore eyes," Jerome responded, cupping her face in his hands and then embracing her again. "What are you doing here? What brought you in town? Is Mother okay?"

"As far as I know, she is," Jade said as she smoothed her hair back and sat down with Jerome. "I haven't gone by to see her yet. I wanted to check in on you first. How are you?"

Jerome almost wished she'd said their mother was ill. At least that would have been a good reason for her skipping her normal visit this week. The disappointment that he thought had diminished began resurfacing, but he found reason to smile. His sister had made a visit and she'd stopped by to see him before anyone else in the family. To a man who was accustomed to feeling like the lowest symbol on the totem pole, it meant more than Jade could possibly know.

"Thank you for checking on me," he said. "I'm doin'. That's all I can say, to be honest."

"I know." Jade returned his smile, but Jerome saw sadness in her eyes.

"How long are you going to be in town?"

"My flight back home is tomorrow night. I have a full day tomorrow, so I wanted to be sure to get by to see you."

The one thing that Jerome could say about his sister was that she never forgot him. Jade didn't travel to Atlanta very often, but whenever she was in town, whether it was for a few days or a few hours, she always made time to see him. He couldn't be certain, but Jerome believed that if Jade lived nearer, as was the case with the rest of the family, she would allot more time than one day a week or one day every two weeks to see him. Like his father, Jerome knew his sister would be more attentive to him, despite the fact that he was the one that many people referred to as the "thorn" in his family's side.

"It's always good to see you, Jade. What kind of business brought you here at the end of the week?"

Jade hesitated, and Jerome knew that there was something that she questioned whether or not she should say to her incarcerated brother. For Jerome, feeling that she didn't have confidence in him brought back the reality that he would never truly be trusted by the members of his family.

"Never mind," he said, trying not to sound offended. "That's your own personal business. Didn't mean to be all up in it."

"No, Jerome. I want to tell you. I mean, I don't know how much of this you already know. There's just so much going on, but I need to talk to *somebody* in the family about it."

Jerome's face brightened. "For real? You want to talk to me about something that you ain't shared with Jackson?"

"Don't act so surprised."

"But I am, sis. You ain't never confided in me."

"That's because you always close me out, Jerome. Even before you ended up here, you never wanted to talk to me. I didn't share everything with Jackson, and when I did, it wasn't always because I wanted to. Sometimes I talked to him because I didn't feel like I had any other choice. I talked to Jackson because sometimes it felt like he was the only brother I had."

Jerome relaxed his back against his chair and sat in silence. Jade was right and he knew it. But it wasn't just her. He'd treated everybody in the family the same way. She was the first to confront him on it, though. Until now, Jerome never thought his physical and emotional absence from the family even mattered.

"I'm . . . sorry." It was the first time he had apologized to anyone in years. "I'm sorry, Jade."

"I'm sorry too," Jade replied as she wiped moisture from the corners of her eyes.

"For what? You ain't got nothing to be sorry for."

"Yes I do," Jade said with a laugh. "If I had told you what a jerk you were a long time ago, maybe we could have been talking way before now."

"Okay," Jerome said as he joined her in laughter. "I had that one coming. Now," he said once the air had been cleared, "you want to talk?"

"I want to, Jerome. I just don't know where to start."

"Well, I don't know about you, but I ain't got no place to be. You can start at the beginning."

The boyish grin on Jerome's face diminished as swiftly as it had appeared as he listened to Jade's rendition of what had been happening between the newspaper and the community. Reading had never been Jerome's preference—another reason he didn't do well in school. Newspapers could be found scattered here and there at the prison and books were certainly available, but only a few inmates chose to read over spending their free time on the outside playing. Contact sports had a way of relieving the stress brought on by being held captive in a place that kept men isolated from the people and places they loved.

Listening to Jade speak of the uproar that resurrecting the letters had caused was startling enough, but to hear her talk about her dreams and reveal the belief that their father was murdered, temporarily left Jerome too shocked to speak.

"I know it sounds crazy, Jerome," Jade said. "You're the only person in the family that I've told about this. I said I wasn't going to tell anyone, but I guess I needed to and you just seemed like the right person to tell. I miss Daddy a lot, Jerome, and I'm trying not to think that I'm just letting my grief get the best of me, but—"

"I believe you."

It was Jade's turn to be at a loss for words. Her widened eyes and dropped jaw indicated that she was visibly shaken by Jerome's admission.

"I don't know why, but I believe you," Jerome added. "Daddy had started coming to visit me a lot lately . . . sometimes more than once a week; and I felt like he had a gut feeling....like a hunch or a . . ."

"Premonition?" Jade offered.

"Yeah. I think he knew something was up, sis. I told Mother that I felt that Daddy knew that something was 'bout to go down, but she didn't want to hear it. She got mad at me. So you definitely can't tell her what you feel, Jade; or else she'll get ticked off at you too."

"But I was thinking about telling her tonight. I need to somehow convince her that Hunter wasn't using Daddy's name and his tragedy to bilk money from the community. If I don't tell her, how will she ever understand?"

"I don't know, but there's got to be another way. Take my word for it, sis. Mother ain't ready to hear nothing like this. You'll have to think up some other way to get her to see it your way. If you tell Mother that you think Daddy was murdered and that he somehow knew that it was going to happen, she'll fall completely apart. *Believe* me. She will never accept it, but I ain't just blowing smoke when I tell you that I believe you. I don't know if you're right about him being murdered, but I know that *something* ain't kosher about all this. I don't think it's as open and shut as it seems."

"That's just the way I feel, Jerome. But Hunter was right. I can't expect him to lose his business over this. I just don't know what else to do."

"I don't either, sis," Jerome said. "Ain't much I can do being locked up in this joint, but I'm on your side. You can't give up, Jade. You and me together . . . we gotta think of something."

Chapter 15

It was well past closing, but Kwame felt glued to his chair. He stared at the telephone on his desk, hoping . . . praying even, that it would ring again and he would be told that it was all a mistake. He'd even settle for the sound of Hunter's laugh as he told him that it was all just a joke; a test to see what kind of reaction would result from the warped humor.

"Please tell me that you were lying, Kwame."

Kwame wasn't the only one who was on edge. He'd called Diane at home and told her of Hunter's message and he knew from her response that she was upset. But Kwame didn't expect her to return to the office for clarification. He glanced up from his desk and saw her standing in his doorway with a look of disbelief on her face that surpassed his own. Kwame's eye-contact with her was brief. Diane's glare was so sharp with displeasure that it seemed to cut into his corneas.

"I wish I could," he whispered, bringing his focus back to the phone in front of him.

The curses released from Diane's lips reflected deep irritation. "This is suicide," she said while taking the liberty of sitting in an unoccupied chair near Kwame's desk. "I can't believe Hunter would do something so insanely stupid."

Kwame wanted to say something in his friend's defense, but Diane was only vocalizing the same words that had been flooding his mind ever since he listened to the voicemail message that Hunter had left for him.

"Are you sure you heard him right?" Diane asked, still not wanting to accept the decision that Hunter had made. "Maybe what he meant was . . ."

"Listen for yourself." Kwame pressed the code on his telephone pad that would replay his last message and then pressed a final button that would allow Diane to hear Hunter's voice through the speakers.

"What's up, Kwame? I got the message you left on my cell of your plan to step away from the office for a bit. I know I'm calling late, but it's not too late for the print department. I tried to call you on your cell, but you never answered and your voicemail never picked up, so I thought I'd call here. After a lot of thought and prayer, I decided to let the letters that I passed along to Lorna be placed in tomorrow's paper. I sent the orders to you in an email for your records. I know you like to have things like this in writing. You don't agree with my decision and I fully respect that, but it's my decision just the same. This will most likely be the final week for the letters, but I can't make a promise on that. I just know that I can't pull them today. If you'd pass that information on, I'd appre-

ciate it. I know you have a lot of questions and rightfully so. We'll talk later."

Another string of curses preceded Diane's next words. "Has he lost his mind? What is he thinking of?"

"*Who* is he thinking of might be a more accurate question," Kwame blurted. He wanted to immediately take back his words, but it was too late.

"*Who?*" Diane said with a look that indicated that the effect of tomorrow's newspaper had suddenly taken a backseat. "What do you mean, who?"

"Never mind."

"Who are you talking about, Kwame? Are Hunter's decision-making skills being jaded by someone?"

Kwame released a short, dry laugh. "Funny you should use the word 'jaded'."

Diane slid forward in her chair and leaned closer toward Kwame with narrowed eyes. "Kwame Williams, what are you hinting at? I'm not going to let it go, so you might as well save both of us the trouble of debating and just come out and say what you're trying to say."

Once again, Kwame rethought his decision to say more, but the initial shock he'd suffered from hearing Hunter's message was melting away and was beginning to be replaced by anger. In his opinion, not only was Hunter being stupid, as Diane had so accurately stated; but he was also being selfish. Hunter knew the effect that this was having on Kwame. It was his church that Reverend Tides had been leader of and it was his church that was protesting the letters. Going to church last Sunday had been tough enough. The combination of Hunter's stubbornness and his apparent weakness with respect to the desires of Reverend Tides' daughter would make it near impossible for Kwame to walk through the doors of New Hope Church again.

"Jade Tides is in town," Kwame revealed.

"Who's that?"

"Reverend B.T. Tides' daughter. She's the one who initiated the idea to start running these letters in the paper again. She had been having these crazy dreams about her father's death being a covered up murder or something." When Diane's eyes widened, Kwame knew that he'd said too much. Hunter had told him all the details in confidence, but right now, keeping his friend's secret wasn't Kwame's concern.

"After all this mess started with the picketing and protesting, Hunter was pretty much all set to end the feature. He called Jade and set up a meeting with her to tell her of his decision. That's why he took the day off. They had a meeting scheduled for this morning."

"You mean he wasn't sick?" Diane said, not trying to mask her mounting envy from the revelation.

"My guess is that Jade got to him," Kwame said while simultaneously answering her question with a shake of his head.

"Are they *seeing* each other?"

"Not that I know of," Kwame said as he stood from behind his desk and crossed his arms. "But who knows? It's apparent that I don't know him like I thought I did. Maybe they are an item and I just don't know it. Something's going on, right? He was definitely going to tell her that we couldn't jeopardize the paper or our jobs by keeping the letters going. Now he calls and says for us to run them?"

Diane stood too, biting her bottom lip and flaring her nostrils like an angry cow. "Well, maybe we're talking to the wrong one. Maybe we should be cornering this . . . woman that's instigating all of this. She might be able to charm Hunter, but whatever she's saying or *doing* to him won't work with me."

"No, Diane," Kwame said as he tried get a grip on his business sense. "We can't go to Jade. If Hunter finds out, that's both our jobs. Mine for telling you about this to begin with, and yours for acting on it."

"You say they aren't seeing each other, but at the beginning of this conversation you implied that she may have had something to do with his decision to run the letters." Diane made the observation with caution and seemed to brace herself for the answer. "You think he likes her, don't you?"

Kwame shrugged and turned to look out the window behind him. It didn't give near the view that Hunter's did, but for now, it would do. He wasn't really interested in whatever the darkness outside had to offer anyway.

Diane sat back down as if she thought, for the next question, she might need the extra support that the chair would supply. "Well, is she his type? I mean, should I be concerned? Is she a worthy opponent?"

Kwame had always known of Diane's infatuation with Hunter, but this was the first time she'd admitted to it in his presence. Diane asked her questions with such self-confidence, as if she honestly thought that she had a chance with her employer. Knowing full well that Hunter had no romantic interest in Diane, Kwame's emotions took a quick turn. In the midst of the anger that had been brewing in his stomach, Kwame felt a fit of laughter forming. He tried to hold it back, but it was too strong for him to forbid. His chuckle turned into a guffaw that bounced from one wall to the other, resulting in an echo that traveled the full square footage of the space that he occupied five days a week. By the time Kwame was finished, he was doubled over, gasping for breath while his hands rested on his knees and water spilled down his cheeks. As he regained his composure and turned to face Diane, Kwame could see her scornful gaze through his tear-blurred vision.

"I'm sorry," he said. "I wasn't ready for that."

Cursing, Diane brought herself to a standing position, and using the backs of her knees, she forcefully slid the chair backward. "I'm glad you find this so funny, Kwame. While you're making jokes, this woman could be manipulating Hunter into running these letters until the city finds some nonexistent killer! Is that what you want?"

"Of course not."

"Then I suggest you man up and help me devise a plan of our own." Diane's tone was stern and Kwame all of a sudden felt as if he was no longer the one who was second in command at the company.

"Devise a plan? Diane, you sound like a crook. The AWC is Hunter's paper. We work here and that's all. We can't *devise* a plan to counter his decisions."

"We can if we don't make it seem like we're going against him. Use your head, Kwame, and stop being such a suck-up."

"*I'm* the suck-up?" Kwame challenged. "You're the one who spends your day kissing Hunter's behind and trying to get your groove back, Stella. Let's not talk about sucking up."

Diane couldn't rightfully deny Kwame's accusations, so she chose not to even try. "All I'm saying is use your ranking, Kwame. You have some status around here, but you're so afraid to use it that sometimes you don't seem to be any more important than . . . than Lorna."

Kwame grimaced. "What kind of status are you talking about? Do you know something that I don't? Whatever my ranking, it always falls below Hunter's and he's the one who said to run the section." For effect, Kwame slid a sheet of paper in front of her that displayed the print-out of the email that had been sent as backup. "I can't counter that no matter what my job title is. You know that, Diane. I never have the right to go over Hunter's head."

"Then go *around* him."

"I don't like the sound of this."

"Do you like the sound of being unemployed?" Diane demanded. "We can do this, Kwame. I'm not talking about being blatantly insubordinate. I'm talking about being *creative* with whatever we do to maneuver this. For instance, you can pretend like you never got his messages. If you don't pass that information to the print department they will print what they have. Have you told them yet? If not, it's late and they've probably already gone to print anyway and we won't have this to even worry about. Just pretend you didn't get the message, say nothing, and no one will be the wiser."

"What?"

"For crying out loud, Kwame; do you need everything in writing?"

Diane snatched up the printout that Kwame had placed in front of her, flipped it over and quickly scribbled a note that paraphrased the idea she'd just pitched to him. When she was finished, a wide grin stretched across her face as she slid the note back toward him. It was obvious that she was proud of the scheme that she'd just brought to the table.

In contrast, Kwame tightened his jaws and swallowed back the guilt that he felt rising in his throat. A part of him wanted to lash out at Diane for her imprudence, but he couldn't.

"Hunter left this message over an hour ago, Diane. The print department has already been informed and they are already in the middle of production. It's too late."

His revelation quickly deflated Diane's triumph, but Kwame was more aware of the bitterness that his words had left in his own mouth. It was what he *hadn't* said, that bothered him the most. The print department was indeed already in full swing, but it wasn't due to Kwame's instruction. Diane's plot to override Hunter's decision had formed in Kwame's head long before she had voiced it. It had been his intention to do just the deceptive thing that Diane had mentioned, but Hunter had foiled it before Kwame could implement it. Not only had Hunter called Kwame and left the message on his voicemail while he was away from the office, but he'd also spoken with his trusted secretary. Lorna had already passed the instructions on to the print department before she left the office for the evening.

"Darn it, Kwame," Diane huffed. "I wish you'd spoken to me before you told them. We could have organized this in a way that would have easily been believable."

"Well, what's done is done," Kwame said, shoving his hands in his pockets. There was no need to tell Diane the whole truth. It would only make the situation worse.

"What now?" Diane asked. Her anger that had turned into arrogance just a few moments earlier had now transformed into anxiety. "What's going to happen to the paper, Kwame? What's going to happen to *us*?"

Kwame turned his face back to the open blinds behind his desk and looked out at the lights that illuminated the back parking lot occupied by only his car. He wished that he had the answers that Diane sought, but all he had were questions of his own. Why had Hunter changed his mind? Did Jade really somehow con him into thinking that the church community wasn't strong enough to make a difference? Was impressing Reverend B.T. Tides' daughter worth losing everything?

"I don't know, Diane," Kwame finally answered through an exasperated sigh. "I guess we'll find out in just a few hours."

It was going to be a long wait.

Chapter 16

Moments of sleep had come few and far between throughout the night. Now, just when Hunter was finally beginning to find peaceful rest, the telephone rang and jolted him into a seated position. Looking at the clock beside him, he saw the bright red numbers that told him that it was an ungodly hour for anybody to be calling him.

"Yeah." It wasn't Hunter's usual greeting, but it also wasn't the usual time to receive a phone call.

"Didn't we tell you that God wasn't pleased with you meddling in His business? Why couldn't you leave well enough alone?" the unfamiliar voice yelled at him through the receiver.

"What?"

"Your day in hell is coming, Hunter Greene," the man hissed, "but right now, it's your business that's going up in flames."

"What?" Hunter struggled to clear his head and free his thoughts.

"You heard me!" the man's voice rose even more. "You just couldn't let it go, could you? Now everything that happens from here on out is your fault."

"Who is this?"

"Ain't no never mind who this is. When you find your little girlfriend's body in your burned down building, maybe you'll get the message!"

"My *what*?"

"Hunter . . . help me!" This time, the voice was very familiar.

Hunter's body stiffened at the sound of the distressed female cries that suddenly amplified through the receiver.

"Jade?"

He'd barely gotten the word out of his mouth before he heard the phone disconnect from the caller's end.

"Jade!"

Hearing himself yell out her name brought Hunter to a seated position for the second time. This time, for real. Through the dark room that was only lighted by his muted television, Hunter looked around. The rapid thumping of his heart pounded against the walls of his chest with vigor. The dream he'd just awakened from had possibly been the most convincing nightmare he'd ever had. It had been too real for him to just turn over and go back to sleep. Kicking off the blankets that covered his legs, Hunter jumped from the warmth of his bed and quickly changed from his pajamas to a sweatshirt and a pair of denim jeans.

"Malik!" He stood at the bottom of the stairs and called for his son while holding his socks and shoes in his hand. "Malik!" His son had always been a deep sleeper and Hunter knew that the chances that he could wake him without going upstairs were slim.

Sitting on the sofa, Hunter put on his socks and then slipped his feet in the shoes he generally wore when he went to the stable to check on the horses. After tying the strings, he climbed the stairs, some two at a time, until he reached the top. He opened Malik's bedroom door and the boy stirred as soon as Hunter turned on the overhead light.

"Malik," he called in a low tone. "Wake up, sport. We need to run an errand."

It took a few more calls of his name, and ultimately, Hunter having to physically pull Malik into a seated position. But gradually, the boy became coherent and began putting on his shoes as instructed. Hunter didn't bother insisting that Malik change from his World Wrestling Entertainment pajamas. He hoped that the trip would be an unnecessary, uneventful one.

The pounding in Hunter's chest continued as he drove down the virtually empty streets. The water that was still pooled on the pavement was the only sign of the earlier rain. Looking through his rearview mirror, Hunter saw Malik's head leaning against the window. He'd gone back to sleep and had not once asked his father where they were headed or why.

Still a block away from the office, Hunter had already begun to relax. Had there been a fire, no doubt there would have been the sounds of fire trucks or other emergency vehicles and even in the darkness a building the size of his would have sent up quite a smoke signal. Hunter's relief escalated as he rounded the corner that led him to the parking lot of the building that produced the *Atlanta Weekly Chronicles*. Seeing the building intact with no protesters outside or flames inside prompted him to do something he hadn't thought to do in the midst of the panic.

"Thank you, Jesus," he prayed softly. "Thank you."

Maneuvering his car so that it would be parked directly in front of the entrance door, Hunter took a look around the well-lit parking lot before exiting his car. Scooping Malik up into his arms, he unlocked the door and let himself in before locking it again behind them.

"Daddy, why are we here?" Malik asked while rubbing eyes that had suddenly been irritated when his father turned on the overhead lights.

"I just need to take a quick look around. You can sit right here."

Hunter directed his son to one of the padded chairs in the front of the business where visitors usually sat until they could be seen for whatever reason. For Hunter, tonight felt a lot like that strange night at his house, minus the torrential weather and the frightened son, when he heard the bizarre noises. Just like that night, tonight he found himself walking softly, this time throughout his place of business, looking for something that had no identity.

Walking into his office, he saw a completed copy of the paper that would be in all the news stands by daylight. Picking it up, Hunter flipped through the sections until he came to Section D. He hoped his plan would work. Instead of placing the letters on the front page of Section C where they had been in all of the previous issues, Hunter had told Lorna to have them moved to the second page of the last section of the paper. That way, if protestors picked up the paper to check it out before purchasing it, they wouldn't readily see the infamous feature.

As he opened the paper to the second page of Section D, Hunter's eyes scanned the letters. The racing of his heart caught a second wind. This could be the death of everything he'd worked so hard to build. He had told Jade that the letters would not continue and she, although disappointed, accepted his decision. Just like at the restaurant during their initial meeting, the coast was clear and he had every opportunity to walk away from this most unpleasant situation, but for some reason, he couldn't let it go. Hunter felt the same passion that Jade felt. Although there was no valid proof, deep inside, he knew that there was more to the death of Reverend Tides and he was risking everything, friendships, clout, reputation and his job, to help her get to the bottom of it.

"Hunter . . . help me!"

Jade's cries from his nightmare resurfaced in Hunter's mind. The fire that the unidentified caller in the dream had told him of didn't exist and Hunter hoped that the same was true for Jade's troubles. It was nearly three o'clock in the morning and calling her now would be absurd, but Hunter's hands seemed to take on a mind of their own. Fishing his cell phone from the pocket of his jeans, he scrolled through the numbers in his address book until he reached Jade's.

"Hello?"

To Hunter's surprise, she answered on the second ring and Jade sounded far too alert to have been stirred from her sleep.

"Jade?"

"Hey, Hunter. Is something wrong?"

"Apparently not. I'm sorry. I just . . ."

"No. Don't apologize. What's going on?"

Hunter paused, wondering if he should reveal his true reason for calling. If he told Jade of his dream, he might upset her and make her overly concerned for no reason. She had enough to worry about and certainly didn't need the additional burden of thinking that her safety might be in danger.

"Hunter?"

"I uh . . . I had this dream and it woke me up. It's nothing."

"What kind of dream?"

It was the question that Hunter hoped she wouldn't ask, but with his inability to talk without pausing and faltering, he wasn't surprised that she had. "Just something crazy," he replied, trying to sound carefree. "I guess, I guess . . . I ate the wrong thing before going to bed. I'm sorry."

"Where are you? Are you at the ranch?"

Jade had failed to catch the humor in Hunter's response. Her prying continued and so did his stammering.

"Uh . . . no. I'm at my office."

"Why?"

Another question he hoped she wouldn't ask. "I, uh . . . I uh . . . I needed to check on a couple of things."

"At three in the morning? Hunter what's really going on? I'm coming over there."

"No," he quickly said. Then taking a much-needed deep breath, he continued. "Look, Jade. I just had a few things to check out after the dream, that's all. Don't come out here. Everything's fine."

"Are you telling me the truth, Hunter?"

"Yes. Everything is fine."

"Cross your heart and hope to die?"

Hunter broke into a light-hearted laugh. He couldn't remember hearing that one since leaving the old Perry Homes. The kids in the new area that his mother moved them to didn't talk like that. Hunter couldn't help but wonder if Jade had used the index finger on her right hand to draw the imaginary "X" across her chest as she asked the question.

"Yeah," he said, still smiling at the thought of it. "Cross my heart and hope to die."

"Okay."

From the sound of Jade's voice, Hunter could tell that she'd found it amusing too. "Good night," he said. "Well, what's left of it anyway."

"Good night."

As he disconnected the call, Hunter felt the weight of a burden being lifted from his shoulders. The business was still intact and Jade wasn't in any danger. The dream had been nothing more than a dream. Tucking the newspaper under his arm and switching off the light in his office, Hunter started for the front of the building where he could see that Malik had curled his legs underneath him and made a bed of the chair that he'd been told to sit in.

"Might as well go ahead and check the other rooms," Hunter whispered.

He walked the full length of the building, peeking in on Lorna's workstation as well as the area where the other full- and part-time employees worked on a daily basis. As he rounded the corner to head back to the front of the business, he stopped and took a quick look around Michelle's office and then stopped by Kwame's as well.

Seeing the open blinds, he stepped inside long enough to peer into the back parking lot before closing them. A complete issue of this week's AWC had been placed on Kwame's desk too. Hunter looked at the front page of it for a moment and was reminded all over again of how much he knew that he and his best friend disagreed on the running of the letters. But whether they saw eye-to-eye or not, he smiled at knowing that he could count on Kwame to stick beside him and back him up on his decisions. Kwame had to know that he'd never intentionally do anything to hurt the business or its employees without good reason.

Just as Hunter walked from behind the desk and was headed to the door, his eyes caught a glimpse of a stray sheet of paper that rested near the corner of Kwame's desk. Picking it up, he noticed that it was the email that he'd sent, outlining his decision to run the letters for another issue. While Hunter was in the process of placing the printout back in its place, the paper slipped from his hand and floated onto the floor beside him, flipping in the process. Hunter stopped to retrieve it and saw the handwritten note on the back.

> *I repeat . . . this time in writing since it's apparently the only form of communication you understand. Follow your heart and do what you need to do. Pretend you didn't get the call or the email from Hunter. Don't pass along this suicidal message. Let the paper run as is, and working together, we can save our jobs. I've got your back, Kwame. Let's do this.*

Hunter stared at the note in disbelief. It was clearly written in haste and not in her usual neat penmanship, but he had no doubt that it was Diane's handwriting. The first line of her note indicated that she and Kwame had already discussed disregarding his instructions. No doubt, the scheme was Diane's creation, but Kwame had apparently toyed with the idea of carrying it out and that, for Hunter, was the most unsettling part. Kwame and Diane were the two employees that he trusted most to carry on the business in his absence. Knowing that together, they'd concocted a plan to override his authority, was more hurtful than infuriating.

Folding the letter into a neat square, he slid it in the pocket of his pants. Again, Hunter retrieved his cell phone and began dialing as he turned out the office lights and headed back toward the front of the building. This time it only rang once before Jade answered.

"Hunter? What's wrong?"

"I need to talk. Can you meet me?"

"I'll have to call a cab, but yes. I'll be there in about forty-five minutes."

After a brief moment of thought, Hunter said, "No. That's too much trouble for this time of morning. It'll be much easier for me to just come to your hotel. Give me twenty minutes."

Chapter 17

Initially, it seemed like a good idea, but as Jade sat on the side of her hotel bed and tried to calm her nerves with deep, slow breaths, she was no longer sure about her decision to give Hunter the room number to her private temporary living quarters. When he suggested that he meet her there, Jade didn't even give it a second thought. But in the eighteen minutes that had passed since hanging up her phone, she'd done little else other than think about it.

Hunter would be arriving any minute. She'd gotten up and changed clothes three times since hanging up the telephone. Her first outfit, a pair of silk black pants and a matching black and grey top, felt too dressy so she had pulled it off and replaced it with a pair of jeans and a tank top. Upon looking at her reflection in the mirror, Jade decided that that one wouldn't do either. The tank top fitted her a little too snugly. She didn't want

Hunter to feel like a trap had been set for his arrival. The only other top that she had was red, and Mildred Tides had taught her daughter at a young age that wearing red on a first date was inappropriate. While Jade was fully aware that this wasn't a date, she was self-conscious of the fact that she and Hunter would be alone in a hotel room and there were very few settings that could be described as more date-like and intimate than that.

Jade had only brought a few pieces of clothing for her brief visit, so she put on the only other outfit that she hadn't tried on and dismissed. It was a lavender sundress that she bought for herself just before coming to visit her father for Father's Day. After getting dressed, she made up the bed that she'd been lying in. All made up, it didn't look as inviting as it did with the covers turned down. Jade had even tidied up the room, placing the clothes and shoes that she'd tossed over the chairs inside the closet. There was a table with two accompanying chairs in the room that would provide the perfect place for her to sit and chat with Hunter, but something about the bed being so close made it feel like an unspoken enticement. The last thing Jade needed him to think was that she was making any covert suggestions, but there was no more time to make changes. The knock on her door was soft, but the banging that echoed in her chest was anything but.

"Calm down, Jade," she whispered to herself as she took one last look in the mirror on the wall. The pep talk offered very little help and Jade still found herself searching for a valid reason to change the location of the meeting. Taking one last deep breath, she walked toward the door and opened it. Relief flushed through Jade's body when she saw Hunter standing there, holding his sleeping son. Seeing the boy was just the perfect thing to help her find the comfort level that she needed.

"Hey," Jade said as she stepped aside. "Come on in."

Hunter returned her greeting and then walked in. Once inside, he stood with Malik still in his arms.

"It's okay," Jade assured him as she rushed toward the bed and pulled back the comforter. "You can lay him here."

"Thanks," Hunter replied.

She carefully pulled the comforter on top of the child after Hunter released him. For a moment, Malik stirred. He opened his eyes briefly and looked from his father to Jade. Seeming to find no surprise in seeing them both standing over him, Malik turned over and pulled the comforter to his neck and closed his eyes again.

"Sorry," Hunter whispered. "He's too young to leave at home by himself. I hope you don't mind." He tossed a folded newspaper at the foot of the bed as he spoke.

"Not at all." Jade couldn't be happier that Malik was too young to leave at home. "I don't drink coffee, but I've heated water in the coffee pot and I have packets of hot cocoa if you want some? If you're hungry, I have a bag of chips and a can of soda you can have."

"What? No stew beef and rice with a side of sweet potato soufflé?" Hunter said with a brief chuckle.

"No," Jade giggled. "And, unfortunately, no cold milk either."

"I'll take a cup of cocoa. Thanks," Hunter replied, smiling that she took note of what he liked to drink. "I don't do coffee either."

Jade walked toward the coffeemaker to prepare a cup for each of them. All the while that she was pouring and mixing, she tossed glances at Hunter, watching his every move. He removed his sweatshirt and the newly exposed short-sleeved crewneck showed off nice tone that looked to be more hereditary than acquired. Just before taking a seat at the table, he walked closer to the bed to check on his son once more.

"They have marshmallows," Jade suddenly said. "I hope that's okay."

Hunter looked at her through the room that was dimly lit by the one lamp that was turned on. "Yeah, that's fine," he responded as he walked back to his chair.

Setting one cup in front of each chair, Jade joined him at the table, sitting directly across from him. Both of them sat in silence and she studied his face as he took a sip of the cocoa and then stared down into the cloudy brown liquid when he rested the cup back on the wooden table.

"Hunter, what is it?" Jade could see the growing disquiet on his face, even with him not looking directly at her.

"The letters," he started.

"You don't owe me any more explanations or regrets, Hunter," she broke in. "It's okay about the letters. I think it's time for me to give up. I don't want to, but I'm starting to feel like I have no choice. I tried to reason with Mother and Jackson tonight and by the time they got finished with me, I felt like a traitor . . . or at best, a stepchild."

Her words brought Hunter's eyes from the cup. "You spoke with them?"

"I *tried* to," Jade stressed. "Neither of them wanted to hear what I had to say."

"Jade, you didn't tell them that you'd asked me to run the letters, did you? There was no need for you to put yourself on the spot like that. They never had to know of your involvement."

Jade shook her head and doing so seemed to immediately calm Hunter. "I didn't tell them that, but I did tell them that I thought it was admirable that you'd resumed the feature. I tried to tell them that it honored Daddy's memory, but it was two against one. I think that if Renee had spoken her mind, it would have evened the playing field, but it was obvious that she didn't want to become involved."

"Renee?"

"Jackson's wife," Jade clarified. "She mostly remained quiet, but I could tell that she didn't see the feature as all bad. Mother and Jackson did though. There was no convincing them otherwise. It seems that Reverend Knight has really won them all over and made them see you as a monster. The things they said about the paper and your intentions were deplorable, Hunter. I just feel so helpless because I'm still not convinced that I'm wrong about Daddy's death. But I know I can't fight this battle alone. Jerome wants to help, but . . ."

"Jerome? You spoke with him about this?"

"Last night after you dropped me off here, I caught a ride to Buford to see him. I knew that if I didn't get around to seeing him before visiting hours ended on last night, I wouldn't get to see him at all. I couldn't come in town and not spend at least a few minutes with him."

"How is he?"

Jade was impressed that Hunter asked about her brother's wellbeing. She knew that there were more pressing questions to follow, but the fact that he'd asked this one first spoke volumes about the type of man Hunter was.

"Jerome is doing well," she said with a slight smile. "We talked about a lot of things. Last week, he finished the requirements for obtaining a GED. It was a surprise that he wanted to give to Daddy and Mother, but with all that has happened, he's never gotten a chance to share it with anyone but me. Mother and Jackson don't get by to see him as much as they used to. He thinks they are still embarrassed that he had to come to the funeral with an armed officer. Like me, he misses Daddy a lot, but other than that, he's doing as well as can be expected."

"What did he say when you told him about all that's going on here?"

"He shared with me that Daddy basically told him, in a not-so-direct manner, that something was getting ready to happen. He thinks Daddy had a premonition of his death and he agrees that the public doesn't know the whole story yet. He warned me about going to Mother with my beliefs and he was right. She immediately asked if I'd gone to see Jerome and when I said that I did, she started accusing him of planting, as she put it, "such foolishness" in my head. I tried to tell her that Jerome had nothing to do with it, but with Jackson backing her one hundred percent, she wouldn't believe me.

"In both their eyes, Alfonzo Knight is an angel sent from heaven and they credit him with the one being used by God to give the *Atlanta Weekly Chronicles* an ultimatum." Jade saw the questioning look in Hunter's eyes, but she answered it before he could voice it. "Either shut up or shut down. That's the challenge he has indirectly handed to you. I wouldn't want to have that on my conscience, Hunter. I wouldn't want the AWC to fold because you tried to help me chase a killer that no one believes exists. So, please don't feel badly about removing the letters from the paper."

Jade watched in astonishment as Hunter released his left hand from his cup and slowly reached across the table. She looked up at him, but his eyes were locked in his own open hand that reached for hers. He said nothing, but it was evident that he wanted her to place her hand in his. Jade swallowed and her breaths became shallow as she dropped her eyes to his hand and wondered why he waited so patiently for her to respond.

In slow motion, she released her cup as well, and then little by little, moved her right hand until it was resting inside his left. His hand was warm and as his fingers closed around her hand, Jade had the sudden urge to pull away, but she didn't.

Although his grip wasn't tight, she could feel Hunter's strength and she struggled to remain composed. Not knowing what to expect, she examined him as he gently brought their locked hands to his face and rested his forehead against them. For several moments Hunter sat in complete silence and Jade was left to her own theory and reasoning. At first, she thought he was going to cry, but there were no sounds or tears. Hunter just sat and as he did, Jade could almost visibly see his perplexity multiplying right before her eyes.

"Hunter?" she whispered. His elongated silence was beginning to concern her. She wasn't afraid for her safety nor did she fear him personally in any manner. Her growing anxiety was in not knowing the reason for his mental torment.

"I couldn't do it." His voice was at a low level, but Jade heard him.

"You couldn't do what?"

Hunter never looked at her. Instead, he withdrew her hand from his face and then cupped it between both his hands. Jade was almost certain that awakening her senses was the furthest thing from his mind, but as he rubbed his hands across hers, Jade could feel every hair on her arm come to full attention. More than ever, she needed to pull away. But more than ever, she didn't want to.

"I couldn't remove the letters."

"What?" To both Jade's relief and disappointment, Hunter released her hand and then turned to pick up the newspaper that rested directly to his left on the bed beside his chair. He held it in his hand for a moment and then placed it on the table in front of Jade.

Staring at the front page of today's paper, Jade found herself almost afraid to open it. She'd thought it was a done deal. When she left Hunter's home on yesterday, there were no uncertainties that he would put the feature to rest for good. Her hands trembled as she fingered the corners of the pages and flipped through, one section at a time, coming to a stop at Section C. Jade looked up at Hunter for an explanation.

"Section D, second page," he said.

Turning to the last section of the paper, Jade gasped softly at the sight of the picture of her father that occupied the upper left corner. Beneath the full-color image was a letter that Hunter had written. Jade's eyes scanned every word. In the first paragraph, he apologized to those who had been offended by the continuance of the tributes. In it, he explained that contrary to popular belief, he was doing none of it out of selfishness, but rather from an unexplainable drive to keep the pastor's life and untimely death fresh in the minds of those who were already forgetting. Hunter apologized to Mildred and all of the Tides children for any anguish that his decision had caused them and extended the invitation for any immediate member of Reverend Tides' family to make an appointment to stop by his office to speak with him personally. All of his words were heartfelt, but it was the final two paragraphs that caused tears to spill from Jade's eyes.

As a child, my family, like every family that lived in Perry Homes, was poor. Sometimes the Greene family went for weeks with no extra money and as a result, we never knew what it was like to have new toys or clothes. The residents of Perry Homes were always shunned, ridiculed and teased about one thing or another, so to cover our hurt, we sometimes, in our ignorance, did the same to each other.

As a young boy, I used to laugh at Reverend B.T. Tides because every Friday he would gather his family together and pray so loudly that his neighbors could hear him in the hallways. Then one night, as I stood at the front door of his unit listening and laughing, I heard him pray for my family. To my knowledge, no one had ever cared enough about my family to pray for us, but Reverend Tides did. He remembered me, my mom and my brothers when our own family members had pushed us to the side. So, today, I remember him. If that makes my readers hate me and cause the closing of my business, then it's a small price to pay for the honor of a man that God used to change an entire community and build one of our area's largest, and most respected churches. I didn't know Reverend Tides very well, and that is a regret that I suppose I'll carry forever. But for what he did for my family, I loved him. And that's something I'll carry forever as well.

By the time Jade reached the last line, she could barely read it through her distorted vision and was nearly choking in an attempt to get her tears under control. She didn't see Hunter rise from his chair, but she felt him as he pulled her from hers and then wrapped his arms around her to provide comfort. She rested her cheek on his chest and wept for several minutes, and not once did he disturb her.

Even after Jade's tears had subsided, she remained there. Hunter's grip around her body loosened, as though giving her the opportunity to pull away if she desired. She didn't, and neither did he.

Taking in a deep breath, Jade inhaled the smell of Hunter's skin. The scent was ordinary, but appealing, like that of a man who had recently showered, but had not put on any fragrant lotions or creams that hid his natural, masculine aroma. It entrapped her and for a split second, served as a source of rapture, taking her to a place she'd never been.

"Jade?"

At first, she thought it was a part of her trance, but it didn't take long for Jade to realize that Hunter was actually calling her name. He had released her, and now it was only Jade's arms that were holding her to him. Jade was left to wonder just how long she'd been adhered to him without his assistance and how many times he'd called her name before she'd heard him.

"I'm sorry," she whispered in embarrassment as she loosed him. Jade didn't know what else to say in her defense, so Hunter's voice was a welcomed one.

"Don't be. It's been that kind of a day, I suppose."

"I suppose," Jade agreed, still fighting to clear her head of its prior thoughts and her nostrils of the manly scent that still lingered. "Is that the reason that you wanted to talk to me tonight? You wanted to tell me about the letters in the paper?"

"Not exactly." Hunter fished his pants pocket as he spoke. "Are you okay about the letters, though? I mean, your tears . . . you weren't upset, were you?"

Looking at the unnecessary concern in his eyes, Jade smiled. "Of course not. I don't want you to lose the paper though, Hunter. I just don't know what I'd do if . . ."

"I won't lose the paper. I admit that doing so was one of, if not my biggest fear just a few hours ago. But after the meeting you and I had, God reminded me that He gave me this paper, and unless He decides that it has run its course, the *Atlanta Weekly Chronicles* will survive all of this madness. God knows my heart and our reason for printing the letters. He's not going to punish me because of the misguided opinions of others."

Jade noticed the folded note that Hunter pulled from his pocket as he spoke and she wondered what it was, but didn't ask. "That's a nice childhood memory that you have of my father," she said. "We were such the churchy family, right down to our names. My parents gave each of us biblical middle names."

"Oh, yeah?"

"Jackson Andrew, Jerome Abraham, and Jade Abigail," she said with a laugh while she wiped residual tears.

"What does B.T. stand for?" Hunter asked the question he'd pondered several times over the years. The question that even Kwame didn't know the answer to.

"Booker Taliaferro," Jade said, laughing. "Just like Booker T. Washington's first and middle names. Daddy told us that as soon as he came of age, he insisted that his family and friends use his initials instead."

"Why?" Hunter probed.

"Because they never said his name right," she said, laughing a little harder now. "Everybody in the family, including my grandparents, would always call him Booger Teef and Daddy couldn't stand it."

Hunter laughed with her, but for both of them, the laughter was short-lived. Reality set in quickly and Jade took the conversation back to the newspaper and Hunter's printed letter.

"This really is nice," she said, looking at the paper once more. "I remember the days of us having family prayer in the living room of our apartment; but I never knew that any of the neighborhood kids made fun of it."

"There were a group of us," Hunter admitted. "I don't think any of us told anyone. We just laughed among ourselves. We all feared Jackson so we definitely weren't going to pick on him and Jerome would sometimes come out and shoot hoops with us, so we didn't mess with him either. We were such stupid kids."

"But look at you now," Jade said as she reached out and touched Hunter's bare arm. "It's who you are today that counts, right?"

Hunter's smile sent a clear message that her words had been received as a compliment. "Yeah. I found out that many of my boyhood friends didn't fare so well. Even my brothers chose the road that headed for trouble. I'm one of the fortunate ones."

"I suppose the same can be said for me," Jade shrugged. "But God has a way of replacing old friends with new ones. I only have one girl in Virginia that I label a true friend. Ingrid can be a bit rigid sometimes and we definitely don't always agree, but I know that when it comes right down to it, I can always count on her."

Jade watched as Hunter's countenance turned sad. He turned away from her and walked to the hotel window, sliding back the curtain and looking out. It was now nearing five o'clock in the morning, but darkness on the outside was still thick. With the lamp on the inside still on, Jade wondered if people on the outside were looking in, but her concern diminished when Hunter's silence remained. She approached him with caution, taking a place beside him by the exposed window.

"Did I say something wrong?"

At first, he said nothing. Then Jade noticed the slow shaking of his head.

"No." His reply was only slightly more audible than a murmur.

Just as she was about to ask another question that would dig deeper into his sudden mood change, Hunter handed her the folded paper in his hand. While she opened it and read both sides, he never moved or spoke. Jade fully understood the email, but the handwritten letter left questions.

"Who wrote this?" she asked.

"I sent the email to Kwame early last evening. He's the editorial director of the AWC, but he's also been my best friend for several years. The note on the back was written by Diane Vickers, my company's managing editor. While we aren't exactly friends, I've always considered her a loyal employee."

The root of Hunter's demeanor slowly began to sink in as Jade mentally put the pieces of the puzzle together.

"It seems that while I was away from the office yesterday, they were trying to create a way to keep the letters from being printed as I instructed. Like you said about your girlfriend, I thought I could always count on Kwame, too. He's always had my back in the past, but I think the heat of all of this got to him this time. He's a member of your dad's church, so this hit close to home for him. I knew he didn't agree with my decision and I respected that. But trying to double-cross me is another issue. I can't respect a man who will try and undermine my authority. If I can't trust him . . ."

"But he didn't stop the letters," Jade pointed out. "You weren't in the office and like this note says, he could have refused to pass along your message. The letters are there, so he didn't go through with it. I mean, I agree that he never should have even given it a second thought, but he's human, Hunter. Perhaps what the lady suggested to him sounded tempting for a minute, but at the end of the day, he did as you asked. Isn't that what really matters?"

"I could be wrong, Jade, but I don't think he passed the information on. After I didn't hear back from him and it was nearing closing time, I called my secretary and had her to pass the information on to the print department to run the layout that included the letters. I think that Kwame was purposely avoiding me. I called both his cell and the office and never could get an answer at either one. That letter proves that at some point, he returned to work and he and Diane mulled over some possible ways to get around executing my decision. Of all the people to abandon ship, I never would have figured Kwame to be in the number."

As Hunter stared out the window at nothing, Jade searched every distinct detail of his side profile. He had such strong, handsome features, but at the moment, every one of them seemed spiked with disenchantment.

"I'm sorry, Hunter," Jade whispered. "I can't help but feel at least partially responsible for all that's going on." She held up her hand to stop him from interrupting and then continued. "I know you were the one who made the decision to stick with the letters, but it was my letter to you in the beginning of all of this that got the ball rolling. I wish I could make this feeling about Daddy's death go away, but I can't. If I could take it all back, I would. It was never my intention to bring you down like this. Now it's affecting your job and your friends and now I just wish I'd never said anything at all."

Hunter suddenly turned from the window and firmly cupped Jade's chin between his index finger and thumb, forcing her to look directly into his eyes. "Don't ever say that again. Don't you see? The reason you can't make it go away is because it's not meant to. This isn't just some whim that we're dealing with. We're not chasing false leads, and if nobody else knows that, we do. This whole thing with your dad's death has turned into a mission, and like it or not, it looks like it's going to be up to you and me to solve the mystery that lies beneath it all. But if we're going to do it, we have to stop wavering. That's the conclusion I came to last evening after I stopped being selfish and sought God for *His* direction. The reason I've been apprehensive and indecisive all this time is because I've been thinking about how it all affects me and my life. But this ain't about me, Jade, and it's not about you either. We're just vessels that God wants to use to do something that everybody else thinks is ludicrous.

"All my life I've thrived on the doubts of people. When somebody tells me that I can't do a thing, it just gives me more determination to succeed. That's how I became the first male in any generation of my family as far back as I've researched who stayed out of jail. When people said all of Patricia Greene's boys would end up in jail, they were almost right. But I was the one who made them liars. I took their expectation on as a personal challenge. When they laughed at me for quitting college and said they knew I didn't have what it took to be successful, I started the *Atlanta Weekly Chronicles.* When they said a man who had no active father didn't have the wherewithal to be a good father, I shut them up when I made the decision to raise that boy right there," Hunter said as he loosed her chin and pointed toward his sleeping son.

"I learned a long time ago that as long as I had God on my side and I was doing what I believed to be right, He'd give me at least one person to believe in me and with me. Now, if push comes to shove, I can do this without the support of Kwame, Diane or any of the people who have stood outside my building misjudging, protesting and ridiculing; but I can't do it without you. You're the only person I need, Jade. Do you understand me? If others come on board, that's fine and good. But I *need* you, Jade. No doubting, no regrets and no turning back. Now, are you with me or not?"

Jade looked up at Hunter, and for the first time, she felt the depth of his dedication and loyalty to a cause that at one time felt like hers alone. His eyes clung to hers and analyzed her reaction. They were intense, fearless and embodied those of a man ready for combat. The darkness of his eyes was so powerful that it weakened her knees and drove her heart to beat at a volume so high that she could barely hear her own response.

"I'm with you."

Chapter 18

It was nearly seven o'clock in the morning by the time Hunter was able to fall asleep again. It had been just after six when he finally gathered his son and left Jade's hotel room. After the two of them renewed their vow to keep fighting for the truth behind the fire that reduced Reverend B.T. Tides to an unrecognizable mass of charred bones and ashes, Hunter and Jade shared her soda and the bag of chips she'd offered earlier. Sleep had begun creeping in on him while they sat at the table watching a late night rerun of *Law & Order*, and Hunter was half-tempted to ask her if he could make a pallet on her floor. It wasn't a good idea and he knew it. The hotel was only a thirty-minute drive from his house. When his eyelids began to get heavy, he said goodbye and left for home.

Now, a knock on his bedroom door broke nearly five hours of undisturbed slumber. As Hunter dug himself from beneath the covers of his bed, he realized that he had slept the whole morning away.

"Daddy!" It was Malik's raised voice coming from the other side of the door.

"Yeah," Hunter called. "Come on in."

The bedroom door was flung open and Malik stood in the doorway dressed in blue jeans and a crewneck shirt and looking frustrated. "Aw, Daddy," he moaned. "You still sleep? We were supposed to ride the horses today, remember?"

"We were?"

"You said that the first Saturday that it didn't rain, we would go riding and I could invite some of my friends."

Hunter couldn't stand it when Malik whined, but this time, he figured that his son had a good reason. Now that Malik had explained himself, Hunter recalled making the promise and he always tried to keep his word, especially where his son was concerned. With the problems that he knew Malik had encountered since the letters started, Hunter did his best to make the rest of the child's life as drama-free as possible.

"There's still plenty of time," Hunter said as he pulled himself to a seated position. "Why don't you call the Lowman boys and tell them they can come over. Give me a few minutes to get dressed and I'll be ready."

Malik's face lit up at the announcement. "Okay. I'm wearing my brown boots. You gonna wear yours too?"

"Yeah, I'll wear my brown boots too." Hunter laughed as his bedroom door slammed behind

Malik's animated exit. He could hear Malik's quick-paced footsteps climbing the stairs in excitement. Hunter's body told him that he could use another two hours of sleep, but duty called.

The water that he splashed on his face after brushing his teeth gave Hunter's tired body a boost and it wasn't long before he could hear the pounding of Malik's feet making a hurried descent from his upstairs bedroom.

While in college a few years back, Hunter recalled one of his professors saying that every man knew his purpose in life when he found a job that he'd be willing to do whether he got paid for it or not. If those words were true, Hunter determined that he'd found his calling in fatherhood. Malik was the one detail of his life that he'd not trade for anything in the world. Hunter loved his job as founder and Editor in Chief of the *Atlanta Weekly Chronicles*, but he could think of a few things he'd trade it for. If some wealthy tycoon walked into his office and offered him the right dollar amount, Hunter had to admit that he'd most likely sell the paper he'd started and worked hard to build into a successful business. But no amount of money matched the worth of his son.

"Daddy!" Malik yelled.

"I'm in the bathroom. Come on in."

Malik walked in with the cordless phone pressed into the front of his shirt to block his voice from the person on the other end.

"What's up?" Hunter whispered.

"Can Kyla come over too?" the boy asked with a pleading look on his face.

The name was a foreign one to Hunter. "Kyla who?"

"Please, Daddy?" Malik begged, not answering his father's question.

His son's eagerness to have this girl come and spend the afternoon riding in their pasture caused Hunter to momentarily lose interest in shaving. Turning off his clippers, he gave Malik his full attention.

"Who is Kyla?" Hunter insisted on an answer.

Malik's feet shifted and his eyes turned to the floor. "She's just this girl. She's new at our school. Her mom and her just moved here and they're staying with her grandma out in Shelton Heights where Willie and Jeremy live. Mrs. Lowman said she can bring her over when she brings Willie and Jeremy. Kyla stays right next door, and she was with Jeremy 'nem when I called and she said she wants to come over. She don't have many friends at school yet, so I thought we might could invite her over here."

Hunter struggled to remain composed while his son talked. Malik never took his eyes off of the floor and it was easy to see that his request for the girl to join them was more than just the gesture of goodwill that he pitched it to be. Hunter didn't know if his reply was to satisfy Malik or himself. He couldn't deny that he was curious as to who this little girl was who had captured his son's affections.

"Yeah, she can come," Hunter said, quickly restarting his clippers and bringing them to his jaw to hide the smile that he could no longer hold back.

As if he were afraid that his father would change

his mind, Malik darted from the bathroom while he relayed the message to whomever was on the other end of the line. Seeing his son's reaction reminded Hunter of his own first crush. He was a bit older than Malik at the time, but he remembered being a seventh grader and totally smitten with a ninth grader named Sarah Gibson. Every now and then, Sarah still crossed Hunter's mind. Back then, she snubbed his every show of affection. He wrote her letters like any lovesick boy would do, but Sarah laughed at them, and once even crumpled one into a ball and dropped it at his feet. She was ruthless and snobbish, but Hunter adored her just the same.

For three years, Hunter hoped she'd see beyond his age and notice that he would one day grow to be mature beyond his years. She never did though, and once Sarah graduated high school, he never saw or heard from her again. That is, until four years ago when she walked through the doors of the *Atlanta Weekly Chronicles* looking for the same man she'd dismissed as a teenager.

When Lorna came to him and told him that a Ms. Sarah Gibson-Shivers was out front to see him, Hunter's heart stopped for several moments and then began beating double-time to try and catch up with the pumps of blood that it missed sending during its brief paralysis. The hyphenated last name brought him back to his senses. Clearly, Sarah was married now. As smart and as beautiful as she was, that was no surprise to him. By the time Lorna had gone to get the visitor and had walked her to Hunter's office, he'd gathered himself and showed no signs of elation when Sarah made her appearance, standing beside Lorna whose eyes gave the visitor a quick warning before she disappeared to return to her own duties.

"Hunter Greene." Sarah said his name as though until seeing him, she was never really sure he was the same person she'd gone to school with.

There was a slight trembling in his legs, but Hunter managed to stand to his feet and walk around his desk so that he faced her. "Sarah Gibson," he responded with an outstretched hand.

"You remember." She beamed as she stepped forward and placed her hand in his.

"How could I forget?"

It was a surreal moment for Hunter, but one that he thought was going to be the start of something wonderful. Sarah wasted no time making her divorced status known, and just a few hours later, Hunter found himself sitting across the table from her as they shared a meal at Red Lobster. She'd told him that it was her favorite eatery.

For five months, they spent time together whenever they could. Sarah lived in New Jersey and they made the long distance relationship work well for a while. Mounting concerns began gnawing at Hunter's consciousness, though. Hunter's mother loved Sarah, as he knew she would. Malik, however, never seemed to warm up to the lady who spent several days and nights at their home, and Sarah didn't seem to be in any hurry to embrace him either. And as the weeks and months passed, Hunter began feeling that his attraction to Sarah was far shallower than he'd first thought it to be. The relationship that they shared felt exploitive, not just on his part, but hers as well.

It became clear to Hunter that he'd allowed a childhood crush to take him over. Sarah was still beautiful, but she was also still condescending towards those who were less fortunate. She'd married rich the first time and now that her divorce was final, Hunter had the feeling that she had no plans of lowering her standard of living. Had he not grown to be a successful business man, Hunter had no doubt that Sarah would still see him as the unworthy kid she viewed him as in high school.

For him, being with Sarah in every way had been his fantasy for years. As the months passed and the thrill of it all faded, he was able to think more clearly. When the fog in his mind cleared, Hunter realized that to him, Sarah was no more than a trophy and to her, he was no more than an insurance policy. He didn't love her, nor did she love him. When their relationship ended, the only heart that was broken was his mother's. Patricia wanted so badly for her sons to marry women who were wealthy. With her other boys in and out of trouble, Hunter was her best hope; but he refused to make the same mistake that his mother made. Hunter refused to allow himself to be used for the sake of security and he'd dare not become another Dwight Rollins: a man who used women for his selfish gratification.

"Daddy, you ready?"

Hunter nearly dropped his electric razor when Malik's voice jolted him from his reverie. He'd been so deep in thought that he hadn't shaved any more of his face than was done the last time his son walked in.

"Not quite, sport." Hunter immediately placed the rotating blades against his skin as he spoke. "I will be by the time the kids get here, though. Why don't you go on outside and wait for them; how 'bout that?"

"A'iight."

Shelton Heights was only a few short miles from Hunter's estate. If the Lowman boys and Kyla were already dressed when Malik called, they would be pulling up to his security gate at any moment. Hunter was glad to know that all of his son's friends hadn't shunned him. Reverend Tides was a resident of Shelton Heights and his wife still lived there. It would have been almost understandable if Willie and Jeremy's family had decided that it was best that their boys didn't associate with the son of Hunter Greene.

"They're here, Daddy!"

Hunter heard Malik's call over the sound of the running water. He dried his face and splashed on his favorite aftershave before walking from his bathroom into his bedroom.

"I'm coming, Malik. Let them in the gate!" Hunter shouted back.

It only took a few minutes for Hunter to change into his riding gear and meet the children outside. Willie and Jeremy were eight and ten, respectively. But as soon as he saw Kyla, he knew she was a bit older. It wasn't until Mrs. Lowman had said her goodbyes and had disappeared through the open gate that Hunter turned to address the pretty girl who stood at least three inches taller than his smitten son.

"Hi, there. I'm Hunter Greene, Malik's father."

She accepted his outstretched hand and displayed a grin that made Hunter understand why his son had been impressed. "Hi, Mr. Greene; I'm Kyla Jericho."

As they all made their way to the pasture, Hunter continued his talk with the girl. He glanced at Malik who gave him a look of disapproval. It was a silent message that he wasn't particularly fond of the way Hunter was monopolizing Kyla's attention. Malik's unspoken disapproval didn't faze his father.

"How old are you, Kyla?" Hunter asked.

"Eleven," she answered. "But I'll be twelve soon."

"I see," Hunter responded. "You just moved to Atlanta?"

Kyla hesitated before she answered, like she was making sure she chose her words with caution. "Yes, sir. Me and my mom moved here from California in June. We live with my grandmother."

"California?" Hunter was surprised. He would not have guessed that she was from the west coast. "I guess moving here from there was a shock for you, huh?"

"Not really," she said, sounding more mature than her age. "I've lived in several states. My dad is a Marine and we've had to move in different places since I was a kid. So I've learned to adjust."

Hunter smiled but then took a moment to think as he opened the gate that would lead them all inside the pasture where his trained horses grazed. By now, Malik was enjoying the company of Willie and Jeremy and didn't seem too bothered that his father was still the one getting all of Kyla's attention.

"Your dad is in the Marines? We don't have any Marine bases here. Is he retiring?"

Kyla quietly shook her head and watched as the boys ran ahead and began admiring the horses. Her eyes were downcast when she began talking again. "He's still there. Daddy is stationed in 29 Palms, California at the Marine Corps Air Ground Combat Center. They . . . him and Mama, had a fight and we moved here to stay with my grandma."

From her demeanor, Hunter could easily tell that this subject was a sore one for the girl. Her true age showed in her sad countenance. His first instinct was to switch gears and take the conversation on another route, but Kyla began talking again before he could think of another subject matter.

"They've been married a long time—since before I was born. They started dating in high school. I don't know what the fight was about, but it went on for days before we moved here."

"Well, it doesn't matter what the fight was about, Kyla," Hunter said. "I hope you know it had nothing to do with you. Your daddy still loves you, I'm sure."

The girl looked up at him and smiled for the first time since she began talking about her parents' split. "I know. He tells me that all the time. He says he loves me and he loves Mama too. Daddy said he's coming to see me first thing when his assignment is over."

Hunter returned her smile and the girl continued. "He's gotta go to Iraq. He leaves in a few weeks and he has to stay for about a year. When he gets back, Daddy says he's gonna make things right."

"Good daddies always do," Hunter said. "Have you made any new friends?"

"Not too many," she shrugged. "The girls at my school have a lot of attitude. So I have friends, but most of them are boys. There's Malik, Jeremy, Willie and K.P."

"K.P.?" That name sounded new to Hunter. He'd not heard his son speak of him.

Kyla nodded as she clarified. "He lives across the street from us. He just moved there with his grandma just like us. But I don't think he likes the neighborhood too good. He's always sad. But he's nice to me though, so I call him my friend."

"I do that with people who are nice to me too," Hunter said as he placed his hand on Kyla's back and led her in the direction of the horses.

While the children rubbed the soft coats of the stallions, mares and ponies, Hunter gathered the saddles. Riding horses was like second nature to Malik and he embraced that advantage by showing off his skills to the pretty girl who watched in awe. Willie and Jeremy were among the children who came by often to ride, so they were capable of holding their own. Kyla admitted that her only experience with riding horses came in yearly visits to various fairgrounds, so she took her time and let her horse walk while Malik and the others allowed theirs to trot and sometimes gallop.

Hunter, seeing that his son needed some pointers on matters of the heart, flagged Malik down as he headed for another lap.

"Hey, Daddy," he said as he brought his favorite horse to a stop. "What's the matter?"

"You're being a little rude, sport," Hunter said. "You have three guests here and you act like you only have two. Kyla's not as good on a horse as you are."

Malik grinned. "I know. Did you see how she looked at me when I started riding so fast?"

"Yeah. And I also saw how lonely she looked when you kept riding with the boys and left her behind. You like this girl, right?"

Malik shrugged as though he wasn't sure what he felt. Hunter knew better and in his mind, today was the perfect time to teach his ten-year-old a life lesson.

"Listen, son. If you really want to impress her, stop showing off your skills and start showing her how to ride. You have to treat a lady like a lady; not like she's one of the dudes. Give her some attention. Why don't you go over there and let your horse walk beside hers? That way, you can talk to her and give her some pointers on how to ride like you do. I'm sure she'd appreciate you for thinking enough of her to do that."

"She would?"

"Yes," Hunter assured him. "When you like a girl, you have to take time to show her that you care. And you'll know if she likes you back because she'll smile a lot and she'll let you show her the ropes. So, why don't you help teach Kyla how to ride before one of your friends does and then she's going to be impressed by them and not you."

Malik followed the direction of his father's eyes and saw Jeremy steering his horse in Kyla's direction. "I gotta go," he said, just before flapping the reins of his horse and kicking into high gear.

Hunter laughed out loud as Malik sped past his best friend and made it to Kyla just in time. He was still laughing when he answered his cell phone without looking at the display screen to see who it was that was calling him on a Saturday afternoon.

"Well, you sound a lot more cheerful than you did last time we spoke."

Hunter stopped laughing, but the sound of Jade's voice made his smile linger. She'd told him last night of how busy her schedule would be today. Hunter hadn't expected to hear from her, but he welcomed it.

"Hey," he replied. "I just had an amusing moment with Malik. Did you finally get some sleep?"

"I did. You?"

"Yeah. Not enough, though. Malik woke me up and reminded me that I promised to let him and a few of his friends ride the horses today."

"Oh. Well, I won't break into your time with him and his friends. I just had some unexpected available time on my hands."

"Oh?" Hunter wondered just how much free time she had.

"Yeah. I thought I'd be in the salon all afternoon, but one of the maids here at the hotel told me about her daughter who does hair right in her living room. I have a beautician here in Atlanta who I go to every time I get a chance, but the wait is almost painful. I thought I'd check this girl out and her mother was right. She did a good job and I was in and out inside of two hours."

"Two hours?" Hunter said with a laugh. "That's fast?"

"Spoken like a clueless man," Jade said with a laugh of her own. "I'll let you go."

"Wait. What time does your flight leave this evening?"

"I rescheduled it," Jade said to his surprise. "I decided that I wanted to go to New Hope tomorrow. I think there may be a few things that I want to say to Reverend Knight and to the congregation."

"Jade . . ."

"I have to, Hunter. I have to do this for my own peace of mind."

The beeping in Hunter's ear told him that another caller was trying to get through. He took the phone away from his ear long enough to view the display screen. It was Kwame, and right now he was quite possibly the last person that Hunter wanted to talk to. Ignoring the call, he placed the phone back to his ear. Jade had mistaken his elongated silence as an unspoken signal.

"I know you have to go, so I'll leave you to your outing. Tell Malik I said hello."

"Why don't you tell him yourself?" Hunter suggested. "Since you have all of this free time, why don't you come out and ride with us?"

Jade's chuckle sounded nervous. "I don't know. I mean, believe it or not, I've never been on a horse in my entire life. I wouldn't know what to do."

Looking across the pasture, Hunter's eyes locked into Malik as the boy steered his horse beside Kyla's and talked to her, demonstrating how petting the horse kept him calm. Kyla smiled and nodded as she followed his lead, rubbing her hand across the horse's mane.

"Hunter?" Jade said, sounding unsure as to whether he was still on the line.

"I'll teach you," he replied.

Chapter 19

Jade heard the ringing of her cell phone, but she pulled the covers over her head, hoping that it was a part of a dream that she tried desperately to hold on to. Realizing that it wasn't, she reached for the stand beside the bed and flipped open the phone before placing it to her ear.

"Hello." She didn't even try to clear her voice before answering.

"Girl, you still sleep?" Ingrid's voice said. "What are you? Jet-lagged? Too bad, boo. It's time to give Jesus His time. I've been standing here ringing your doorbell forever. When you didn't answer your phone, I thought I was going to have to call the police. I'm glad I called your cell before I did. You 'bout to make me look like a fool, having the cops come out here when you're in there snoring. I knew I should have kept that house key. Come open this door, girl."

With the phone in hand, and still somewhat disoriented, Jade kicked her covers back and climbed out of bed. She groaned through a stretch and then walked slowly to the door. Opening it, she saw no one; just the brightness that waited on the other side.

"Where are you?" Jade asked.

"I'm at your front door, crazy girl. Come on, now. You're gonna make us late for church."

Only then did reality sink in for Jade. She closed her hotel room door and rested her back against it as she spoke. "I'm sorry, Ingrid. I should have called you. I changed my flight. I don't get home until late tonight. My flight leaves at ten."

A profane word slipped from Ingrid's lips and Jade could envision the look of disgust that accompanied it.

"See what you made me do? I was doing good. The cussing demon hadn't spoken through me in a long time—at least two weeks. Now, I got to go to church for real and ask forgiveness."

Jade shook her head. It would have been funny if it weren't so true. Ingrid had come a long way from where she was when they first met, but cursing, for her, was like an addiction, and two weeks really was a long time for her to have "been clean." Jade was working on her, though. Ingrid was having a hard time breaking a habit that had been passed down for three generations. She had told Jade that in her childhood household, using swear words was just as normal as speaking standard English. Jade knew that it was only a matter of time. She had no doubt that God had something great for Ingrid to do and the change that Jade had seen in her best friend over recent years reassured her that Ingrid was going through a transformation that would just take a little more time.

"I'm sorry." Jade repeated her earlier apology. "I just decided that I needed to talk to some of the church people and the best time to do that was after Sunday morning worship."

"Well, what are you waiting for? It's eleven o'clock. What time does church start?"

"Oh my God! I overslept! I didn't know that it was this late. I have to go, Ingrid. I need to be checked out of here by noon and I still have to shower and pack my stuff and. . . ."

"Well, don't be talking all fast like it's my fault," Ingrid said in a tone two octaves higher than her normal. "You're the one who overslept and not only made yourself late, but me too. If I had known you weren't even home, I could have saved the drive over here and gotten to church in time enough to get a good seat *on my own.* Now, because of you, I'm gonna have to endure Sister Gordon making an embarrassment out of both herself and me. For the life of me, I don't know why Pastor Rhodes still has psycho usher on staff."

Jade chuckled at the thought of it. In her mind, she could see Emma Gordon irritating people by insisting that they tighten up on a row near the front of the church to make room for Ingrid instead of her just seating the latecomer in the rear to avoid distracting the services. It was a regular practice of the middle-aged attendant that no one understood. Sister Gordon, although a nice woman, had been dubbed "psycho usher" by Ingrid ever since she began attending church with Jade.

"I'm sorry, Ingrid. I didn't mean to put you in

the position to have to deal with Sister Gordon, but I really did mean to call you. I was just up so late last night with Hunter and when I finally fell asleep, I was out like a light."

"You were up late with Hunter?" It seemed to be the only part of Jade's response that sank into Ingrid's mind.

Jade sighed. She could hear the real questions behind the posed one, and getting into it with Ingrid right now would make both of them even later for Sunday morning service than they were already. "Go to church, Ingrid. I'll talk to you tomorrow over lunch."

It was just after noon when the cab driver delivered Jade to the church. The usher at the back door broke into a wide grin when she saw Jade walk in the sanctuary. The woman, whose black and white uniform looked as if it had more starch in it than needed, helped relieve Jade of her shoulder bag and dutifully pushed it under the back row pew.

"I'll just take one of the rear seats," Jade whispered in her ear.

"Nonsense," the usher insisted. "You're a part of our first family. I'll take you to the front to sit with your mother."

"No," Jade responded quickly while touching the usher's arm. "I *want* to sit near the back. Somewhere in this area is fine."

Remembering the exchange that she'd had with her family on Friday, Jade wasn't at all sure of what her mother's response would be at seeing her today. She hadn't even told her that she'd changed her flight. Mildred thought her daughter had left on

Saturday as planned. Jade felt that it was in the best interest of all parties involved that she didn't allow herself to be ushered to the front. Besides, her lower body was still sore from the horse-riding yesterday. The quicker she sat down, the better.

The usher's response was somewhat delayed and apprehensive, but she bestowed a compassionate smile upon Jade and nodded as if to say she understood. This was Jade's first visit to New Hope since Reverend B.T. Tides' casket lay at the altar nearly two months earlier. No doubt that was the reason for the usher's empathetic smile. Looking ahead and seeing the pulpit filled with ministers, but void of her father, gave Jade an uneasy feeling. It was fleeting and quickly overshadowed by the sudden urge to laugh. As the usher led Jade to the corner of a pew that was only one row from the back, a quick image of the scowl on Ingrid's face as Sister Gordon walked her all the way to the center aisle's third row at Gospel Tabernacle flashed through her mind. Jade welcomed the more tolerable thought.

Jade's arrival couldn't have been better—or worse, depending on what was about to happen next. The members of the praise team were relinquishing their positions on the platform, church members who had been standing in worship were now returning to their seats and Reverend Alfonzo Knight was taking his position at the podium, holding the newest copy of the *Atlanta Weekly Chronicles* in his hand. Feeling a lump rising in her throat, Jade swallowed hard and held her breath.

* * *

Only a few feet separated Hunter from Jade, but she hadn't noticed his presence. He and Malik had arrived before the services started and mingled in the thick crowd of people who entered early so that they wouldn't be noticed. Hunter took a seat on the back row, directed Malik to sit beside him and then buried his head in his open Bible, not really reading the words on the page facing him. It was just a tactic to discourage anyone from making small talk with him and seeing through his feeble disguise, which consisted only of a pair of fashion frames that gave him a slightly different appearance than normal.

Sleep deprived from the full day before, it didn't take long for Malik to drift off to sleep. Hunter had been scanning the thick crowds for any sign of Jade. Even with the thousands that poured into the church's edifice, entering the two passage-ways and filling the pews, Hunter was sure that he would spot Jade if she was among them. She stood out. If Jade was there, he knew he wouldn't miss her.

When he saw no sign of her, Hunter began wondering where she was or if Jade had perhaps changed her mind about walking into what could easily turn out to be a den of lions. When Hunter finally saw her enter, he smiled. He should have known that a woman as brave and as determined as she wouldn't let the threat of this crowd intimidate her. Jade was stronger than any woman he'd met in years. Not just mentally, but spiritually as well. Unlike most women he'd spent as much time with as he had with Jade, she had not made herself available to him. She carried herself with dignity and refinement, all the while never compromising her femininity. Even in those moments where she'd been angry or in the ones where she had been brought to tears, Hunter could still see her grace and her strength. He liked that.

Kwame, however, was a different story. Hunter had scanned the crowd for him as well. He wasn't surprised, though. He imagined the AWC's editorial director was somewhere hiding from what he figured would be a massive uprising from the members of New Hope. As infuriated as Hunter still was with Kwame for the part he played in the ploy to dismiss his orders, Hunter couldn't exactly blame his right hand man. Hunter too, expected the price of his decision to run the letters to be steep and the fallout to be enormous. The weekend sales had exceeded Hunter's expectations. His tactic to move the feature on Reverend Tides to a different section had worked; apparently, so had Hunter's editorial letter.

"Let's give God another hand clap of praise." Reverend Knight's voice drew Hunter's eyes from the woman sitting on the end of the row in front of him and to the man standing in the distance. Because Hunter was so far from the front, he, like most of those around him, looked to the monitor on the wall that displayed a clear view of the goings on in the pulpit.

The newly appointed pastor raised the newspaper in the air and spoke into the microphone simultaneously. "I can't say that I understand it or agree with it," he said, "but in my time with the Lord on last evening, He gave me peace. I wish that the paper and everybody affiliated with it would just let our late pastor rest in the arms of the Lord, but just because I don't like it, don't make it wrong."

A few responses of "Amen" ran through the building and the sound of agreeable hand claps resonated. Hunter took a quick look at Jade and could visibly see her body relax against the back of the pew. It was as if she'd just released a breath that she'd been holding in preparation. Reverend Knight's voice took Hunter's attention once more.

"Before I bring the sermon today, Brother Williams, who most of you know has a high ranking position at the paper, has a few words that he would like to say to the congregation. Please receive him with the love of God."

Hunter's eyes narrowed as Kwame took the stand, dressed smartly in a dark suit with a striped dress shirt that he wore without a neck tie and with the top button undone. Hunter had not seen Kwame enter and was fully prepared not to see him at all. Using his index finger to nudge his frames up on his face, Hunter gave Kwame his undivided attention.

"Good afternoon," Kwame said into the microphone that the pastor passed to him as he walked toward the speaker's stand.

The audience responded to his greeting, but their replies were overshadowed by a screeching reverberation that had many of the churchgoers, Hunter included, cringing in their seats. Awakened from his peaceful sleep, Malik jolted to an upright position and covered his ears. The noise was brief, but more than a little annoying. Kwame repositioned himself behind the podium and began talking again once the high-pitched noise subsided.

"I apologize," he started. "I guess that's why God never called me to be a preacher. I'd drive the congregation to drink."

Kwame's remark brought a chorus of laughter from the audience, but Hunter wasn't among them.

"I wanted to speak for a couple of reasons," he continued. "First, I want to thank Reverend Knight for calling me to meet with him this morning so that we could clear the air. On behalf of the *Atlanta Weekly Chronicles*, I would like to assure you all once again that no harm was intended in our decision to revisit the feature that we'd once removed from our periodical. We only did it because we felt that this was something that would be a great way to honor a man who deserves to be regarded at a standard as high as any preacher in this city and state."

Agreeable comments ran through the audience of listeners and Hunter found himself simmering with a fury that threatened to reach a boiling point. He couldn't understand why Kwame was using pronouns like "we" and "our." He had been dead set against the feature being restored. Hunter's eyes made a quick movement in Jade's direction. Her jaw had dropped and she stared ahead as though she couldn't believe her ears.

And rightfully so, Hunter thought. He could hardly believe what he was hearing either. Now that the flames had been quenched, Kwame was making a full about-face. But when the heat was on, his stance had been a far cry from supportive. Hunter looked down at the Bible that he had clasped between his hands. If he opened it to its last page, he'd see a copy of the handwritten letter that had been scribbled on the back of the email that proved his point. But seeing the letter that indicated Kwame's willingness to betray him wasn't high on Hunter's list right now.

"Our intentions were nothing less than honorable," Kwame added. "But as was stated in the editorial letter of this weekend's edition, we render heartfelt apologies to all of those who were given reasons to feel otherwise. Especially to you, Mrs. Tides."

Kwame said a few more words, but they were lost amid the thoughts in Hunter's mind. It wasn't long before applause rang out and Reverend Knight was reclaiming his spot at the podium. Hunter thumbed through the pages of his Bible, searching for a scripture that he'd not even heard the pastor direct them to. The woman beside him, figuring him to be a new convert or perhaps just a plain old sinner who didn't know any differently, volunteered to help him find the familiar passage.

"Thanks," Hunter mumbled.

"Hey, Ms. Jade!" Malik tried to whisper, but his sudden words were loud enough for those seated closest to them to hear.

Hunter tried to shush him, but it was too late. At least twelve or fourteen eyes turned in their direction, but all but two of them quickly returned to the Bibles in front of them. Jade continued to stare in their direction. She immediately realized that it was Malik who had called for her and she returned his smile and wave. But it took her a little longer to recognize the identity of the man beside him. For a while, Hunter's eyes remained glued to his open Bible, but feeling the burning sensation of Jade's stare, he finally looked up and then briefly removed his glasses to clear the question that remained in her mind.

At first, her facial expression was one of sheer surprise, but it didn't take long before what began as a pleasant smile spread into a full-fledged grin. Once Jade was sure of his identity, Hunter replaced his frames and turned his eyes back to his Bible. His mind, however, lingered on the enthusiasm that he saw in Jade's smile. She had spent several hours with him just yesterday, but her reaction after recognizing him clearly said that she was happy to see him again.

The last time Hunter attended a Sunday morning worship service at New Hope the weather outside was brisk. It was early in the year just as the winter was coming to an end. At least six months had passed since then. Although Reverend Knight spoke well, Hunter couldn't view him as a preacher of the same caliber as his predecessor. Reverend Tides' delivery was more impassioned and his knowledge of the scripture definitely exceeded that of Reverend Knight. Still, Hunter enjoyed the sermon and he stood with the rest of the congregation as the new pastor rendered a special prayer for those who had gathered around the altar and he then gave the official dismissal.

Hunter grabbed Malik's hand and they maneuvered through the crowd that gathered quickly near the exit doors. The foremost issue on most of their minds was to try and get to their cars and get out of the parking lot before the rush. Uppermost on Hunter's mind, however, was getting to Jade.

He saw her speaking to the usher at the back door and he made it to her just in time to reach beyond her and take her overnight bag from the usher just before Jade got her grasp on it.

"I'll take that," he said.

"Excuse me?" the usher demanded.

"It's okay." Jade chuckled at the usher's school teacher demeanor. Then she turned to Hunter and said, "Thank you."

In silence, the three of them made it through the exit doors and out onto the front lawn of the church. No words were spoken until they were in the parking lot and standing beside Hunter's Range Rover. He was the first to break the silence.

"So is that why you were late? You spoke to the pastor?"

"No," Jade answered in a matching whisper. "I never got the chance to speak with him. It was all you. The letter was what did it." She beamed as she spoke. "It was like a miracle. If we weren't out here on the church grounds, I'd hug you."

Hunter laughed as he used his index finger to push his glasses up. "What? God has something against hugging on His property?"

Jade laughed with him. "I guess not."

Their carefree giggles came to a screeching halt as they embraced. It was the second time in three days that Hunter had held her in his arms, but to him, this time felt different. Friday night, it was to soothe her, and he assumed her firm grasp around his waist that night in the hotel was because she needed comforting. Today there were no tears and no need for consolation; yet her hold was just as solid. Hunter could feel his heart pounding against the side of Jade's face as she rested her cheek against his chest. He could smell the fragrance of her freshly shampooed hair. Once again, like the day when they had the altercation, Jade had used a hot comb, or perhaps a blow-dryer, to straighten out her hair's natural waves. Several strands of it tickled Hunter's face as it blew in the gentle breeze.

"Daddy, there goes Uncle Kwame."

Hunter winced and he felt Jade quickly pull away from him. He could only guess that like him, she too had forgotten that Malik was standing with them.

"Get in the truck," Hunter ordered all of a sudden.

"Can I speak to Uncle Kwame first?" the boy asked, looking up at his father.

"Get in the truck," Hunter demanded again; this time through clenched teeth with a stern face.

Malik's eyes were filled with questions, but he knew better than to voice any of them. Following his father's instructions, the boy walked to the passenger side of the SUV and climbed in.

"Hunter . . ." Jade began.

"What are you doing with the rest of your day?" Hunter asked over the sounds of a distant roll of thunder.

"I'm gonna catch a ride with Jackson and Mother," she said, throwing a glance in Kwame's direction and then looking back at Hunter. "I'll probably stay for dinner and then catch a ride to the airport afterwards."

Opening the door to his vehicle, Hunter said, "Call me before you leave?"

"Yes, I will. Thanks for everything, Hunter."

Hunter tried to peel his eyes away from Jade, but they were momentarily imprisoned. His intent was to get in his truck and leave before Kwame had the chance to notice him, but Hunter's brief delay was just enough time to blow his cover.

"Hunter?" There was a hint of uncertainty in Kwame's voice the first time, but when he repeated his name the second time, all doubt had disappeared. "Hunter. What are you doing here, man?" he called from five parking spots away.

"Go." Hunter's lips barely moved as he gave Jade the one-word order.

"Hun—"

"Now, Jade." His voice was firm, but not threatening.

Taking her overnight bag from his extended hand, Jade turned and walked in the opposite direction, never facing Kwame or acknowledging him. Hunter wasn't sure whether Kwame realized who the woman was that he'd been chatting with, but at the moment, it was of no great concern to him.

"Hey, Hunter," Kwame said as he came to a stop in front of Hunter with an outstretched hand. "I didn't know you were here, man. I been trying to call you since yesterday morning. Where you been?"

When Hunter remained silent, Kwame's eyes became probing. He looked from his own open hand to the hand that Hunter made no effort to offer in return "What's up with you? You gonna leave me hangin'? You ain't got no love for a brotha today?"

Hunter reached in his Bible and retrieved the folded copy of the original email. "Nah, I ain't got no love for you, but I won't leave you hanging either. Here." He placed the paper in Kwame's hand with more force than necessary and added, "By the way, I'm sure glad that *we* were on the same page in *our* decision to run the letters in the paper."

With that, he climbed into the driver's side of his truck, closed the door and started his engine. Hunter avoided Malik's curious eyes and pulled out from the parking lot, joining the line of vehicles that waited their turn to exit onto the street ahead. In his side view mirror, he watched Kwame open the note, run his fingers through his locks and then fall against the car beside him, using it to support his weakened knees.

Chapter 20

"What do you mean *he knows*?"

Kwame closed his eyes as the words oozed from the telephone into his ear. He had been able to think of little else than his brief confrontation with Hunter. The words spoken had been few, but the look in his friend's eyes told him that there had been a full-blown war going on between them that Kwame had been totally unaware of.

"Just what I said, Diane. Hunter knows that we were talking about going against him on printing the letters."

"But *how*?" she pressed. "No one was in the office except you and me. That means one of us would have had to tell him and it sure wasn't me. Why would you tell him something like that, Kwame?"

Her assumption stirred anger inside of Kwame. "How stupid do you think I am, Diane?"

"Well, if you didn't tell him, how could he know?

Does he have the place bugged? If Lorna had been anywhere around, the culprit wouldn't even be in question, but she had long gone. This doesn't make sense, Kwame. How could he have heard our conversation?"

"He didn't hear it, Diane; he *read* it." Kwame's words were received with confused silence and after a heavy sigh, he continued. "It was the note that you wrote."

"What note?"

"The one you scribbled on the back of the email that I showed you. The one where you were telling me not to tell him that I'd gotten his telephone message. When we walked out of the office we must have left the email on my desk somewhere. That's all I can conclude. Somehow, he got his hands on the note and that tells him all he needs to know."

Diane grunted a single swear word and then Kwame heard her blow a vexed breath into the phone. "What did he say?" Diane's voice was filled with the same terror that Kwame felt when he initially became aware of why Hunter hadn't answered any of his telephone calls.

"He really didn't say much at all. He just shoved the paper in my hand and informed me in no uncertain terms that he was aware of what had gone down." Even now, as Kwame spoke of something that had transpired more than two hours ago, he could still vividly see the look on Hunter's face just before he climbed into his SUV and backed away. There was unmistakable anger on Hunter's face, but his eyes were glazed with hurt and betrayal.

Kwame was so deep in thought that he barely heard Diane's next question.

"So he gave it back to you?" Diane asked.

"What?"

"Hunter," Diane clarified. "Did he give you the paper? Do you still have it?"

"Yeah," Kwame nodded. "Got it right here in my hand."

"Destroy it."

"What?" This time Kwame heard Diane, but he couldn't believe her command.

"Destroy it, Kwame," she repeated. "Get rid of it and no one will be the wiser."

"What?"

"Use your brain, Kwame. You've got the paper in your hands. It's the only evidence that we had our little ill-advised exchange . . ."

"You sound stupid, Diane!" Kwame said in a raised voice. "You act like Hunter ain't already seen it. I can destroy it all day long, but he's still seen it."

"But it would then be his word against ours. We can convince him that he misread the note as long as he doesn't have it to refer back to. We could . . ."

"Diane, you're about as dumb as a piece of sheetrock! You sound like a two-bit wannabe crook that flunked out of Crime 101! I'm sick of listening to you! That's what got us into this!"

"Don't you dare try and blame me for this, Kwame!"

"Who wrote the note, Diane?"

A brief silence was all at once broken by more swearing. It had been some time since Kwame had heard Diane curse so much. She had always been the employee at the *Atlanta Weekly Chronicles* who swore more than any other, but in the office it was kept to a minimum and she rarely, if ever, cursed around Hunter. Diane was so busy trying to impress her boss and win him over that she made it a point to do what it took to make Hunter believe she was far more wholesome than she actually was.

"I only wrote what you were thinking, Kwame!" Diane barked after she'd taken a break from words that were less suitable. "Besides, it was in your office. How could you leave it without checking to be sure all of your junk is put away? Oh, but you're so meticulous," she said, her tone becoming condescending. "Always need things to be done by the book . . . always need everything to be in writing for your stupid little files. Well, of all emails, why wasn't it important to file away *that* one?"

"I don't need the third degree from you, Diane. I have bigger fish to fry. In fact, I can't think of anything that means less to me right now than what you think of me!"

"We could lose our jobs over this, Kwame. This is *not* about me. This is about . . ."

"Oh, shut up, Diane! Just shut. . . . up!" Kwame struggled not to reach back into his own past and pull out a few choice words he hadn't used in a while. "That's the same crappy line you used to get us in this mess. It's always about holding on to the job to you, isn't it? Well, maybe we ought to lose our jobs, Diane. Maybe that's just what should happen. If it does, we can't blame nobody but us!"

Kwame was almost sure that he heard sniffles on

the other end of the line, but he couldn't find any sympathy for himself, let alone Diane. He couldn't believe he'd allowed himself to doubt Hunter's decisions so much that he'd contemplated breaking the chain of command in the name of saving face with his church family and salvaging a job that he might have put in more jeopardy in the process.

"We're as good as fired, aren't we?" The harshness in Diane's voice had diminished and there was no doubt left in Kwame's mind that she was in tears. Knowing it softened Kwame too, but he couldn't offer her an honest answer to calm her fears. He didn't own the AWC and he didn't call the shots. Whether he or Diane still had a secure position there was out of his control.

Kwame had been Hunter's best friend for years. He knew him to be a good man. He knew Hunter to be a fair man. But he also knew him to be a businessman and Kwame knew that he'd not only breached Hunter's faith as a friend, but as a businessman too. Because of that, Kwame knew he'd entered a realm of double jeopardy and he had no idea what the outcome of his gamble would be. He wished he did, but he didn't.

"Daddy, how do you know when a girl likes you?"

Hunter had been sitting on the side of his bed, slipping his feet into his best pair of Johnston & Murphy black dress shoes when he took note of the voice coming from his open doorway. Looking up, Hunter's eyes did a quick scan of his son's choice of clothing before he answered, and even then, he was stalling.

"What do you mean by how do you know when a girl likes you?"

There really was only one meaning to what Malik had asked, but in truth, the question had caught Hunter unprepared. He'd known the day would come when he would have to talk to Malik about girls and all the things that surrounded the topic, but not this early in his son's life. Ten, in Hunter's opinion, was far too young to indulge in such adult matters.

"I mean, how do you know when a girl likes you?" Malik responded in a matter-of-fact tone, not bothering to rephrase the original question.

Patricia Greene had once told Hunter that she would know when he'd been struck by Cupid's arrow, because only something as strong as love would make him take a day off from work just to spend time with someone of the opposite sex. To date, he'd never missed a day of work solely for the sake of spending a day of relaxation with a woman, so she was probably right. Still, that was his mother's opinion. Hunter had never given any thought to how *he'd* know if a woman loved him, so Malik's question required some deliberation.

Glancing at the clock on the wall, Hunter realized that he had very little time to spend on stalling his answer. Jade had telephoned half an hour ago and invited Malik and him to dinner at her mother's home. She'd said that Mildred Tides wanted to meet him and speak to him personally. According to Jade, the coast was clear. Her family was no longer angry. That eased Hunter's initial hesitation, but now a new kind of anxiety was mounting.

"Come sit down, sport," he said.

Malik obeyed and the two of them sat in silence for several moments. Hunter turned to his son and looked him straight in the eyes.

"Is this about Kyla?"

Malik's only reply was a quiet nod of his head, prompting Hunter to take a deep breath and then release it before speaking again. "Son, you're ten. You have a long, long, *long* time to wait before you are even mature enough to date. Why are you getting so whipped this early? You got a lifetime for that stuff."

"It ain't like I'm in love with her or nothing." Malik curled his top lip and shrugged as he spoke. "I'm just saying I think I like her. A ten-year-old can like a girl, can't he? I mean, I don't want to date her, but I want to get her a gift for her birthday. But I don't want to do it if she don't like me too, 'cause then I'll look like a big dummy. How can I find out if she likes me? How did you know that Mama liked you?"

Hunter smiled. As much as he and Yvonne didn't see eye-to-eye and as poor of a parent as she'd been to their son, he was glad that Malik hadn't forgotten her. What pleased him even more was that Malik seemed to have no memory of the negative things surrounding his mother. The few times he mentioned her were always in a positive tone.

"Well, you can't really go by what happened with me and your mom because we were grownups, Malik. Grownups act differently than children."

"Okay, well what about somebody else, then?" Malik challenged. "I know you had to like somebody before you got all old and stuff. Didn't you ever have a girlfriend in school? How'd you know she liked you too? I just need to know if Kyla's feeling me."

Feeling me? Hunter wasn't unfamiliar with the slang phrase used to describe the attraction between two people, but it was the first time he'd heard Malik use it.

"First of all," Hunter said, "I am *not* all old and stuff. Secondly, to be honest with you, when I was your age, no, I didn't have a girlfriend."

"Oh."

Malik looked disappointed and Hunter knew that he couldn't let him leave that way. As young as he was, it was obvious that Malik was dealing with what, to him, was a serious matter and he needed his father to get over his own hesitations and talk to him. Hunter knew that if he didn't, Malik would likely get advice from one of his friends or someone else who might lead him wrong.

"You know she's older than you, don't you?" Hunter said, breaking the ice that had begun forming between them.

"I know."

"So what are you saying? You like older women?"

Malik grinned and shrugged. "I don't know. I just think Kyla's cool; and she's pretty too."

"Yeah, she is." Hunter had to agree.

"And she's on the honor roll."

"I'm not surprised. I figured she was smart."

"But Jeremy told me that he thinks K.P. likes her

too. And he keeps coming over Kyla's grandmother's house to see her."

It was the second time in as many days that Hunter had heard K.P.'s name referenced. "Who is K.P.? Is he new at your school?"

"He's not new at the school, but he never hung around us until Kyla started going there. He's not really our friend. He's *her* friend. Jeremy says K.P. lives across the street from Kyla and he always sees them talking outside."

"So you see K.P. as a threat?"

"Not if we had a fight." For special effect, Malik stuck his chest out as he spoke. "He's older than me, but I can beat him if we fought. K.P.'s a cry baby."

"That's not a nice thing to say," Hunter said, all the while trying not to laugh at the new posture that Malik still held. "We don't call names, remember? Name-calling is hurtful. You wouldn't want people calling you ugly names, would you?"

"Sorry," Malik mumbled as he slowly deflated his chest.

"Do people at school pick at him? Is that why he cries?"

"He don't cry because they pick at him; they pick at him 'cause he cries all the time."

"Why?"

"I don't know. I don't take no classes with him, but I know some kids who do and they say he'll just start crying for no reason."

"Maybe he just needs some friends," Hunter suggested.

"But Daddy, don't nobody want to be friends with nobody who cries all the time."

Hunter's first thought was to reprimand Malik for his comment, but he imagined that he'd feel the same way if he was his son's age. Boys were always expected to be tough. Even the girls expected them to be that way and shunned them if they weren't. It wasn't until a boy became a man that people of the opposite sex expected them to be sensitive. After sitting in momentary quiet thoughtfulness, Hunter decided to use this situation as an example of something deeper.

"Remember your Sunday School lesson just a couple of weeks ago? Didn't your teacher talk to your class about how important it was to be friendly to others? Didn't you all read about Jesus and how He made friends among sinners and other people that were shunned by the rest of society?"

"Yeah, Daddy, but them dudes were just gamblers and cheaters and stuff," Malik pointed out. "They weren't no cry babies. The teacher didn't say that Jesus had friends who were cry babies."

"Malik . . ." Hunter's tone was warning.

"Sorry."

"The next time you have friends over to ride the horses, why don't you invite K.P. too?"

"But Daddy, he likes Kyla."

"Let me tell you something, Malik. If you're scared to have another man around your lady, then you might need to move on anyway. If she likes you, then you don't have to worry about that."

"But that's just it," Malik said, looking at Hunter with pleading eyes. "I don't know if she likes me or not. That's what I'm trying to find out. If I knew she liked me, then I wouldn't worry about K.P. and he could come over here and ride all day long if he wanted to."

"Does Kyla like to be around you?" Hunter asked.

"Uh-huh."

"Does she smile more at you than she does the Lowman boys?"

"I think so and Jeremy says she does."

"What about at school when other boys who are her age and in her grade are around? When you come around, does she still acknowledge you?"

"Yes," Malik said with noticeable pride. "Friday, she let me hold her books while she tied her shoestrings too."

"Then I'd say you've got yourself a winner."

Hunter watched as a victorious smile broke through on Malik's face. The boy didn't speak, but his grin made his glee known. Looking at the clock on the wall again, Hunter slipped his other foot into its shoe and stood. "You ready to go?"

"Been ready," Malik responded as he ran for the door that led to the garage, leaving his father to lock up the house.

Touching his wrist to make sure that he had his watch, and tapping his pocket for his wallet, Hunter headed for the door as well. Just as he reached for the doorknob, the telephone rang. He wrestled with whether to answer or allow it to roll into voicemail, but curiosity won. Sunday was the day of the week that his mother generally called him. Walking to the unit that sat on the table beside his bed, Hunter noticed the image on the caller ID just before picking it up. His hand froze. It was Kwame.

As if there was some chance that his footsteps

could be heard on the other end of the phone that still rested on its cradle, Hunter backed away in soft, slow steps. Once again standing at the door that led to the garage, he stopped, rechecked his pocket for the wallet he'd checked for moments earlier, then made his exit.

Chapter 21

Jade's mind darted from thought to thought as she and her sister-in-law set the dishes on the table in preparation for dinner. Even though she was fully aware that this situation was entirely different, Jade couldn't help but be aware of the fact that she hadn't invited a man to eat with her family since George Bannister. Taking a step away from the table, she picked up the glass of tea that she'd poured earlier, took in some of the sweet drink and swished it around her mouth before swallowing. Just the thought of George had put a bad taste there, and as quickly as she rinsed it away with the tea, Jade pushed the distasteful experience from her mind.

Her second thought was of Jerome. At the oddest, yet somehow most appropriate times, Jade would think of her incarcerated brother. Most times she'd think of him when she was driving down the highway, shopping in various stores or preparing for dinner. She supposed it was because these were common everyday matters that she, and most people that she knew, took for granted. They were simple things, but things that Jerome hadn't been able to do freely in nearly ten years. Almost unconsciously, Jade sighed, closed her eyes and said a quick, silent prayer.

"So is he as cute in person as he is on paper?"

The whisper that came from over Jade's left shoulder startled her. She steadied the glass in her hand and turned to see Renee standing there, sporting a knowing smile.

"What?" Jade questioned.

"Jade, you're standing here trying to calm your nerves over a man who is coming to share a dinner with your family. I know it's supposed to be business, but from where I stand, it looks like a bit more than that."

As Renee spoke, it became clear to Jade that she'd gotten the wrong impression of her closed eyes. While it was true that she was becoming increasingly nervous about Hunter's arrival, Jade was glad that she could honestly refute Renee's theory.

"For your information," Jade began as she set her glass back on the counter and headed back to the dining room, "I was thinking about Jerome and how I wished he could be here to enjoy family gatherings like this with us."

"Oh," Renee said with a giggle. "Guess I misread that one."

"Don't quit your day job," Jade said in jest. "Motherhood, you've got down pat, but a fortune teller, you're not."

The two shared a laugh, but Jade found out

rather quickly that Renee wasn't quite ready to release the issue of Hunter Greene.

"But is he as cute in person?"

Buying herself some thinking time, Jade replied. "Renee, he's been to New Hope. You've never seen him?"

"Girl, a million people come through New Hope. How would I know him from any other visitor? I don't know most of the members, so I definitely wouldn't know someone who came only on occasion. The letter in the paper said that he grew up with you guys. You remember him from back then?"

"Barely, but yes," Jade said, hoping her face wasn't as flushed as it felt. She continued to set the table as she spoke, being sure to avoid eye-contact with Renee. "I remember him and a few of the other guys who used to live in the neighborhood, but I don't really remember any of their faces. I just recall them playing on the basketball court, mainly. Hunter used to play with them. That's about as much as I can remember."

"So, is he cute?" Renee asked for the third time.

"Cute is such a juvenile word, Renee. I don't generally define grown men as cute. If you're over twenty-one, cute no longer—"

Both women stopped speaking and took on the characteristics of a freeze frame as the doorbell rang. Back in motion, Renee placed the last set of silverware on the table and they both stepped into the living room as Jackson emerged from the hallway and threw a glance in their direction before heading to the door.

"Good evening," Jackson said as he extended his hand toward Hunter and stepped aside. "Jackson Tides; but I hear that you already know me from Perry Homes."

"You heard correctly," Hunter said, flashing a pleasant smile. "Few people from our neighborhood didn't know the boy who wore number fourteen."

It was easy to tell that Hunter's remembrance of his jersey number flattered Jackson. His ball playing days were long behind him, but Jackson still loved the sport and having someone, years later, recall the number he wore was humbling.

"He *is* cute," Renee whispered in Jade's ear.

Jade fought to hold back her smile and a nod of agreement. Hunter wasn't exactly her date for the evening, but for some reason it pleased her that her sister-in-law approved. And Renee wasn't alone in her line of thinking. Jade thought Hunter looked particularly dashing at the moment. As distinguished as his appearance was in church earlier today, Hunter's current look topped it. Perhaps it was the way he wore the simple, yet dressy, ensemble. Jade wasn't sure what magnified the exclamation mark on Hunter this afternoon, but she somehow found it hard to take her eyes away.

"This is my son," Hunter said to Jackson while pointing toward the child who stood beside him, but slightly behind.

Immediately extending his hand toward Jackson, the boy said, "Hi. My name is Malik Greene."

Jade smiled, remembering him saying those same carefully enunciated words to her not long ago. She noted that Malik seemed a bit unhappy, not wearing the smile he did yesterday at the pasture and this morning at church. She assumed it was because he was in an unfamiliar and perhaps uncomfortable place.

"Hi, Malik. I'm Mr. Jackson Tides. Nice firm handshake you've got there, lil' man. Why don't you both come in?"

"Thank you," Hunter said.

Both he and Malik accepted their invitation and stepped into the carpeted living room where the women stood at a distance. Just as Jade was preparing to step forward, Renee moved in front of her and took the short walk that brought her to the gentlemen.

"Good afternoon, Mr. Greene, I'm Renee. It's wonderful to finally put a face to a name and meet you in person."

"This is my wife," Jackson added, throwing her a look that scolded her for not introducing herself as such. Jade nearly burst into laughter at her brother's insecurities.

"Please, call me Hunter," Hunter replied.

Slipping his arm around his blushing wife's waist, Jackson gently pulled her away and after Renee had acknowledged Malik, Jackson gestured in Jade's direction. "I believe you've met my baby sister."

Hunter broke into a wide smile as he nodded and said, "I've had the distinct pleasure."

Even knowing that her family was present, Jade couldn't help but close her eyes and inhale the manly fragrance that she'd become familiar with as Hunter embraced her. The hug was brief, but long enough to send Jade's heartbeat into overdrive. When Hunter released her, Jade turned to Malik and hugged him as well. It resulted in the first smile she'd seen from him since his entrance.

Walking toward the hallway, Jackson said, "I'm going to get Mother. She laid down for a nap earlier, but I'm sure she's about ready now." Halfway down the hall he stopped and looked over his shoulder at Renee. "Honey, can you help me please?"

"Huh? Oh, yes," Renee said, looking from Hunter to Jade. "We'll be right back. Dinner is ready, so we'll sit down and eat as soon as we return."

Jackson and Renee had barely cleared the room before Jade released the laughter that had been trying to set itself free for the past several minutes. Hunter looked at her, not verbally speaking, but asking a very clear question with his expression.

"I'm sorry," Jade said. "But I think my brother is just a bit jealous that you're getting more attention from his wife than he's comfortable with."

"Am I?" Hunter asked with raised eyebrows.

"Yes, you are," Jade assured him. "Please sit down and make yourselves comfortable."

Jade sat first and Hunter followed. Malik chose, instead, to walk to the opposite corner of the room and admire the colorful fish that swam in the tank beside the grandfather clock. It was a fairly new addition to the home's décor that Jackson had purchased as a means to bring cheer into the home that seemed to be drained of life after the death of their father.

"Is he okay?" Jade whispered.

"Woman trouble," Hunter replied, prompting a double-take from his couch partner.

"What?"

Hunter laughed at Jade's facial expression, throwing his head back in the process. Jade liked his healthy, hearty laugh. In fact, the more time she spent around Hunter, the more she liked *him*. When he finally spoke, his tone was soft so his words wouldn't be overheard by his son.

"When we were driving in the subdivision, we passed a house where this girl lives—a girl that he likes. Remember Kyla from yesterday?"

Jade nodded.

"Malik sort of has a crush on her. She lives on the corner of the next street up and when we passed her house, Kyla was sitting on the front steps with a classmate named K.P. He thinks that K.P. likes Kyla and I think he's a bit put off by seeing the two of them talking."

"I see," Jade said. To herself, she thought of how young the children were and how her dad would have never even tolerated the thought of her or one of her brothers speaking of having a girlfriend at Malik's age. Deciding to change the subject, she said, "What happened after I left today? Did you speak with your friend?"

As soon as she posed the question, Jade wished she hadn't. A moment ago, Hunter was by all appearances relaxed and comfortable in her mother's home, but Jade noted a clear and instant change. Hunter sat forward on the sofa and wiped his hand across his lips before responding.

"Kwame's not my friend and if you don't mind I don't wish to discuss him this evening."

Hunter's words weren't exactly harsh, but they were certainly edged with a sternness that hadn't been heard until now. Jade was quiet for a moment, not sure how to respond or react. Even looking straight ahead, she could see Hunter turn to her and could hear him sigh, regretting his response. But before he could speak, Jade's family emerged from the shadows of the hallway. Hoping they didn't feel the tension in the room, Jade stood and Hunter followed.

"Did you sleep well, Mother?" Jade asked.

"I don't know what that is anymore, baby, but I thank God for the rest He gave me," Mildred answered before looking toward her dinner guest. "Hunter Greene, I presume."

"Yes ma'am," Hunter replied, taking her hand and cupping it between both of his. "It's been a long time, but we've met before."

"So I hear," she said. "I remember when y'all were little back then in Perry Homes. I can't say I remember you in particular, but I do remember our neighbors and I sure do remember how B.T. used to pray for you. You grew up to be a nice looking young man. Prayer works, don't it?"

Jade had eased into the kitchen to avoid her sister-in-law's pondering eyes. Renee had caught a glimpse of the rigidity that had briefly settled between Jade and Hunter. But now, Jade could hear them all laughing in the living room from Mildred's remark.

"Yes ma'am," Hunter finally replied. "I suppose it does. This is my son, Malik."

"Well, hello there, Malik. How are you?"

"I'm fine, thank you. And you?" Malik said.

Jade smiled in spite of the confusion she still had over Hunter's reaction to her earlier question.

Malik was a very well-raised boy. His father had taught him well.

Renee joined Jade, and together, they placed serving dishes on the table. It didn't take long for the aroma from the spread of food to fill the house and the nostrils of those waiting to partake of the prepared meal of stew beef, wild rice, corn on the cob and sweet potato soufflé. As Renee called them all to the dining room, Jade felt a sense of accomplishment when she saw Hunter break into a grin and pat his stomach three times when he caught sight of the menu.

"Did someone tell you all what my favorite meal is?" he asked aloud.

"Well, Jade prepared the meal," Mildred revealed.

Hunter looked at Jade but she turned away to head back to the kitchen, wondering if Hunter recalled the night in the hotel room when he casually mentioned the meal. Jade took a chance that there might have been some significance. It appeared that she was right.

After Jackson had said grace over the food, serving dishes were passed freely. Hunter's mouth watered in anticipation, but he reminded himself that he was a guest in the Tides' home and served himself much smaller portions than he wanted.

"Eat up now," Mildred urged, noting Hunter's reservation. "There's plenty to go around."

Hunter smiled. As unsure as he had been when he first walked through the doors of the house, he was now at ease. There was no shortage of conversation at the table, but he noticed that very little was offered from Jade. Instead, unless a question was directed at her, she sat quietly, only contributing a smile or a laugh on occasion. It was a far cry from her warm reception when Hunter and Malik first arrived and Hunter knew why.

"I'm sure it's no secret as to why we invited you here, Hunter," Jackson said as he wiped his mouth with a napkin.

Others were still enjoying their meals, but the chatter had quieted. Hunter looked at the second helping of stew beef that he'd not long ago put on his plate. He wanted to eat it, but with the atmosphere suddenly becoming more serious, he felt compelled to give Jackson his attention instead. Hunter was fully aware of why he'd been summoned, but he chose not to reply to the statement that had been presented.

Jackson continued. "On behalf of myself and my family, I'd like to give a personal apology for all of the ruckus that we caused. I hope you can at least understand why we felt the way we did. However, we were wrong, and for that we are sincerely sorry."

"I do understand," Hunter started.

"No you don't," Mildred interjected. Her eyes immediately filled with tears and her hands trembled slightly while she twisted the napkin in her hand. "'Till you've lost the person in your life who was your everything, you can't really understand."

Jackson immediately vacated his seat and stood behind his mother's chair to offer support. Mildred's breakdown had a domino effect among the women at the table. Within a few short seconds, laughter turned into tears and both Renee and

Jade had their faces buried behind napkins. Jackson stood strong, but Hunter could even see the sadness in his eyes. Even Malik had stopped eating and now had his eyes fixed on the table cloth in front of him. Hunter wrestled with whether he should go on, but when no one else did, he chose to.

"You're right, Mrs. Tides. I can't understand on the same level as you and your family do. Maybe I can't even understand on the same level as the members of New Hope, but I do understand why you may have felt the way you did. I understand why you may not have wanted the letters printed, and perhaps in knowing that, I should have been more mindful but we . . ." Hunter stopped and made a conscious effort not to look in Jade's direction. Taking a breath, he continued. "I felt that this was something that God wanted me to do. I don't have all the answers nor do I have a good explanation, but I know that the reason that He had me keep the letters running will soon be realized."

A hush rested among them and then Jackson spoke. "How long are you going to run them?"

His question was quiet, but Hunter could hear an underlying sternness. It was clear that Jackson wanted this to be a short-lived project, but Hunter knew that he couldn't give him the answer that he wanted to hear.

"I wish I knew," he replied. "I'm not accepting new letters, so only the ones we received prior to Reverend Tides' death will make the paper. I can promise you that much."

"What are you trying to accomplish?" Mildred

asked, wiping away residual tears. "I mean, I know you say that God is leading this, but you must know what it is you're looking for."

Hunter could feel Jade's eyes on him, but he still refused to look in her direction. The last thing he wanted was for Mildred to suspect that her daughter had any involvement in his decision. "I can't tell you much more, Mrs. Tides. You'll have to trust me on this. I would never do anything to hurt you or your family and I will not drag this out any longer than God directs me." Looking across the table, Hunter locked his eyes into Mildred's. "I *need* you to trust me," he said in a pleading voice. "I need that, Mrs. Tides."

The silence that followed seemed infinite. Everybody's eyes were on Mildred now except Jade's. Hunter could still sense hers on him.

"Do what you must." Mildred's words were forced and said with little enthusiasm. Still, Hunter received them and thanked her for her quiet, somewhat apprehensive blessing. He wanted this to be over just as much as they did.

"I'm sorry everyone, but I have to be going," Jade said, standing up all of a sudden and changing the air. "It's after seven o'clock and my flight leaves at ten and you know Hartsfield-Jackson Airport; I need to get there at least an hour and a half early to be sure that I get through security lines and to my gate in time."

"I'll get your bag and wait for you in the car," Jackson said as he walked to the living room to get the leather shoulder bag that sat on the floor beside the sofa.

Hunter followed him. "Listen, Jackson. Why

don't you let me take her? Your mother is still a little emotional right now and she may need you for a while."

Jackson eyed Hunter and then glanced toward his mother who had Jade in a tight embrace, telling her how she wished she could have stayed longer. Hunter felt a bit guilty for using Mildred's fragile state as a reason to spend a few more minutes with Jade, but he had the feeling that Jackson hadn't been fooled.

"You don't mind?" Jackson asked.

"I don't mind at all," Hunter said, taking the bag from Jackson's grasp.

Jade had a bewildered look on her face when she noted the change, but she didn't ask any questions. Instead, she kissed her brother's cheek and then walked out the door that Hunter held open for her.

Knowing what to do, Malik headed for the backseat and Hunter opened the passenger side for Jade. Hunter admired her calves in the denim skirt that she wore. Her outfit matched perfectly, even down to the denim accented sandals.

"Ready?" he asked as he closed his own door and buckled himself in.

"Yes."

Chapter 22

Traffic on Interstate 85 North was heavier than normal for a Sunday night. The rainfall was slowing motorists down and forcing them to take it a little slower than usual, but Hunter had no complaints. He needed the extra time to talk to Jade and the rain was only one turn of events that made it possible to do so without reservation.

As Hunter drove away from Mildred Tides' home and into the community, he and his passengers spotted Kyla and K.P. still sitting out on the porch where they'd been two hours earlier. They were no longer alone, though. Jeremy and Willie had joined them. Despite Malik's protests, Hunter pulled his vehicle over to the side of the road and got out to speak to the children who were excited to see him. They immediately asked if they could come to Greene Pastures again on the following Saturday.

"Sure," Hunter said as he looked into the cloudy

sky that was beginning to darken. "That is, if it doesn't rain."

"Will you teach me to ride some more, Malik?"

It was that question that broke Malik out of his funk. He smiled at Kyla and nodded with excitement. "Sure! We can trot next time if you want."

"Okay. But not too fast," Kyla said.

"You can come too, K.P.," Hunter said after noting the boy's look of abandonment. "Would you like that?"

"Yeah, K.P.," Willie urged. "It's really fun. Mr. Greene's got lots of pretty horses out there to ride."

Malik's countenance dropped briefly before looking upward to where his father's eyes were waiting. Hunter gave him a silent nod, indicating that everything would be okay and the reassurance seemed to help.

"I gotta ask my grandma," K.P. answered.

"Go get her," Hunter directed.

As he waited for the boy's guardian to make her exit from the home, Hunter looked back into the SUV where Jade waited patiently. The brown sunglasses that accentuated her face hid her eyes, but Hunter was almost certain that she was watching him. When K.P.'s grandmother finally joined them, she introduced herself as Gertrude Price, the boy's paternal grandmother. It didn't take much convincing to get her to agree to allow her grandson to join the other children in Greene Pastures.

"That would be wonderful," she said as she leaned on her cane and studied Hunter closely over her reading glasses. "He be so quiet 'round the house and there ain't much I can do to keep him entertained. I'm seventy-two years old and done had two surgeries to remove the water from my knee, so I can't do too much."

As Gertude spoke, she lifted her skirt to her thighs and rolled down her stockings to give Hunter and anyone else who was in looking distance, a clear view of the scars. It was not a pleasant sight. Hunter glanced again back at his SUV and saw Jade laughing at his misfortune.

"I'm gonna have to get cut again before long 'cause I can feel the water building up again. See? Feel this right here," Gertrude said, reaching for Hunter's hand.

Drawing his arm out of her reach, Hunter replied, "That's all right, Ms. Price. I can see it from here. So, it's okay if K.P. catches a ride with the other kids?" He wanted desperately to change the subject.

"Oh yeah, sugar. He can go. You know his folks been having problems lately, so that's why I got him staying here with me." Gertrude dropped her voice to a low level as if K.P. and all of the other children who were standing with them couldn't hear. "My son been on that stuff for years."

The telephone rang just as she finished her sentence. "That's probably him right there. Go get the phone and talk to your daddy, Ko-Ko."

Malik exchanged glances with Willie, Jeremy and Kyla, but none of them spoke. K.P. dropped his eyes to the ground and then went inside to catch the ringing phone. Hunter couldn't determine whether he was more embarrassed by the story that his grandmother had just shared, or by the nickname that she'd just used.

"You ain't got to rush off," Gertrude said, noting that Hunter had begun backing away. "I got ice cream and cake inside for the children and there's plenty for you and your boy."

Malik looked at Hunter with hope in his eyes. "Can we, Daddy?"

"I gotta get Ms. Jade to the airport. It's already getting late."

"Well now if you got something to do, why don't you let the boy stay and enjoy dessert with his friends? You can come back and get him when you're done running errands. I don't mind."

Hunter looked at Gertrude as she made her offer. He didn't know the old woman and he never left Malik with people he didn't know. Jeremy must have seen Hunter's hesitation.

"Mama's coming over too, Mr. Greene," the boy said. "She'll be here in just a minute and then when we're done, Malik can just go with us to our house and wait for you."

Hunter was still a bit apprehensive, but he knew the Lowman family well as they'd brought their boys to his home on several occasions. "Okay," he said to Malik's joy. You call me on my cell if you need to."

"I will, Daddy. Thanks."

"Good thing I booked a late flight," Jade remarked as they drove along the highway. It was the most she'd said all at one time since they'd left

Shelton Heights. It was the most she'd said to Hunter since before dinner when he scolded her for mentioning Kwame's name. He had been trying to find a fitting time to apologize and now was as good a time as any.

"I didn't mean to snap at you earlier," he said as he tossed a glance in her direction before looking ahead through the falling rain.

"Then why did you?" Jade's tone almost dared him to try and create an excuse for his actions.

"I don't know."

"Did you and Kwame get into an argument?"

"No, we didn't have an argument. We didn't say much of anything to one another. I gave him a copy of the note I'd found and left him standing there." Hunter pulled his vibrating cell phone from his hip and then tossed it into the cup holder beside him. "He's been calling me all day, but I've not spoken with him."

The rainfall was beginning to ease and traffic was starting to move more freely. Hunter saw Jade glance down at her watch, but he wasn't worried. They had plenty of time to make it to the airport for her flight. The closer they got to their exit, the lighter the traffic became. Most of the cars kept straight when Hunter took the Atlanta Airport exit. It would only be a few minutes now.

"You have to see him at work tomorrow," Jade said. "What are you going to do?"

"I haven't decided yet," Hunter said, readjusting his rearview mirror to get the high beams of the vehicle that followed too closely behind him out of his eyes.

"You can't let this one incident overshadow all

that the two of you have been through over the years."

"Whose side are you on?"

"I'm not taking sides, Hunter. It's *my* father that he didn't want to honor in the features. If I can forgive him for his misguided thoughts, then you can too."

"That wasn't misguided, Jade. That was a blatant attempt on his and Diane's part to undermine my authority."

"Maybe so," Jade said with an understanding nod. "But God doesn't hold us responsible for what other people do. That's not within our control. However, He does hold us accountable to how we respond to what others do. That part, we can control and we can't lose our Christianity no matter what other people do. Just think where we'd all be if God held our sometimes blatant sins against us like that."

Hunter looked in her direction and smiled. "You sure it's Jackson who's the preacher in the family?"

Jade smiled back. "I don't mean to preach at you, Hunter. I'm only saying that true friendships come few and far between. Kwame was definitely wrong in what he was contemplating doing, but that was the human side of him."

"You mean the *selfish* side of him."

"Maybe."

Their conversation came to an instant halt when they both lunged forward, as the truck behind them ran into Hunter's back bumper.

"He hit us," Jade said, looking behind them.

Hunter put his foot on the break. "It wasn't too

hard," he said as he maneuvered the vehicle to the side of the road. "It's probably not any damage so if he's cool, I am."

"He's pulling up beside us," Jade said, just as Hunter was about to reach for the handle of his door.

Looking up, Hunter tried to see through the mixture of water and mist that clouded his window. The person in the vehicle beside them didn't move. He made no effort to drive or to get out of the truck.

"What are they doing?"

"I don't know," Hunter said as he double-checked to be sure the locks were engaged on all of his doors.

Two minutes passed. . . . then three. Still there was no movement. Both vehicles remained powered and Hunter was beginning to get the feeling that what seemed like an innocent fender-bender might be more. Picking up his cell phone, he dialed 9-1-1.

"What are you doing?" Jade's voice was panicked.

"Just sit still," Hunter said, just as the operator answered. "I've been in an accident," he told her. "Can we have a policeman to come out? I'm on the Atlanta Airport exit ramp off of 85 North."

"Is anyone in your vehicle injured? Do you need an ambulance?"

"No. It was a minor accident."

"Is another vehicle involved?"

"Yes. A dark colored pickup truck. Black . . . maybe blue."

"Is anyone hurt in that vehicle?"

"Not that I'm aware of. No one has gotten out of the truck, but like I said, it was minor. They just bumped me from behind."

"What is your name, sir?" the operator asked.

"Hunter Greene."

"I'm sending someone out right away, Mr. Greene."

"Thank you."

Hunter returned his phone to the cup holder and looked at Jade. He could see mounting concern on her face.

"Why are they just sitting there?" she asked.

"I'm not sure. It's dark out and it's raining. It could be a female who was driving alone. I can't blame her for not getting out. You can't be too careful nowadays." Hunter's explanation sounded so good that he almost wanted to pat himself on the back for coming up with it on such short notice. And what he'd told Jade could easily be the case. If he were a woman driving alone, Hunter knew he wouldn't be so eager to climb out of the safety of his vehicle at this hour of the night.

"But why would she pull up beside us like that? Why didn't she stay behind us where she was when we first pulled over?" Jade's voice was full of concern.

The seed of doubt that had never truly been uprooted was now flourishing again. Jade had a good point and Hunter couldn't deny that. It was very odd that the driver of the pickup had chosen to pull alongside him instead of staying on the safety of the shoulder. In the current position that the driver had put his or her car in, approaching cars were forced to go around it as they headed toward the airport.

Deciding that he was unbearably uncomfortable with the position of the other vehicle, Hunter shifted his SUV into drive and pulled slightly forward, so that the truck, although it was still in the road, was behind him and not beside.

"Better?" he asked Jade, making it seem as if he hadn't made the move to ease his own doubts as well.

"Yeah," Jade admitted with a slight smile.

Only a moment passed before both Jade and Hunter flinched. Not only had the dark truck moved up beside them again, but in the process, the driver moved closer and scraped the side of Hunter's vehicle. Jade gasped in fear and Hunter shifted into drive and pressed the gas. Whether or not this was an accident was no longer in question.

No sooner had Hunter pulled away than the truck was in hot pursuit. He tried to focus on the road as he heard Jade frantically talking to a 9-1-1 operator, telling her what was transpiring. The steep curve ahead forced Hunter to ease his foot off of the gas pedal, but when he did the pickup truck gained on him and pulled in the lane beside him.

"Oh my God!" Jade gasped as she reached for the door to help steady her as they took the curve at a speed faster than they should have.

"Hold on, sweetie," Hunter said, trying to maneuver the SUV away from the truck whose driver showed no signs of letting up.

All of a sudden, Hunter saw the truck weave

away from them, and for a fleeting moment, he thought that his pursuer had given up. But that was not the case at all. Hunter could hear the motor of the pickup rev in an almost angry manner and he knew that the danger had just begun. Flooring his gas pedal despite the dangerous road conditions, Hunter tried to head for safety—wherever safety was. Only a moment later the pickup was beside Hunter again. Then with all the force the opposing driver could muster, he seemed to direct the truck in their direction, slamming it into the side of Hunter's SUV and forcing him off the road into the steep embankment. For a moment, all Hunter could hear were Jade's cries as she screamed for God's mercy and protection. And all he could see were the trees that closed in on them. The soft soil under the grassy embankment rendered his steering wheel useless and Hunter could not keep his truck from flipping once, landing on its wheels and then hitting a tree head-on.

The airbags in front of them imploded and the force of his made Hunter see large white spots where clear vision once was. After he caught his breath, he slowly began to move, pushing himself away from the inflated safety device. He sat motionless for a moment but when his vision finally cleared, the first thing Hunter noticed was his passenger, still leaning forward into the airbag in front of her. She wasn't moving.

"Jade?" When she didn't respond he panicked. "Jade!"

Chapter 23

Feeling strong hands gripping his shoulder, Jerome jolted into an upright position in his prison bed and wiped the beads of sweat from his forehead. He could see the dark outline of his cellmate's frame standing over him, adding to Jerome's initial disorientation and fright. Swiftly, Jerome scooted backward, pressing his back against the cold wall.

"Wake up, fool," the six-five, two hundred fifty-pound convicted drug dealer said in annoyance. "How am I supposed to get any sleep with you making all that noise?"

The man that Jerome only knew by his street name of Rocky, cursed, climbed back to his own bed, and sat on the edge of it. "You need a fix or something? I got something I can give you, but it's gonna cost you."

Rocky was broad and burly, but in the four months that they'd been cellmates, Jerome had heard some things about Rocky that made him question whether the man who slept in the bottom bunk beneath him had gotten the nickname because he dealt in crack cocaine or because he was mentally unstable. Rocky was a fighter and had gotten into many brawls with inmates he shared space with. So far, Jerome had managed not to push him over the edge. The last inmate he'd beaten accused Rocky of trying to rape him. Rocky denied it and the claim had never been proven, but Jerome trusted no one.

"Naw, man, I don't need no fix," Jerome said, making sure his tone stayed even. "I just had a bad dream, that's all. Sorry I woke ya." With that, Jerome repositioned himself on his mattress, laid flat on his back and closed his eyes to try and find sleep that was more peaceful this time.

Another swear word came from Rocky and then he added, "I'm woke now, nigga. All that noise you was making messed up my dream. I was on a date with one of Hollywood's finest, too. But I'm woke now so you might as well tell me what had you moaning and squirming over there."

"I don't remember. It was just a dream, I guess."

Rocky must have seen right through Jerome's lie and he didn't sound at all pleased that Jerome chose not to share the nightmare. "Talk, nigga," he demanded. "If you think I'm gonna let you roll over and go back to sleep after you done messed up mine, you got another think coming."

While Jerome hoped that a good night's sleep was still in his future, he had no intention of rolling over to find it. He was still unsure as to whether the "Hollywood's finest" that made Rocky's dream so entertaining was male or female. And quite frankly, it didn't matter. Even men who had been straight on the outside were known to act differently out of desperation on the inside.

"It's my dad," Jerome said, allowing his eyes to scale the ceiling above him. He didn't know what time it was, but hardly any light was being provided from the slit in the cell wall. He figured that it must have been around midnight though. He hadn't been sleep that long before he started dreaming of his father calling his name. In the dream, Jerome could hear his father's voice, but couldn't find where the call was coming from. Jerome had been answering and even calling back, but his father hadn't seemed to hear him either.

"Jerome!" his father's voice called.

"Dad!" Jerome responded.

"Jerome!"

"Dad!"

Back and forth, they called for one another, but to no avail. The dream was so real that it was frightening. Jerome's heart still raced with residual panic.

"Well, that part I know," Rocky said, bringing Jerome's thoughts back to the cell. "I heard you call for him, but why? Your daddy's dead," he said as though Jerome had forgotten.

"I know that." Jerome was irritated by the senseless reminder, but he tried not to let it be heard. "Just 'cause he's dead don't mean I can't dream about him, does it?"

"Guess not. I used to dream about my old man too," Rocky said. Jerome could hear him lying back on the mattress below.

"Is he dead?"

An offensive word slipped from Rocky's lips and it was followed by a chuckle that was laced in animosity. "I *wish,*" he said. "I used to dream that he got killed and I was the one who did the world the favor. Sometimes when I think about him now, I wish I had killed him. If I was gonna have to spend all these years in jail, I wish it was for something worth my time. Killing my dad and knowing that he was six feet under would have been worth being locked up in this joint."

Jerome lay in silence. His immediate thought was of how cold Rocky sounded. He thought within himself that only an animal could be so cruel as to wish death upon his own father. But then reality slapped him and then forced him to look it directly in the eyes. Jerome had to admit within himself that he was no better than Rocky. He could remember times in his younger years that he wished he was someone else, living somewhere else and doing something else other than having to deal with parents who were so strict and heavy-handed. Jerome remembered thinking on more than one occasion that if his daddy would just keel over and die, living at home would be much more tolerable. He could often deceive his mother and pull at her heartstrings, but his father was much more steadfast. Jerome wished he couldn't recall his thoughts back then, but he could—and he could recall them clearly.

"I know what you thinkin'," Rocky said. "You up there thinking 'bout what a jerk I am for what I just said."

Jerome wanted to tell him otherwise, but instead he lay quietly while Rocky used more than a few offensive adjectives to describe the man who was the authority in his childhood household. In all of the weeks that Jerome and Rocky had shared a cell, they'd never discussed anything that even resembled personal information. In fact, until now, the two men had barely spoken to each other at all.

"My old man thought he was God," Rocky said. "Whatever he said was the law and nobody else in the house had a say so. That included my mama. If she said anything or did anything to go against something he said, that fool would smack her just as easy as he'd hit me or my brothers and sisters. He ain't never cared nothing about nobody but himself. Me and my two brothers all dropped out of school before we got to the tenth grade. My oldest sister got to the eleventh grade, but she dropped out when she got pregnant. My youngest sister was turning tricks by the time she was fifteen. You think that nigga cared anything about that?" Rocky answered his own question with another expletive and then continued.

"All he ever cared about was that whatever money we made, *however* we made it, came home and he got to call the shots on how it was spent. When I was a teenager, I was more scared of what my old man would do to me if I didn't bring my cut of the drug money home than I was of what would happen to me if I didn't do right by the man I was making drops for."

Jerome continued to focus on the ceiling and listen to Rocky's depiction of his life. Jerome was grateful for the darkness that surrounded them. He didn't even bother to wipe away the tears that seeped from his eyes into his ears. He was careful not to sniffle, though. He needed to keep his emotions private.

All B.T. Tides ever did was love his family. He treated his wife well and only wanted the best for his children. Yes, he meddled in their lives on occasion, but as Jerome thought back over it all, he understood more clearly than ever that all that his father was doing was trying to steer them in the right direction. And of all of the Tides children, Jerome knew he'd been the worst. As a matter of fact, he was the only one who gave his parents such heartache. All of his life he had been selfish and stupid and it had taken nearly ten years in Phillips State Prison for him to realize it.

"I'd give anything to be in your shoes right now, man," Rocky was saying. "You ain't got to worry 'bout your daddy once you blow this joint. You ain't got much longer in here, and when you get out, you're home free. When I get out of here—whenever that is—I'm still gonna have to look that nigga in the face anytime I go to see my mama. I can't even believe she's still with him after everything he's done to her."

Jerome sat up and wiped his face in the process. "Well, I'd give anything to be in your shoes too," he revealed, clearing his throat. "I'd do just about anything to bring my daddy back."

"Oh. Your daddy must have been a good one. I figured he was. At least yours came out here to visit you. I ain't seen mine since I been in here. But it ain't like I want to see him, so he's doing me a favor as far as I'm concerned."

Jerome chose to pull away from the subject of

Rocky's unfit father and talk about his own. "Yeah, my daddy was good to us, but I hated him just like you hate yours."

Rocky sat up too. Jerome couldn't see him, but he heard the creak of the mattress and he knew he'd gotten his cellmate's full attention so he kept talking.

"My daddy is . . . was a preacher. He had been a preacher for all my life and just about all of his. Everybody loved him; everybody but me, that is." Jerome paused to gather himself. His chin had begun to tremble but he knew he couldn't cry; not in front of Rocky. When he felt more in control he continued. "In my house, I was the bad one. I kept so much chaos going that I think my folks wondered if I was on drugs or something."

"Were you?"

"No. Believe it or not, I've never done drugs in my whole life . . . not once. But I sold it to other kids in the neighborhood and did drops just like you. Sometimes I'd sneak out of the house on Friday nights and my family wouldn't see me again until Sunday night or early Monday morning."

"And you tryin' to tell me you wasn't doing drugs?" Rocky sounded like he didn't believe Jerome's story.

"Hey man, I ain't got no reason to lie at this point," Jerome answered with a short laugh. "I partied though. I did booze, women. . . . just about everything else but hard drugs. I guess I'd seen enough of what drugs did to people and I didn't want to go quite that far. I still had my other addictions though and they controlled me just like drugs would have."

"So why'd you hate your old man? What did he do?"

"He loved me." Jerome's voice cracked, and that time he couldn't catch himself before choking up. Tears began to spill down his cheeks again and he was embarrassed knowing that Rocky was aware. He expected the thug to laugh at him, call him cruel names or just ridicule him for losing composure, but he didn't.

The cell was completely quiet for a few minutes. Every now and again Jerome would take a gasp of air as his face remained buried behind his hands. It wasn't that he no longer cared what Rocky thought. Jerome just couldn't hold back the tears. When they broke forth, they did so without his consent. He could only be grateful that Rocky was being cordial . . . at least for now. Jerome imagined that by morning the "church boy" jokes would rise to a new level.

When he removed his hands from his face, he looked down, but the darkness hid whatever was there. Jerome hadn't heard any stirring. He knew that Rocky was still sitting beneath him and waiting. Taking his cell mate's silent cue, Jerome spoke again.

"I just wanted to be like all the other boys." His voice had dropped even lower than it had been earlier. "I did what it took to fit in. I knew the kids in the neighborhood picked at my family 'cause my daddy insisted that we pray every day. But they didn't pick at me because I wasn't like the rest of my family. I was cool; or at least that's what I thought. When the rest of my family was praying, I was knocking off convenience stores, beating up other boys, or snatching old ladies' purses. When they were in Bible study and Sunday morning worship, I was at the club or sexing it up with some girl or doing drops and collecting money. All my daddy ever did was love me and I was too stupid to appreciate it. That's why I'm locked up in this joint, man. Not 'cause I was with the rest of those guys when they shot that dude over a few dollars. I'm in here 'cause I had too much devil in me to see Jesus in my daddy. I was too stupid to know that all he was trying to do was save me from going to hell.

"Now that he's dead, I feel like everything I've been trying to do recently to better myself has gone to waste. I got my GED and I made sure that I've lived by the rules over the last few months. I did it all so that I could get out of here at my parole hearing and show my daddy that I could be good too. I wanted to show him that I could make him proud. I wanted to show him that I could go to church and listen to what he had to say, knowing that he'd been right all along when he told us about the need to serve God and keep His commandments. Now I ain't got no daddy to show nothing to. I got to live the rest of my life knowing that he died while I was still a failure."

Rocky let out a grunt and at first Jerome thought it was the prelude to an outburst of laughter, but it wasn't. Instead, Rocky said, "Nigga what you talkin' 'bout? You ain't no failure. Yeah, your old man is dead, but your GED is still your GED and you still probably gonna get to blow this joint in a couple of weeks."

"Yeah, but then what?" Jerome asked, sounding like he truly valued whatever Rocky had to say.

"Then make your old man proud, that's what," Rocky answered in a matter-of-fact tone. "Shoot. You sound like you got a little preacher in you yourself. That right there that you just told me . . . that was deep, man. That's one heck of a story. Men like you make a lot of money doing group talks and junk, nigga. You know, sometimes all folks need is a little hope to feel like they can make it and be somebody. If you can serve ten years and come out with a good head on your shoulders, you straight, dude. When you get out of here you can teach them niggas on the outside how not to ever have to come in here."

Jerome sat up straight and his mind floated back to his last conversation with his father. "Yeah," he said thoughtfully. "Or maybe I can teach the brothers on the inside how to survive and how not to ever come back."

Chapter 24

The rain was still falling, but as Kwame drove toward Cleveland Avenue, he was thankful that the downpour had slowed considerably. He glanced at Malik who sat quietly beside him and knew that the boy was worried about his father. Unclear information had Kwame grasping for straws, but he had to find out what had happened.

"So you're sure he didn't say he was at Grady Hospital?" Kwame asked Malik for the second time.

Kwame shrugged his shoulders and said, "He didn't say which hospital he was at. He just said he was at the hospital, but he was fine. It was Ms. Jade that might have been hurt."

That didn't tell Kwame much, but he knew that if Hunter had a say so in the matter at all, the ambulance wouldn't have taken them to Grady. The hospital specialized in acute care, but it also was a magnet for the uninsured, causing the waiting room to be packed on any given night. Realizing that

South Fulton Medical Center was less than ten miles from the airport, Kwame figured that he'd take his chances there. He found a vacant spot in the parking lot, pulled the hood of his sweater over his head and waited for Malik to get the umbrella. Then they both climbed from the car and dashed for the entrance doors to the hospital's emergency room.

"Daddy!"

It only took a second for Malik to spot his father standing in the corner next to a leather shoulder bag, looking out of the window. Malik dropped the wet umbrella on the floor and darted toward Hunter. Kwame watched as Hunter turned and flashed a look of surprise before catching Malik who had all but flung himself into Hunter's arms. Although Kwame stood a few feet away closing the umbrella, he could hear Hunter's first questions.

"Hey, sport. What are you doing here? How'd you get here?"

"Uncle Kwame brought me," Malik answered.

Kwame knew that by now Hunter was looking at him, but he pretended to be so busy wrapping the umbrella that he hadn't overheard the conversation between father and son. Kwame hoped to hear a reply of some kind. At least then he'd have an idea of whether or not Hunter was still upset at him. Kwame was sure that he was. It was only a few hours ago that Hunter had left him standing in the church parking lot alone.

Wrapping the umbrella was a simple task and Kwame had already made it more of a chore than was necessary. He couldn't keep fiddling with it, pretending not to be able to get the Velcro strips to cling. Sooner or later he'd have to face what was his immediate greatest fear and Kwame decided on sooner. With the umbrella in one hand, he straightened his back and walked toward Hunter and Malik. Hunter said nothing, but the message behind his narrowed eyes was almost frightening.

"What are you doing here?" Hunter's tone wasn't nearly as friendly as it had been when he asked his son the same question only moments earlier.

"Malik told me about the accident. I just wanted to make sure you were okay," Kwame stated.

"I'm fine. You can go home now."

Hunter's lingering disappointment could be seen on his face and heard in his voice. Kwame knew that his friend's anger wasn't misplaced, but he wanted to somehow make it better.

"Can we talk?" Kwame didn't hold out much hope for a favorable answer, but he had to at least try.

Hunter took a quick glance toward Malik and then back at Kwame. "This is not the time or the place," he responded, barely moving his lips.

"When, then?" When Kwame saw Hunter's jaw tighten, he knew he was pressing his luck. But Hunter had been avoiding his calls all weekend and this might be the only chance he could get to try and redeem himself. Kwame's pressing was an act of desperation.

Hunter took a deep, calming breath and then pointed in the direction of an empty chair in the corner as he pulled a half-eaten pack of M&M's from his pocket. "Go have a seat over there, son. I'll be there in a minute."

Whatever questions Malik might have had about the strange interaction of his father and the man he called 'Uncle Kwame' took a backseat at the sight of the candy. Malik took the offering from Hunter's hand and walked across the room, politely begging the pardon of the people who he had to cross in front of to get to the vacant chair.

Without saying a word, Hunter walked away and Kwame watched him come to a stop in front of the window he'd been staring out of when he and Malik first arrived. His back faced Kwame and Kwame had worked with Hunter long enough to know that such a stance was a silent way of saying, "I want to be left alone." Under normal circumstances, Kwame wouldn't challenge Hunter's desire, but in his opinion, this particular situation went far beyond normal. Taking cautious steps, Kwame walked toward Hunter, coming to a rest standing beside him, staring at the same darkness that Hunter looked into.

"I'm sorry," Kwame whispered.

He heard Hunter release a short, but heavy breath. He'd worked with him long enough to know what that meant too. The almost huffy-sounding sigh said, "Yeah, right. Whatever."

"Come on, Hunter. We've been through too much. It was a moment of bad judgment; a fleeting thought. You know Kwame Akil Williams all too well to think that I'd do anything maliciously."

"I also know Thaddeus Lee Williams all too well."

Kwame quickly looked at his friend. Hunter's voice had remained at a whisper as he spoke, but his tone was so sharp that his words seemed to cut into Kwame like a two-edged sword. Kwame couldn't believe he'd heard correctly.

"What? What did you say?"

"You heard me," Hunter said, turning to face Kwame with unapologetic eyes. "Man, I knew you way before you were Kwame Akil Williams. And you're right, Kwame wouldn't do something like that, but Thaddeus would."

"I can't believe you said that, Hunter. That's not fair and you know it. I made a mistake. That's no reason to bring up the old me."

"I didn't bring him up, Kwame; you did. You brought him up when you decided to scheme with Diane."

"I wasn't scheming with her," Kwame said, thinking fast and hoping that he wasn't lying in an attempt to justify himself. "Diane wrote that note."

"Don't patronize me," Hunter snapped, drawing the attention of those closest to them. "This wasn't all her idea and you know it."

Kwame could feel beads of perspiration gathering on his forehead. As much as he wished he could refute Hunter's accusation, Kwame knew he couldn't do so convincingly. "Okay," he conceded, hoping that Hunter's voice level would lower to match his own. "No, it wasn't all her idea. I've already admitted that the thought had crossed my mind. But it was just that . . . a thought. I didn't carry it out. Doesn't that count for anything?"

For several moments Hunter was quiet and Kwame found hope in the silence. He'd been Hunter's friend long enough to not only read his body language, but sometimes his thoughts. Because Hunter had returned to his window stare, Kwame couldn't look directly into his face. All he could see was Hunter's jaw line, clinching and then relaxing in an almost rhythmic manner. There were very few times that

Hunter was at a loss for words, and for a moment, Kwame felt that he'd had a rare advantage. He was just about to speak again to say something to convince his friend even further, but Hunter spoke first. His face never turned from the glass in front of him, but Hunter's words were clearly directed to Kwame.

"Can you honestly tell me that you didn't actively plan to carry out the thought that you and Diane discussed? Can you look me in my face and tell me that had I not told Lorna to pass the word to the printer, my orders still would have gotten relayed?"

Kwame tried to swallow, but his mouth could find no moisture. Not looking directly at him, Kwame could still see Hunter as he slowly turned from the window and looked in his direction, waiting for a reply to a question that he probably already knew the answer to.

"Hunter?"

At the sound of Hunter's name both men turned and saw Jade walking toward them. Hunter quickly vacated the spot beside Kwame and met Jade. He took a moment to inspect a small Band-aid that was near her left temple and then took her in his arms for a firm embrace that, in Kwame's opinion, seemed full of emotion. From the window where he remained standing, Kwame watched as Hunter interacted with Jade. His touches to her face were tender and the eyes that had just minutes earlier been full of bitterness were now filled with concern.

As they spoke to one another, both their voices were lowered to little more than a whisper, but from where he stood, Kwame was able to hear a few words.

"I'm sorry. I'm so sorry."

Those were the words that Hunter kept repeating during and after the embrace that he and Jade shared. In response, she told him over and over that it wasn't his fault and that everything was okay. Kwame heard the words "contusion" and "prescription" and then he heard Jade tell Hunter that the doctor said she was fine and was free to go home. As Kwame took a few steps closer, he heard more.

"You've missed your flight," Hunter told Jade.

"I know, but I should still be able to catch another," she replied.

"Tonight?"

"I have appointments for tomorrow, Hunter. I have clients to see."

"Can't you reschedule? You've been through a lot tonight, Jade. I'm sure your mom would be glad to have you stay over one more night . . ."

"You didn't call her did you?" Jade's voice was filled with worry.

"No."

"Good," she said through a sigh of relief. "I don't want to tell her about this. She'd be too upset."

"Sweetheart, you're going to have to tell her eventually."

Sweetheart? Kwame thought. He hadn't heard Hunter make reference to a woman with a term of endearment in years. He couldn't help but wonder just how close the two of them had become.

"Hunter, whoever was in that truck tried to kill us. I can't tell Mother that. Not now. She's still struggling with what happened to Dad. She'd be devastated if I told her this now. Please," Jade begged. "Please let's not tell her right now."

Kwame couldn't believe the words he'd just heard. From what Malik had told him, he'd thought that it was a simple accident. His assumption was that Hunter had hit a patch of water in the road and had lost control of his vehicle. He had no idea that another person was involved, much less that this was no accident.

"Okay, you're right," Kwame heard Hunter say. "It's probably not best to tell her right now. But are you sure you want to take your flight tonight? It's late and you might not be able to find one anyway."

"I'm sure they have something available. I have to try."

"My truck was towed, but if there's a red-eye flight available, I'll make sure you get there in time to catch it. Let me see what I can do."

"Thanks."

Kwame stepped forward just as Hunter pulled out his cellular phone and began to dial. "I'll take you guys wherever you need to go."

"Don't bother." Hunter's reply was quick and dry.

"Come on, Hunter. Let me do this. I can take her to the airport and I can take you and Malik home too. It's not a problem."

"No."

"Hunter." Jade touched Hunter's arm as she said his name. Kwame watched as Hunter turned to her. Immediately, his eyes softened when they met hers. Jade continued. "I need to get there as quickly as I can. Let him take us . . . please."

A familiar tightening could be seen in Hunter's jaws as he focused back on Kwame. Without saying a word, he turned and walked toward Malik who had fallen asleep, holding an empty bag of M&Ms. As Hunter awakened his son, Kwame walked back to the window, picked up Jade's carry-on bag and brought it to her.

"Thank you," Jade said with a smile.

"I'm sorry," Kwame whispered. "For everything."

It was all he could say and Jade didn't have the opportunity to respond before Hunter rejoined them. He relieved Jade of the shoulder bag that Kwame had just given her and then turned in the direction of the exit doors, holding Malik's hand. Kwame watched in silence as the three of them walked away. Then, releasing a burdensome sigh, Kwame followed.

Chapter 25

One by one, Orlando blew out the candles that had been lit in his living room. He was tired and his shoulder pained him from the place where it had hit against the door of his pickup as he jerked his stirring wheel to avoid tumbling down the same slope that Hunter had.

That darn newspaper boy, he thought. If Hunter had just let go of the subject of Reverend B.T. Tides' death, none of what had happened in the last few hours would have been necessary. Orlando was anxious to know the outcome of the accident, but with no power in his home, he couldn't watch his television. The crash appeared to be violent enough to kill them, but just as Orlando was about to get out of his truck and make sure the job was complete, he saw headlights approaching from behind and had no choice but to speed away to avoid blowing his cover. Just like before, he found the nearest phone booth and called 911 to report the accident. But unlike with the Reverend Tides mission, this time he couldn't follow up to see the televised report to revel in his moment of victory.

Orlando screamed an oath and then followed the distant flicker of light and found his way to his bathroom. There was no one to hear his blasphemous scream—no one he cared about anyway. The one person he called his friend was dead and Orlando lived a lonely existence with only the voices in his head to keep him company, and in his mind, Reverend Tides was the reason for it all. Noises came from Orlando's basement. He hadn't fed his dog in two days and he knew the whimpering half-bloodhound, half-mutt was hungry. Orlando hated that dog and didn't know why he didn't just put him to sleep. Perhaps it was because Toby was all he had left.

Taking his candle with him to the kitchen, Orlando searched his near-bare cabinets. He didn't care much for the dog, but he knew he'd get no sleep if he didn't feed him. Orlando didn't like baked beans and since he was the only one left in the house, he chose those to feed to the dog. With the candle in one hand and the opened can of food in the other, he opened the door that led to his basement and walked down the steps into the dark, wet area that smelled heavily of feces and urine.

"Shut up! You're here because this is where dogs belong!" he yelled and then added swear words to drive his point home to anyone who cared to listen.

The frightened dog yelped and then retreated into a corner. Orlando dumped the can of cold beans into the dog's dish and then used his foot to kick it into the direction where the dog had run. Orlando didn't bother to try and bring Toby any fresh water. He figured that there was enough water leaking from the house's worn pipes to keep the mutt from dehydrating. Either way, as he walked back up the stairs into his home, Orlando didn't care. He was worn out and still wet from the rainfall he'd gotten caught in. It was quite a distance to walk to his house from the thick wooded area behind it where he'd left the truck so it wouldn't be found in his yard if officials came snooping.

Sometimes Orlando had the urge to talk to someone about what was going on inside of him, but there was no one he could trust. He didn't have money to hire a professional to listen and he sure couldn't tell anybody in his family. Nobody understood him. Nobody cared. The home Orlando lived in was built with his own hands. He built it so that his wife and children could have a decent place to live. But because of Reverend Tides' stubbornness and stinginess, his family was now divided in three places and none of them shared the home Orlando had built for them.

In anger, Orlando pulled off his wet clothes and dropped them on the bathroom floor. He took one look at himself in the dimly lit mirror on the bathroom wall and rubbed his hand through his scruffy beard. He looked like the shell of the man that he once was. For a fleeting moment, Orlando felt remorse for what he'd done to Hunter and Jade, but then he returned to his vindictive thinking.

"They deserved it," he said to his reflection. "That paper boy asked for it by sticking his nose where it didn't belong. And Jade . . ." Orlando stopped in thought and then yelled at the top of his lungs. "Well, I ain't got my children so why should you have yours!"

He felt his body trembling. Orlando wasn't sure whether it was the chill from the dampness of his skin, the anger that was growing inside of him, or something more. He reached in his medicine cabinet and pulled out a prescription bottle that had been empty for three months. Orlando was well overdue for the refill, but he hadn't taken the initiative to follow his doctor's orders.

"I don't need this anyway," he mumbled as he tossed the plastic container into the empty basin. "They ain't tryin' to help me. They tryin' to kill me."

Not even bothering to shower, Orlando blew out the candle in the bathroom and felt his way through total darkness to his bed. He was hungry, but he didn't feel like eating tonight. Even if he had, there was very little to choose from in a kitchen where only nonperishable items could be stored. He'd convinced himself that that was Reverend Tides' fault too.

The covers on Orlando's bed carried the stench of sheets that hadn't been laundered in weeks, but he had become accustomed to the disgusting smell. Pulling back the bed linen, Orlando climbed in and then pulled the covers over him. Sounds from his basement continued, alternating from whimpering to tapping. Ignoring them, Orlando promised himself that he'd take care of it in a few days. Everything would be taken care of soon.

Chapter 26

Jade's first appointment wasn't until eleven o'clock on Monday morning and she was relieved that she'd booked it for that time. It had been a long night and an even longer day, it seemed. Had she just listened to Hunter, things wouldn't have been nearly as hectic.

It was very late by the time they reached Hartsfield-Jackson Airport after leaving South Fulton Hospital. Upon their arrival, Jade quickly found out that there were no late flights leaving Atlanta and heading for Norfolk. The earliest flight out was at 7:50 a.m. and that was an almost six hour wait.

When she suggested that they leave her there, Hunter wouldn't hear of it, so they got back into Kwame's car and headed back to Stone Mountain. Not a word was spoken between Hunter and Kwame during the trip. In fact, Hunter instructed Malik to sit up front with Kwame while he shared the backseat with Jade. Jade had no qualms, but for different reasons. With each passing minute, she felt closer to Hunter and felt a growing attraction to him. He'd seen her injuries as his fault, but in Jade's eyes, Hunter was her hero. He'd done what it took to save both of their lives. There was no avoiding it. Last night, they were going to either live or die and they were alive because Hunter stayed alert and kept a level head in spite of the danger that was all around them.

As they pulled into the driveway of Hunter's home, the rain was falling lightly. Jade thanked Kwame for transporting them, but Hunter said nothing as he got out of the car and dashed to the door to open it so that she and his son could get inside quickly. Malik had fallen asleep again in the car, so he didn't show any signs of resistance when Hunter instructed him to take his bath and go straight to bed.

After he had his son settled in for the night, Hunter stayed up with Jade and they talked for hours about the ordeal that they'd endured. It was only then that Jade became aware of how frightened Hunter had been throughout the chaos.

"I was scared but I think anger was my biggest emotion," he'd said. "That whole thing was senseless. I didn't get really afraid until I called your name and you didn't move right away."

Jade looked at him as they shared the couch and she could see the concern on his face. She wanted to respond, but before she could, Hunter spoke again.

"Somebody wants me dead, Jade, and I need to find out who it is."

"Maybe somebody wants *me* dead," she replied. "What if . . ."

"What if it's the same person who killed your father?" Hunter had read her thoughts precisely. All Jade had been able to think about as she sat in the outpatient room being seen by the doctor at South Fulton was that whomever it was that was behind the wheel of that truck had been the same person who had killed B.T. Perhaps he'd run her father off the road in the same manner.

"What do you think?" she asked, fishing for Hunter's opinion.

Hunter took a drink from his cup and then nodded his head. "It's definitely a possibility. If the police could find the truck, that would be a big help. But with me not being able to give them an accurate description, I don't know how successful they'll be in their search."

"You told them it was a dark color."

"Yeah, but there are a million dark pickup trucks in Atlanta. The guy who stopped and helped us out of the truck said that it looked black to him, but couldn't be certain."

"Didn't you say he got a portion of the license plate number?"

"Yeah; but only the last two numbers. I don't know how much that will help, but I think it's a good possibility that if we could find out who that person was, we could find answers to the mystery of your dad's death."

Jade had sat in quiet thoughtfulness, sipping from the cup of green tea that Hunter had made for her. Her mind was flooded with so many thoughts that it was difficult to separate them. She vividly remembered the whole frightening experience, but she felt an overwhelming sense of safety in Hunter's house. Jade considered the fact that the assailant could know where he lived and could be waiting right outside the door, but she felt secure with Hunter sitting beside her.

"I wonder how he knew where we were," Hunter said aloud, breaking her train of thought. "Somehow, the person in that vehicle knew that we would be headed to the airport last night. That's the part that's been puzzling me the most. Before Kwame arrived with Malik at the hospital, I kept thinking to myself, '*Who else knew and how did they find out?*'"

Jade remembered drifting off to sleep on Hunter's couch last night, still wrestling over his question. It was an appropriate one. In a strange way, it seemed to point accusing fingers at her family, but Jade was certain that they had nothing to do with it. Jackson was the only one who would even chance going out in that kind of weather and Jade refused to even allow her mind to consider that her brother would do something so volatile. But Hunter was right—somehow the person in the truck knew.

At five o'clock this morning, Jade awakened to Hunter's gentle shaking of her shoulder. He looked as if he'd just woke up as well and Jade wondered if they'd fallen asleep together on the couch. She didn't ask though. Instead she rushed into the guest bathroom to wash up and prepare herself for her flight home. When she came out of the restroom, Jade went into the kitchen where Malik stood at the counter with a school backpack strapped to his back and eating a bowl of Cheerios. She spoke to him, gave him a brief hug, and helped herself to a glass of orange juice.

"You're up early," she remarked.

"Daddy said he's gonna take me to school after taking you to the airport. That way he doesn't have to leave me at home by myself."

Jade smiled. "That's smart."

It was quiet for a moment, but Malik broke the silence with a question that Jade wasn't prepared for.

"Ms. Jade, you like my daddy?"

Jade had almost choked on the mouthful of juice that she'd been swallowing at the time. After her coughing spell ended, she used a paper towel to wipe her mouth and then turned to Malik, staring at him for a moment as she tried to convince herself that she'd heard him wrong.

"Do you?" he asked when she made no attempt to answer.

"Do I what?" Jade still wasn't sure that Malik had asked what her ears had heard.

"Do you like my daddy?"

Her heart raced as if it wanted to run right out of her chest. Within herself, Jade knew that she'd developed feelings for Hunter, but she didn't think that it showed and she wasn't sure that it was reciprocated. She wasn't ready to admit them yet and certainly not to Hunter's ten-year-old son.

"Hunter and I are friends, Malik," she said. "Friends like each other, so yes, I do like him. You don't mind us being friends, do you?"

Malik shook his head slowly. "No, but I wish you liked him more 'cause I really like you."

"Jade, you ready?" Hunter called from somewhere in the living room.

Malik's words left Jade needing a moment to catch her breath, but there was no time to. "We're in the kitchen," she called back.

Hunter appeared around the corner and Jade could only pray that she didn't look as flustered as she felt. She hadn't at all been prepared for the boy's revelation. Hunter didn't seem to notice. After grabbing a glass of juice of his own, they all filed out to Hunter's BMW and headed for the airport.

Now back in Virginia, all the happenings of Jade's last few moments in Atlanta were still on her mind, but it was the one that took place just before she headed for security lines that had her staring into space as she sat behind her desk, waiting for the arrival of her first client for the day.

Malik had chosen to sit in the car inside the parking deck while Hunter walked Jade inside. Hunter had instructed Malik to keep the doors locked and to use the emergency cell phone he'd given him to call if he needed him. With a portable GameBoy in hand, Malik said goodbye to Jade and immediately became absorbed in his game.

"Is he going to be okay out here by himself?" Jade thought that a child of ten was too young to leave alone in a public parking deck, but she didn't press when Hunter assured her that Malik would be fine.

Though Jade had plenty of time to catch her flight, she and Hunter took quick strides toward the building as did most of the people who were headed there. She looked at Hunter in amusement as he checked his pocket for keys that he'd just placed there. It wasn't the first time she'd taken note of his habit.

Jade had expected Hunter to hand her the carry-on bag after she successfully made it inside, but he took her arm and continued to walk with her as she walked in the direction of her gate. When they reached the security line, Hunter stopped. Regulations wouldn't allow him beyond that point without a ticket of his own.

"It's only 6:30," he said, looking at his watch. "You should get through security and to your gate with no problem."

"Thanks, Hunter," she replied.

"No problem."

"I don't mean just for the ride to the airport," Jade clarified. "I mean for everything. Situations about my father's death just seem to be getting more and more weird and I just don't know what I would have done if you hadn't been there."

Jade blinked back tears that she wasn't expecting and Hunter had reached out and whisked away the moisture that had gathered in the corner of one of her eyes. Then he took her in his arms and embraced her as if he didn't want to let her go. Jade melted in his arms and inhaled the scent of his skin as she returned his hug.

It was Hunter who had reached out to embrace her. That part Jade was sure of, but even as she sat at her desk and replayed the moment in her mind, she still wasn't sure who had initiated the kiss that followed. All she could remember was them releasing one another from the lengthy embrace and the look in Hunter's eyes when she looked up at him. For the sake of everything that her mother had always taught her, Jade wanted to believe that it was Hunter who pulled her close and kissed her lips. But a part of her whispered that it was she who had pulled him to her.

Whatever the case, Jade remembered her mind racing and her head spinning. Hunter's lips were gentle, but demanding, and they covered hers perfectly. The kiss sent a melody through her veins and threatened to weaken her knees. When Hunter released her, Jade felt as if he held on to her waist just a little longer to give her an opportunity to stabilize herself. Not a word was spoken. Hunter simply stepped back, ran his own thumb across his lips and then walked away.

Four hours had passed since then, but Jade could still feel the tingling that the touch from Hunter's lips had left behind. She started in her seat as she heard the knock at the door. Jade looked at her wall clock and frowned. She didn't like it when her clients arrived early. Now, she wouldn't have time to dim the lights ahead of time.

"Come in," she called while standing from her chair in preparation to greet Mrs. Childs.

"Hey girl."

"Hey," Jade said, taken aback by the sight of Ingrid.

The two embraced and then Ingrid's eyes immediately latched on to the Band-aid on the side of Jade's head. "What happened? You bumped your head?"

"Actually, yes," Jade said, glad she could answer truthfully, but anxious to change the topic of concern. "How are you?"

"I'm good," Ingrid said, making herself comfortable on Jade's couch. I saw that fine Demetrius Miller on my way in. Lord have mercy . . . I don't know how you can resist."

"It's not that difficult, Ingrid. I don't find him nearly as intriguing as you do. Demetrius does nothing for me."

"I don't get you, Jade. He's single, he's successful and he's about as handsome as a brotha can get. What are you looking for?"

"Can I hear the word Christian?" Jade asked.

"He might be a Christian; you don't know," Ingrid challenged.

"If I don't know it, then I doubt it's true. Christianity generally isn't a hidden attribute."

Ingrid smacked her lips. "Child, please. Just because he's not shouting all over the church and saying 'Have a blessed day! at the end of all of his conversations don't mean he's not saved."

"I never said it did. Just because a person does those things don't make them saved either. I'm talking about his lifestyle, Ingrid. I work with Demetrius five days a week. The life he lives doesn't mirror Christianity. And even further, every man who puts on the mask of Christianity isn't necessarily where he needs to be either. You just can't ever be too certain nowadays."

"George really messed it up for every man who crosses your path, didn't he?" Ingrid said. "No man is going to measure up as far as you're concerned because you'll always see them as another George . . . looking good on the outside, seeming to be good on the inside, but ready to destroy your world if you let them get too close."

"That's not true, Ingrid."

"Prove it."

Jade laughed at her friend's challenge. She didn't know what Ingrid had in mind, but if she were daring her to go out with Demetrius to prove that she didn't view all men the same, that wasn't going to happen. "Been there; done that. I'm not going out with him again to prove any point to you, Ingrid. If you're so sold out on Demetrius' dignity, then you go out with him."

"If he asked me, I would," Ingrid said without hesitation. "Besides, I'm not asking you to go out with him. I'm telling you to prove that you don't view every man as untrustworthy by naming one that you do. And please don't name your dad. I mean any other man. Name one man that you'd go out with if he asked you."

Jade opened her mouth to take on the dare, but decided that the win wouldn't be worth it. Sure, she could say the one name that would have so easily rolled off of her tongue, but then she'd have to answer probing questions about Hunter and what had taken place in the three days she'd spent in Atlanta. Eventually, she'd tell Ingrid about Hunter and the intimate moment they shared at the airport. But not today.

"Ingrid, I have a client arriving in about fifteen minutes and I need to prepare my office for her. Can we talk about this later? I have to fill you in on my trip back home anyway. How about dinner tonight? My treat."

Jade added the last part for incentive. Ingrid was never known to turn down a meal; especially a free one. She had a healthy appetite, and when it wasn't on her dime, it got even healthier. Jade's strategy worked perfectly.

"Okay, great. And I have to fill you in on church yesterday. I'm writing a letter to the pastor about that psychotic woman that they have manning the door. She's a certified nincompoop and somebody is going to hell just for allowing her to serve as a church usher."

Jade couldn't wait to hear the details of what had happened. She was sure that Ingrid was going to embellish whatever had truly taken place, but Jade needed the laugh. Maybe it would help her forget how close she'd come to death just a few hours earlier. If she could forget the stalking of the still unidentified driver, her time in Atlanta could be remembered with complete fondness.

"I'll meet you in the parking lot after work," Ingrid said as she opened the door to let herself out.

"Okay," Jade answered. Then one by one, she turned off the lamps in her office and began lighting the scented candles in preparation for her first client of the day.

Chapter 27

All morning long, Hunter's office door had been closed. That wasn't just a rarity, it was a first. He wasn't sure how much the staff knew and he didn't care. As usual, Hunter had spoken to the early birds when he walked into the office at 8:00, but he hadn't spoken a word to anyone since.

Kwame and Diane were not due to clock in until nine, and although Hunter was sure that they had arrived on time, he hadn't seen or heard from either one of them. He was sure that they were just as anxious to steer clear of him as he was of them. In his mind, Hunter supposed that they, with bated breath, were wondering what he was going to do with the information that he had uncovered. Hunter had reluctantly decided that he wouldn't fire either one of them, but he had already typed up their warning letters. As far as Hunter was aware, the act of insubordination was a first for both of them. As a businessman he had to be able to separate his professionalism from his personal feelings. Personally, he wanted to dismiss them both and replace them with people who he knew would be happy to take their positions and make the money he paid them. But professionally, it would be unfair. Both Kwame and Diane had given him years of dedicated service, and on a business level, they deserved a second chance.

A knock to Hunter's door caused his muscles to tighten in anticipation. He fully expected to see Kwame on the other side since Hunter had never allowed him to say whatever it was that he desired to say last night as they left the hospital.

"Come in," Hunter said.

"Mr. Greene, are you okay?" It was Lorna. Hunter looked at her standing in his doorway holding a folded newspaper in her hand and looking at him in concern.

Today, she wore a black skirt that stopped just above her knees and a multi-colored silk blouse, whose pattern almost made Hunter's eyes cross. Every time Hunter looked at her and listened to her speak, he thought of Lovita Jenkins from *The Steve Harvey Show.*

"What can I do for you, Lorna," he responded, not addressing her question.

"I just got a call from Diane's sister," Lorna automatically frowned when she said the name. It wasn't out of character. Lorna always frowned when she spoke of Diane.

"What do you mean a call? She's not here?"

"No."

"Is Kwame here?" All Hunter needed was a reason to change the blue slips to pink ones, and if both Kwame and Diane had conspired to be absent today, Hunter wouldn't hesitate to fire both of them.

"He's in his office," Lorna answered.

"Well, where is Diane?"

"She's in the hospital. Her sister said she had an accident last night."

"Is she alright?"

"Yeah, she's okay. Her car got totaled though. When her sister told me what happened I thought it sounded like a major enough accident to make the papers." There was a smile on Lorna's face as she approached Hunter's desk. "I was right. Here it is."

Hunter took the section of the *Atlanta Journal-Constitution* from her hands and scanned the short piece. His eyes narrowed when he read the area where the accident had taken place and they widened when he read the rest. Had it been any other employee who had brought him the news, Hunter might have remarked on what he'd read, but he couldn't with Lorna.

"Her sister said that you could call her at this number if you had any questions or wanted any updates. Diane will probably be released tomorrow."

"Thanks," Hunter said as he took the slip of paper.

"I'm going to lunch now." Lorna's voice was full of satisfaction as she closed the door behind her.

Hunter's eyes immediately went back to the article. Diane's accident had happened less than two miles from his house. She didn't live any where near him, so it baffled him as to why she was headed in his direction at that hour of the night. What puzzled him even more was the portion of the article that defined Diane's alcohol level as barely legal and described her as wearing only a raincoat over an otherwise nude body.

"What on earth?" Hunter said with a scowl.

Just as he was about to take his eyes away from the paper, he saw an article that covered his own accident last night as well. Fortunately for him, the AJC didn't have the names of any of the people involved. The piece simply said that the couple rescued from the vehicle didn't have life-threatening injuries. The accident, it said, was under investigation while the police were still trying to find the driver of the dark-colored pickup that had left the scene.

"Thank God," Hunter whispered. He was sure that knowing that it was him behind the wheel of the SUV that had been forced off of the road would have made the article much longer and it would have been placed in a more prominent place in the paper.

Hunter looked at the telephone number that Lorna had given him and was glad when he heard an answering machine pick up on the other end. He didn't feel like talking to Diane or anyone in her family. However, as her employer, he felt obligated to check on her wellbeing.

"Hello, this is Hunter Greene from the *Atlanta Weekly Chronicles.* I just got word of Diane's unfortunate accident and I wanted to check on her progress. Please inform her to take care of herself and take as many days as necessary for her complete recovery. We wish her well and will see her upon her return. Thank you."

As soon as Hunter hung up, he picked up the

phone again and called a florist to have an arrangement delivered to Diane at Grady Hospital. That was usually something he would ask Lorna to do, but to insure that what was sent was something decent, Hunter decided to send them himself. After he ended the call with the florist, Hunter sat back in his chair and tried to organize all of the thoughts in his head. The past few days had seemed like one long dream. Some parts of it were bad, but others were good.

All morning Hunter had considered calling Jade, but decided not to. He didn't want her to feel that he'd read more into their departure than was really there. To him, Jade's kiss alluded to something that she'd never voiced, but what if it didn't? What if it was just another "thank you" like the one she'd expressed shortly before it? What if he was inflating it to make it into something that he wanted it to be?

Hunter closed his eyes and slowly ran his tongue across his lips, hoping for a hint of the taste that Jade's kiss had left behind this morning. He knew that the flavor he savored was most likely only in his mind, but Hunter didn't care. He relished the thought of holding Jade in his arms and seeing the look in her eyes just before she slipped her hand behind his neck and pulled him down to meet her waiting lips.

At first, her actions stunned him and Hunter had almost pulled away. Instead, he chose to wrap his arms around her waist and deepen the kiss that she'd started. It seemed that he had waited his whole life for that moment. It was a moment that he had fantasized about earlier when he helped Jade climb from the horse she'd been on as he taught her to ride. Hunter recalled the instant that he'd thought of kissing her just before he lowered her feet onto the ground in front of him. The temptation was so strong that it alarmed him. Hunter was almost certain that Jade sensed his desire to share the intimate exchange with her, but she said nothing as she rubbed the coat of the stallion that had provided her with her first horseback-riding experience.

Hunter almost laughed at himself as he took note that his eyes were still closed in a moment of reminiscence. In a way, he felt like a school boy who had just been kissed by the girl of his dreams. But then, as Hunter thought about the time in his life that that had actually happened, he had to withdraw the comparison. He still recalled the moment he'd kissed Sarah. She'd been the object of his affections throughout high school and he had to wait until he was an adult to have the chance to do something he'd dreamed of time and time again as a teenager. Still, as moving as that moment with Sarah was, Hunter couldn't fairly compare it to what had happened with Jade. For him, the kiss with Jade was much more intense and profound. There was a deeper meaning behind it and Hunter wondered if Jade felt the same.

A new knock snapped Hunter from more pleasant thoughts than the last one had. He opened a file on his desk to appear more submerged in business than he actually had been.

"Come in," he said.

When the door opened this time, it was Kwame. The two men locked eyes briefly before Kwame pulled his away. He had already been given permission to enter, so he did, and closed the door behind him.

"Can we talk for a minute?" Kwame asked.

It was a moment that couldn't be avoided forever and Hunter knew it. He'd written up the warning for the part that Kwame played in the unexecuted scheme and eventually he would have to meet with Kwame to discuss it and have him sign it for his employee file. Without speaking, Hunter pointed in the direction of the chair across from his desk and Kwame followed his directions and sat. After clearing his throat—a sound that seemed to echo in the otherwise silent space—Kwame spoke.

"Look, Hunter; I'm not going to make any excuses for what happened. I was wrong and I'm sorry. I was scared and wanted to try and do anything to save both my reputation with my church and my position here. I thought you'd made a selfish decision to impress Jade and it angered me that you'd put her wishes before mine and what I thought was best for the paper. You asked me at the hospital whether or not I would have carried out your orders had you not passed them along to Lorna. To answer that honestly, no, I don't think I would have. I thought running the letters again was an act of suicide and if I could have prevented what I thought would be the professional death of us, I would have.

"But you have to know that this wasn't the return of Thaddeus. I know that you remember my hustling days and a time when I'd do anything to undermine the next man to get what I wanted, but that's not me now. This wasn't the rebirth of a bad man who is up to no good. This was about a good man who made a bad decision. That's all it was, Hunter. I thought I was smarter than you. I thought I knew better than you. And I thought I had a more level head than you had at the time. It's apparent that I was wrong on all counts and I admit that. But I don't want you thinking that you can't trust me ever again because of it. You can. I don't know what else to say, man. All I can say is that I'm sorry and it won't ever happen again."

Hunter sat in silence. He had been all prepared to lay into Kwame about his transgressions. They were at work now and he had the green light to say all the things that he wanted to say about how unethical and unprofessional Kwame's actions had been. Now none of it seemed necessary. A part of Hunter, the part that desired to continue to hold the grudge, wanted to think that Kwame's spiel was rehearsed and insincere. But he knew better. Hunter knew that Kwame meant every word of what he'd said and he also knew that no lecture he could give would make Kwame feel any worse than he already did. He had beaten himself up enough already. Lashes from Hunter would fall against nerves that had been deadened by Kwame's own brutal self-imposed punishment.

"Diane's been in an accident," Hunter said as he pushed the newspaper in front of Kwame and pointed at the article.

At first Kwame looked puzzled by the fact that Hunter hadn't addressed the matter he'd just unloaded his heart about, but news of Diane's accident forced him to look at the paper in front of him.

"She was naked?" Kwame said aloud as his eyes searched through the article. "Why was she naked?"

"I don't know," Hunter shrugged as he gathered the blue warning slips, stood, and put them in a drawer of the file cabinet behind him. "Her sister called and told Lorna about the accident. Why she was dressed in only a raincoat and dress pumps, or why she was even on that end of town, I don't know."

"She was right near you," Kwame observed. "Why was she over there at almost mid . . . ?"

Kwame's voice drifted, causing Hunter to turn from the file and look at him. He could determine from Kwame's dropped jaw that he was putting pieces of a mental puzzle together.

"What do you know?" Hunter asked.

"Uh . . . I don't . . . I'm not . . ."

Hunter slammed the file drawer and leaned across his desk so that his face was within inches to Kwame's. "You just asked me for another chance, Kwame. You just told me that I could trust you. Now here you are trying to hide something else from me. What do you know about this?"

"I'm not trying to hide anything, Hunter. I'm just not sure, that's all.

"Sure about what?"

"Yesterday afternoon after I got home from church, Diane called me. She called me several times as a matter of fact. I told her you had found the email with her note on the back and she was worried about losing her job. She kept trying to get me to come up with a plan to somehow get us out of trouble. I knew that half of what she was saying, she was saying only because she was drunk."

"She was drinking when she called you?"

"Yeah. She was talking like a desperate woman, saying stuff that just didn't make much sense. She started attacking my character and trying to make me feel less of a man for not stepping up to the plate to come up with a solution. I knew we just had to face the music and that's what I told her, but I don't think she wanted to accept that. She was determined to do something to smooth all of this over. I'm just wondering if she thought she could come by your house and . . . *you* know."

Hunter's eyes widened. "And what? Seduce me? You think Diane thought that she could show up at my house naked and convince me to change my mind?"

"Well, I think showing up naked was just the beginning of a much more . . . *involved* plan, but yes, that's what I was thinking. I could be wrong, but in the state of mind that she was in when I last spoke with her, it's possible."

"This is crazy," Hunter whispered as he sank back into his seat, but his voice rose in increments as he continued speaking. "Was there a full moon last night? Has everybody in the city of Atlanta gone mad? First some imbecile tries to kill me and Jade and now I find out that my managing editor got into her vehicle half drunk and half naked to possibly come to my house and what? Work me over into a sexual frenzy to the point that I'd forget what you two conspired to do? What in God's name is going on?"

"I'm not making excuses for either one of us, Hunter, but this whole thing with the letters, the picketing and the backlash from the church was a new level of stress for me. Apparently it affected Diane a lot more than was first thought too. You were the only one that was equipped to handle it on any level, Hunter. It doesn't take a genius to see that Diane and I weren't prepared for it at all."

Hunter rubbed his temples in an effort to massage away the threat of a tension headache. It was good to be talking to Kwame again, but the subject matter wasn't one that Hunter was enjoying. "I need to get out of the office for a while," he said. "As a matter of fact, I think I'm going to take the rest of the day off."

"You? Taking the day off?" Kwame asked in disbelief.

"I'll be working from home," Hunter said, prompting an 'I should have known' look from Kwame. Picking up a box from beside his desk, Hunter added, "I'm going to be pulling more letters for this week's edition. If you need me for anything, give me a call."

Chapter 28

It was Wednesday and Mildred was having a particularly rough day as she folded laundry. In the past, Wednesdays in the Tides home had always meant two things were going to happen. One, Mildred would wash all of the soiled clothes and bed linen; and two, dinner would consist of fried chicken, cabbage, corn bread and macaroni and cheese. For at least the last ten years of their marriage, those two things were automatic. Apparently, in the final weeks of his life, according to her incarcerated son, B.T. had taken on another habit that didn't involve her. He had begun going to the prison to see Jerome every Wednesday as well.

Mildred had tried to totally rid her mind of the last telephone conversation that she'd had with Jerome. It wasn't hard for her to believe that B.T. had doubled his visitations with his youngest son without insisting that she come along. Mildred hated the once-a-week routine of going to see Jerome in prison and B.T. knew how she felt. Mildred told him often. She loved her son, but it sickened her that Jerome had lived such a life that the only way she could see him was by going into such an ungodly place. A part of her was glad that her husband hadn't talked to her about the additional visits. She wouldn't have wanted to go along anyway. But Jerome's claim that B.T. somehow knew that his death was imminent disturbed Mildred.

In the days that had passed since their conversation, Mildred had searched for any recollection of B.T. saying anything that hinted at his untimely death, but she couldn't think of anything. The thought that he would disclose such information to Jerome and not to her was preposterous as far as Mildred was concerned. She had already concluded in her mind that she would confront Jerome about it the next time she visited him. Mildred wanted him to look her in her face and tell the same lie he'd told over the phone. Today would have been a good day to pay him a visit, but Jackson was on the road and wouldn't return until Saturday, and by then she would be in the Georgia Mountains on a much needed spiritual retreat with some of the sisters at New Hope. At first, Mildred had declined the offer to join them, but she needed the change of atmosphere and she needed the prayers of the Women's Ministry. That would mean that she'd have to delay her talk with Jerome until next week. Mildred had never visited the prison alone and she had no intentions of starting to do so today.

"Ten whole years," Mildred said, shaking her head in sadness as she folded the last of the laundry.

It was hard for her to believe that Jerome had spent a whole decade locked up in prison. He had missed so many monumental family moments. The birthday service that New Hope had thrown for B.T. when he turned sixty and Mildred's own sixtieth birthday party that had been given by the family, Jade's graduation from college, Jackson and Renee's wedding, Alexis' birth—Mildred had to sigh when she thought of her granddaughter. Because of Jerome's determination to defy his upbringing, he had never even met his only niece. And the only time he'd seen his sister-in-law was on those rare weeks when she joined them when they visited the prison. All Renee had ever known her brother-in-law to be was a jailbird.

"Lord, I just don't understand it," Mildred said. The weariness in her voice reflected the way she felt. It was an accurate outward display of how her entire being had felt ever since B.T. died. She didn't understand a lot of things.

At the funeral, Jackson spoke powerful words of hope and reassurance to the members of the family. But Mildred hadn't felt much of either of those things since the night she received the horrible news. Every day, it felt as though a piece of her was dying. Some nights, as she knelt beside her bed, she prayed that God would take her in her sleep. When she opened her eyes again, she wanted to see B.T. waiting to embrace her. Mildred constantly dreamed dreams of her walking into heaven and being greeted by the man she loved so dearly. The dreams were so real that there were mornings when she woke up thinking she was dead—or that B.T. was alive. Whatever the case, they were together again and it *felt* good. Mildred had lived to see her children grow up to be adults and two out of three had grown up to be assets to society. If dying now would mean that she could share a home with her husband again, Mildred would choose death over a day-to-day existence without her beloved B.T.

"If only I had gone to the hardware store with you that night. I would have been with you in the accident. I would have been with you now."

Mildred looked up into the ceiling as she whispered the words and tears drained from the corners of her eyes. Nobody knew the pain that remained in her severed heart. She tried to remain strong in the face of the church members and keep her composure when her children were around. But in moments like this, when she was all alone, Mildred sometimes allowed her true emotions to flow freely. Doing so didn't necessarily make her feel happier, but it made her feel better.

Using unnecessary care, Mildred opened her drawers and put her folded clothes away. Half of the dresser drawers were empty now that she had boxed all of B.T.'s clothes and stored them away. Next, she gathered the small stack of towels and headed for the bathroom to put them in the linen closet. The blue set that B.T. always used hadn't needed washing in two months.

Tears broke as Mildred was reminded once again that she was a widow. She buried her face in the thickness of one of the towels in the stack and wept heavier than she had in weeks. Mildred knew that she needed to talk to someone; but who? Jackson was on the road and contacting him during this time of the day would be impossible. She loved her daughter-in-law, but they had never had the type of relationship wherein Mildred shared her heart.

As much as she could, Mildred dried her tears with the towel, put the stack away and walked into her living room. She picked up the phone and dialed, only to get Jade's voice mail. It was what she expected. Mildred knew that her daughter's days were filled with counseling grief-stricken women, and in the middle of the day, she would be in a session. Mildred chose not to leave a message. Instead, she walked into the kitchen to pour a glass of water.

The cool liquid sent a blanket of refreshment down Mildred's throat but did little to comfort her. The water couldn't drown the real issue that haunted her. Knowing that both Jackson and Jade were out of reach made Mildred realize even more how lonely she was. Since B.T. was gone it almost seemed that no one needed her anymore and that made her feel like a burden rather than useful. Mildred knew they loved her, but both of her children were grown and had their own lives and careers to keep them busy.

Both? You have **three** *children, Mildred.*

The glass in Mildred's hand crashed to the floor and she turned quickly, pressing her back against the door of the refrigerator. The voice was audible and came from a place very near her. At least, that's the way it sounded. And to add to her terror and cause her breaths to come in short, quick pants, was the fact that the voice sounded far too familiar. It sounded like B.T.'s.

Mildred clutched her chest and prayed in silence that her heart would slow its racing. Her eyes scanned the space around her, but nothing seemed out of sorts. There was no one there and the voice that had sounded so close and so near was now silent. Still, Mildred's knees buckled and she remained attached to the fridge, praying that her legs didn't completely give way.

Several minutes passed before Mildred felt comfortable enough to let go of her crutch and stand on her own. Reaching for the broom in the corner beside the refrigerator, Mildred began slowly sweeping the glass into a pile. Her hands shook as she struggled to move past the brief, but frightening experience. With each stroke of the broom, Mildred's mind drifted farther away from her task. She recalled numerous times that B.T. had reminded her that she had two sons. Mildred had never forgotten about Jerome nor had she disowned him—at least, not in words. But as many times as she had scolded B.T. for the needless reminders, Mildred knew that her behavior justified every one of them.

"Actions speak louder than words" was one of Mildred's mother's favorite adages and Mildred had fallen victim. She thought of all those times when B.T. had to nearly beg her to go with him to visit their son in prison and the many times that she'd sighed heavily and rolled her eyes when she heard the operator on the other end of her phone line telling her that she had a call from Phillips State Prison. And Mildred cringed when she thought of the times when she'd looked at the caller ID and allowed the voicemail to pick up so that she wouldn't have to speak to her incarcerated son. Mildred knew that in her own way, she'd turned her back on Jerome for the mistakes that he'd made, and finally admitting it to herself, on top of all of her other grief, was almost too much to stomach.

"Lord have mercy on my soul!" she wailed through a new batch of tears. "I'm so sorry, Lord. I'm so sorry!" Dropping the broom, Mildred covered her face with her hands and wept until there seemed to be no tears left.

Actions speak louder than words, she reminded herself.

As she gathered herself and headed to her room to change from the duster into something more presentable, Mildred reasoned that now was the time to swallow her bitter, unwarranted pride.

Chapter 29

"I don't understand the problem. Why don't you just call him?"

Jade looked across the table at her bewildered best friend. Yesterday, Jade had told Ingrid most of what happened during her long weekend in Atlanta, but it wasn't until today, when they sat down to eat lunch, that she added the intimate detail that she'd purposefully left out before.

"I'm not going to call him, Ingrid. The woman isn't supposed to be the first to call. It's an unwritten rule. And my mother taught me that a woman should let the man take the lead. She never indicated that I should ever be the one to call a man first."

"I'll betcha she didn't ever tell you to be the first one to kiss a man either, but you did that with no problem."

Jade took a moment to wipe her mouth with her napkin. It was more so a stall tactic to give her time to think of what she could say in her own defense. "I told you that I wasn't sure that I initiated the kiss."

"If you're not sure, then you did. I mean, don't get me wrong. I don't think there's anything wrong with a woman making the first move, but if you're going to be all adamant about a woman not being the aggressor, then you don't need to be giving away kisses without first getting an invitation from the man. And since you already did that, then maybe you should be the one to pick up the phone and call him too."

For days Jade had been trying to hide the confusion she felt in not hearing from Hunter. It had been three days since she boarded her flight back home and she was beginning to wonder what he thought of her. Jade was all but certain that she'd been the one to make the first move when they kissed at the airport on Monday and she was already beginning to regret a moment that had at first seemed special.

Jade still remembered the look in Hunter's eyes when their lips parted ways. He looked stunned, but not at all displeased. She had enjoyed their brief display of affection and had spent many hours, both awake and asleep, reliving the moment. But now Jade wasn't sure what to think. Hunter's silence was deafening. The possibility that he thought she was too forward or overly aggressive haunted Jade. What if he defined her actions as unseemly or downright disrespectful? On the flight back to Virginia, Jade searched for a reason to revisit Atlanta, but now she hoped that nothing would happen that required her to.

"Are you just going to not say anything to him?" Ingrid asked.

"What's there to say? Should I apologize?"

Ingrid laughed. "Girl, you're a trip! What would you be apologizing for?"

"For crossing the line."

"Look boo," Ingrid said, "if Hunter Greene has been supporting you the way you say he has, you haven't even come close to crossing the line. As a matter of fact, you're too far away from the line to even see it, let alone cross it. I'm all for believing that there are brothers out there who just have genuinely good hearts and will go the extra mile just for the sake of helping a sister out. But that's not the vibe I get from what you've told me about this guy."

"But he *does* have a genuinely good heart. He's been helping me since the beginning when even my *best friend* thought I was losing my mind."

"That just proves my point," Ingrid said, ignoring the words that Jade chose to stress. "From all of this stuff that you've been telling me over the last couple of days, I think he was hooked at 'hello'."

Jade rolled her eyes to the ceiling and shook her head, but the whole time she wondered if Ingrid was right. Jade could only speak for herself, but she knew she'd had an immediate attraction to Hunter. Whether or not the fascination was mutual, she wasn't sure; but it was true that he'd remained in her corner even when he had doubts and when the fate of his business hung in the balance.

"Girl, that man almost lost his business over you," Ingrid said as though she was reading Jade's thoughts. "Your Mr. Greene has been tried in the fire and has come forth as pure gold. I don't think he could be tried any more than that."

"You wanna bet?" Jade said as she took a sip from her glass.

Ingrid's mouth didn't move, but her eyes demanded more information. Jade pointed to the small dark bruise on the side of her forehead. "This scar came from an accident that we had while he was transporting me to the airport."

"I know. You told me."

"But I didn't tell you the whole story," Jade said, gaining Ingrid's full attention once more. Jade brought her voice to a whisper and said, "I think somebody was trying to kill us."

"What?"

Jade placed her finger to her lips and made a shushing sound. As she told Ingrid the whole story, Jade had to quiet her friend more than once, stopping Ingrid from making an outburst of some kind.

Once she finished, Ingrid asked, "Did you call the police?"

"Yeah. They were looking for the truck, but we couldn't give all that great of a description and the driver could be long gone by now. I just kept thinking how Daddy died in almost the same type of accident that we were in. We survived, but he didn't. Mother said he'd gone to the hardware store that night to buy some stuff to do some improvements around the house. He'd also stopped by the gas station and filled an empty gas can with fuel to use in the lawn mower that weekend. All of those chemicals and flammables he was transporting are all that made the difference in his outcome and ours."

"You still don't think it was an accident, do you?" Ingrid asked.

"I never have; you know that. But after Sunday night's ordeal, I'm more convinced than ever. I mean, the whole story may never come out. Maybe Dad's death will always be considered an accident, but I'll never believe it."

A brief silence passed between them and then Ingrid asked, "What reason would anybody have to kill your father, Jade? I'm not saying you don't make a good point; I'm just playing devil's advocate here. Is there a reason that someone would want your father dead? Did he have any enemies that you all knew of?"

"No, but neither do I. I don't know of any enemies that I have and I don't know of a reason that someone would want me dead, but apparently somebody does. And I think that whoever it was that ran Hunter and me off of the highway did so because they think we got too close."

"To each other?"

"No silly," Jade said with a scowl. "To the truth. The whole city of Atlanta was fighting mad about Hunter putting those letters back in the paper, but in last week's issue, when he completely revealed his heart in his editorial letter, it calmed everything. It was like some kind of miracle and I don't think the person who killed Daddy was counting on that. I think the killer was banking on the fact that the city's disapproval would either stop the letters or shut down the *Atlanta Weekly Chronicles* all together. Either way, it would have silenced the mission that Hunter and I are on. When Dad's church and the folks around the city didn't kill our message, *somebody* decided that they'd kill the messengers instead."

"Umph," Ingrid grunted after swallowing a gulp of tea and taking a quick look around the restaurant. "I might need to stop hanging with you then 'cause I can't be getting killed. I don't look good in black and those folks at the funeral home don't ever put your makeup on right. And you know the beauticians that do dead folks' hair are all old ladies. They have your hair looking all jacked up with one of those dos from the eighties. All because of you, I'm gonna be laying up in some casket looking like some ashy-faced sixty-year-old while psycho-usher is walking latecomers up to the front of the church and making the folks who got there early move down to make room for them. Girl, fooling with you, there will be a fight breaking out at Gospel Tabernacle. First good fight I could have witnessed in years and I'll be too dead to enjoy it."

Jade laughed at the shallow details that her friend chose to highlight, but inside she was still concerned. Whoever it was that had launched the vicious attack on Hunter and her was still on the loose. But what was currently most prevalent on her mind was that she still hadn't heard from Hunter. She had been certain that he was just as drawn to her as she was to him. How could she have ever read him so wrong? How would she ever face him again?

Chapter 30

"Congratulations, Mr. Tides. Your parole is hereby granted."

Jerome had thanked the members of the board, promised to never make them regret their decision and was escorted back to his cell to gather his meager belongings. His release was immediate and he should have been turning flips, but Jerome felt as though he was in a daze. Nothing about the last three days seemed real to him.

Wednesday, his mother had dropped by for an unexpected visit, and for the first time in years, they talked . . . *really* talked. It hadn't been an easy visit for Jerome and he knew it was hard for his mother as well. Years of disappointment and frustration lay between them. Blame and accusations were tossed from one to the other followed by the admittance of mistakes and misgivings. Some of the things that Mildred said to Jerome were painful, but he accepted them realizing that for the most part, they were also true. His mother listened as he shared with her all of the things that he had done in his life, some of which she'd had no idea. Jerome knew that it was difficult for her to sit and listen when he explained his rebellion.

Jerome told her how he had wanted nothing to do with Christianity because of all the pain and poverty that they had endured. In Jerome's mind, his father was praying to a God who didn't care about him or his family. To Jerome, being a Christian meant being boxed into a lifestyle that allowed no time for recreation. As children, all they'd ever done was go to church. Jackson wasn't even allowed to play in football games that fell on the nights that church services were scheduled. Jerome hated the demand that church placed on his family. It meant being picked on and ridiculed by schoolmates and he rebelled so that he wouldn't have to endure being ostracized by those that he longed to be accepted by. Back then, it was far more important for him to meet the approval of his friends than his family. As he spoke, Jerome swallowed back the tears that pressed against the back of his eyes, but Mildred made no attempt to hide hers. Water flowed freely down her cheeks and Jerome tried, with little success, to comfort her.

When all was said and done, Jerome felt purged and relieved. Much of what he told his mother had already been shared with B.T., but having said it to the parent who he seemed to have disappointed the most made a world of difference.

"Come on church boy." Jerome snapped from

his daze and turned to see his least favorite compound officer standing in the doorway of the cell that had been his home for far too long.

"It ain't like this is a penthouse and you're Donald Trump," the man said with a laugh. "If I was as lucky as you, I'd be high-tailing it out of here so fast that all anybody would feel was the air I stirred up when I passed them."

The CO made a good point. All Jerome had was a few books and some copies of the AWC that he'd saved for the sake of reading the letters that kept the spirit of his father alive. It wasn't the gathering of his belongings that had him moving in slow motion, it was his thoughts. Jerome had known for weeks that his parole hearing would be today, but he had been so afraid that his parole would be rejected that he hadn't told any of his family of his possible release. And even in the event that his parole was granted, Jerome didn't know that he'd be released the same morning of his hearing. He thought it would take a few days to get the paperwork together. That's the way he'd seen it happen for fellow inmates time and time again. Parole would be approved, but their release would be gradual.

This unexpected wave of events had forced him to try and call his mother, but got no answer. When he called Jackson's house, Renee answered and told him that she would get in touch with Jade. Jerome didn't see how Jade could help from Virginia, but when he called Renee again to follow up on the plan that had been set in motion, he was told that he would be released into Hunter Greene's care. Although all Jerome knew of Hunter was what his sister had told him, he had no qualms with the arrangement. He was just glad to be leaving.

Without saying anything to the CO, Jerome brushed past him when he walked out of his cell. Rocky was headed his way and Jerome stopped and waited for him to join them at the mouth of the cell that they had shared.

"So you out, dog? I mean, right now?" Rocky asked.

"Yeah," Jerome said, pressing his closed fist against Rocky's. "I was surprised too. You take care of yourself, man. Like I told you last night, don't let these guys mess you up and have you fighting. It ain't worth it. In here, it takes a lot more strength to use your brain than your fist."

"Yeah, but a fist will knock a nigga out much faster," Rocky said with a laugh.

Jerome laughed with him. He and Rocky had chatted back and forth to each other for much of last night. They stopped when one of the inmates in a neighboring cell swore threats at them through the darkness and ordered them to shut up. Rocky invited the man to come over and make good on his threats, but Jerome kept silent. He was only a few hours away from his hearing and if obeying the man's rude command meant that he could go home, Jerome was more than willing to oblige.

"I can't make no promises about being good and all," Rocky said, "but I'll do the best I can."

"Your best is all God requires." Jerome was taken aback by his own words. The new prayer life that he adopted in the past few days was already having an effect on him.

Rocky shook his head and released a short laugh. "Have a good life, dude."

"You say that like we won't see each other anymore. I'll be back to check on a brotha."

"You better than me. You turned out to be cool and all, but if I was busting out of this joint, none of y'all wouldn't see me no more."

"I won't hold that against you," Jerome said with a laugh. "But I've got to come back. Not just to see you, but to see some of the other cats too. I think God is letting me out of here for a reason. I made a promise to Him and to my daddy's memory and I gotta keep it."

"I hear ya," Rocky said.

Jerome offered his hand and Rocky accepted and shook it firmly. "See you later, Rocky."

"I ain't going nowhere for at least another five; so take your time." Rocky laughed when he said the words, but Jerome was certain that he saw sadness in his eyes just before turning to follow the guard.

As Jerome walked past the cells that he'd walked past many times before, he felt mixed emotions. He was elated to finally be able to be free of the walls that had held him in confinement for the last ten years, but Jerome also felt a sudden fear of the unknown. For years, this had been home. He wondered how he'd even function on the outside. He had his GED, but all he was really skilled at was cleaning toilets. Reality was frightening.

As he rounded the corner, Jerome passed faces he'd seen many times before and some that he'd never noticed. Those must have been fairly new inmates and Jerome felt a sense of sympathy for them. In prison, every day felt like a week and nobody could truly be trusted. In ten years he'd not made any real friends. Until he and Rocky connected just a few days ago, Jerome had been pretty much a loner.

Instinctively, Jerome turned and looked behind him. He could still see Rocky standing at the cell door, watching. He turned back around and continued to walk. All around him, he heard calls from inmates who took advantage of their last chance to needle him with the "church boy" taunt. Jerome smiled. Those things that had mattered in the past no longer had the same effect on him. For the first time in his life, he was proud to be his father's son. Holding his head high, Jerome set his sights on the doors that waited just a few feet ahead. They were his access to freedom.

Things hadn't quite returned to normal at the *Atlanta Weekly Chronicles*, but they were getting there. Today, Hunter and Kwame were sharing lunch together for the first time since the fallout and it had afforded them the opportunity to have their first heart-to-heart talk. They probably never would have talked about what had happened had it been up to Hunter. Kwame had apologized, he'd finally been able to forgive him, and in Hunter's mind, that was enough. But Kwame was having trouble letting the issue rest and Hunter reasoned that it was because Kwame hadn't yet forgiven himself.

"Are we cool, Hunter?" Kwame asked.

"For the umpteenth time, Kwame; we're cool. Now just drop it."

"I just don't want you seeing me as the old Kwame."

"You mean as Thaddeus?"

Kwame sighed. "Yeah, him. I'm just so disappointed in myself, you know? If anybody had told me that I would have tried to be disloyal in my position, I would have called them a liar."

"Like Peter did when Jesus told him that he'd betray Him?"

"Unfortunately, that's a good analogy."

"So what do you want me to do, Kwame?"

"I don't know. I guess it feels like I'm getting off too easy. I think I'd just feel better if you hauled off and punched me in the mouth or something. I feel like I owe you."

"That's probably because you do," Hunter said. "But like Jesus, I'm trying to see your mistreatment as sinful ignorance and let you off the hook."

Kwame sighed again, dropping his eyes to his plate. When he didn't respond, Hunter continued.

"Look, Kwame; what's done is done. I'm not happy about what you and Diane did and to be honest, I do feel like I have to be more watchful than I used to be. I mean, I used to think that I could pass any responsibility on to you and not even give it a second thought as to whether it would be carried out like I asked. I thought we had each other's backs like that. My level of trust has been lowered and I can't lie and say it hasn't. But I need for us to move on from this place. You screwed up, you've owned up to it, you've apologized and I've accepted. It's going to take some time for everything to be on the same level as before, but I'm working on it. You don't need to apologize anymore nor do you have to fear for your job or our friendship. We're cool."

The third sigh from Kwame was the heaviest of all, but Hunter didn't give him a chance to reply before he began speaking again.

"I mean it, Kwame. I don't want to keep revisiting this topic. All the things that you think I felt about you and this whole situation, I'll admit that they are probably all true. I was hurt, I was angry and I felt betrayed; especially by you, and I think I deserved better than that. Kwame, I believed in you when nobody else would give you the time of day. I put my money where my mouth was when I said I believed you were ready to make a change, man. Then I proved even further that I trusted you when I put you in a respected position at the company that I built from the ground up. All of that and then you still go and try to stab me in the back? Yeah I was mad and I had every right to be.

"But a very dear friend recently made me see that I couldn't judge your whole being on that one mistake. The good you've done over the years had to count for something, and when I put it all on the scale, your good far outweighed this farce. I didn't want to accept that at first because at the time nothing would have pleased me more than to fire you and watch you have to try and see when the next person would come along and give you the same opportunity that I did."

Hunter watched Kwame's eyes drop at his harsh words. If Kwame had only let the subject drop as Hunter had been trying to convince him to do for the past two days, he wouldn't have had to hear

Hunter's repressed thoughts. Kwame had asked for it as far as Hunter was concerned, and now he'd have to deal with it.

"I finally got to the point that I could forgive you and chance rebuilding my trust," Hunter said. "But like I said, if I'm going to be able to do that, I need you to do it too. We both have to work together to make this happen. Even when Diane returns on Monday, I'm not going through this with her. I'm already over it. She was never my friend anyway, so all she has to do is show me that I can trust her to do her job. That's all I pay her for and that's all I expect from her. With you, I expect more because our relationship goes beyond business. But I still don't want to keep rehashing the same stuff. I'm not saying to act like it never happened, I'm just saying let's move on."

Kwame returned Hunter's stare and shook his head in agreement. But just as he was preparing to comment, the ringing of Hunter's cell phone interrupted them. Hunter pulled the phone from the pocket of his suit jacket and paused when he saw Jade's office number displayed on his ID screen. He'd been impatiently waiting to hear from her, but had almost given up hope. Hunter wished Jade's timing had been better though. He would have much rather spoken with her privately.

"Hunter Greene," he answered.

"Hi, Hunter. It's Jade. How are you?"

"I'm fine. It's good to finally hear from you. How are you?"

Jade paused and then said, "You say that like you were expecting a call from me."

"Expecting might be too strong of a word. But I was hoping that you would call. I mean, by no means were you obligated, but considering . . ."

"Considering what?"

Hunter paused and looked across the table at Kwame who was clearly trying to figure out who he was speaking with. Excusing himself from the table, Hunter walked out the front door of the restaurant and stood a few feet from the entranceway.

"Do I have to remind you? Was it really that insignificant?" Although no one stood near him, Hunter spoke in low tones.

"Insignificant?" Jade sounded insulted. "No it wasn't insignificant but after I didn't hear from you I thought that maybe you were upset with me. I figured that maybe you were offended."

"Jade, you kissed me. How in the world could I find that offensive?"

"I don't know. I just thought I'd done something wrong. Why didn't you call?"

"Because I didn't want to seem pushy," Hunter said. "I'll admit it's been a while for me, so when I didn't hear from you, I thought maybe you tasted the rust."

Both of them shared a laugh and then Jade said, "Actually I would have guessed that you got a lot of practice."

Hunter couldn't control his grin. Instinctively, he rubbed his finger across his lips in remembrance. "To be honest," he said, "I wasn't sure what to make of the kiss and I didn't want to be presumptuous. I knew what I wanted it to mean, but I wasn't sure what it actually meant."

Jade remained quiet.

"So, are you going to tell me what it meant or should I just keep guessing?" Hunter probed.

In the silence that followed he could feel tension on both ends of the phone. But this time, it was *good* tension. His own heart pounded in anticipation of her answer.

"Can we talk later tonight?" Jade asked.

"Sure." Hunter didn't want to wait, but he didn't want to pressure her either. "Should I call you or will you call me?"

"I'm coming back to Atlanta on a late flight."

"Tonight?"

"Yeah. That's the purpose of my calling you. I need your help. I'm in a bind and I've exhausted every other avenue that I could think of. I really hate to bother you with this but . . ."

"You're not bothering me, Jade. What's the matter? What do you need?" Hunter's mind immediately went to financial matters. Jade's voice now sounded strained and he was all but certain that it was the pressure of having to ask him for money that made her seem so burdened.

"It's my brother."

"Jackson? What happened?"

"No, not Jackson. Jerome. He was granted parole today."

"Really? That's wonderful, Jade." The good news made Hunter even more baffled as to why she didn't sound cheerful.

"I know. But Renee said that Jackson won't be home until Saturday evening and Mother left this morning for a retreat with the Women's Ministry at the church. She won't be back at home until late Saturday as well. Jerome is kind of stranded right now and policy won't allow the prison to release him on his own accord. He has to have someone there to pick him up or have a reserved room in a halfway house. Renee and Jerome are virtually strangers and she doesn't feel comfortable picking him up and having him at the house with her and the baby without Jackson being there. And I know you don't know him any better than she does and I don't want to inconvenience you but . . ."

"I'll go and pick him up," Hunter said, wanting to do whatever was necessary to calm the growing anxiety that he heard in Jade's voice. "It's not a problem. I'll do it."

Jade's relief was detectable as she thanked him. "I'll be there as quickly as I can. My flight will land around ten tonight. Jerome is basically homeless right now and I'm going to have to try and make accommodations for him, at least until Mother gets back home. After that, we'll have to play it by ear. I don't know how she'll feel about him moving in with her."

"Okay," Hunter said. "I'm sure I can find something for him to do at the paper for the rest of the afternoon. We're getting ready to print this weekend's issue. We're shorthanded by one employee in the pressroom today, so if he doesn't mind working a little bit . . ."

"He won't," Jade assured him. After a brief pause, she said, "Thank you."

"I'm happy to do it, Jade. I'll head out there right now, and don't worry about him eating or whatever. I'll make sure he gets what he needs. He can hang out with Malik and me at my place. You just concentrate on getting here. I'll take care of everything."

"Thank you so much, Hunter," Jade repeated. "I don't know how I'll ever repay you."

Hunter smiled as he closed his phone and headed back inside where Kwame patiently waited. He tossed enough money on the table to cover the check and the tip. "I've got to run."

"What do you mean you have to run? We rode together," Kwame pointed out.

"Then, *we* have to run."

"Okay, but I was going to take care of the check."

"It's not a problem. Besides, I might need to cash in on that desire you still have to repay the debt I'd written off."

"Name it," Kwame said as he stood and began taking quick steps to catch up with Hunter. "Where are we going?"

"To Phillips State Prison to pick up Jerome Tides. He's been released."

Chapter 31

The walk from her terminal to baggage claims at Hartsfield-Jackson Airport had become very familiar to Jade. Over the past two months, she'd made the trek as many times as she had in the past two years. She was excited about the chance to see Hunter again and even more excited to see her brother as a free man. But the frequent trips combined with her busy workload at the office were beginning to drain her.

"Hey baby sis!"

Jade turned and had to blink twice before she was certain that she wasn't hallucinating. When she realized that it really was Jerome who was walking toward her, Jade dropped her shoulder bag and broke into a sprint. Jerome practically caught her in mid-air as she dove into his arms.

"Jerome!" she exclaimed through a teary-eyed grin. "Oh my God; you're here! I didn't know you'd be here," she said, wrapping her arms around his neck and squeezing him tightly.

Jerome laughed and spun her around before lowering her to the floor in a standing position. "Well, that was a welcome almost worth spending ten years on lockdown. Come on and let's get your luggage."

Together, with their arms wrapped around each other's waists, Jade and Jerome strolled back to the area where Jade had abandoned her bag and then they joined other passengers of the flight Jade had just disembarked who were standing, waiting for the bags they'd checked to make their appearance on the metal conveyer.

"It is so good to see you," Jade said, tightening her grip around her brother. "Did everything go well with your release?"

"Yeah," Jerome said, looking around the airport as if he'd never seen one before. "Man, Jade; the whole world has changed since I saw it last. Atlanta was always busy, but I've never seen so many cars, houses and businesses in my life."

Jade laughed at her brother who sounded like a teenager who had just migrated from farm life into the city. "You've got a lot of catching up to do, huh?"

"One day at a time, sis. I'm trying not to be in a hurry 'cause when I first walked out of those prison doors, I was completely overwhelmed. I didn't expect to be like that, but I was. Hunter and Kwame were cool though. They didn't look at me funny once. Those cats in the jail would have had a field day if they had seen me crying like that, but your friends were real cool and I pre'shate that."

Jade had been so overjoyed at seeing her brother

that she'd totally forgotten about Hunter. "Where is Hunter? Did he bring you here?"

"He's back there somewhere," Jerome said. He was just about to turn to point Jade in Hunter's direction when the alarm on the conveyer sounded, signaling that the luggage was about to be delivered.

Jade turned slowly and scanned the room as much as the crowd would allow. It took several minutes, but she finally spotted Hunter, standing beside Malik as the boy sat in a vacant spot on one of the few inside benches provided for those who had to wait on their transportation to arrive. Malik was busy playing with what looked like a GameBoy, but Hunter's eyes were fixed on Jade. She could only imagine the thoughts going through his head. He'd been kind enough not only to give her brother a ride from prison, but also to entertain him all day until she could get there. From the distance where Jade stood, she couldn't read the expression on his face, but her active imagination saw locked jaws and cold eyes.

Jade turned to her brother. "Jerome, can you get my luggage when it comes through? It's only one suitcase and it's black leather, just like this one. I have a white ribbon tied to the handle so that it will stand out in case someone else happens to have luggage just like mine."

"Sure. I'll get it," Jerome replied.

"Thanks. I'll be right over here with Hunter and Malik."

Jade was nervous as she walked the distance that separated her from Hunter. The closer she got to him, the less his expression looked like the one she'd conjured in her mind, but Jade was still ashamed of the way she had behaved.

"Hey Ms. Jade," Malik said, jumping between Jade and Hunter and embracing her around the waist.

"Hi, Malik," she replied.

"You still got the bump on your head?"

"It's much smaller now," she said with a smile as she stooped to give him a clearer view.

Malik returned her smile and then retreated back to his chair to again focus on his game. In slow motion, Jade took her eyes from the boy and brought them to Hunter. To her surprise, there was no sign of the disappointment that she expected to see in his eyes. Instead, she saw admiration and approval. Jade felt the blood flush from her face.

"Hi," Hunter said with a slight smile.

"Hi."

"Well, you dropped your luggage, screamed and jumped around your brother's neck and then you came over here, grinned and gave Malik a nice little hug. I admit that I want a little more than what you gave him," Hunter said, tossing a look at Malik, "but as much as I'd like you to throw yourself at me, I don't expect to get as much as you gave Jerome. But can a brotha get some love?"

With a wide grin breaking across her lips, Jade stepped directly in front of Hunter. He reached out and pulled her closer, wrapping his arms around her waist. As Jade inhaled his fragrance, she placed her arms around his neck and closed her eyes.

"I'm sorry I didn't call. I missed you," Hunter whispered.

Jade could feel the hairs on her body stand upright as his warm breath caressed her ear. "I missed you too," she replied.

Hunter ran his fingers through the thick waves of her hair. Jade had wanted to straighten and curl it before coming but didn't have time. Hunter's next words made her happy she hadn't.

"I love your hair like this; when you wear it natural," he complimented. "You're so beautiful."

His admiring comments brought a smile to Jade's lips as their eyes locked. She wanted nothing more than to have Hunter kiss her and she was almost certain that it would have been his next move had Jerome not interrupted the moment.

"What all you got in here, girl?"

Jade broke into laughter when she turned to see Jerome approaching with her shoulder bag in one hand and her suitcase in tow in the other. Hunter reached out and relieved him of the rolling suitcase and Jade grabbed Malik's hand as they walked out of the airport en route to Hunter's car. Jerome and Malik climbed in the backseat and Jade walked to the rear of the car where Hunter was placing her suitcase in the trunk.

"I can't thank you enough for this, Hunter," she said, touching his cheek with her hand.

Hunter looked at Jade and she felt as though she was being hypnotized. His eyes were smoldering like that of a volcanic rock, failing at its attempt to hold back the heat that was inside. "I think you can," he whispered.

"Daddy, can we stop by Chick-Fil-A?" Malik called as he opened the back door.

His voice echoed in the parking garage, causing both Jade and Hunter to flinch. Jade stepped back and allowed Hunter to close the trunk before he walked around to open the car door for her.

"Yeah, sport," he said to Malik as Jade climbed into the passenger seat. "We'll grab something."

Another moment had been broken, but only for a while. During the ride from the airport to Stone Mountain, stolen looks were frequently exchanged between Jade and Hunter between conversations shared with their backseat guests.

"I made a reservation at the Hampton Inn for me and Jerome," Jade said to Hunter as they turned onto Mountain Industrial Boulevard.

Hunter glanced in her direction, but didn't respond. As promised, he stopped and bought food for everyone, and by the time they made it to his ranch, everyone had finished their meals.

"You have an early day tomorrow with your friends," Hunter told Malik. "Go on and get your bath so you can turn in."

The weariness could be seen in Malik's eyes and he offered no resistance to his father's command. "Okay. Good night, Daddy."

"Goodnight, sport," Hunter said, kissing his son's forehead.

After hugging Jade and saying goodnight to Jerome, Malik bounded up the stairs and headed to the guest bathroom. Jade looked at Hunter as he told her and Jerome to make themselves comfortable and offered them both something to drink. When they declined, Hunter sat on the couch adjacent to the sofa they shared and used the remote to turn on the television. For an hour they sat, watching reruns of *Frazier* and *Will & Grace*, and at 12:30, Jerome began a light pattern of snoring.

"Hunter," Jade whispered. "I think we'd better get to the hotel. Jerome is tired and I know you are too. We don't want to keep you up."

Hunter stood from the sofa. "You're not keeping me up, Jade." He walked toward Jerome and shook him. "Wake up, man. Let me show you to your room for the night."

"Was I sleep?" Jerome asked as he stood and stretched.

Hunter chuckled. "Yeah. Come on."

"A'ight," Jerome said as he bent down and kissed Jade's cheek. "I can't believe I get to sleep in a real bed. I may not ever wake up. Goodnight, sis."

Jade managed to return his bedtime farewell, but she watched in shock as Hunter led her brother up the stairs. Now her mind raced. Hunter had given the guest bedroom to Jerome and Malik had been sent to his own quarters. That left one bedroom: Hunter's. Jade's heart pounded as she wondered what plans Hunter had for her. The look in his eyes as they stood at the trunk of the car and his remark that implied that he knew ways that Jade could thank him, all came rushing back in Jade's mind.

"Oh no," she whispered. "Please don't be like this, Hunter. Please don't."

Jade's body stiffened when she heard Hunter descending the steps. Without thinking, she closed her legs and squeezed her knees together. She'd been excited about being able to spend time with

Hunter, but this wasn't what she had in mind. When Hunter made his new residence on the space beside her instead of where he'd been sitting earlier, Jade wished she'd accepted that earlier offered drink. She needed anything to moisten her mouth.

"You ready to talk now?" Hunter asked, taking her hand in his.

"Why did you take Jerome upstairs?" Jade blurted. "I told you I reserved a room at the hotel."

Not detecting her apprehension, Hunter brought the back of her hand to his lips and kissed it twice before looking into her eyes. "It made no sense for you to spend money on a hotel room when you could stay here."

"But . . ."

"Jade, when I said I'd take care of everything, that meant *everything*—including you," Hunter said, bringing her hand to his lips once more.

Snatching her hand away, Jade jumped to her feet and pulled down her skirt. Her hands trembled as she began speaking. "Okay, Hunter. Maybe I owe you an apology. Maybe I came on too strong and sent the wrong message when I kissed you last weekend and maybe I did the wrong thing by asking you to go out of your way to accommodate Jerome until I got here. I didn't mean to make you think that when I got here I'd be spending the night with you. I mean, I admit that I really care for you. I mean, I like you a great deal. But this . . . this isn't me. I don't do this kind of thing and I'm sorry if I did anything to make you think otherwise. Please, just take me to the hotel."

When Jade finished her ramble, the room seemed to be in complete silence in spite of the sounds coming from the television screen behind her. She stared at the floor, not knowing how Hunter was going to respond but hoping this wouldn't be the beginning of a bitter end. She knew Hunter loved the Lord and he'd been nothing but respectful and courteous to her over the weeks that had led to their ultimate bond. She didn't want to lose what they had, but she couldn't do this.

"You think I'm trying to sleep with you?"

Those were the words that finally broke the silence between them and they brought Jade's eyes from the hardwood floor to the man who had spoken them. Hunter's arms were folded in front of him and he looked at her with disbelief.

"Is that what you think of me, Jade? You think I'm trying to get you into bed?"

Jade was so ashamed that she couldn't speak. In her mind all signs pointed in that direction, but she had misread Hunter once more.

"How shallow do you think I am?" Hunter asked.

"I'm sorry."

It was all that Jade could say and she knew immediately that her apology fell on deaf ears. Hunter stood and then walked into his bedroom where he retrieved his car keys. Grabbing the handle to Jade's rolling suitcase, he walked past her to the door that led to his covered carport.

"I'll meet you at the car," were the only words he said to her.

The door didn't exactly slam behind him, but it closed with additional force. Jade stood motionless and full of regret. Why had she jumped to such a rash conclusion? How could she have indirectly accused Hunter of wanting to take advantage of her?

When are you going to stop treating all men as if their names were George?

Jade had been asked that question by Ingrid, and each time it was presented, Jade had denied its validity. This moment was her wakeup call. Until she'd accused Hunter and seen in his eyes the look of a man whose honor had been attacked, Jade hadn't realized how right Ingrid had been. Using her bare hands, Jade brushed away the moisture from her cheeks and dried her hands with a single stroke down the sides of her skirt. She took the slow steps of a woman three times her age and opened the door. From the doorway where she stood, Jade could see Hunter sitting behind the wheel of his cranked car. He had to see her step outside, but his eyes were fixed straight ahead.

Jade walked to the passenger side and climbed in the seat beside Hunter. Just as he was about to shift gears to back out of the driveway, Jade reached across and turned the key, shutting off the engine. Still, he didn't look in her direction. Both of them sat quietly for several minutes, Hunter staring straight ahead and Jade looking at his side profile under the moonlit sky.

"I'm sorry," she said, repeating the last words she'd said to him before he stormed out of the house.

Jade expected a reply. She thought he'd snap at her, tell her how foolish she was; maybe even tell her how misplaced her confidence was if she thought he couldn't keep his hands off of her or control himself around her. Jade expected something, but Hunter didn't speak or move.

Reaching out, Jade placed her hand on top of

Hunter's. He'd not moved his hand from the gearshift since placing it there when she first got into the car. Hunter didn't pull his hand away, and for Jade, that was the first positive sign she'd gotten from him since the misunderstanding began. Gathering more confidence, Jade lifted Hunter's hand from the gearshift and sandwiched it between both her hands.

Under the glow that his security lights provided, Jade saw movement. Hunter's jaws tightened and his head took a slight turn to the left, away from her and toward the driver's side window. He also took a silent breath that caused his chest to visibly rise and fall. In all of his negative body language, he still didn't pull his hand away from her.

"Hunter." Jade reached out and brushed her hand across Hunter's cheek. She saw his eyes close as though he was savoring the moment. He opened them when she used her hand to turn his face toward hers. Even in the dim light, Hunter's stare was intense.

"I need to talk," she whispered. "And I need you to listen."

Chapter 32

Perhaps his body was still on a prisoner's schedule. Whatever the reason, Jerome's eyes opened at exactly five o'clock in the morning, same time they had for the past ten years. He sat up and stared at the space around him. There were no bars, no sounds of inmates who cursed the sight of another day, and he was alone. He hadn't been forced to share his space with anyone else.

As that thought passed through his head, Jerome thought of Rocky and wondered how he was. Just before going to bed last night, Jerome had said a prayer for all of the men who hadn't shared in his fortune to be released. But he said a special prayer for Rocky. With Rocky's temperament, it was going to take a special anointing from God to keep him on a path that would lead him to freedom. God had done it for Jerome, so he saw no reason why he shouldn't believe He could do it for Rocky.

Jerome kicked off sheets that felt softer than

anything he'd slept on or under at Phillips State Prison. Rolling onto his knees, he took a few minutes to pray and give thanks to God for all that he'd gone through and all that he'd learned. Praying first thing in the morning was one of the life practices Jerome had begun during his last few days of confinement. He had promised to give God the first minutes of every day. It was his way of putting God first. It was something Jerome had seen his father do throughout his childhood.

Completing his time of meditation, Jerome walked to the window and looked out. The sun hadn't come up yet and darkness still blanketed the beauty of Hunter's property. Jerome had had a chance to get a good view of it all yesterday when he'd come home after spending five hours working side by side with the employees at the *Atlanta Weekly Chronicles*. While there, Jerome felt like one of the staff; and when the day ended, Hunter handed him a crisp fifty-dollar bill for his assistance. It was more money than Jerome had seen all at once since he was arrested. Hunter offered him a permanent job in the pressroom too, and Jerome couldn't wait to get started. Life was already looking more promising than ever.

Immediately after leaving the job site, Hunter took Jerome to a menswear store and purchased him two pairs of slacks, two pairs of denim jeans and about ten shirts that he could mix and match. To top it all off, there were a dozen pairs of socks, two pairs of dress shoes and a pair of Nike tennis shoes, all being scanned for Jerome's sake. Jerome's eyes glossed over with tears several times during the process. He had one breakdown, but the moment was a private one as he looked at himself in the mirror of the stall in the men's dressing room. By the time he came out and showed the ensemble to Hunter and Malik, Jerome had replaced the tears with a smile.

"I'm gonna pay you back, man. I promise. As God is my witness, I'm gonna pay you back." That's what Jerome told Hunter as they walked back out to the car with his bags in tow. Hunter's response was one that Jerome hadn't expected.

"I love your sister," he said after Malik had closed himself in the car. "I feel the need to tell you that because there's a possibility that I'm doing this for the wrong reasons, Jerome. I mean, don't get me wrong. You seem to be an all-around good guy. I wouldn't have offered you the job or gotten Kwame to let you rent the spare room in his house if I didn't. I like you and I wish you all the best that God has to offer, but I'm not just doing this for you. I'm also doing it because I know it will make Jade happy and her happiness is really important to me."

As Jerome now stared out into the night, he remembered staring at Hunter in much the same fashion. Jerome was still trying to get used to the idea that normal windows really were much larger than the slits in the prison walls, and yesterday he found himself trying to digest the news that Hunter was in love with his little sister.

"Oh. I didn't know y'all were dating," he had replied to Hunter's comment on yesterday. "She always referred to you as a friend."

"I didn't say she was in love with me. I said I'm in love with her."

"So what are you saying?"

"I'm saying that in my heart of hearts, I think she feels the same way about me that I feel about her, but we've not really discussed it. Matters of your father's death have kept us pretty occupied with other things. We're supposed to talk when she gets in town tonight."

"Well, for what it's worth, I hope she digs you the way you want her to. My sister's one of a kind, man. And if you'll buy me three hundred dollars worth of clothes, give me a job and a place to live just to make her happy, then you're alright with me."

The two men shared a handshake and a brief brotherly hug before climbing in the car and heading to Hunter's home. Several things had changed about Stone Mountain since Jerome's incarceration and he'd been almost swept off of his feet by some of it. But when they turned the corner and he saw Hunter press in a code at the gate that brought them to his house, Jerome was impressed most of all.

"Man, you're living the dream of every cat that ever lived in Perry Homes," Jerome had said as Hunter walked him from one end of the property to the other.

Now Jerome looked at the clock that sat on the dresser and wished the hands on it would rotate faster. Hunter had invited him to ride the horses with the other guests that would be coming by later today and Jerome was counting the minutes. As he climbed back under the crisp covers, Jerome thought about the last time he'd been on horseback. B.T. and Mildred had taken their three children to one of the local carnivals when Jerome was still a kid in grade school. Back then, his dream was to be a cowboy and ride the horses like the guys who lived on the Ponderosa on *Bonanza.* Jackson wasn't very impressed with the tall animals with long-haired tails, and Jade had been too afraid to get on one, but Jerome remembered riding those horses and promising himself that one day he'd have a few of his own. For now, he would gladly settle for living vicariously through Hunter.

One day at a time, Jerome reminded himself as his level of excitement rose. The horses were only one reason for his enthusiasm. In a few hours he'd also be able to surprise his mother who had no idea that she had been Jerome's last visitor before his parole and release. He and Jackson had never been close growing up and Jerome knew he was to blame for most of that, but Jerome hoped that he and his brother could get a new start too. This would be a chance for a new start with all of his family . . . except his father.

Jerome shook the thought from his head. He missed B.T. sure enough, but all he could do now was honor his promise to live a better life from this moment on. Jerome knew he couldn't keep mentally beating himself for how he'd brought such heartache and shame to his father and to the entire Tides family. It was a new day, a new time, and for him, a new beginning. Going forward, Jerome had vowed to live so that B.T. would smile down on him from heaven. He hoped it would make up for all that had happened on earth.

* * *

Jade awakened to the sight of sparkling sunshine that broke through the corners of the window shades and to the smell of bacon and eggs. It was nine o'clock, an hour later than she normally got up on Saturday mornings, but the combination of the flight in yesterday and the late hour that she'd gotten to bed made her hug the covers tighter with no intention of getting up anytime soon.

Last night, after she'd finally recovered from her embarrassment and had convinced Hunter to allow her only five minutes to explain herself, Jade opened her heart. She shared a secret with Hunter, that until last night, she'd only told Ingrid. For years, Jade had kept the information confidential because she had been too ashamed to share it with her family. In her mind, knowing it would have crushed her father and killed her mother.

"It was a mistake and a regret that I'll carry with me for the rest of my life," she told Hunter in the prelude to sharing the night she'd lost her virginity.

Jade watched as compassion glossed over Hunter's once-hardened eyes. Just as she'd asked him to, Hunter sat quietly and listened as she tearfully told him of the night that she'd found herself in a place and a predicament that she'd never have guessed she'd be in. The whole ordeal lasted less than five minutes, but it forever changed her testimony of purity and virtue.

"I don't even know how it came to that," Jade had said, sniffling between every few words. "We'd taken a trip to Jacksonville, Florida, so that I could meet some of his friends who were going to take part in the wedding ceremony. Afterwards, George suggested that we take a walk on the beach and watch the sunset before heading back to Atlanta. The sky was beautiful and we sat on the sands of the near-empty beach and talked as we enjoyed the scenery.

"After about an hour, it was dark and I told him that we should get on the road before we both were too sleepy to drive. He started kissing me and telling me how beautiful I was and how much he loved me. I allowed it for a while, but then I started to feel uncomfortable with the way he was touching me. George had never made me feel uncomfortable before so this was a new place for me where our relationship was concerned. I asked him to stop and I tried to get up so that I could initiate the walk back to the car, but when he said he just wanted some time with me and told me that he just wanted to kiss me under the moonlight, I believed him. Maybe I shouldn't have, but he'd never given me a reason not to trust him.

"The kissing continued for a while, and it was nice. I can't say I wasn't enjoying it, because I was. When he directed me to lie down, that was my cue, but I didn't take it. He was still only kissing me at the time, so I didn't feel an immediate need for concern, but when the exploration of his hands escalated, I started trying to push him away. Before I knew it, he was on top of me, and with his lips so tightly pressed against mine, I couldn't speak or scream. I moaned as loud as I could to try and voice my objection, but I think he thought the moans meant something else . . . like maybe he thought I was enjoying it. It was over just as quickly as it began and I was crying and trembling beneath his body weight.

"It was only then that he seemed to realize that I was in pain, both physically and emotionally. He apologized repeatedly and told me that everything was okay. He loved me. We'd be married in just a few weeks and all would be well. Then he left me standing at the altar without any explanation. It was like his whole agenda had been to bring shame on me and my family."

Jade broke into heavy tears when she said, "I couldn't tell my daddy that his baby girl had gone against God's will and everything he'd ever taught me. And Mother . . . well, I don't know if she could have stomached knowing the truth. I was so glad to be living in Virginia so that I wouldn't have to face either one of them on a regular basis. I rarely ever came home for anything prior to Dad's death because every time I saw them, I was reminded of this horrible, horrible secret."

Hunter had held Jade in his arms and allowed her to cry until her heart was content. He'd whispered comforting words that she needed to hear. Jade clung to Hunter as if she needed every bit of his strength to survive her heavy crying spell. When Jade finally released him, Hunter took her hands in his and prayed for her and with her. It was a powerful prayer, and in the end, Jade felt an incredible release. Before that moment, she hadn't realized the magnitude of heaviness that harboring the secret had placed on her.

Not many words had been spoken between Jade and Hunter after she shared her story with him. He just held her and repeatedly apologized for anything he'd done to make her feel that he would put her in the same situation as George had. It was an apology that Jade felt she wasn't owed, but she respected him even more for offering it.

Once they were back inside the house, Hunter showed her to her room. His home had five bedrooms, four of which were upstairs, and Jade kicked herself for assuming that it only had three. When Hunter said goodnight and turned to walk out of the room, Jade caught him by the arm and brought him close to her. This time, there was no mistaking that she initiated the kiss that followed. It was longer and deeper than the one they shared a week ago at Hartsfield-Jackson Airport and Jade felt her body relax in Hunter's arms. Even with the look of fervor that she saw in his eyes as their lips detached, Jade knew that she could trust him and that their relationship would not cross the bounds of their commitments to God.

"I love you," he whispered in her ear during the embrace that followed.

Jade's heart skipped a beat even now as she reminisced. Tears trickled from her eyes onto the pillow beneath her head as she relived the moment. She'd been too captured at the time to reply, but Jade knew that Hunter knew how she felt. Sometimes words weren't needed.

Jade pushed away the memories of the night before as she began hearing noises from downstairs. She could hear Hunter, Jerome and Malik laughing and talking. Jade kicked the covers off of her body and sat up on the side of the bed. This was a new commencement for her and she could feel it. But as exciting as it was, it made her miss her father more than ever. Her brother was free after ten years of imprisonment and Jade was more than sure that she'd met the man who she'd someday marry, but knowing that B.T. wasn't here to join the celebration and he wouldn't be there to give her away or to officiate her special day, ushered in a cloud of sadness on what should have been a day of rejoicing.

Chapter 33

Because of Jade's late rising, breakfast had been served later than normal. Hunter hadn't cooked breakfast for more than just him and Malik since the first time Jade had come to his home for their initial meeting concerning the letters in his paper. He enjoyed both the additional company and the compliments they showered him with while enjoying the meal he'd prepared. Several times during breakfast, Hunter stole looks at Jade and remembered the secret that she entrusted him with. He loved her more knowing that she'd placed such confidence in him without fear that he'd pass it along.

Hunter could determine that Jade had some level of concern that perhaps he would view her differently knowing that she'd been with another man. In all honesty, Hunter had no qualms with it. After all, he couldn't present her with a clean history either. However, he did struggle with the manner in which Jade had been introduced to such an act of intimacy that should have been saved for marriage. Hunter desired to find George and punish him for what Hunter saw as an act of blatant sexual misconduct. He fell just short of considering it rape, and Hunter had gone to bed seething at the man who'd taken something so precious and then thrown it back in Jade's face when he failed to honor his commitment. Knowing that George's loss was his gain was the factor that gave Hunter peace.

When Malik's guests began to arrive, all of them made their way out to the pasture. Hunter laughed at Jerome, who seemed more excited than the children to be riding the horses again. Malik, holding the reins of Kyla's horse, wasted no time claiming his territory. Although Hunter wanted to spend all of his time with Jade, he had to divide it between her and K.P. who was the most inexperienced of all of those there. In order that he would not lose any time with Jade, Hunter secured K.P. on one of the horse's backs and then climbed on the horse with Jade as he held the reins to both horses and walked close to the fence to stay out of the path of the others.

"This is Ms. Jade," Hunter said to K.P. while enjoying the feel of Jade's arms around his waist as she sat behind him.

"I know," K.P. said.

"You do?" Jade asked.

"Yes. From church."

Jade smiled. "Do you go to New Hope?"

"Yes ma'am."

"I'm sorry," Jade said apologetically. "There are so many people at the church that I have no way of knowing most of them."

They rode for a while before Hunter asked K.P. if he felt comfortable enough to ride alone. The boy nodded again and Hunter handed him the reins; he and Jade followed a few feet behind while K.P. took the lead.

"You're really good with children," Jade told Hunter.

"I guess Malik gave me good practice."

"Do you want more?"

Hunter took a quick look over his shoulder and then turned back around. No one had ever asked him that question before, but those in his immediate family knew that Hunter had always desired three children.

"Yes. I'd like to have another son and a daughter. I want my daughter to be my youngest."

Jade laughed. "Then you'll be just like my parents and your daughter is going to be spoiled."

"You're not spoiled. Not yet anyway."

"Are you offering to spoil me, Hunter Greene?"

"That depends."

"On what?"

"Are you offering to give me a son and daughter?"

Hunter felt the grip of Jade's arms around his waist loosen. He guided their horse to a stop and looked over his shoulder again. "Does it take that much thought?"

"No," Jade answered. "I . . . I guess I'm not quite sure what you're asking me."

Hunter climbed from the horse and then helped

Jade do the same. He scoped the pasture and saw K.P. still maneuvering his horse at a safe speed along the side of the fence and the others trotting behind one another in the center of the pasture with Jerome leading the pack. Turning, he looked Jade in her eyes and smiled.

"The one thing your brother said to me yesterday that made a lot of sense was that people don't know how precious life is until they lose the ability to live it as they please. He said that those of us on the outside don't really value life as we should. We rush through every day with the attitude that that day is just in the way of us getting to the next day. In prison, he said that inmates long to be where we are so that they can just inhale and exhale. Every day is precious to him now, and you can see it."

Hunter tossed a look toward Jerome and then continued. "I love you, Jade. I'm asking you for one day at a time. That's how Jerome lives now and I think it's an awesome way to take on life and the things that God offers in every day that He gives us the opportunity to inhale and exhale. Give me the chance to show you that every man is not George. Life is too precious to rush it. A lot of miles rest between Atlanta and Virginia, but if you're willing to give me a chance, I'd like to try and see where life takes us."

"I know you're not George," Jade whispered through a shy smile. "You proved that a long time ago, Hunter. I love you too and I'd like nothing more than to give us a chance."

This time, it was Hunter who found Jade's lips. As her arms embraced him, Hunter felt as though he was wrapped in a silken cocoon of euphoria.

He didn't want to release her, but he knew he had to. When he did, Hunter instinctively looked around him to see who, if anyone, among his guests might have noticed them. Everyone seemed too absorbed in their own merriment to see or even care, and that was just fine with Hunter.

Mrs. Lowman would be along in less than an hour to pick up Malik's friends so Hunter reluctantly left Jade's side, excusing himself to prepare lunch for everyone.

You're really good with children.

Hunter laid the slices of bread on the table as he thought of Jade's words. Without realizing it, he shivered. It wasn't what Jade said that sent chills through Hunter's body, but rather his unspoken thoughts that followed. Hunter couldn't believe how close he came to proposing. The words were on the tip of his tongue when she asked him to explain himself. And the scariest part of all was that a part of him wished he'd followed his heart. Asking Jade to marry him despite the limited time they'd spent together felt right, and the fact that he was standing in his kitchen regretting that he hadn't done so made Hunter believe that asking her *would* have been right. But he relished knowing that it was only a matter of time. There were fewer things in life that Hunter had been surer of than the knowledge he and Jade would make a life together. She was the woman he'd unknowingly been searching for, the mother that his son deserved.

Those last few thoughts had barely run their course through Hunter's head when the front door opened and his hungry and still-excited guests entered. Even K.P. was smiling as he boasted to the others that he had ridden his horse without once falling off.

"Wash up for lunch, guys!" Hunter yelled from the kitchen.

In a matter of minutes everyone had gathered in his living room snacking on sandwiches and juice and chattering about their time in Greene Pastures.

"Wrestling's on, Daddy. Can we watch?" Malik said.

Hunter tossed his son the remote and Malik fiddled with the buttons in an attempt to find what he was looking for. Instead, he pressed a button that activated footage that Hunter had recorded two months earlier. As soon as he realized what it was, Hunter reached for Malik's hand.

"Give me that, Malik."

"No," Jerome said. "I never saw this. Let it play."

Hunter looked at Jerome and then at Jade. She probably hadn't seen it either. In slow motion, Hunter sank back on the couch. He'd forgotten about the recording that he'd made the Sunday after Reverend Tides' funeral and certainly had no intention of playing it in front of the deceased pastor's children.

"I know heaven's always been a place of unending joy. But with B.T. Tides up there, I know Jesus and the angels are just straight up showing out!"

"That's Sister Price," Jade said when the hat-wearing woman that the news reporter had just interviewed broke into a holy dance on the front porch of New Hope.

The next scene brought the entire living room to an eerie hush, and slowly, every eye gravitated to K.P. when they realized it was him on the screen.

"God don't make no mistakes," the man who K.P. stood next to said. "So we got to believe that there is a reason why the good Master saw fit to take him this-a-way. Reverend Tides was a good man. Many, many times, he gave me money from the benevolence offering to pay my bills when things got tight with my family. I know we all got to go some time, but it's a shame he had to suffer like this. It's a doggone shame."

"K.P., that's your daddy," Kyla pointed out.

The boy who had been laughing just minutes earlier had climbed back into his shell and sat on the living room floor staring at the hardwood beneath him. His sudden change in demeanor baffled Hunter and he could tell that it had done the same for the other grownups in the room.

"K.P.," Hunter said as he slid to a spot on the sofa that brought him closer to the boy. "Is that your father?"

K.P. nodded and Hunter saw visible trembling.

"What's the matter, son?" Hunter probed. "Why are you shaking?"

When tears began spilling down the child's cheeks, Hunter looked at Jade who read his thoughts. "Come on, guys," she said to the other kids. "Let's take our food and finish eating it on the porch. That way we can still watch the horses until your mom comes to get you."

"He's always crying for nothing," Jeremy said, gathering his leftovers. "He makes me sick."

"I know," Malik mumbled, gaining him a firm swat to his behind.

"Get your stuff and go out on the porch like you were told." Hunter's voice was firm. "And I don't want to hear another word or else *you'll* have something to cry about. Do you understand me?"

Tears that were more so due to embarrassment than pain welled in Malik's eyes, but he blinked them back. "Yes sir."

Once they were alone with K.P., both Hunter and Jerome moved to the floor where the boy was sitting. Jerome's eyes were filled with questions and Hunter knew that he wasn't certain as to why he and Jade had sent the children away. At first, Hunter was tempted to ask Jerome to leave too, but his gut feeling told him that Jerome needed to stay.

"K.P., what's the matter?" Hunter asked. "Why are you crying? Did something happen to your father?"

A silent, tearful shake of K.P.'s head was all that Hunter got in return.

"What then? Why are you crying?"

"It's just us, buddy," Jerome added. "It's just you, me and Mr. Greene. We your boys, K.P.; you can tell us."

K.P. looked up at Jerome and behind his tears was sheer fright. Jerome lifted his hand, palm down, and extended it in K.P.'s direction. "It's just us, dude. You can trust us."

Hunter caught the look that Jerome threw in his direction and in response he reached out and placed his hand on top of Jerome's. "Yeah, K.P., man. It's all for one."

"I c..c . . . can't," he stammered.

"Yes you can, dude," Jerome said. "Don't leave us hanging."

K.P. stared at the men's hands in front of him and then slowly placed his on top.

"There you go," Hunter said. "Now that means we've got your back. Tell us, son. Tell us everything."

Chapter 34

Police cars swarmed the property surrounding the wood-framed house set in an almost secluded spot off of an otherwise busy area of Redan Road, not five miles from Shelton Heights. From across the street, Jerome stood with Hunter and Jade and watched the drama unfold with fear and expectation.

The police cars were joined by black SWAT vehicles that men bailed from, rushing for the front door, yelling for Orlando Price to come out of the house and surrender. Jerome had seen action scenes like this on television, but real life surpassed it by far. Being around so many armed officers made him nervous to the point of perspiring. The last time Jerome had seen so many of them all in one place had led to ten years in confinement.

"Oh, please, God; please God; please God." Jade prayed the words over and over as she rested in Hunter's arms for additional comfort.

Over the loud speaker, the police continued to demand that Orlando vacate the premises while members of the swat team, protected by large black shields, moved in closer. Just when it seemed that the house was vacant, shots rang from the inside. Jade screamed and Jerome reached for her, but she had already grabbed Hunter and buried her face in his chest.

"It's okay," Hunter said in an attempt to calm her. "I got you, baby. I got you."

A single shot came from the gun of one of the outside officers and then suddenly everybody seemed to rush the house at once.

"They got him," Jerome said. "They got him. Let's go."

"Wait, Jerome!" Jade yelled, but he had already gone.

Jerome ignored the commands of one of the officers that he stay back, and by the time he reached the front door, Hunter was right on his tail.

"Jerome, wait," Hunter urged as he grabbed for his arm, but Jerome wasn't obeying him either.

Through the house Jerome ran, pushing officers and gunmen who were searching the premises as well.

"Jerome, calm down," Hunter said, still trying to keep up as Jerome ran from one room to the next, opening doors and yelling.

"Daddy!"

"Jerome, let the cops do their job."

Ignoring Hunter, Jerome called out again. "Daddy!"

"Jerome!"

The sound brought the whole house to a standstill. Nobody moved. It was weak and muffled, but they'd all heard it. Jerome's heart pounded so fiercely that his body shook. He could feel blood pumping through every vein in his body.

"Daddy!" Jerome's voice broke, mirroring the tears that leaked from his eyes.

"Jerome!"

The barking sounds that joined in were louder, helping them to get a more accurate feel for where the calls were coming from. All at once, everyone rushed for the same door. Hunter reached it first and Jerome was one step behind him. The two of them, along with SWAT team members and policemen took the basement steps like a herd of cattle as they followed the dog's woofing. All the while, both Hunter and Jerome ignored the officers' commands that they step aside.

The stench was overwhelming. Many of the officers gagged as they walked into the dark space that reeked of a mixture of foul odors, but Jerome didn't.

"Daddy!" he called just as one of the officers turned on a flashlight and began scanning the room.

"Jerome."

Chapter 35

Reverend Tides was frail and in need of immediate medical attention, but he was alive. He'd defecated and urinated on himself so much in the more than eight weeks that he'd been tied to the pipes in Orlando Price's basement, that the doctors were amazed that his body wasn't diseased or that he hadn't at least formed a rash many times worse than that of a baby whose diaper hadn't been changed in weeks. Reverend Tides' biggest health challenges were malnourishment and dehydration and there were bandages around his waist where the ropes that held him attached to pipes had torn into his skin in his attempts to free himself.

From his hospital bed at Piedmont Hospital, Reverend Tides allowed Hunter to interview him for the *Atlanta Weekly Chronicles* and the hospital had made special allowances for the after-hours visit. The AWC was the only newspaper that had been allowed inside B.T.'s private room. Holding a handheld recorder, Hunter talked candidly with the man whose family he'd lived next door to for years in Perry Homes.

When Hunter asked Reverend Tides how he survived, the pastor said, "Remember how God sent crows, some of the most unclean birds in the world, to feed Elijah? Well, He provided an unclean dog to feed me. Every time that fellow threw food down there for Gabriel, he would eat some and then he'd share some with me."

Hunter pushed the image of the preacher eating food from a dog's container from his mind and focused on a more pressing question. "Gabriel? Mr. Price's son tells us that the dog's name is Toby."

Reverend Tides released a weak chuckle. "I never heard the man call the dog anything other than something slanderous. I named him Gabriel because it means 'hero of God.' That's what that dog was for me—a hero of God."

Hunter smiled. In the three days that Reverend Tides had been in the hospital, the staff had bathed him and given him a fresh shave. Beyond the feebleness of the man who was at least thirty pounds smaller than normal, Hunter could see an image of Jade. She had her father's dark eyes, wavy hair, smooth skin and his high cheekbones. And as much as the preacher had taught miracles to his family and the members of his church, everyone, including Mildred and their children, was having a hard time accepting the fact that their pastor, husband and father was still alive. This had been the first time

Mildred had left B.T.'s side in three days. She'd said she never let him out of her sight again and her words weren't idle ones.

"No one could fault you for being hostile about all of this. Do you have any animosity?" Hunter asked.

"I've known Brother Price for years. He's not a bad man. He's a sick man. I knew he wasn't pleased with me, but I never thought it would come to this. I found out that he was mishandling money I was allowing him to receive from the church's treasury for the purpose of paying bills. The last time he came to me, I refused his request. It wasn't fair to allow money that had been donated for the less fortunate to be used frivolously. As a result of him mindlessly spending his subsidized income and my not granting him the offering that he asked for, all of his services were disconnected and his family eventually scattered. He blamed me for all of it. No, I'm not angry. As bad as it was, it could have been worse."

"He's been diagnosed with paranoid schizophrenia," Hunter said, sharing the news that Jade had told him out in the hall as she and the rest of the family were leaving. "The police found an empty bottle of Thorazine in his bathroom that had not been refilled as directed."

"I know. I didn't know what it was, but I knew he was mentally ill. I understand that his parents never knew. They always thought he was on drugs. He was sick and I'm glad the gunshot from the police didn't kill him. That boy was screaming in the house, talking to people who weren't there. He didn't need to die. He needs help."

Hunter hesitated before he asked the next question because he wasn't sure Reverend Tide knew all the details surrounding his own abduction and ultimate torture.

"When the police found your burning vehicle, there were charred remains inside, which is why you were determined to be dead. Do you know anything about that?"

"I talked to the police earlier today and I told them that Brother Price had another gentleman with him when they ran me off of the highway that night. I'm convinced he was disturbed too. He looked like a homeless bum . . . had a wildness about his eyes that wasn't normal for a sane man. Brother Orlando told him to set the van on fire. I had gas and other chemically-based stuff in the back of the van that was flammable. I think he set the fire in the wrong area of my van and couldn't get out of the van fast enough before the flames swallowed him up.

B.T. Tides shook his head in pity as he recounted. Hunter thought it spoke volumes that the pastor held no grudge against Orlando, whose obvious intention was to torment and eventually kill him, and the fact that the pastor chose to honor the man with the title of "Brother" even though Orlando had treated him as anything but.

"Reverend Tides, you've given God your whole life. You struggled and endured hardship and poverty as a man whose only aim was to please God and build a church in His honor and for His glory. You seem like the most unlikely candidate for something like this. How do you explain why God chose you? Are you angry at Him at all? Were you *ever* angry during any of this?"

"Let me tell you something, son," Reverend Tides said, placing his hand on top of Hunter's. "No man gains anything from being angry with God. When I gave my life to Him I told Him to use me as He pleases. In a strange way, all of this is an answer to my prayers. In all of my preaching, praying and serving God's people, my own family was coming apart at the seams. I had a daughter who would rarely come home, a son in prison, a wife who could barely stand to look at him and another son who was beginning to act like he was the only child in the family by distancing himself from his siblings. In the last three days, I've been able to see all of my family come together in peace. My youngest boy has been set free by both man and God, and he's been given a new chance at a new start. My wife has come to embrace all of her children and she's been able to forgive Jerome for the hurt that he caused her. Jackson has rededicated himself to being a brother to his younger siblings. My daughter is talking of moving back to Atlanta to start a practice here where she'll be closer to family. I can't be mad at God for that. I love Him for that and if I had to do it all over again, I would.

"What good am I as a shepherd to God's flock if my own sheepfold is in disarray? God kept me through it all. I had days and nights when I felt like I was going to die, but I knew I wouldn't. God had prepared me for this trial, but it was far more trying than I ever imagined. Everyday I had to remind myself that He was by my side. I repeated the Twenty-third Psalm every single day. I knew He was my shepherd. I knew He'd lead me to green pastures. I knew He'd restore my soul and lead me into righteousness. But I also knew I had to walk through the valley of the shadow of death and be strong until He did it. He promised He would provide me with mercy and see me through and He did. God stayed true to His word and I'm alive. When I count all of the blessings that I've gained from this, I'd be a fool to be anything but grateful."

Hunter experienced an emotional moment that he wasn't expecting, and he turned off the recorder and wiped the appearance of tears from his eyes.

"You are the most inspirational man I've ever met. You gained my respect when I was a kid and you've never lost it. I think that you are the reason I chose the way of salvation. I mean, I tried other avenues before getting there, but I never forgot the preacher in Perry Homes and I'd think about you often when I found myself doing things that were wrong."

Reverend Tides patted Hunter's knee and rendered a tired smile. "It's testimonies like that that make living for God worth anything I might have to endure. My wife tells me that you helped the family a lot through this difficult time. She said that you and Jade never gave up. All the while, neither of you thought this was an accident. Thank you for being there for them even when they didn't want you to be. And to top it off, you convinced a friend to give my son a place to stay and you gave him a job at the very establishment that you nearly lost at the hands of my family, New Hope and the community as a whole. I apologize for that, but charge it to their heads and not to their hearts."

Hunter returned the pastor's smile. "Reverend Knight and the church have formally apologized and I've accepted their regrets. And as far as Kwame is concerned, he served time some years back because of bad decisions he'd made too. He was given a new start, so he had no problem with helping another brother do the same. Jerome deserves that."

"You're quite the inspiration yourself, Hunter," the preacher said.

"It's like you said, Reverend Tides. If going through all of that would bring me where I am, I'd do it all over again too. Had none of this happened, I probably never would have reconnected with your family, which means I would have never reconnected with Jade. I love her," Hunter whispered the last three words and then raised his voice to a more audible level. "I love your daughter."

Reverend Tides' face showed no surprise at Hunter's words. "I know. She told me. I look forward to getting to know you better, son."

At that moment, a nurse entered and interrupted the men. "Mr. Greene, the doctor is requesting that you let the reverend get some rest now."

Hunter turned to her and nodded and then reached out and shook Reverend Tides' hand. "Thank you for allowing the *Atlanta Weekly Chronicles* to do this story. This is one that the world really needs to hear. And thank you for accepting me as a part of Jade's life. That means the world."

Hunter stepped out into the hall and began walking toward the exit doors. Between his talk with K.P. yesterday and his own detective work, Hunter had finally put all the pieces of the mystery together. He had already determined that K.P. was the same child who'd written the letter to the AWC weeks earlier. His letter had been among the first to appear once Hunter resurrected the feature. The letter had been signed 'Kobe', but Hunter knew that they were one and the same—Kobe Price, also known as KoKo.

Last night, Hunter had read it again and many clues were given, even then. K.P.'s letter was written in the present tense because he knew Reverend Tides was still alive—at least that he was still alive at the time that the letter was written. When K.P.'s mother left Orlando, the mentally unstable man hadn't allowed her to take their son. Mrs. Price hadn't been privy to the information that K.P. had. It was only after she'd fled that Orlando abducted and tortured his pastor, and K.P. had been there at the house and had witnessed it all before being sent to live with his grandmother.

The voices in Orlando's head told him that Reverend Tides was the blame for everything and everyone he'd lost. After Orlando captured the preacher, he'd sent his son away to stay with his grandmother and K.P. had been too afraid to say anything, which led to his depression and constant sadness. It was too big of a burden for any adult to have had to carry, let alone a child. Hunter also deduced that it was K.P. who innocently told his father that Hunter and Jade were headed to the airport. The boy had told Orlando when the man called that evening as Hunter was preparing to leave K.P.'s grandmother's house. The child had no clue of what would come of his revelation.

And K.P.'s letter was the reason they needed to keep running the feature, but neither Hunter nor Jade had caught the clues in the letter that seemed so juvenile. But all of that was in God's plan too.

Had they caught it early on, Hunter wouldn't have had the chance to fall in love with the preacher's daughter.

Hunter digressed when he thought of Reverend Tides and his choice to count his blessings rather than look at the downside. One blessing Hunter could count for himself was his increased awareness of the power of forgiveness. He'd finally completely forgiven Kwame and Diane, but listening to Reverend Tides made Hunter ashamed that he'd taken as long as he did to get to the point where he could release the anger. As much as he'd felt betrayed by what his employees and friend had done, it was nothing in comparison to what Reverend Tides had gone through. Yet, the pastor had not even struggled with forgiving his torturer.

Hunter climbed into his car and gently placed the recorder on the seat beside him. He'd never had a father or even a father figure that he could look up to. Now, Hunter felt like he had one. It was another blessing he could count that had risen out of the mayhem of the last two months. He had a mother and siblings, but aside from Kwame, he had no one in his inner circle who loved God like he did. In the Tides family, Hunter had found everything he needed and more.

Snapping his seatbelt into place, he started his engine. At this time of night, the drive to his house would take about thirty minutes, nearly half the time it would take during rush hour in Atlanta. As he shifted into gear and headed out of the hospital parking lot, Hunter's cell phone rang. Glancing at the caller ID, he flipped it open and placed it to his ear.

Not giving Jade a chance to speak, Hunter said, "Hey, baby. I was thinking that tomorrow I'd take the day off and just relax. No AWC work; just me and you. I was hoping that maybe we could talk before you make plans to go back to Virginia Beach."

"I'd love to," Jade replied. "What did you have in mind?"

"Oh, I don't know. I thought maybe we could ride in the pasture and talk about the possibility of changing your name to Green Greene."

READERS' GROUP GUIDE

IN GREENE PASTURES

Kendra Norman-Bellamy

DISCUSSION QUESTIONS

1. Christians are sometimes expected not to become overly emotional, even in the most traumatic times. But Mildred went from shock to hysteria when the police woman broke the news of her husband's accident. What are your thoughts on that?

2. What did you think of Hunter's immediate reaction to the letter he received from Jade Tides?

3. Do you think Hunter was wrong for not letting Kwame know ahead of time of his planned visit to Virginia to meet with Jade?

4. At what point could you, as the reader, feel a romantic connection developing between Hunter and Jade?

5. Reverend Tides' church quickly banded together to fight Hunter's decision to restart the section featuring letters concerning the pastor's fate. Do you think they were justified in their actions? Why or why not?

6. Was Hunter too harsh in his dealings with Kwame after finding out about the scheme to undermine his authority? Would it have been more "Christian-like" for him to immediately forgive and forget?

7. When the city of Atlanta turned on Hunter and the friendship between Hunter and Kwame was put to the test, Malik seemed to get trapped in the middle although he had nothing to do with either. How much do children suffer when parents are caught in adversity?

8. What were your feelings about Jerome and his incarceration? Did your heart go out to him or did you feel that whatever hardships he endured in prison were exactly what he deserved?

9. How did you feel about Ingrid and her sometimes rigid personality? Did you view her as a supportive friend to Jade or just a fair-weathered one?

10. Discuss your take on Diane and her workplace arch-rival, Lorna. Did you hate them both? Like them both? Find yourself rooting for one over the other?

11. The subject of date rape was addressed to some degree in this story. Share your feelings on this and discuss whether or not you think that's what took place in the story that Jade revealed.

12. As you were reading, did you realize how important K.P. was to the mystery before it was ultimately revealed?

13. The entire Tides family had unresolved issues. Discuss each of them and how you think they developed and got so out of hand.

14. Orlando Price was diagnosed with paranoid schizophrenia. Within your group, talk about this illness and whether you think genuine Christians suffer with such personality-altering disorders.

15. Hunter Greene is a single father who is gainfully self-employed, financially stable and loves his son unconditionally. Do you believe that such men exist in real life?

16. Did the ending of the book surprise you? Why or why not?

17. Who was your favorite character in the story? What made him/her so memorable for you?

18. Who was your least favorite character? Why?

19. If you could rewrite any part of this story, which part would it be? Why would you change it? How would your revised version read?

20. What was the most prominent message that you received from reading this story?

Other Titles by Kendra Norman-Bellamy

For Love & Grace (BET Books)

Because of Grace (BET Books)

Thicker Than Water (BET Books)

More Than Grace (Kimani Press)

A Love So Strong (Moody Publishers)

Crossing Jhordan's River (Moody Publishers)

Three Fifty-Seven A.M. (KNB Publications)

The Midnight Clear (KNB Publications)